Knox Hollow

Murder on Mayflower

Knox Hollow

Murder on Mayflower

Grace Kuhn

To Mark Kate

Grace Kuhn

3

ISBN-13: 978-0-578-75174-0

Library of Congress Control Number: 2020920614

PRINTED IN THE UNITED STATES OF AMERICA

For Mamou, Papa, and Grandma
I wish you were here to read this

CHAPTER 1 - Home Sweet Home

The moment John's grey pickup truck turned the corner on to Mayflower Circle, I knew something was strange. It was just . . . a feeling. I don't know how to explain it. Luke always says I'm not very good with my words, which I've come to realize is true. I can never think of the right thing to say in the moment or how to word what I want to express. But I had a strong feeling — one that comes up out of nowhere and sucker punches you right in the gut — that there was something not right about this place. Maybe it was that the houses were a bit too glamorous or maybe it was the storm that loomed in the distance as we made the long road trip. Or maybe it was the fact that Mom had plucked us up like weeds the day after school ended, threw us into a car, and forced us to leave the only place we had ever known as home. I don't know. It was just a feeling.

*****

"T-minus ten minutes Iz!" John's excited voice pierces through the music blaring from my headphones.

I pretend not to hear him and keep looking out the window, staring at nothing but trees and sky. Tall, green trees and a smoky grey sky that looks like it is about to break out into a storm at any moment. I ignore him when he repeats his cheesy line and don't look up until he's tapping me on the shoulder, and I can't avoid talking to him any longer.

I glare at him, "What?"

"We'll be there in ten . . . well . . . now, nine minutes," he says cheerfully, pretending he can't tell how annoyed I am.

"Great," I retort with as much sarcasm as I can manage.

I want him to know how mad I am. I want him to be as miserable as I feel at this moment. I want him to know that I hate his cheesy jokes. But most of all, I want him to know that he is and always will be the man who ruined my life. I know, I'm a terrible person. It's just . . . nope. There's not even an explanation. I'm just a terrible person.

"Come on, Iz, you're going to love the new place! It's so much bigger than back in Portland. Your room is double the size! You can't tell me that doesn't excite you just a little bit."

"Oh yes, John! A bigger room does make up for forcing me to leave Portland and all of my friends and my dad and basically everything I care about. It's really just so exciting," I snap.

I can see the shock and hurt in his eyes, and for a split second, I feel awful for going off on him. But then I remember what he's done and the feeling dissipates pretty fast. Forcing me to leave Oregon and move three thousand miles away to some small Massachusetts town. I shouldn't feel bad for him. He doesn't deserve that much.

"I know this is hard on you and your brother. It's hard on all of us, but I promise it will only get better from here. And it's ok if you're mad at me, it really is, but I think you should give Knox Hollow a chance," he reassures.

I hate his whole glass half full mantra on life. It really is sickening. How does it get better from here when I know it's just a long road of misery ahead? Really, John? Tell me where this magical silver lining is.

I don't say anything to him, so he takes it as his cue to keep going. "I know change is really hard, especially at your age. One day you'll see that your mother and I were just trying to do our best for you kids, trying to give you the best we could. I think deep down you know that. This anger and these silent treatments are all just your way of coping with the changes. A way of — "

I cut him off with so much anger, so much rage. The sound of my voice echoes through the truck. "YOU'RE NOT MY FREAKING SHRINK!"

I'm pretty sure I just went from passive aggressive eyerolls to a full on aggressive blow up. I'm also pretty sure that I'll be getting in some trouble for what just came out of my mouth. And I'm *absolutely* sure that John won't be giving me life advice anytime soon. What can I say? I'm a terrible person.

We turn the corner onto Mayflower Circle, and instantly, the street becomes the most glamorous thing I have ever seen. Two solid stone pillars connected by an intricately designed slate gate open automatically as our car approaches. Striking red and baby pink roses bloom by the entrance. As we begin to drive down the street, I am struck by the sight of gorgeous, four thousand square-foot houses that stand like mountains set high up on rolling hills of perfectly manicured, golf course green lawns. John was telling me these houses have been around since Abraham Lincoln took his first steps into the Oval Office. Off in the distance the sun is melting into hazy oranges and pinks, looking like a bowl of rainbow sherbet. The view of sharp mountain peaks is incredible. It seems like the sky has decided against a storm and settled on a pink masterpiece instead. I've never seen anything like this. This is definitely a rich neighborhood; I already feel like I don't belong here. But in all honesty, when have I ever felt like I've belonged anywhere? I didn't fit in at our old house in our old town and I'm not going to fit in at our new house in our new town. Why am I so unsettled by this? It's just a proven fact of my life.

Ever since we left our little yellow house on Evergreen Avenue, which was our very first home, I've felt like I didn't belong. It was like my place in this world had somehow disappeared. Most of my life has been spent wandering through the lost and found, hoping to find a place where I belong. I just don't fit anywhere. It's like when you're putting a puzzle together and you try to jam two pieces together that don't really go. They kinda sorta fit, but it's never comfortable or permanent. I wish I could go back to when I had a place in this world, when life was safe and comfortable.

When I was little, we lived in this three bedroom yellow house with a big backyard. The house wasn't big, but it was perfect. It was home. My room had these calming purple walls and a purple bean bag chair that I liked better than my own bed. At least half of my room was filled with stuffed animals that were my best friends. We had this old brown couch that my mom was always complaining about and a fireplace in our living room. Most nights, the four of us would snuggle up on the couch with a movie in front of the fireplace, completely happy. Luke and I would fall asleep every time, and Dad would carry us up the stairs and into bed. The two of them would tuck us in and kiss us goodnight before kissing each other good night. We had this clumsy old golden retriever named Casey who could play fetch for hours. Mom was still in school getting her doctorate and Dad's construction company was just starting to take off. And then they got divorced. We were shuffled around to different babysitters while they went through marriage counseling, court dates, and volatile fights that got ugly so fast. We were thrown around from house to house while they battled for custody and tore each other to threads. We looked at our parents utterly confused at what was going on as they fed us lie after lie. We were pushed to choose sides. We watched our dad pack his bags and move away. We were living in a happy ending. And then they got divorced. And Dad moved out. Casey died. We sold the house. Mom met John. They had two little girls. And suddenly Luke and I were just a reminder of Mom's old life, not a part of her happy ending.

This depressing trip down memory lane hasn't done anything to improve my mood. Neither has Mr. Positivity in the seat next to me or the storm that I know is brewing even though the sky has put on a temporary show for us. I better tell you that if you're going to read my story — my very own mystery novel — you need to expect a lot of negativity, a lot of eye rolling, and a lot of depressing memories. If you're okay with that — with me as terrible as I am — then go ahead. Read.

*****

"Izzie! You actually said that to him!" Luke looks at me completely bug-eyed.

The two of us sit on our old bean bag chairs, in what will be my room, eating Chinese food from the carton.

"Does it really surprise you?" I ask.

"Well, no, but still! Mom's gonna kill you!"

"Do you really think John's going to tell her?"

"Well, no, but she would kill you if she found out."

I shrug and give him a half smile. At least I still have Luke. Luke who's been my best friend even when I do and say stupid things. Luke who always knows what to say even though he's a year younger than me. Luke, the only person that I can count on.

"I still don't know why you chose to drive with him," Luke laughs.

"Because there was no way I was driving across the country with a baby who won't stop crying. I had to pick my poison."

"I get it, but at least you wouldn't have gotten into a fight with Olivia."

"I probably would've."

Luke laughs again. "Yeah, you're the only person I know who could find a way to get into a fight with a three-month-old."

11

"Izzie!" I hear my mom yell.

Luke shoots me a worried glance. "Oh no!"

I smile at him and walk out of the room ready to face Momzilla. I'm honestly not afraid. She forced me against my will to move across the country. Compared to that, being grounded for a week or two is nothing. I mean, am I even going to really be leaving my room anyway? It's not like I have a social life or anything now.

Mom's sitting at the swirled grey and copper granite countertops with Chinese food cartons and a glass of her favorite chardonnay in front of her. Her thick, milk chocolate colored hair is thrown up into a messy bun and she wears her old, green UVM track sweatshirt. The baby is nuzzled against her shoulder almost asleep. Almost asleep is as close as Olivia comes to actual sleep. The girl has lungs of steel and can wail with the best of them. She's basically attached to my mom — our mom — at all times.

She turns slightly, trying not to wake Olivia, and whispers, "Is she asleep yet?"

"Almost," I reply.

She jokingly rolls her icy blue eyes. For 40 years old she looks so young. Her skin is smooth and wrinkle free. You can see the life in her eyes, in her smile. Everyone says I'm her mini me and as I've gotten older and matured, we look almost identical. The only difference is my hair is baby blonde, and I'm nearly a foot taller.

"I just wanted to check in with you quickly, hun. We haven't seen much of each other these past few days," she places her hand lovingly on my shoulder. "Are you doing ok?"

At this moment, I completely melt into a puddle. One pat on the shoulder, one reassuring smile, one word from her soothing voice and I want to break down in tears. I want to tell her I miss home so much it physically hurts. How these past few months I've been holding on to this giant bucket full of anger and lashing out at everyone who's just trying to help me. How John won't even look me in the eye anymore. Saying horrible things and snapping at adults, that's not me. I feel like I'm playing a character in a movie. Dramatic teenage girl with anger issues. But I won't cry in front of her. I won't let her know how much this hurts. I feel the sadness inside me transforming into bubbling anger. It's not like she cares anyway. If she cared, I wouldn't be here right now. I look away from her, trying to get my emotions in check before I react. I suck at emotions.

"Look at me, baby. Look at me," her calm voice fills my ears.

This is her super power. Her soft, steady voice. It can convince you of anything and make you feel like everything is going to be okay. But I won't let her do it to me this time. I won't let her convince me that life is going to turn out just fine when nothing is okay right now. I've decided how to react. I *want* to be mad. I *need* to be mad.

I clench my hand into a tight fist and slam it down on the counter. "No, I'm not okay! How could I possibly be okay? You've ruined my life! But your new family is happy so I guess everything is just perfect for you!"

I storm away to my room and slam the door so hard the floor vibrates. I can hear the baby's cries as I dash up the stairs. As soon as the door is shut, I collapse to the floor. I feel the hard wood against my back, while hot tears roll down my cheeks and burn my face. I throw my head back, hitting the door. All of this bottled up anger has exploded. Being here, in this house has broken me apart. All at once, everything becomes so real to me, not just something that loomed in my future. This is reality; this is my new life.

"Izzie," Luke's voice is quiet, scared almost.

I forgot he was in here. I look up at him with sadness consuming my entire face. At this moment I am the queen of the ugly cry, but Luke still rushes over to me. He puts his arm around me, and I rest my head on his shoulder. I open my mouth to talk, but no words come out.

"I got you, Izzie. I got you."

We sit like that for either five minutes or forty-five minutes. I've lost all concept of time. I'm just sitting there crying like a toddler who was told she couldn't get a toy at the store.

Eventually, Luke says to me, "I know you're going through a lot right now, but the longer you sit on this floor the sadder you're going to get."

"I'm just so tired, Luke. Emotionally, physically. I'm just tired."

"I know, but — wait, hold up a second. Why are you physically tired?"

"I carried all those boxes inside from the truck and the cars."

"All those boxes? Izzie, you carried in one box and then quit! And you didn't even carry it inside. You made it halfway up the driveway," Luke almost yells.

"It was heavy!"

"It was filled with our reusable grocery bags! It barely weighed anything!"

"Well I'm sorry I have noodles for arms!" I try to keep a straight face, but before I know it I'm cracking up at how stupid I sound.

"Alright noodle arms, go wash your face and maybe find some chamomile tea while you're at it. Get a good night's sleep, and I promise you'll feel better in the morning."

"Why do you always know what to say?"

"One of us has to," he smiles.

I head out of my room and into the bathroom in search of a face mask in my bag of toiletries. Maybe if I put on a face mask, make some tea, and read a book I'll feel a bit better. It helped when Logan Thomas dumped me. I quickly find what I'm looking for, but on my way out of the bathroom, the mirror catches my eye. I stop and stare like a child mesmerized by a TV show. The shiny glass reflects an image of a girl who has been broken down one too many times. The tears in my eyes make them an even brighter shade of blue. My face is red and blotchy, and when I try to smile, it doesn't look the same. *I* don't look the same. Since when did smiling start to feel unnatural? It used to be second nature. I stand there and picture the spotless mirror breaking into millions of tiny pieces. Millions of sharp shards would come from this one whole piece. If it shattered into a million little pieces, could they put it back together? Or would there just be too much damage? Can somebody put me back together? Or am I too broken to be fixed?

Ring! The sound of the doorbell forces me out of my mirror induced trance, which I realize makes me sound like a narcissist. I'm a lot of things, but I promise I am not a narcissist. This was just a low moment. Anyway, who in God's name is ringing our doorbell this late at night? I hear John's footsteps down the hallway and him pushing down the handle to greet these mystery guests. With my face mask in tow, I creep to the top of the staircase and peer out from behind the banister. I stay kind of hidden just in case . . . you know . . . whoever is ringing our door is a serial killer or something. I sound insane, but you never know what kind of people are out there. John reaches out to shake hands and greets the guests, and I can hear their muffled voices.

"Please, come in! The house is kind of a mess, but we do have wine glasses. That may have been the first box we opened," John jokes.

"Well of course, you can't have it any other way! And please don't worry about the house. Ours is a hot mess, and we've lived here for years," says an unfamiliar woman's voice. It sounds semi high-pitched and confident. Like the voice of someone who is used to being in charge.

I hear her high heels clicking as she walks through the door before I see her. She's as striking as this neighborhood is; she just looks like someone who commands the control of everyone in the room. The lady is tall with her legs taking up eighty percent of her body. She's thin and has unusually long arms that carry a bottle of wine. Her hair is the color of black coffee and hangs in loose waves halfway down her back. I can't make out her face too well from up here, but I can tell she's beautiful. She wears a light cheetah print dress that just reaches her knees and black high heels that click with every step she takes.

As she walks in, I hear another voice. This one is deep and flat. "Stephanie and I were on our way back from an event and we saw the moving trucks. We wanted to bring your family a little housewarming present."

"Well, I appreciate it. You can never go wrong with a good pinot noir," I recognize this voice as John's.

"That's what I always say!" It's the woman's — Stephanie's — voice again. You can hear the enthusiasm radiating from it, but I'm getting a sense of over the top excitement that can only be fake.

These new people are intriguing — or maybe it's just that I've spent the last five days in a car with Mr. Positivity and his 80's rock music and really just people in general are interesting. I sit and continue to watch as they talk for a moment by the front door. My eyes are focused on John as he makes some "funny" comment that Stephanie finds hilarious. She must be either drunk or insane to find him funny. As he turns his head, his eyes meet mine, and they lock for a split second. There is nothing worse than being caught staring. I know he knows that I've been watching. The danger alarm is pulsing in my brain. Shoot! Shoot! Shoot! Now I'm going to look like I'm an actual stalker. All I can think is *Please don't call me out and make me come down and introduce myself. Please just let me be.* Of course, he doesn't.

16

"Izzie, why don't you come here and meet Mr. and Mrs. Kester!"

He's the actual worst. I guess this is what I get for having a tantrum in the car. Well played John, well played.

After internally debating about whether I should act like a normal human and go introduce myself or run quietly back to my room and pretend like nothing happened, I decide to make the awkward trek down the stairs and make even more awkward small talk.

Before I'm even down the stairs, Mrs. Kester is practically jumping out at me with an outstretched hand.

"Well hello, it's so nice to meet you. You can just call me Stephanie. Mrs. Kester makes me feel old. My family and I live next door," she laughs.

I shake her hand and reply, "It's nice to meet you Mrs. . . . uh . . . Stephanie. I'm Izzie."

Now that I'm closer to her, I can see that she really is beautiful. Stephanie has these bright hazel eyes that scream with intensity and command you to look at them. Long, coal black eyelashes fan out delicately like little umbrellas for her eyes. Her skinny nose gently protrudes from her face and curls up slightly to a point. You can tell she's spent some time lying on the beach on an expensive tropical vacation because her skin is perfectly sunkissed. Her overall appearance and energy is intimidating.

"Aren't you gorgeous!" she exclaims. "John your daughter is a beautiful young lady. You're going to have the boys from Knox Hollow lining up at your doorstep!"

I am NOT John's daughter! I feel the anger bubbling up inside me again, and I suddenly remember why I was on the hunt for face masks and tea.

"She certainly is. She's a great kid, that one," he says with a smile while patting me on the shoulder.

His tone and his words are so genuine. John doesn't do sarcasm, and he always tells the truth. I guess it's part of his whole being a therapist thing. A dishonest therapist who takes cheap shots at their patients would not have a job for too long. John may be the worst for trying to give me advice and making me socialize with these neighbors, but he's a real one for not calling me out and still pretending to think I'm a decent human being.

I give John a small smile and follow him as he leads the Kesters into our kitchen.

"Izzie, can you grab the Kesters some wine glasses while I find your mother?" John asks before turning to Stephanie and her husband. "My wife's just putting the baby down. I'll be right back."

I nod my head as John leaves me and these two strangers in an empty kitchen with nothing to talk about.

"I don't think I introduced myself," the man's voice emerges from the silence as he reaches out his hand, "I'm Richard Alexander."

I'm a little curious as to why he introduced himself using his first and middle name. I hate to be rude, but I don't even care to learn his first name. I just want to escape back to my room. Standing next to Richard makes me feel like an ant standing next to a giraffe. He's so tall that it seems like his head could almost touch the top of our high ceilings. His body looks to be pure muscle. His arms seem to burst out of his perfectly ironed collared shirt, which makes him fill more space and appear taller than he is. His face is soft and welcoming, except for his sharp, angular jawline that gives his face some much needed definition. Two deep blue eyes settle above his high-bridged nose that give me an eerily peaceful feeling. Something about his presence makes me feel calm, but also unsettled. Like when you know you've forgotten something, but can't figure out what it is. His dark brown hair is swirled into a small, gel-slathered poof at the front of his head. The two of them together make a glamorous couple, in a very JFK and Jackie fashion.

I shake his hand and say, "I'm Izzie, it's nice to meet you."

I hand the strangers — whom I guess I should start referring to as my neighbors — the wine glasses and try to think of something I could bring up to break the awkward silence. What about, *"hey, my life kinda sucks right now,"* or *"what's your favorite color?"*

Nope. Those are both ridiculously stupid. Luckily, Stephanie speaks up before I can make this situation more uncomfortable than it already is.

"So will you be going to Knox Hollow High?" Stephanie asks.

"I'm pretty sure that's the school name my mom told me," I respond disinterestedly.

Stephanie claps her hands and gasps, "Oh you're going to love it! It's really a gorgeous school, and you'll love the kids and the teachers!"

Oh yes I'm sure I'm going to love the snotty rich kids and uptight teachers. I keep that thought to myself and just smile at Stephanie. See, I do try to control my reactions.

Stephanie continues to talk, "And there's quite a few kids in this neighborhood who go there. How old are you?"

"Seventeen," I can barely get the words out before she's talking again.

"Wow, so you'll be a senior! How exciting! I loved high school. My senior year I was prom queen and homecoming queen. But yes! There's quite a few your age on Mayflower. Let's see, there's Hazel and Shea. Oh and Saige, sweet girl, a little unhinged, but sweet. And Graeson," she rolls her eyes as she says the last name, "Take it from me, you want to stay away from that boy!"

Woah this woman is intense. Her mouth is moving so fast my brain can't physically process what she's saying. I think she may have just told me that a girl on my street is mentally insane, but I'm very intrigued about this Graeson kid.

"You seem to have all the gossip," I joke, but I can already tell she's one of those ladies who inserts herself in other people's business and spreads rumors anywhere and everywhere.

Richard's eyes go wide, and he shoots Stephanie a look that screams "stop talking, now!" He places his hand gently on her shoulder and says with clenched teeth, "I think that's quite enough, honey." His tone is calm, but you feel the underlying anger and annoyance. It's the voice my mom uses when I say something sassy in public.

"I'm fine, stop being so uptight," Stephanie jerks away from Richard's hand. "You never let me have any fun."

I realize I'm twisting my hair around my fingers, and I can hear the beating of my heart echoing in my ears.

Stephanie pipes up in defiance to Richard's friendly reminder of public manners, "I have all the gossip, Isabelle! And there's plenty of it to go around! Everyone is always hiding something." She pauses and sees my slightly stunned reaction, which I did not mean for my face to make. She adds, "I'm kidding of course."

I look at the clock and realize it's only been three minutes since John left. I glance over to Richard's face, which is glowing with discomfort. Can my parents move any faster?

"Do you play any sports?" Richard asks to change the subject, which I'm very grateful for.

"I play basketball."

"Very cool. Do you think you'll try out for the team at Knox Hollow?"

"I haven't really thought about it, but probably," I smile.

He seems like a nice guy. I don't have much to go off of, but my first impression of him is that he's overshadowed by Stephanie's compelling "life of the party" personality, but is the one putting in all the behind the scenes work. She's the Oscar winning actress, but he wrote the whole movie. It reminds me of a mystery book I read a few weeks ago. It was about an overpowering wife who was having an affair with one of her husband's friends. It didn't end well. When he found out, he killed her point blank. I probably shouldn't be comparing my new neighbors' relationship to a murder I read about though. It just sounds like a bad omen. But I'm a true crime junkie. I love to read it, write it, watch it. The thing that fascinates me the most about true crime isn't the actual crime; it's the people. Their personalities, their minds, their pasts. It's all about why people do the things they do. People are intriguing. Luke always says my love of true crime novels has warped my brain into thinking everyone I meet has some sort of ulterior motive or suspicious background. I mean, he's not wrong. It's made me an observer — I stay quiet and spend more time listening and paying attention to the little details. My brain analyzes people. I know that sounds weird and slightly insane, and maybe I am, but you'd be surprised how much you can learn about people when you pay attention.

Stephanie starts talking again about either her high school glory days or the boys I should maintain a far distance from. I'm not paying attention, just watching Richard's face grow more annoyed with each word she says. She sounds like a 12-year-old girl who's consumed way too much caffeine. Her arms are flying, her hands are moving, and her eyes are bouncing all around in their sockets as she speaks lightning fast in a sing-songy tone. My brain can't keep up with her.

"Hello!" I hear my mom's bubbly voice approaching behind me.

She emerges into the kitchen, immediately lightening the mood of the room. Everyone makes their introductions — Stephanie's far too over the top for anyone's liking — and settles into a light conversation. It's so easy for my mom to talk to people, even total strangers. I can barely keep a conversation going even with my best friends, who I haven't reached out to since we left Portland. But it's not like they've made any effort either.

"I just have to tell you, Brenna," Stephanie starts and I can't even imagine where this sentence is going. "Your daughter is gorgeous!"

My mom smiles brightly and replies, "Thank you so much! She's amazing."

I feel my cheeks blush a violent shade of red, and I wonder if I'm supposed to say thank you or not. I mean, the compliment was kind of directed at my mom, so I just stand there awkwardly unsure of my place in this setting.

"Those long legs and blonde hair," Stephanie walks towards me and places her hands on my cheeks. "Ugh! And those beautiful blue eyes! You, my dear, are stunning."

My eyes bulge as I resist the urge to scream. This stranger is rubbing her hands on my face and telling me I'm pretty. This sounds like a textbook case of what my preschool teachers would call "stranger danger." It's like Stephanie is scouting me out to go parade around in beauty pageants or something. I mean, you typically don't slather your germy hands over a stranger's face. At least it makes me feel like I'm not the weirdest person in the room.

After what feels like hours later, Stephanie removes her hands from my face, and I stand there like a mannequin, still trying to process the weirdness of the situation. This woman is sending me a strange vibe.

My parents continue on talking with the Kesters for a while, while I try to figure out a way to exit the conversation without being rude. I'm not sure you could even consider this a conversation, seeing that conversations usually entail two or more people speaking, and Stephanie hasn't zipped her mouth long enough to let anyone else get a word in.

After a while Richard says dryly, "It was wonderful to meet you all, but it's getting late, so we better head home. Thank you for your hospitality."

Surprisingly, Stephanie doesn't protest, and the two of them say their goodbyes and head for the front door. Before they turn to leave, Stephanie grabs my arms and gives me a hug. My body goes as straight as a board in total shock. This woman sure is very touchy-feely.

She cranes her long giraffe like neck down and whispers softly in my ear, "We're plagued with secrets . . . and *he* knows them all."

And with that, Stephanie and her cheetah print dress strutted out of our house, one step closer to the hangover that was inevitably on its way.

CHAPTER 2 - Joy Ride

"Where are the damn plates?" my mom asks herself as she walks aimlessly around our first floor, which has turned into a sea of half unpacked boxes.

I sit at the kitchen counter pretending to be intently reading a book so she won't ask me to help. We've already covered the fact that I'm a terrible person, so this is really just in character for me. I can't stop thinking about my strange interaction with the Kesters last night. The way Stephanie spoke like she was on camera and acted in a larger than life fashion is weird enough, but what was up with her being all over me and telling me that "he knows everyone's secrets." Who's he? And what does he know? She was most likely so drunk she didn't know what she was saying, and I'm just searching for an issue where there isn't one. But still, this doesn't settle well with me.

I'm still on edge after blowing up at my mom last night. Okay, maybe yelling and throwing digs at her was not my finest moment, but I have no regrets. I'm not going to apologize for being mad at her for ruining my life. It's her fault. We still haven't acknowledged our fight — aka the major elephant dancing around the middle of the room. She's probably scared to make me fly off the handle or too tired to have this fight *again*, seeing it's the same one we've had at least twenty times before. I have no intention of bringing it up because that would entail an apology, and I surely will not be giving her one of those. We can just add this to the list of things we don't talk about.

I can hear my mom moving boxes around and shuffling through our endless mountains of stuff.

"Where are the *plates?*" she says again, but this time with a slightly raised voice as if she's waiting for the plates to call out to her and say, "I'm right here!"

At that moment, I hear Olivia start crying as my mom lets out an over-exaggerated groan. It's not funny, but I can't help but laugh a little at the situation. The woman just wants to find her plates.

I watch the digital clock on our new oven change from 12:03 to 12:04 as I realize I have run out of things to occupy myself. I can only organize my scrunchies so many times before I lose my mind. If this is what life in Knox Hollow is going to be like, I'm really in for it. I need some sort of action to break me out of the mind-numbingly boring week I've just had.

Hoping that a little vitamin D will boost my mood, I decide to head outside. I step out the sliding glass door and instantly feel the sun's glowing rays warming my skin. It's one of those sweet summer days where the sun bounces off your skin, but doesn't smother you with its heat. I can already feel the freckles on the bridge of my nose popping out with every second I spend in the light. I grab the basketball from the passenger seat of John's pickup and start shooting it in the hoop that was left behind by the people that lived here before us. Playing basketball has always helped me organize my thoughts and release my emotions in what John would call a "constructive way." Apparently yelling at people and slamming doors doesn't fall under that category, so basketball it is. Right now, I have so many thoughts and emotions to sort through. Between moving across the country away from my dad and my friends, losing it on John, the fight with my mom, and the strange interaction with Stephanie and Richard, my mind is filled to the brim with issues to sort through. With each basket I shoot, I feel the tension releasing in my shoulders. Dribbling the ball, bending my knees, extending my arm, and following through with my wrist. It makes me feel good. It makes me feel at home.

I'm not sure how much time goes by, but I feel the built up anger leaving my body slowly, but surely. It's funny how therapeutic launching balls as hard as you can against a backboard can be. One shot gets away from me and bounces off the board so hard it ricochets back and then down the steep driveway. With my long legs pumping, I jog after the ball letting my momentum carry me down the hill.

All of a sudden, I hear the rev of a car engine and turn my head to see a baby blue antique Cadillac with no top barreling towards me at full speed. My brain doesn't react quick enough to move away, and the car shows zero sign of stopping. When my body and my brain finally connect, it's nearly too late. As I lunge to dive out of the way, the car screeches to a halt, stopping and creating a deafening noise as it skids against the pavement. I watch the two boys in the front seat as their eyes bulge. The one in the driver's seat exhales a giant sigh of relief, but the one in the passenger seat looks like he's turning a concerning shade of blue from holding his breath.

"What the hell?!" I yell, feeling the calmness that I just recently acquired already slipping away.

The boy in the driver's seat opens his door, steps out of the car, and begins to walk towards me. He helps me to my feet and appears to be genuinely relieved that he stopped the car in time.

"I'm deeply sorry for the trouble," he says with a thick British accent that makes me forget that he almost just hit me going eighty down a residential street.

I take a closer look at him, and wow he's hot! His eyes are an icy shade of blue, like a crystal clear sheet of glass. His hair is the color of honey with deep brown streaks, and there's a ton of it that sits in a cute ruffled mess on his head. And his smile! It's one of those smiles that makes your cheeks instantly blush and your mind go fuzzy. I like Knox Hollow a little more now.

"Do you always drive that fast?" I laugh.

He flashes his smile at me again, and I feel myself melting into a puddle. "I would say no, but that, my friend, would be a lie. As my mother would say, 'I raised you better than that young man!'"

I roll my eyes at him and his annoyingly compelling charm and suddenly remember why I was mad at him. His smirk is working a lot harder than his apology is.

"You almost killed me," I say letting the annoyance seep through my tone of voice.

"Aww don't be like that! It's all in good fun, an innocent mistake," he smirks.

"Fun? Is this what you people do for fun?" I retort.

"Oh yes. Haven't you heard of the game 'run your neighbors down'? All the cool kids are playing it."

"Oh, I bet," I say sarcastically,

"Well, I don't believe we've made a proper introduction yet," he says as he extends a muscle toned arm in my direction. "I'm Graeson Frederick Tailor Ambrose . . . the third. You must be the new neighbor."

What's up with these people and their need to introduce themselves by their full names?

"That I am. We just got in last night. I'm Izzie," I introduce myself and then add sarcastically, "It's been a pleasure meeting you."

So this is the infamous Graeson I was told to stay away from. Maybe Stephanie wasn't so far off with this advice.

He laughs, and his dimples pierce his cheeks making it difficult for me not to smile. He says, "Well, Isabelle, might I say that you are quite beautiful."

"Do you say that to all the girls you almost run over?"

He puts his hands on his hips and shakes his head playfully, "Funny, real funny. You're quite the comedian."

I glance behind Graeson to his car and see his friend still looking utterly shell-shocked from the near accident. I forgot he was even here.

"Hey, is your friend okay?" I ask half concerned and half searching for a way to keep this conversation going.

"My friend?" he looks like he's wracking his brain to remember everything before our little conversation. "Oh, right, my friend!"

He looks behind him and yells, "Shea! Get your arse out of my car and come introduce yourself!" He looks back to me and says, "Please excuse him. He's a bit shy."

Shea tumbles out of the car and awkwardly makes his way up to us, clearly unsure of what to say. Graeson seems amused with the whole situation, but I feel for the boy in the passenger seat. Meeting new people has never been my forte. I find it difficult enough to keep a conversation going with the people I've known forever.

"Shea, this is our new neighbor, Isabelle. Isabelle, this is my best friend Shea Donahue."

He extends his hand for me to shake, unsure if that was the right move. I take it, feeling the clamminess of his hand.

"Hi," I say. "You can just call me Izzie. It's nice to meet you."

He takes a second to process my words, but then speaks up, "It's nice to meet you too. I'm . . . um . . . really sorry about that. You know . . . um . . . almost killing you and everything. That's not normally how we introduce ourselves to new people."

He lets out a small nervous laugh and I return his little joke with a wide, toothy grin to hopefully make him feel more at ease.

When he looks up from nervously staring at his feet, he sees my smile and moves his eyes up to meet mine. We lock eyes for a moment, and I can see him relaxing a little. It makes me release the breath I didn't even know I was holding. Looking at him close up now, there's something about him that's very comforting. It may be his bright blue eyes that catch my attention and seem to be a river of thoughts and emotions. Or maybe it's the slight awkwardness I see in him that I also recognize in myself. Or maybe it's just that I'm happy to be around people my age that I actually have a chance to possibly be friends with. I'm not really sure what it is. But now that he's in front of me, I see that he's handsome in his own charming way. He's not like Graeson who comes right out and screams "come look at me, I'm gorgeous." Shea is cute in a subtle way that sneaks up on you and catches you off guard, but is so very intriguing. His hair is caramel colored, with blonde undertones that pop when the sunlight hits it a certain way. He's tall and thin, with long, gangly arms that hang awkwardly at his side that he doesn't seem to know what to do with. It's like he hasn't yet grown into his body. His skin is gently sunkissed, and he has two humble dimples that hang out on each of his cheeks. Subtle, but captivating.

We stand in the middle of the road for a while longer with Graeson's car still running while we break the ice and learn the basic information about each other. I learn that they're both going to be seniors and Knox Hollow High next fall with me, Shea runs cross country and track, and Graeson plays soccer and lacrosse. I tell them a little bit about Portland and my love for basketball. And for those few moments, I forget about everything else and just enjoy talking to them. In the middle of the street with the sun shining down on us, I feel like a normal teenage girl for the first time in God only knows how long. And right now, it's enough.

"We were headed to meet another friend at a spot downtown. Would you like to join us, Miss Isabelle?" Graeson asks, turning his charm up into full gear.

I consider my options: running off with two kind of strangers who almost killed me or going back to angrily shooting hoops by myself. It's not a difficult decision, even for me who usually overanalyzes every situation.

A sly smile spreads across my face, "That depends on who's driving."

Graeson shoots me another one of his smirks and says, "I'm an excellent driver."

"You almost *killed* me ten minutes ago!"

"Yeah, *almost*, meaning that I, in fact, did not kill you. Therefore, I am an excellent driver."

Shea, eager to add to the conversation, says, "I'm not sure that's how that works, buddy."

"Oh sure, take the pretty girl's side! I see how it is," he says pretending to be all hurt as we all start laughing at the ridiculousness of the conversation.

"You really should come," Shea adds quietly.

We lock eyes again and I say, "Why not?"

It's true. What do I have to lose? This sounds reckless and impulsive and fun and exactly what I need right now.

Graeson starts cheering and says, "Let's roll!"

I follow his lead to the baby blue Cadillac, and he opens the backseat door for me.

"Wow, you really are a gentleman," I joke.

"It's those English roots," he snaps back.

I buckle up, yanking the seatbelt extra tight — Graeson's track record speaks for itself — as he hits the gas and turns the radio up until it's blaring in my ears. He drives incredibly fast with the car gliding over the pitch black road as if it were a sheet of ice. The sunlight bounces off my back and the top of my head, perfectly contrasting the cool breeze that blows my hair in every direction. Graeson sings along off key to the song blasting from the speakers, and the smell of their cologne combines with the aroma of the fresh air and mowed lawn clippings. My mom might actually kill me later, but I can already tell that this is going to be totally worth it. I can't even wipe the smile off my face. The rushing air, the music, the speed, the freedom. It's all perfect. Most likely unsafe, but perfect. A joy ride for a girl in desperate need of some joy.

*****

Graeson whips into the parking lot, basically diagonal in the space. As fun as that car ride was, a part of me is grateful to be on solid ground with my life out of Graeson's hands. The kid only takes full speed, sharp turns and is a little too fond of the gas pedal. Shea opens my door and helps me out of the car. I hold onto his hand for a moment longer than I should, but he doesn't seem to notice or mind.

The destination before us is a cute, old-fashioned diner modeled after one from the fifties. Neon pink and blue signs hang from the windows and the smell of salty french fries and charcoal fill the air.

"Are you sure I'm not imposing on your plans?" I ask as we walk up to the front door.

"I almost ran you over today. I figured the least I could do was invite you to lunch," Graeson reassures me.

It's weird how easy it is to talk to them. I'm typically terrible at making new friends. I'm not shy, I'm just awkward and always say the wrong thing, which then makes me self-conscious and more awkward. It's a vicious cycle. But something feels different with Graeson and Shea. It feels comfortable, like I've known them for years.

The three of us make our way into the diner. The inside of the mom and pop shop is even more endearing than the outside. Black and white checkered stools line the counter that stands before the kitchen, and fire engine red booths are placed alongside shiny metal tables. It's the kind of place where everybody knows everybody, and the waiters have your usual order memorized. The smell of french fries and charcoal is even stronger now and hits my nose full force. It's a place straight out of Grease; I didn't even know they still made restaurants like this. All around, people are laughing and talking cheerfully, sipping coffee out of cream colored mugs or biting into juicy cheeseburgers. Before we even sit down, I'm in love with this place.

"It's not much, but it's our favorite place in town," Shea tells me.

"It's perfect," I respond.

As we walk through the diner, Graeson is greeted by almost every single person in there. Swooning high school girls, old couples sipping their coffee, and young kids running around seem to all rush to say hi to him. He returns them all with a charming smile and a cheerful hello.

Shea looks over to me and says, "He knows everybody everywhere, basically Knox Hollow's resident celebrity for whatever reason. We like to refer to him as 'the mayor.'"

I whisper quietly, "Is he always this . . . ," I search for the word, but can't seem to find one that sums Graeson up. "This . . . I don't know."

Shea laughs and whispers back, "Yes, he's always the star of the show."

When we reach the booth farthest to the back, I notice a girl about my age sitting there. Her face turns into a pout the moment she sees the boys.

"Where have you guys been? I've been waiting here for half an hour!" Her voice is higher pitched and sweet, even though she's annoyed.

Graeson looks pensive as he attempts to figure out how best to answer her question, "Minor detour. We met a new friend!"

"He almost ran her down with his car," Shea adds laughing.

Her eyebrows furrow as she says almost in a yelling voice, "Graeson Frederick Tailor Ambrose I swear to God Almighty if you were speeding again!"

I can't help but laugh and say, "Oh, this wasn't the first time?"

Graeson blushes a violent shade of red and hangs his head as she continues going off, "No! It was not the first time! One more speeding ticket and he loses his license! And yes, hang your head. You should be ashamed of yourself." She turns to me, and the anger in her eyes melts into sympathy as she stands up to greet me, "I am so sorry about him. My name's Hazel Huntington, I take it you're our new neighbor."

"I'm Izzie, it's really nice to meet you," I smile and slide into the booth across from her.

Hazel is a tiny girl full of so much spunky, vibrant energy. She has thick, golden blonde curls that fall in loose waves a little past her shoulders. She can't be more than five feet tall and has a tiny, thin frame. From her build to her features, everything about her is petite. Her eyes are an ocean blue, complemented by deep black lashes and light eyebrows that have a natural curve. Her tiny button nose is decorated with freckles that pop against her pale skin. And even though I've only known her for a few seconds, I already love this girl.

Shea sits next to me, and I can tell it's taking all of the self control in his body to bite back the laughter. Hazel catches on and shoots him a serious look that dares him to laugh.

"Don't laugh at him, Shea! You're encouraging his idiocy!" she adds.

"Hey!" he defends himself. "What did I do? I'm not the one who almost killed someone on my way over here."

She rolls her eyes and motions for Graeson to slide into the booth, "Izzie, I'm very sorry that this is your first impression of us. I promise we're not normally this insane."

"It's all good. I've spent the last week trapped in a car with my stepdad. I could use a little crazy."

With that, Hazel's hilarious rage fades into a bubbly persona. The four of us order some food and settle into a conversation with Graeson's ego slightly hurt after being rightfully shoved into his place.

*****

Between mouthfuls of his cheeseburger, Graeson asks, "Have you met anyone else yet? I know you only got in last night."

I think back to my encounter with Stephanie and smirk, "I met Stephanie and Richard Kester last night."

They all start chuckling and Graeson says, "I'm deeply sorry that they were your first impression of Knox Hollow."

"At least they didn't almost run her over with a car," Hazel adds slyly.

Graeson's lips fold into a pout, "Why is everyone so caught up on that one little thing?!"

Shea, seemingly interested in my story, says, "So you met them last night?"

"Yeah. We got in around six o'clock, and then they knocked on our door pretty late last night. They said they were on their way home from a party and wanted to stop in and introduce themselves."

"What'd you think of them?" Graeson smirks.

I think about how to respond and settle on, "They were . . . uh . . . a little weird. Not so much him, but Stephanie was . . . a lot."

"I'm telling you," Graeson starts, "That woman is bat shit crazy!"

Hazel seems slightly alarmed and says, "That's not very nice. She's just a little intense, especially when you first meet her."

"And she loves her red wine," Shea adds.

"Yeah, it was a little overwhelming. Her husband seemed annoyed at her, and she said some really strange things."

"Ah Richard!" Graeson says, "He tries to keep her in check, but it's quite useless. What did she say?"

I spend the next few minutes filling them in on my interaction with the Kesters. I tell them about how Stephanie kept hugging me and touching my face and telling me how pretty I was. When I tell them about what she whispered to me, Graeson laughs, but Shea and Hazel seem to have that same uncomfortable feeling in their core that came over me last night.

"That sounds about right for Stephanie. She's a loose cannon when she's been hitting the red wine," Graeson jokes.

Hazel furrows her eyebrows and wrinkles her nose, "That's weird, even for Stephanie."

"Who's he? And what does he know?" Shea asks, confused.

"That's exactly what I was wondering. She just gave me this really weird vibe. She strutted in like we've known her for years, and she was so over the top and enthusiastic. It was like she was filming a reality TV show. She kept talking about secrets and how she had all the gossip, which really isn't that surprising. Richard kept trying to get her to stop, and when he wasn't listening, she whispered that."

Shea and Hazel are actively analyzing the situation, deep in thought about it all.

Graeson shakes his head and laughs, "Stop reading into this! It's classic drunk Stephanie causing problems."

"You're probably right," I start, "It was just weird."

"It could be normal Stephanie," Hazel starts. "She likes drama. She likes it so much that she creates it when things are quiet around here. I have some stories for you, Izzie. I don't doubt what she said about knowing all the gossip, but the "he knows" part was probably just to mess with you."

"I don't know, something doesn't sound right with that," Shea juts in.

"That's kind of messed up," I say.

"That's Stephanie for you," Hazel replies.

Graeson rolls his eyes, "You guys worry too much."

Maybe I worry too much, but the fact that Hazel and Shea are unsettled by this makes me even more confident that something odd is at work.

"Does Stephanie have any kids?" I ask trying to obtain some basic information like all the private investigators and detectives do in the books I read.

"Three," Hazel says. "Alex, Alison, and Ella."

I make a mental note of that information, and I ask a few more questions, unsure what I'm planning on doing with the knowledge I've acquired. I learned that Stephanie is 39 years old. She's an adolescent psychologist, SoulCycle teacher, head of the PTO at the elementary school, and a thrower of very flashy and glamorous parties.

"Alright, enough. Let's have some fun, instead of worrying about Mrs. Kester and her drinking habits," Graeson finally says.

I decide to put it to the side for now and just enjoy that I've made some new friends. It's a big deal for me. We spend the next two hours getting to know each other and laughing so hard we almost pee in our pants. For that time, I forget about everything else that I'm dealing with.

At around three o'clock, we vacate our booth and make our way to the parking lot.

Shea says to Hazel on the way out, "You're sure you're good driving yourself home?"

"Are you kidding me?" she fires back at him. "I refuse to get into any vehicle that *he* is operating. I want to continue living on this side of the ground. I'm not heading home anyway. I told my mom I'd pick Jack up from his friend's house."

I say goodbye to Hazel and thank her for letting me hang out with them.

"Don't thank me!" she says. "Thank you for coming. We *need* to hang out. I'm always stuck with these bozos."

I watch Hazel drive away as I hop into Graeson's Cadillac, anxiously but excitedly awaiting the drive ahead of me.

*****

"ISABELLE KATHERINE ANDREWS!" I hear my mom's angry voice booming as her feet make loud thud noises down the staircase the second I open the front door.

I knew she was going to be angry, but the sound of her voice is still making me shudder. She never calls me Isabelle. I'm definitely in for it. I probably shouldn't have ignored all of her texts, especially the ones asking where I was. You live, you learn.

I resort to the only defense I have in this situation — playing with her motherly emotions. Hopefully, she'll be so proud that I made friends and so relieved that I don't hate life here as much that she'll forget she's mad at me.

"Before you yell at me, I want you to know that I made some new friends. Who are my age! And live in this neighborhood!"

"I don't care who you met! I was worried sick! I was seconds away from calling the police. You can't just leave and not tell me where you are. You didn't even text me back!"

"I was outside, and I met two boys who live a few houses down, and they invited me to lunch. I forgot to check my phone."

"That's unacceptable. I thought something bad happened."

"I'm fine."

"And thank God for that. You got into a car with two strangers. That was reckless. Do you know how badly that could have ended? You could have been kidnapped or worse."

So I guess this is a bad time to bring up that they almost hit me with their car? Probably.

"Nothing bad would've happened."

"Izzie," her volume lowers. "I need you to understand that impulsive decisions have consequences. I will not let you put yourself in danger."

Ugh, there she goes droning on about me and my impulsivity. I'm not impulsive, I'm spontaneous. There's a difference. I swear.

The next thing I say I choose carefully because I know it will make her mad. "I don't really care about consequences Mom. I've lost everything that I had."

Her face melts from angry to hurt, and I feel a little guilty ping in my heart.

"Don't say that, Izzie. You still have me and Luke and John and the girls. I know this move was beyond difficult, but you cannot go around saying you lost everything. I — "

I cut her off and say, "I really don't want to talk about this move. I'm trying to cope with it and move on, I really am. I don't want to keep going over the details. I may have made a spontaneous decision today, but I met three really great people who seem to really like me. I made three new friends, which is more than I ever had in Portland. I'm trying to get through this in my own way. Can't you just let me deal with it on my own terms?"

She pensively thinks about what to say next, stuck between her fear of my recklessness and her happiness that I'm making progress. Finally, she says, "I'm so happy you made friends. I am, Iz. I want you to hang out with friends and enjoy being a teenager, instead of being angry and sad. But I want to be in the loop. I am not ok with you running off and leaving me worried sick about where you are or if you're ok."

Her words run through my brain, calming my nerves and making me feel a little bad that I didn't apologize. But I won't apologize. I can't apologize.

"I hear you. I won't run off again without telling you," I say, purposefully avoiding the phrase I'm sorry.

She puts her hand on my shoulder and smiles softly, "And promise me you'll answer my texts and think about your decisions a little more? No more jumping into random boys' cars."

"I promise. Can we just take this little incident as a learning curve and leave it in the past?" I smile.

She giggles and says, "I can do that."

She wraps me up into one of her signature bear hugs and holds me so tight that I realize how scared she was.

When we disengage, she says, "I only worry because I love you so much."

"I love you, mom."

*****

After dinner, I sit out on our front porch steps because we don't have chairs yet with the new book I'm reading and a glass of iced tea. The sun is tucked gently behind a puffy white cloud as the sky's bright blue coat slowly fades into warm pinks and oranges. The emptiness that had been gnawing a hole in my heart doesn't feel quite as . . . well . . . empty. I met three new people who I really like, and my mom and I seem to have a better understanding of each other. I'm shocked to say it, but I actually had a good day. I haven't been able to say that in a while.

I look up from my book and see Shea walking down the street in my direction.

"HEY!" I call out to him.

I think I catch him off guard, but he looks up, and a wide smile spreads across his face.

"Hey!" he calls back.

He turns and starts walking up our driveway, and for some weird, unexplainable reason I feel a little flutter in my chest.

When he reaches me I say to him, "I would offer you a chair, but we don't have any."

His smile stays glued to his face and his arms are awkwardly crossed. He replies, "It's all good. Chairs are overrated anyway."

He sits down next to me on the step and asks, "What are you reading?"

"It's called *The Monogram Murders*. It's by Agatha Christie, she's one of my favorite authors," I say eager to keep his attention.

"Sounds interesting."

It goes quiet for a moment, and I search for something to say to keep him on my front porch a while longer.

"I wanted to apologize again for almost running you over. Definitely not our finest moment," he says, stumbling over his words in a way that makes me like him a little more.

"Did you come all the way down there just to tell me that?" I smile.

"Well, I was on my way down to that house over there," he points to a white siding and brick house across the street. "There's an old man who lives there. He has dementia and is in a wheelchair, so a couple days a week I go down and help him out. But I saw you were outside and wanted to apologize and say hi and now I'm just babbling on." He drops his head back and says, "I'm just going to say it. You're really pretty, and I can't string a sentence together anymore."

His words send a tingling feeling throughout my entire body, making it feel like there's an electric current flowing between us. All words are failing me now as I feel my cheeks blush a rosy pink. Without even thinking, I place my hand over his. For a moment I'm worried he'll pull away, but instead, he turns his hand over so his palm is pressed against mine, and our fingers intertwine.

"I've had a rough couple of weeks," I say point blank. "And today. Today made everything feel a little bit better."

He turns his head so we're face-to-face, and I can see the bright sparkle of his blue eyes, "I know a little about rough weeks. I've had a few bad patches recently. I know we just met, but if you ever want to talk, I'm here."

Shea's words fill me to the brim with a warm feeling that quickly infects my whole body. Sometimes, all you need is for someone to tell you they understand. To tell you they're there for you. Sometimes, that's enough.

A small smile spreads across my face that Shea seems to understand as my way of showing how much this means to me. I just can't even express any of my thoughts right now. It's all a bunch of incoherent words and feelings that float around in my head like ice cubes floating in a glass of water. It's like there's some unspoken understanding between us that I can't even describe.

We sit like that for a while longer, letting our feelings swirl through our minds. It's silent, but not an awkward silence. It's a silence that speaks better than any words could. It's a silence that comforts you and makes you feel a little less alone. A silence that fills you with crazy, wonderful possibilities.

"Well I better get going," he says reluctantly.

I don't want him to leave, but the fact that he's going to help an old man is making me fall a little harder for him.

"Maybe I'll see you tomorrow," I say.

"Maybe you will."

With those words filling my mind with endless feelings and questions, Shea walks down my driveway, his figure glowing against the hazy orange sky. I think to myself: maybe this joy ride is just beginning.

CHAPTER 3 - Bearer of Bad News

"Hey, kiddo," I hear my dad's voice on the other line.

I'm slumped in my purple bean bag chair, lost in a novel and snacking on crisp, green grapes.

"Dad!" The excitement radiates through my voice. "I missed you."

There's a pause, and the line goes quiet for a minute until I hear him clear his throat, "I know, sweetheart. It's been busy over here."

"How's working for Jackson's company going?" I ask.

Another pause and another throat clear, "That didn't work out. I've been picking up odd jobs wherever I can. But let's not talk about me honey, I want to hear about you. How's life up in Massachusetts?"

He's gearing away from work, which I can tell is a touchy subject. I know it's been tough on him, so I don't press the matter.

"It's good. I've made some new friends," I say, trying to keep the conversation positive.

"Well, that's great," his voice is coarse and slow. "I'm glad you're doing good. How's your brother?"

I was waiting for that question. Luke won't talk to our dad. Other than a few awkward, two minute phone calls or quick hellos when he would come to a sports game or music concert, Luke hasn't spoken to him since they got divorced seven years ago. Remember how I said we were pushed to take sides? Well, Luke took my mom's. I took my dad's. It's funny because Luke and I talk about everything together. Sometimes, I feel like he's my only friend. But the divorce is the one thing we don't talk about. We don't talk about it because we both have very different, but very strong feelings about it. I'll defend dad, and he'll protect mom. It's an unspoken contract between the two of us to pretend the whole thing doesn't exist.

I can hear the hurt in his voice when he asks about Luke. I don't understand Luke's reasoning. He won't talk about it, and I won't ask. Mom always says that time faded them into different people who had different visions and wants. I've always felt like my mom has tried to push him out of our lives as much as she can. It's like she doesn't want to be reminded of or tied down to the divorce and what life was like before things collapsed. Ever since then, our lives have been divided into two different eras: pre and post divorce. We were one happy family, and then we were just pieces of it held together by tape and glue and fake smiles.

"He's good," I say with fake happiness. "He misses you."

The line goes silent again as he pretends not to notice my white lie. Sometimes, I feel like there's so many elephants in the room, so many things we don't talk about, so many issues we ignore that it's difficult to have a conversation. It's like constantly walking on thin ice, always scared that at any point you'll plunge into the icy water below.

"Good to hear. I tried calling him earlier, but he didn't answer. I know you kids are busy. But if you could, would you tell him to give me a call when he has a chance?" he asks even though he already knows that Luke won't even consider dialing the first number.

"Of course. I miss home a lot Dad."

"I know, sweetheart, I know. I miss you being close by, but your mom's trying to do what's best. You're not giving her a hard time, right?"

"I'm doing my best. It's hard sometimes."

"Me and you are a lot alike. We take some time to warm up. Luke and your mom have always been able to adapt and talk to anyone. You'll find your place, sweetheart. Just give it time."

His words send a feeling of comfort and warmth throughout my body. It gives me the reassurance that only he can provide me with. God, I wish he were here now. My face feels wet, and I realize that tears have been streaming down from my eyes. I just feel like I'm moving so far away from him, like a planet falling out of orbit.

When I was in second grade, I was accused of clocking some terribly annoying girl in my class in the nose after she made fun of me. My dad marched into the school and fiercely defended me against my teacher's accusations. Of course they were true. I totally threw a fist at her insanely large nose. But later that day, my dad came into my room and pulled me onto his lap. I remember feeling safe and secure in his arms, like the world was a little bit smaller.

He looked at me with his warm chestnut eyes and said, "Punching people is not okay . . . but I'll always be on your side, bud."

He was always on my side, even when I was wrong. Even now, when I'm hundreds of miles away from him, he's rooting for me.

"Wipe the tears from your eyes," he says softly.

"How do you know I'm crying?" I say, trying to deny the fact that I show emotions other than anger.

"Because I know you. Just like I know that you are going to be okay. You're going to be better than okay, Isabelle. Just give yourself time, bud. I promise it will all work out in the end. It always does"

"Okay," I cry quietly.

"And you can come visit whenever you want. The apartment's small, but there's always room for you," his voice is lined thick with sympathy.

"I love you Dad."

"I love you kiddo."

And with that last simple phrase, I hung up the phone stuck between the terrible ache in my heart from missing home and his reassuring words that truly made me believe that I would be okay.

*****

When I finally leave my room that morning, I make my way down the stairs in serious need of some one-on-one time with my basketball. I find John packing snacks into a lunch box while Madison, my three-year-old half sister, is telling him some story that no one can keep track of. Her mocha brown hair sticks out in every direction, permanently tangled under a silver tiara. She wears her favorite princess costume — my mom has given up trying to get her to wear anything other than princess dresses — with matching plastic high heels that would cause anyone over the age of four to break an ankle.

"Izzie!" I hear her squeaky voice.

"Wow, Princess Madison you look beautiful today," I compliment her.

She blushes and tucks her chin down to her chest like she always does when she's embarrassed, "Thank you. Guess what!?"

"What?"

"Daddy's taking me to the park!" she says with pure excitement.

I would give anything to go back to the days where a playground was all it took to make me happy. The days where you would swing so high, believing that you might actually touch the clouds and feeling the rush of air against your face. The days where you would run wildly around without a care in the world, feeling the blades of grass on your tiny bare feet. The days where the scariest thing was crossing the monkey bars, fearful of falling into the mulch below so you would latch on so tight that little blisters would form on your palms. Madison and Olivia are so lucky. They have two parents who love each other, two parents who can be in the same room. They're not going to be anything like me, angry and stubborn, the essence of a broken home. My sisters will always remind me of what I don't have, what I lost.

"That's exciting," I say back, unamused with the conversation.

"We're packing some snacks and heading over to the park a few blocks down. Any interest in joining us?" John asks.

I furrow my eyebrows and give him a slight scowl, "No, I'm all set."

Madison goes back to singing to herself, as I watch John fight the urge to not say something about my attitude. He's scared to overstep, but he's ready to break. It's not my fault he stormed into my life and changed everything. He's going to have to deal with this. With me. Right now, I'm just in one of those extra terrible moods where I almost want to cause an issue. It's like I just want an excuse to be angry so I don't have to feel sad. I know, that's weird and twisted, but it's how I feel. Anger makes it easier to avoid all the pain. I just don't want to feel all the sadness rushing over me, swallowing me up like a wave. Sadness is like an undertow, sucking you down and trapping you until you can no longer breathe. It's weird, but talking to my dad makes me even angrier with John. He serves as a permanent reminder of what was taken from me. Like a replacement because my dad wasn't good enough.

"What?" I say to him, daring John to make a move.

He contemplates what to say next, "I think that you could've said it a little nicer, that's all."

I stare him down, ready to take my opportunity to be mad, "Do you think I care?"

Now this phrase particularly sets him off. It makes the brightness of his sky blue eyes dim and his mouth twitch a little. This should be good.

He takes a big breath in, desperately trying to maintain a calm front, "You're not going to talk to me like that, Izzie."

"I will if I want to," the words escape me before I have a chance to think about them.

Okay, so maybe that was a little harsh. I quickly turn to make a run for the stairs and find my way out of the mess I've just made.

"Stop. Right. There," he enunciates each letter in each word.

I internally debate either booking it to my room or facing John. I don't want to take the coward's way out, but I really didn't expect John to fight back. Slowly, I turn my body around so I'm looking at him straight in the eye. Silence. Both of us trying to mentally calculate the next step.

"Okay, so I found all the boxes with our Christmas decorations. Those need to —" my mom walks up the stairs from the basement and interrupts herself when she reads the room. "What's going on here?" Her voice is skeptical and accusatory towards me.

The tension in the kitchen is so thick, you could cut it with a freshly sharpened knife.

"We were just chatting," John pipes up casually as I heave a massive sigh of relief.

I'm not sure why, but John will never rat me out to my mom. As far as I know, he doesn't say anything to her when I act like this. Is it because he's scared to overstep? Or because me acting like this has become so normal to him? I'm not sure. But I don't have the brain capacity to analyze that right now.

My mom shoots me a "what did you do?" look, so I quickly move my eyes to the floor, staring at the laces on my grey Nike sneakers.

"Madison and I were headed to the park," John adds.

A forced smile spreads over my mom's face, probably to keep from alarming Madison, as she says, "I've been working so hard to unpack. I think a little fresh air would do me some good. Mind if I tag along Miss Madison?"

Madison, oblivious to the scene that was unfolding in front of her, cheers and runs over to hug our mom. She wraps her hands around her legs because she's too small to reach any higher. It makes me think of the days when I used to run at her full force, throwing my whole body at her, wrapping my arms around her legs. She would bend down and hold me tight, clinging onto the days where I still voluntarily hugged her. Watching Madison do that now sends a lonely feeling into the pit of my stomach. I can't stop thinking about how Madison and Olivia are both so lucky they didn't have to grow up as a part of a broken family.

When Madison releases her, my mom turns, hands me a box cutter, and says, "Stephanie let me borrow this the other day. Would you mind running it back to her?"

I nod my head, unsure of how much my mom has gathered from the situation.

She leans in and whispers, "We'll talk about this when I get back."

I'm dead freaking meat.

*****

The Kester's front door is made of solid birch wood. I feel uncomfortable standing on their porch all alone. I keep getting the strange feeling that somebody's watching me, hidden in the lush green bushes and shrubbery. The logical part of me knows that's not true, but I can't shake the feeling.

I'm about to walk away when a young girl who looks to be about seven years old with hair the color of butter slowly creaks the door open. Her wide blue eyes stare intently out at me — a mix of nerves and curiosity. Half of her ghostly pale face is hidden by the door.

"Hi," I say cautiously. "Is your mom home?"

I would've just given the boxcutter to her, but I felt weird handing a sharp bladed object to a seven-year-old. Sometimes, I have good judgment. Not all the time, but sometimes.

She doesn't speak, but nods her head instead while motioning for me to follow her. I'm guessing this is one of Stephanie's three kids. She's a lot quieter than her obnoxious mother.

I follow the little girl's lead into the entryway of the Kester residence. A crystal chandelier hangs from the high ceiling. Our footsteps echo as we walk along the dark hardwood floor, causing the noise to bounce all around the area. On each side of me are large, gradually winding staircases with black slate steps that extend to the upstairs landing. In front of me is a small, white-washed table decorated with a vase of sunflowers resting upon a stack of old books. From what I can tell, this house was professionally decorated by a famous interior designer.

The little girl leads me down a hallway straight ahead, but still doesn't speak. The sound of my footsteps echoes in my ears, making me even more self conscious about being here. I wish this child would say *something*.

The hallway opens up to a massive kitchen and a set of french doors that the sunlight pours through, creating streaks of light that dance across the floor. Through the glimmering glass is a high deck, equipped with pots of thriving flowers, an outdoor sectional and chairs, and a table where the middle is a strip of a gas fire.

Finally, I decide to speak up, "So, is your mom here?"

49

The little girl nods as the two of us stand awkwardly in the kitchen.

"What's your name?" I try to get her to talk again.

There's an awkward silence until I hear her tiny, raspy voice, "Ella."

Her eyes stay glued to the floor, and I start to feel bad for her. She seems afraid of her own shadow. My presence is probably making her cringe with anxiety.

"My name's Izzie," I say softly with a smile on my face, "I just moved in next door. I like your bow." I point to the little pastel pink bow that holds back her shoulder length hair.

"Thank you," her eyes don't leave the ground. "I'll go find my mom."

I can't tell if she's actually going to look for Stephanie or just looking for an excuse to stop talking to me. Either way, I'm now standing completely alone in a stranger's kitchen. I thought I was uncomfortable before, but now the beads of sweat on my head are starting to drip down my face and my hands ferociously twirl my hair in knots. I guess that nervous little girl gave me more comfort than I thought.

An eerie silence settles over the entire house. I hear the faint noise of classical piano music, and wonder if someone's actually playing the piano or if it's all in my head. Well, this is great. I guess this is what I get for trying to start a fight with John. Sometimes I feel like the world is just out to punish me. Or maybe I'm punishing myself. I notice a loose piece of paper on the white marble countertops. A scribbled grocery list is scrawled across it in red ink. I hear footsteps quickly, but smoothly running down the stairs, and I thank God that Ella's coming back for me. But then I hear a hushed voice.

"You said you'd have it by Thursday," the voice is quiet, but harsh, definitely not that of the little girl who seemed stunned by the sound of her own voice. No, this voice is confident with an underlying sense of urgency.

I instantly recognize it as Stephanie, and quickly realize she's not talking to me. She comes down the stairs and turns the corner into the dining room instead of heading straight down the hallway where I'm standing. Curiosity gets the best of me as I impulsively inch towards the staircase and crouch behind it so I can better hear her conversation. I feel like a detective investigating a suspect. It sends a rush of adrenaline and nervous excitement through my body. It feels kind of . . . good.

"You said you'd have it by Thursday," she repeats the line, but with a more vicious tone.

She's clearly angry, but trying to keep the phone call a secret. Why else would she be whispering?

"NO! You will have it for me by Thursday," she snarls with an intense level of conviction. I would not want to disobey whatever it is she wants. She seems like the type who will turn the tables on you as soon as you go against her. And from the looks of it, she has the power to make your life a living hell if you don't give her what she wants. I mean, that's only speculation — my best guesses on her personality — but I just know that it's true. My dad taught me to always follow your gut feeling, and most of the time, my assessments of other people aren't that far off. Having good instincts makes you a good judge of character.

It's silent for another moment, and I can hear the muffled sound of the voice on the other line, but can't make out the mystery caller's words.

"Listen to me, right now. If I don't get it by Thursday I will go over there and tell her. I'll tell her everything."

This sounds serious. Stephanie knows something about someone that sounds like it could cause a lot of damage. This woman has so many levels of crazy.

I hear her voice cut through the quiet, "If you even try, I swear to God I'll kill you."

Her words send chills down my spine. The danger alarm is shrieking in my brain, telling me to run. I don't know what this is, but she doesn't sound like she's messing around, and I do not want to get caught in the crossfire of whatever mess this is. All of a sudden, my hand releases the box cutter, and it falls to the ground with a thud that echoes throughout the silent house. Shit! My body and brain go into complete panic. My only thought now is *get out*. I move as silently and quickly as I can, praying to God that I don't catch Stephanie's eyes. I hear her footsteps coming closer, but I don't stick around long enough to know if she saw me. As soon as I'm outside, my legs start pumping, and I don't stop sprinting until I'm safely inside my house with the doors locked.

It looks as if I've created yet another mess for myself, except the fall out of this one is far beyond my imagination.

*****

I hear a soft tap on my bedroom door and break into a cold sweat worrying that it's my mom ready to serve me a very harsh punishment, or worse, talk about my feelings. But it's just Luke.

"Hey," he says. "Mom wants to talk to us."

Oh no. So I *am* about to pay for my actions, and Luke was just delivering the message.

I throw my head back and put my hands over my eyes.

"What did you do?" Luke asks. "I just want to know what I'm about to walk into. I've got your back, but I want to know what I'm defending."

"I mean it wasn't that bad," I lie, trying to hide the uncertainty in my voice.

Luke gives me an all-knowing stare and doesn't even have to use words to get me to break into a nervous word vomit.

"I was talking to dad, and then I may have kind of yelled at John, and then he told me I couldn't talk to him that way, and I told him that I could talk to him any way I wanted and that I didn't care and . . . I messed up!" The words just keep flowing out of my mouth, making absolute zero sense.

Confusion is written all over Luke's face, "I have no idea what you just said, but I'll tell you what I always tell you. It's going to be okay. You just gotta think before you say something, especially when it comes to John. But it's going to be okay. This storm will pass."

I half smile at him and wonder how someone so smart and wise could be related to someone as much of an idiotic mess as I am.

"On a side note," he starts. "Are you ever going to unpack these boxes?"

He's referring to the mass of brown cardboard boxes that cover almost every inch of my floor. It's funny to think that my entire life is packed into those four cardboard walls. And I don't feel like opening all of that up right now, or ever.

"Nope," I answer. "Oh, hey dad wants you to call him." I remember to tell him.

He nods nonchalantly and then motions for me to head downstairs with him.

The second I make it into the living room, I'm already regretting ever leaving the comfort of my bean bag chair. My mom sits cross legged on the couch with a polish pottery mug full of green tea in her hand. John sits next to her, staring out into the distance at the window. His face is filled with worry, instead of his typical relaxed look. Worry lines crease his forehead as he stares out into the navy blue sky. I didn't realize how late it had gotten. Madison and Olivia are safely tucked into their beds, oblivious to the troubles on the floor just below their bedrooms. My toes curl and my body cringes as I sit in the arm chair across from John. This is not going to be good.

"Hi, you two," Mom's voice is soft and kind, the type of voice she uses when she has to deliver bad news to us.

I stare at the two of them awkwardly, unsure if I'm supposed to be apologizing or waiting for them to talk some more. John's focus is shifted from the window to me and Luke.

"Is everything okay?" Luke asks.

Mom takes a big breath while an uncomfortable silence fills the air, "I have some bad news. This is not going to be easy to hear, but I want you to know how much we love you."

This sounds like the start of the conversation mom and dad had with us when they told us they were getting divorced.

"You're scaring me, mom," Luke says.

I can see tears pooling in the corner of her eyes, "I got a call from your grandma, dad's mom, a few hours ago. Dad was in an accident. He was drinking and driving, and he crashed into a tree. His injuries were pretty severe, but they took him to the hospital, and they're hopeful he'll recover. I am so sorry."

I can't hear anything but static filling my ears. My heart drops into my stomach. The entire world freezes. Time stops. No one moves. My brain shuts down. Mom's words hang heavily in the space between us, but don't quite make it into my brain. I don't think I understood her. I don't think I heard her right. There's no way I heard her right. Right?

The world around me goes completely black as a numb feeling settles over me. Am I supposed to cry? Or am I supposed to lash out and scream? Or am I supposed to feel like my entire body was injected with novocain and block out the noise?

"I'm sorry, what did you say?" I ask, trying to keep my voice steady.

"Honey, I'm so sorry," Mom says as she walks over to hug me.

I shake myself free of arms, and say with a rising volume, "Stop! What did you say? Mom, what did you say? I didn't hear you right."

The panic suddenly crashes over me the way a wave crashes into the shore. My breath is rapid and shallow, my heart working overtime to keep me from passing out. I look over to Luke whose face displays zero emotion, his eyes locked on a spot on the wall.

"Izzie, look at me," she begins. "Look at me. It's going to be okay, honey. It's —"

I cut her off. I've lost all control of myself — my voice and my body.

"NO!" I scream. "Tell me again. It's not true!"

Tears are streaming down my face faster than I can wipe them away. They sting my cheeks and drip down my neck. I abruptly jump up from the couch and start pacing in circles. I'm shaking my head back and forth, ferociously rubbing my hands over my face as if it will help take the pain away. I feel like the room is closing in on me. I can't breathe. I can't breathe. I can't breathe. I'm gasping for air, but I keep choking on the lump in my throat.

All of a sudden, John grabs my hands firmly, but gently at the same time. I'm hyperventilating faster and faster as he pulls me into a sitting position next to him on the couch. He wraps his arms tightly around my shoulders, pulling my head into his neck. It's weird, but I don't fight it. The pressure from his arms holding me tight slows my breathing and calms me down slightly. The tension in my body lessens.

His face is back to his natural calm appearance. John is in his element. Being a psychiatrist and everything, he's used to helping people with emotional trauma. I just didn't realize I had become one of his unstable patients.

His voice is steady and firm, but soft, "Breathe. Just take a deep breath in. You're okay."

I hear the sound of my breathing — in and out, in and out, in and out. I let myself relax in his arms for a moment, and then suddenly, everything clicks into place. The storm of emotions crashes over me again.

I start shaking my head again, "NO! You're not my dad! You're not my dad! You can't do this! You're the reason he crashed the car. You're the reason he might die. NO! You can't do this!" I scream.

I try to storm away, but mom grabs my hand.

"Izzie, stop! I understand that you're mad, but this is not John's fault. You have every right to be mad, but you cannot take this out on him," she says.

John stands up, his face still calm and cool.

"I take a lot from you, Izzie. I take all the eye rolling and the yelling and rude comments. I let you treat me like I'm less than human. I keep my mouth shut, and I let you take your anger out on me. And if it helps you get through your day, I'll take it all. Because, whether you like it or not, I love you. I'm not going anywhere, Izzie. I'm here for you. I try, Izzie. I try every single day to be there for you and show you that I'm not the bad guy. To show you that we're on the same side. And you know what, I am *never* going to stop trying. I'm never going to stop being there for you. So whenever you realize that, I'll be here."

John finally fought back, but it's a lot different than I thought. It feels . . . strange. I pictured him screaming and blowing up after years of dealing with me. But he just delivered an Emmy award winning speech. Beautifully worded, calmly said, and kindly delivered. He wasn't angry, just firmly reassuring me that he's never going to stop trying to get me to accept him. I always pictured this moment with me yelling back at him, finally engaging in an argument that's been brewing for six years. But now I just feel empty. Empty and hurt and disgusted in myself. John and my mom were just the bearers of bad news, not the actual wrongdoers. And I can't be angry with them for that.

The words flow out of me without thinking, "I'm sorry."

I turn around and slowly walk back up to my room, ready to bury myself in a cocoon of blankets. I don't bother waiting to watch their stunned reactions, and before I leave, I notice Luke is already gone. All of this has just been too much for one day.

C H A P T E R 4 - The Red High Heels

Chrysalism is the tranquility of being indoors during a thunderstorm. I learned that word a few days ago, and it's fitting right now. I sit at my bay window huddled under a blanket, watching the rain angrily fall from the sky. I can hear the water droplets as they slap the window and roll down the glass. It makes me think of when I was little and pretended the rain drops falling down my window were having a race. Thunder booms off in the distance and lightning strikes flash in bright bursts. I've always loved thunderstorms. I love the feeling of being safe inside, like my own little bubble away from the world. Which brings me back to the word chrysalism. I've spent the last two days self grounded in my room. I've been looking up new words to express emotions seeing that I have the emotional maturity of a two-year-old. After everything that happened on Tuesday, I've been living in a state of numbness. I'm just going through the motions. It's like I'm physically here, but my mind is off somewhere else. I don't feel upset or angry — surprisingly — or even annoyed. Just like I'm floating through each day and night, unable to process or understand everything. But honestly, not feeling at all feels a lot better than being angry. It's like living in a world where my problems don't exist.

I'm not sure who I'm supposed to be mad at. It's like I need someone to blame to make it easier to process, but I can't find anyone to fault. I can't blame my mom, and despite my tantrum Tuesday night, I can't fault John either. I still can't believe I told John it was his fault my dad got into a car accident. Not my best moment. I was so upset about the accident that I didn't realize that my mom had said he was drinking and driving. I'm not sure what that means for him or for me, but I have no interest in diving into that. I'd rather be numb. My grandma's been calling a few times a day to keep us updated, but he's still not awake. He broke his shoulder, right leg, and a few of his ribs, plus the trauma to his head. I just can't think about all of this. It's too much to process.

I haven't talked to anyone in the last two days, so you can imagine my surprise when I receive a call from Hazel on this rainy morning. I think about declining the call and returning to my bubble, but there's something about seeing her name on my phone that's comforting. It's nice to know somebody cares enough to reach out to me.

"Hi, Izzie. It's Hazel. Are you doing anything today?" her energetic voice bursts from the phone.

"Hey, I'm not doing anything." My voice comes out raspy; I don't think I've uttered a word in the last two days.

"Well, it's so dreary outside, and I *cannot* sit in my house any longer. You want to go get coffee?"

This is what it's like to have friends, I guess. The thought of hanging out with Hazel is changing some of the numbness to a small sliver of happiness.

"That sounds really great."

"Awesome! I'll pick you up in 20!" Her voice is so excited, and it makes me think that maybe Hazel and I are more similar than I thought at first. Maybe she needs a friend too. I mean, I would if Graeson was my only source of friendship. He's hilarious, but definitely not someone you can have a serious conversation with.

I scramble to get ready, throwing my long, thick hair into a high ponytail complete with a bandana print scrunchie. I throw on a pair of jean shorts that I'm sorta sure are clean and my Rolling Stones t-shirt. I slip on my low top white Converse, not high tops because those bug my ankles. It feels kind of good to get ready and have somewhere to go. Now, I'm just hoping I can make it out to Hazel's car without running into my mom or John.

As my luck would have it, I run right into mom, quite literally, on my way out. I'm moving so fast that I basically launch myself at her.

"Slow down, Iz," she says with a smile, probably genuinely happy to see me out of my room, "How are you doing, honey?"

"I'm fine," I try to plaster a smile on my face so she'll leave me be.

"I just want to talk to you, Izzie. I know how hard this is," her voice is passionate; I know she's trying really hard.

"I promise, Mom, I'm fine. Hazel asked me to go hang out, so can you just let me go, please?"

"I'll let you go if you promise we can talk about this later. I don't want you keeping all these feelings inside and then exploding again. This is a lot to deal with, and I need you to realize that you're not going through it alone."

"Fine, we can talk later, but I really am fine."

She sighs and lets me leave, probably already knowing that I have no intention of actually talking to her later. There's nothing to talk about, anyway. My dad drinks too much. Everyone already knew that, except me, I guess. He made a bad choice and now we all have to live with the consequences. What else is there to discuss? My life sucks. I don't want to go over the details with a fine-toothed comb. I'm just happy that Hazel doesn't know anything about me or my broken family. At least with her I have a clean slate and don't have to be constricted under a label or a mistake that wasn't even mine. Correction, a lot of the mistakes are mine, but I still don't want to talk about them.

"Wait, honey," she says.

"What?"

"Mrs. Kester invited us to her kickoff to summer party Saturday night. I guess it's this whole big block party, and everyone in the neighborhood goes. I think it'll be a great chance for us to meet new people, and you can introduce me to your new friends. Will you come?"

"Sure, mom," I say, telling her what she wants to hear without really listening. "That sounds great."

Hazel is sitting in her car waiting for me as Shawn Mendes blares through the speakers. Her car is a small silver Altima, which is fitting for her. Her wild, curly hair hangs in loose beach waves a little past her shoulders. She wears large, cheetah print sunglasses that take up over half of her face.

When I open the car door, she turns down the music and smiles brightly, "I'm so glad you could come!"

I slide into the seat and say, "I'm happy you called. I needed a break from . . . all of that." I point to my house and laugh nervously because I can't really find the words to sum everything up.

"How are you liking it here? I can't even imagine how hard it must be moving at this age," she asks sympathetically.

I wonder where to start, "It's been alright. It's weird, starting over this late in high school. Like I'm supposed to make all these new friends and find this whole new life, just to move away to college in a year."

"I hear you. You should know, though, that you always have a friend in me. I know I just met you and everything a few days ago, but I just feel like we clicked . . . sorry, that was probably too much. I'm a very loving person, which is too much for a lot of people. I only do it because I care too much about everything. And I'm also very positive, which annoys a lot of people. And I talk way too much, especially when I get awkward and don't know what to say. So you know . . ."

I feel a wide smile appearing on my face, "I love you already."

And I truly mean it. Hazel has a lot of the qualities that I'm lacking in my life. She talks too much, I don't talk enough. She's always positive, I'm always negative. She cares too much, I don't care enough. We balance each other out in the best possible way. The kindness she's shown me since I've been here is more than that of some of my friends back in Portland. Her reaching out to me and going out of her way to include me has been one of the only things keeping me from just leaving everything here and running.

"So you're not a fan of the rain?" I ask to make conversation.

She sighs, "No, I'm not a fan of my brothers. The rain keeps me trapped in my house with the four of them and that's what I *cannot* stand."

"You have four brothers?" I say wide-eyed.

"Yes, four gross boys who take over the entire house. Literally everywhere you turn there's one of them. They're loud and wild and annoying. And, they bring friends. The amount of boys in my house multiplies like bunnies."

"Wow, I see why you wanted to get out," I laugh.

"Oh yes. I decided to make a break for it when they announced that they were turning our house into one big game of capture the football."

"Smart move. My parents would kill me if I turned our house into a football field," I laugh.

"Not mine! They eat, breathe, and sleep football. My dad used to play in the NFL, so football is the only thing that matters in my house. All of my brothers play. It's like a weird cult."

It's funny listening to her family problems. It makes me think that I'm not the only one whose family has issues.

"Who's your dad?" I ask curiously.

"Carson Huntington," she says casually.

"Your father is Carson Huntington?! Like *the* Carson Huntington?!"

I cannot believe I'm hanging out with one of the greatest NFL running backs' daughters. Carson Huntington was a running back for the Steelers for five or six years before he took a crazy hit that left his right knee so messed up he could never return to the field. He was one of the best running backs in the history of running backs. He was so good he ended up in the Hall of Fame, even after such a short career.

Her cheerfulness turns into annoyance, "Yes, but trust me, he's not that amazing. Or maybe he's amazing to anyone other than me. He basically doesn't even realize I exist because I'm not a boy and I don't play football. I'm first in my class, but I can't throw a spiral, so . . ." she laughs.

"I understand that. Family is hard. I've had a tough time with family issues. We all have our stuff."

She smiles, most likely relieved that I'm not just another fangirl who wants to meet her dad. Hazel and I seem to understand each other. We both have our issues. Just knowing that someone else is fighting through something makes you feel a little less alone in a world of struggles.

We sail through the roads, as if the car was a boat and the pavement was the ocean. Hazel is a much smoother driver than Graeson. Her speed matches the one on the speed limit sign, her turns aren't dangerously wide, and her eyes are actually on the road.

After a little while of basic getting to know you conversation, Hazel says, "Okay, so I have to ask! What did you do to Shea?"

My brain fumbles to find what I could've possibly already done to mess him up as my cheeks blush a harsh shade of red.

"What do you mean?" I say flustered.

63

"I've never seen him so happy, Izzie! I haven't seen him smile like that in weeks. Seriously, how did you do it?" she says laughing.

"Uh . . . I . . . I don't think I did anything but talk to him. He's really nice."

"Oh my God! You're blushing!" she basically yells in excitement.

"I am not!" I say even though I'm clearly pretending that there's nothing between us.

"You totally are! Do you like him?! I promise, you can tell me anything. I'm so good at keeping my mouth shut, and we're like best friends now."

"I swear, there's nothing going on between me and Shea."

It's quiet for a minute, and then she turns to me with a mischievous half smile and says slyly, "Do you want something to be going on?"

"Hazel!"

"I'm sorry, but this is just so exciting. Shea's had a really tough past few months, so to see him happy again is huge. He was literally glowing when we all went out to lunch together, and he hasn't stopped talking about you since. And when he talks about you, his face lights up. He hasn't been this happy in so long."

Well, this information changes everything. So I wasn't making all of these feelings up in my head. Shea and I really connected that day. I felt like he understood me in ways no one else did. His smile and his blue eyes and charming awkwardness created all these giddy feelings inside of me. He was so far away from the boys I would go for back in Portland. That day on the front porch, holding his hand just felt right. It felt like something I had been doing my entire life, as natural as breathing. I know a big part of me wanted something with him, wanted to kiss him right then and there on the stairs, but after everything that happened with my family, I almost forgot about it. But now, I remember. I remember as clear as day the sensational feelings and hopes he filled me with. And if Hazel's right about this, maybe there's a chance. Maybe, it's safe to stop denying my feelings.

"You promise you won't tell anyone, especially Shea?"

"As your new best friend, I swear on my life that I will not speak a word of this to anyone else!" she pleads.

"I really like him, Hazel. I —" I'm interrupted by Hazel's extreme enthusiasm.

"I KNEW IT!" She's so excited I think it may actually kill her.

Her smile is so wide it reaches her ears, and her eyes are wide and bright.

"Oh, Hazel, stop making that face at me!"

"I'm sorry, I'm sorry," she apologizes. "This just makes me so happy. I can't control my reaction."

When Hazel finally stops gushing long enough to let me speak, I tell her about my little moment with Shea on the front porch. Now that sends her into an excited frenzy, shooting questions and happy comments at me. I think she may be more excited about this than I am.

Hazel pulls into the parking lot of a cute coffee shop called Cool Beans with bright blue awnings and boxes of creamy yellow, vibrant pink, flashy red, and fire orange tulips growing in boxes under the windows. The smell of freshly ground coffee beans wafts through the air.

After we've ordered, Hazel and I find a small marble table in the back. The frothy foam from my maple latte dissolves as the warm liquid fills my mouth with a bitter sweetness, completely satisfying my coffee addiction.

"You said Shea's had a tough couple of weeks. What happened?" I ask.

Hazel looks skeptical, "I don't think it's my place. I'll let him tell you about it."

"I totally understand."

I wonder what happened to Shea. It must be pretty serious if Hazel won't talk about it. But it does make me feel better about literally pouring my soul out to her about Shea, knowing that she takes the whole promise thing very seriously.

"So are you and Graeson a thing?" I ask, genuinely curious.

The two of them seemed really close when I first hung out with them. I don't really think they're together, mostly because I don't think someone as sharp-minded as Hazel would go for a player like him. I'm curious about Graeson and don't want to flat out ask if he's seeing anybody.

I instantly regret asking her because her jaw drops in utter shock. Coffee comes flying out of her mouth, coating the table with brown spit.

"Are you kidding me?! Absolutely not! I wouldn't date him if he were the last man on earth and the entire fate of the world depended on it!"

I start cracking up, "Okay, okay, I hear ya." I can't stop laughing, and before I know it, I can't even speak. "You really just flipped out."

Hazel's no longer in a disgusted panic over my words. Instead, she's laughing along with me.

"I just can't even fathom that. He's cute and charming in a jerk kinda way, but he's a real ass."

"Does he have a girlfriend?" I question.

"Ha, like five of them. Every girl in Knox Hollow is obsessed with him. It's so annoying how easy it is for him. He can get girls easy, but he never keeps any of them. There's always a new one," she laughs with a level of annoyance.

"So, what about you?"

"I don't have a boyfriend. I wish, but I'm so focused on school and the future that I just don't have the time. There's been one, but nothing all that serious. I wish though," she replies.

"This can be *your* summer, Hazel. It's your chance to do something wild! And now that you're friends with me, I can teach you a little bit about living on the edge."

With a sparkle in her ocean eyes, she says, "I think this is going to be one of the best summers yet."

*****

I hear the plates clattering downstairs as John loads the dishwasher. I actually ate dinner with my family at the table tonight, something I haven't done much since we moved here, so I'm making progress. I didn't talk much, but I made some basic conversation and used more manners than normal. I'm still a terrible person, but now I'm a terrible person with some table manners. Now, I'm back to being bundled up at my bay window watching the thunderstorm. Hanging out with Hazel made me feel really good, especially when she told me that Shea has a thing for me, but I still feel that numb emptiness lingering in my chest. There's still so much crap I'm refusing to work through. It's weird not being able to just reach out and call my dad. Who am I supposed to talk to when I'm at my lowest point? Who is supposed to talk me off the ledge? Who is supposed to tell me that everything is going to be alright when life is falling apart? It's such a weird feeling, not knowing if he's going to pull through. But even if he does pull through, I'm not sure what to do. I feel like he's a stranger now.

The sky is charcoal grey, with wispy clouds that look like smoke. The cackling boom of the thunder and the flashes of white and yellow light calm the nerves in my body. Yes, I understand that that's insanely strange. What kind of person is comforted by thunderstorms? For whatever reason, I am.

I hear my phone buzz and see that I have a text from Hazel.

It reads, "Hey Izzie, today was so much fun! I meant to give this to you earlier, but totally forgot. Here's Shea's number, give him a text!"

I smile at my screen. Hazel really is rooting for me.

I reply back to her, "Today was great, I really needed it. I'll give Shea a text tomorrow, thank you :)."

She texts back instantly, "Text him now, he's awake!"

This girl will not give in. I tell her I will and then go back to staring out the window, but my mind keeps floating back to Shea.

When I can't resist the urge to reach out to him any longer, I add his number to my contacts and spend the next 30 minutes trying to type out a message that isn't awkward. It's a harder task than it might sound.

I settle on, "Hi Shea, it's Izzie. Hazel gave me your number today and I wanted to say hi."

So, the message was still awkward and cringey, but at least better than some of my original ideas. I've never been good with words.

A few minutes later, the bubbles appear on my screen and my leg starts anxiously tapping. He's probably going to think I'm some psycho stalker. I shouldn't have texted him. Oh God, this is making me nervous. Can he text any slower?

His reply reads, "Hey, I'm glad she did."

Ok, this is good! This is really good! My brain is working at top speed to come up with a reply.

I text back, "Me too," because I can't think of anything to say that won't embarrass me.

"Can't wait to hang out again," he texts back.

Those words send a surge of electricity down my spine. I feel like there are stars flying around in my head. I wish Hazel were here to tell me what to say next. But then I remember mom talking about a big block party on Saturday.

I type back, "I heard about Stephanie's party on Saturday. Maybe I'll see you there?"

He replies, "I'll be there, hopefully with you."

I feel my cheeks turning pink, and an involuntary smile spreads over my face. I wonder if Shea's smiling at his phone the same way I am right now?

"Definitely, I'm looking forward to that."

*****

It's two a.m., and I can't tell if I can't sleep because of my worries about my dad or my excited anxiousness about seeing Shea. I've been lying in my bed, staring at the ceiling and trying to make shapes out of the surface's pattern. My mind keeps running; I wish there was a button to turn my thoughts off. The storm has died down, but it left an unsettling darkness that fills both the outside world and my room, swallowing me up. I remember reading something once that said if you can't sleep you should move to a different location and that would help. I might as well try it because I'm losing my mind staring at nothing but darkness and hearing nothing but the sound of my own obnoxious thoughts.

I move over to my bay window that overlooks the houses across the street. Every house is quiet, with dark and empty windows. Nighttime brings an unusual silence. Everything seems still and quiet, like time has stopped moving. But time *is* moving. Life's problems are brewing and unfolding as everyone lays their heads down to rest. It's a false silence. It makes you think that everything has finally slowed down, but in reality, things are developing even faster than when we're awake. We just don't know it because we're living in a dream world. It's eerie, sitting here, staring out into the darkness where nothing is moving and everything is painted the same shade of grey and black, like a noir film.

Suddenly, I catch a burst of color out of the corner of my eye. A flash of red and a figure illuminated by the streetlights. The suspicious silhouette catches my attention, pulling me further away from sleep. Am I really seeing this? Or is it a figment of my sleep deprived imagination? Or a dream? No, this is real. This is actually happening. The tall figure is running cautiously and sneakily down the street in the direction of my house. It appears to be a woman who keeps looking behind her shoulder every few feet as if she is worried that someone is after her. I can't make out her face that well. I can only see her profile and it's blurry from this far away, which makes me remember that I still haven't found my glasses since the move. Not that I've bothered looking, but anyways. The woman wears a blazing red dress that is far too short for her long legs. I would be surprised if the dress reached halfway down her thighs. She runs awkwardly, like a baby just learning to walk. Her feet are bare, her toes slapping against the pavement, and in her hands she clings to a pair of cherry red high heels. I watch the woman run until my vantage point won't allow me to see any farther. I have no proof of who this woman is or where she is going or what she was doing. But I know, with 100 percent certainty, that the woman with the striking red high heels stumbling down my street in the dead of night was in fact Stephanie Kester.

CHAPTER 5 - By Morning

I've never been a big believer in coincidences. Crazy and suspicious things don't just happen independently of each other. Everything is connected. Coincidence is just something people use to explain things they don't understand or to hide from the truth. It's a statement of oblivion, something used to bring comfort in uncertain times. In basic words, coincidence is a load of crap. So, this brings me back to Stephanie. The weird whisper in my ear, the threatening phone call, the late night jog with a pair of cherry red heels. It's all related. It has to be. This is why I spent the rest of Thursday night writing out all the information I had on Stephanie into a fresh notebook. I knew that mental file would come in handy eventually.

So, as I sit in my room of unpacked boxes straightening the frizz out my hair, I read over my notes. This is what I've got:

Stephanie Kester (39)
- *adolescent psychologist*
- *head of the PTO*
- *SoulCycle and yoga instructor*
- *married to Richard Kester*
- *3 kids*
- *Ella Kester- strangely quiet*

06/12- First meeting with Stephanie
- *Kept mentioning that she had all the gossip- blackmail?*
- *Said "we are plagued with secrets, and he knows them all"*

06/16- Stephanie's House
- *Something is going on with her daughter*
- *Phone call to mystery person*
- *Told the person he/she needed to get something to her by Thursday or else she'd reveal his/her secret*
- *She threatened to kill him/her*

06/19- Early Friday Morning
- *She was running towards her house around two a.m. with a tight/short red dress and red high heels*

I've written down all the facts that I have. With a little investigating, I can start making connections and figure out what this woman's deal is. You may be wondering why I don't just let all this go. For starters, it keeps my mind off of my dad and all of the issues I don't want to face. Second, I'm bored. And third, how could I not be interested in this? It's like one of my favorite mystery novels is unfolding right before my eyes. So, tonight is the big kick off to summer party, and I'm on a mission. Well, two missions. I'm going to try and find out more about Stephanie and what she's up to. I have a strong feeling in the pit of my stomach that something is going on deep under the surface of all of her glamour. And if I happen to spend some time with Shea while I'm at it, well that would complete mission number two.

I spend extra time getting ready for this party. I'm not trying to impress Shea, but — no that's a lie, impressing Shea is exactly what I'm trying to do. Once my hair is no longer a frizzy mess from the humidity, I start my makeup. I brush pale rose colored blush onto my cheeks, the sprinkles of the powder looking like fairy dust. Mascara coats my eyelashes, the thick paste making them delicately fan out. I gently rub a light pink lip gloss over my lips to give them some more definition. It's not much, but it's more than I usually wear. I'm not one of those girls who coats their face so heavily with makeup that you can't tell what she actually looks like. And I'm not one of those girls who won't leave the house without it on. But tonight is a worthy occasion for a little makeup.

I pull on a black halter top that doesn't quite reach the top of my light denim shorts, leaving a small portion of my stomach uncovered. We'll see if mom lets me leave the house like this. I wear a pair of black sandals with a burlap bottom, showing off my periwinkle nail polish.

When I'm done getting ready, I head over to Luke's room to talk to him about tonight. I forget to knock on the door and barge right on in.

"Izzie!" he yells. "Can't you learn how to knock?"

"Sorry! I forgot," I say.

He rolls his eyes, "What do you need?"

His voice sounds angry and annoyed. I've never heard Luke use this tone before, especially not with me.

"What's your problem?" I answer him with a question.

"Just leave, Izzie. I'm trying to get ready."

"What?" I say both confused and hurt.

"I asked you to leave," he says firmly, but quietly.

"Seriously, what's your problem?"

He inhales deeply, before saying, "What's my problem? You're the problem, Izzie. I can't deal with it anymore."

What is he talking about? I've made a lot of mistakes in the past week, but none of them were directed at him. I sit there quietly, unsure what to say or do. Luke never gets mad at me.

"I don't —" I start.

"No," he interrupts, "I don't want to hear it. You wanted to know what my problem was, so listen to what I'm saying."

"No!" I say, raising my voice, "I'm not going to sit here and let you talk to me like this when I didn't even do anything."

He shakes his head and inhales deeply again, "That's the

problem, Izzie! You don't even realize that what you do impacts other people. Ever since we moved here all you do is flip out and melt down. You know, I'm dealing with the same crap! I had to leave my friends and my life in Portland too. And it wasn't just your dad who crashed his car into a tree! You lose your mind and scream at everyone, but you don't realize that you are not the only one with problems. Every time you get like that, I'm there for you. I pick up all the broken pieces, and I do everything I can to make you feel better. But you don't even notice when I'm going through something. Because it's all about you! You're selfish, Izzie. You're selfish. All the attention is on you because you blow up at people all the time. You're like a little kid begging for attention from her parents. You know when they told us about Dad, Mom and John were only worried about you because of how you react to things. I just fell through the cracks once again. But that news hurt me too, and you don't even see that because you're so caught up in yourself!"

I feel the blood boiling in my body. I never thought Luke would turn on me. And he's wrong! He's so blatantly wrong! This explains why he slipped away when they told us, but it's not my fault that I'm angry.

"You don't get to choose how I react to issues that hurt me. You don't have a say in that," I fire back at him trying to keep myself under control.

"I'm not trying to control your reactions. I'm just saying that I can't do it anymore. I can't keep dropping everything to help you and give you advice and defend you just for you to go and blow up again. Do you know how draining it is? You never even ask me how I'm doing, Izzie. It's all about you. I can't keep doing this. Especially because I can't defend you after the way you keep treating John," he delivers the message calmly, still not raising his voice above a casual conversation level.

"You're taking John's side?" I'm about to lose it.

"I'm not taking sides, but you're awful to him. And I can't keep defending you when you can be downright nasty. He's trying his best, Izzie. He stepped up to take care of us. He didn't have to do that. He does everything for us, and all you do is yell at him."

"We already have a dad, Luke! John took him away from us!" My voice is rising rapidly.

"John didn't do anything! The divorce was seven years ago, Izzie. You can't keep holding onto that. We've all moved on. At some point, you're going to have to too."

"I'm sorry I don't want to just toss Dad out of our lives like you do!" I yell.

I can see Luke's face turn into bitter anger as he curls his fingers into his palms, pressing his nails as hard as he can into his skin.

"Dad left us. I didn't throw him out. He left us," his voice is quiet and shaky.

"That's not true. They got divorced, he didn't leave us. You abandoned him. You won't even call him! You're probably part of the reason he crashed his car and is fighting for his life!" I'm screaming now.

I went too far. Everything was balancing on the edge, and I just tipped it all over. It was so easy to throw that in his face. It's not going to be so easy to clean up this mess. I went too far. I took it one step farther than I should have, like I always do. Except this time, I don't think there's any chance of coming back. So, I have to keep going down this road. I made a bold move, now I have to back it up.

He digs his nails harder into his palms and looks out at me with a mixture of hurt and shock in his emerald green eyes.

"I can't believe you," he pauses. "You have no idea what you're talking about. You know why Mom and Dad got divorced? Dad's an alcoholic, Izzie! Mom told him he had to choose between

75

drinking and us. He chose alcohol. He left us." his voice is getting louder and louder. I've never heard Luke raise his voice before.

"That's a lie!"

"It's the truth! We only saw him once a month when we were kids because he was in and out of rehab! He didn't want to see us! You know why he can't keep a job? Because he keeps drinking!"

"You're lying! You're a freaking liar, Luke!" I scream.

"The reason Mom didn't tell you was because she knew you'd react like this! You tear her apart. You're awful to her! She's the parent who stayed and you hate her!" His voice is booming, so loud it echoes throughout his room.

I hear footsteps in the hallway and Mom runs in with a deeply confused look on her face, "What is going on in here?!"

"Luke said Dad's an alcoholic!" I'm still yelling, "He's lying, right?"

For a minute, we are all frozen, trapped inside a moment in time. Luke and I both wait for her answer, each of us needing our side to be the correct one. Mom stands there, trapped between her two kids and the truth.

"This is not the time to have this conversation. We're about to leave for a party. This is not the time," her voice is unsteady.

"She needs to know the truth, Mom! She needs to stop defending him!" Luke screams desperately.

I can tell that Mom's heart is hurting for Luke, who can't take the weight of the lie anymore. I don't think I *want* to know the truth, but I think I *need* to know it. Mom wants to take his side because he never gets angry or loud or upset. He's always level-headed and calm. But I can't take another curveball.

"I've always tried to protect you. I've always tried to do what's best for you. That is all you need to know," she says, trying not to choose sides and giving herself more time to figure out how to navigate this situation.

"Mom, I need to know the truth." Tears are streaming down my face, erasing all the makeup I just put on.

She takes a deep breath and looks around the room as if she's waiting for some sort of sign to tell her what to do.

"Fine. Your dad is an alcoholic. Life got very bad before the divorce. He spent so much of our money on alcohol that we struggled to put food on the table for you guys to eat. I told him he needed to stop drinking or we were done. I tried everything to help him, but he couldn't stop. We got divorced because as much as I loved him, I needed to step up and protect you guys. I didn't want that kind of life for you. He's been in and out of rehab, but he always found his way back to the bottle. The consequences of drinking caught up with him the other night. I didn't want to ruin your image of you father. Your brother found out by mistake. He heard a fight we had a long time ago. The way you look at him, Iz, I didn't want to do anything to change that. He's not a bad person. He just made some bad decisions. He's still your dad, and nothing I say needs to change how much you love him."

Luke pipes up, "She should love the parent who stayed."

"She should love us both," Mom says back to him before turning to me. "All I've ever done was protect you. I just want you to live a happy life, Izzie. I'm done arguing and fighting; I'm tired. I never wanted you kids to feel like you had to choose a side. You can love your dad and you can love John and you can love me. It doesn't have to be one or the other."

The wave of emotions is back, smashing over me and engulfing me in a sea of feelings. I'm mad at Mom and Luke for keeping this from me for this long and letting me believe in this story of a hero I had worked up in my head. I'm disgusted with myself for defending him and resenting my mom when all she was trying to do was protect me. I feel abandoned that my dad chose drinking over his own daughter. I'm angry at myself for pushing Luke away and ruining our relationship. I feel a terrible ache in my heart that I may never see my father again. I'm full of so many emotions that contradict each other so much that they all cancel each other out, and I'm back to just feeling numb.

*****

The afternoon sun begins to dim as the early evening hours rush in. My family and I make our way out to the outdoor party, and I take in the scene. Adults mingle in various areas with drinks in their hands. Little kids run around wildly throughout the grass and pavement, barefooted and bright-eyed. Tables of food are set up along the outer perimeter of the cul-de-sac and some of the guys man flaming grills. Music from a speaker settles over the lively event. And in the center of it all is Stephanie Kester. She wears a bright yellow sundress with tiny white and navy blue flowers that pop against her tanned skin, making her stand out in the crowd of people. Her long, coffee colored hair flows down her back in loose waves. She's the sun, and everyone else is orbiting around her. Stephanie stands in a group with a mixture of young and middle-aged women who drink wine out of sparkling glasses. She's clearly the center of attention, and she knows it. But what's going on behind this life of the party act?

I redid my makeup before we left so no one would know that I've been crying. Our family has put on some happy smiles and bandaids on bullet hole wounds. We're just trying to hold the mess together for now. Hazel finds me right away, which I'm very grateful for. I get awkward with new people, so I'm already feeling intimidated. I'm not in the mood to go and socialize and meet my new neighbors. The original excitement I had from before has worn off. My argument with Luke has made me realize I need to stop creating these sloppy messes for myself. I need to stop bringing trouble into my life and throwing a fit when it all goes askew. I've decided to give up looking into Stephanie. She's probably just as shallow as she seems, and it really isn't my business. And if my original thinking was right, I don't want to be caught in the middle of the disaster she brings with her. Tonight, I'm here to see Hazel and Graeson and Shea. That's all.

"You look gorgeous!" Hazel greets me.

She wears a flowy cheetah print skirt that falls about three quarters of the way down her thighs and a black tank top with ruffled straps.

"So do you! I love that skirt," I say excitedly. I'm getting very good at this whole putting on a smile and forgetting what is going on at home thing.

Hazel extends her hand to my family one by one, "Hi, I'm Hazel! It's wonderful to meet you all!"

"This is my mom, my . . . John, my brother, Luke, and my sisters, Madison and Olivia," I say pointing to each one of them.

Luke looks miserable, and John looks kind of hurt about how I stumbled over his introduction. Madison is wearing a princess costume and Olivia still won't stop fussing. Hazel must think we're the weirdest bunch on the block. Both Mom and John seem to genuinely love Hazel. I mean, how could you not love her? After they get to know Hazel briefly, she takes me to go find Graeson and Shea. I've pushed myself back into my state of numbness where I don't feel the pain and ignore the issues that keep piling up. But even with the anesthetized feelings, I can't help but notice the flutter in my heart when Hazel says Shea's name.

She leads me behind the Kester's house where we find Graeson and Shea hanging out on the lower deck. Little kids are weaving in and out of her backyard, playing some sort of tagging game. I don't even bother trying to look at Stephanie's gorgeous backyard because my eyes are instantly drawn to Shea. He's wearing a baby blue, plaid Vineyard Vines button up shirt that makes his eyes pop with a pair of grey golfing shorts. I have to remind myself to stop staring because I'm making a total fool out of myself.

"Well hello there, Miss Isabelle! Don't you look stunning," Graeson flashes one of his charming smirks.

"Why thank you," I smile. "Run anyone over lately?"

He jokingly rolls his eyes, "Why can't you people leave the past in the past? It was one mistake!"

Hazel scoffs at him, "One mistake? Would you like me to remind you that you are one speeding ticket away from getting your license suspended?

"Ah, that means nothing!"

Hazel rolls her eyes and laughs at his stupidity. I feel my palms growing clammy because I'm not sure how to interact with Shea. Yes, I understand that this is just a basic conversation and should be easy for someone my age, but my brain is just not working, especially when I catch a glimpse of his blue eyes.

I turn to Shea and say, "Hey," while Hazel and Graeson argue about whether or not 100 miles an hour is, in fact, considered speeding.

"Hey," he says casually, giving me a wide, nervous smile.

I'm just not sure what I'm supposed to do. Am I supposed to just talk to him like normal? Or am I supposed to come right out and tell him about my feelings? No, I'm definitely not going to do the latter.

Hazel, seemingly perceptive of my awkwardness, says to me, "Let me show you where the bathroom is, just so you know for later."

I furrow my eyebrows confusingly, but I don't question her.

When we're inside she says, "Okay, you're not going to get anywhere by not talking to him."

I consider her point and reply, "I don't know what I'm supposed to do!"

"Just talk to him. He's an easy person to talk to. Let everything happen naturally."

"So all I need to do is talk to him?"

"Yes," she says before adding, "And you should stop staring at his eyes. It's a dead giveaway, and it's making your communication skills tank."

I smile and take a deep breath, "Okay, I can totally do this."

"Of course you can! And I've got your back."

We step back outside and resume conversation with the boys. I try my very best to play it cool, and for the most part, it's working. Once I stop worrying about saying the wrong things and being awkward, conversation flows naturally and easily between us. The sun brings out the blonde undertones in his hair, and his smile doesn't leave his face.

"Hey, Graeson," Hazel says, "Can you come help me get another drink?"

"Why do you need help? You're perfectly capable of finding your own drink," he retorts.

"I need your help," she says sharply.

His face is filled with confusion, but I know exactly what Hazel — aka the playmaker — is trying to do.

"Why?" he asks.

"Stop asking questions and give me a hand," she says in her 'I'm not messing around' tone.

"Alright, relax. I'm coming," he says with his face all scrunched up and then turns to us. "I guess I'll be back in a jiffy."

I hear Graeson as they walk away muttering questions and complaining to Hazel who keeps pulling him by the arm without cluing him in on her plan. Shea and I both nervously laugh.

"How have you been?" he asks while moving to sit down on the outdoor sectional on the patio.

"It's been a week," I say as I take a seat next to him.

"That doesn't sound too good."

"It wasn't," I laugh awkwardly. "But it's fine."

"I take it you don't want to talk about it."

81

"I don't like talking about a lot of things."

He says quietly with an underlying nervous tone, "Can we talk about the fact that you look beautiful tonight?"

A smile attaches itself to my face before I can stop it, and I feel my cheeks turning red, "Yeah, we can talk about that."

*****

A little while later, Shea and I head down to the cul-de-sac. As much as I wanted to just stay up there and talk — or flirt — with him, I don't want to seem completely anti-social. Shea takes the lead, which makes my nerves a little calmer. An elderly man in a wheelchair approaches us. He wears a Vietnam veterans baseball cap and glasses with a wide, black rim that rest on his large nose. A thick, dark brown mustache hangs out above his mouth. His face is coated with lines of age, but you can tell that he used to be handsome back in his day.

"Shea!" he greets, his voice rough and raspy, but cheerful. "Who's this young lady?"

"Mr. Cavanaugh, this is Izzie. Izzie, this is Mr. Cavanaugh. She just moved in over there," Shea says as he points to my house.

"What?" he yells. "What did you say?"

"I said . . . Mr. Cavanaugh, you need to turn your hearing aids on."

"What?!" The old man says louder.

Shea raises his volume while pointing to his ears, "Your hearing aids!"

I'm doubled over laughing. It looks like he's doing an interpretive dance number. Mr. Cavanaugh finally understands the message.

"I forget I can't hear like I used to," he laughs. "Can't see too well either. All the senses are going. So, what were you saying, young man?"

"This is Izzie. Izzie, this is Mr. Cavanaugh."

I shake his outstretched hand, feeling his saggy wrinkled skin against my palm.

His eyes seem to light up as he says, "Aha, so this is the girl you've been talking about."

Shea's eyes go wide and awkward panic settles over his face, "I haven't been talking about any girl."

"Yes you have. The blonde one. You were telling me about her the other day," he smiles, pushing Shea to be further alarmed.

"I'm just messin' with you, Shea. Take a breath, boy!" The old man has cracked himself up. As Shea tries to recover from the embarrassment, Mr. Cavanaugh looks at me and says under his breath, "I'm not kidding."

For such an old man, Mr. Cavanaugh has so much life inside of him. He's out here partying with a drink in his hand just enjoying himself.

Shea and I continue to make our way through the party of people.

"So," I joke, "You're talking about me?"

His face is dyed a permanent shade of red, "I . . . um . . ."

"It's okay," I laugh. "I'm just giving you a hard time. And I kind of liked hearing that you're talking about me."

He smiles at me, and I can't help but feel a rush of happiness surge through my body.

As we're walking, Mom catches my attention and calls me over. She and John are standing with a woman who appears to be in her early thirties. She has light chestnut colored hair that is pulled up into a thick, curled ponytail. She holds an infant in her hands: a little boy with strands of blazing red hair and an adorable smile that shows off his first tiny teeth.

"Hi," I say. "He's adorable."

"Aww thank you! This is Boston, and I'm Hannah," her voice is soft and bright.

The little boy waves at me and makes a squealing noise that Hannah explains as his way of saying hello.

"I'm Izzie," I introduce myself.

"Hannah's a teacher at the high school you're going to go to," Mom explains to me.

The baby squirms in her arms as she says, "Yes, I teach English and creative writing. Your parents were telling me that writing is your favorite! It's a really good school; I promise you're going to love it. Shea knows all about it, right?"

Shea smiles and says, "I've had Mrs. St. James the past two years. By far my favorite teacher." He laughs.

"Hey, why are you laughing? Of course I'm your favorite teacher," Hannah laughs.

The little boy reaches his arms out to Shea and pulls away from Hannah. Shea takes Boston in his arms and holds the baby while he giggles. I think my heart might combust at the sight of this. Hannah begins telling me about the courses she teaches, and I listen attentively, actually interested in what she's saying. Writing and reading are one of my favorite things to do, even outside of school. I also thought everyone in this town would be stuck up and prissy, so meeting someone as genuinely kind as Hannah is comforting. She doesn't look like a rich supermodel, and I mean that in the best way. She's not unrealistic and unnatural looking. Hannah has deep hazel eyes that pop against her pale skin. A thin layer of natural makeup coats her face, and her nose is small and slightly pointy. I find her far more pretty than someone like Stephanie, who looks like a Photoshop image and someone who tries too hard. Speaking of the devil . . .

"Well hello there!" Stephanie's voice pops up from behind.

Oh boy! I'm just praying to God she doesn't start hugging me again. Her yellow dress flows behind her as she inserts herself into our group and interrupts our conversation. I swear I see Hannah roll her eyes, but maybe it was just in my head. Shea continues to hold the red haired baby and bounces him gently when he gets fussy. Stephanie makes her way around our little circle. She hugs both of my parents before turning to me. I shoot Shea a wide-eyed stare as she wraps her arms around me in an uncomfortable embrace. He almost falls over laughing at my face, but then it's my turn to laugh at him as she gives him a hug. She pinches the baby cheeks and utters something in some sort of baby talk, which causes Boston to let out an annoyed cry. After she wraps her arms around Hannah, she looks at her and says, "Wow, Hann, you look great! Have you finally started losing the baby weight?"

Oh yikes! That's a dig if I've ever heard one. Hannah takes it well by just smiling and nodding. I would've smashed my fist right into her perfectly symmetrical face if she said it to me. And Hannah isn't even overweight. Sure, she's not as perfectly slim and toned as Stephanie, but she's still beautiful.

"So, how much fun is this party!? It's such a blast when we all get together," Stephanie says with her over the top excitement as she makes her rounds.

"Thank you so much for inviting us," Mom says to her.

"Of course! You guys are part of the neighborhood now. We're all one big family," Stephanie adds.

Dear God, it sounds like she's auditioning for a soap opera. Like seriously, this woman comes from a different planet. It's taking all of the strength I have in me not to start asking questions about the suspicious things I've witnessed her doing. I promised myself I would keep myself out of her business. Hannah makes a face of disgust at Stephanie's cheesy line. There seems to be some sort of riff between the two of them.

Stephanie starts a conversation about how fabulous her party is, engaging Mom and John. After a few minutes, Hannah makes a graceful exit by telling us she needs to go check on her other two kids who are off running around somewhere. I'm pretty sure she just wanted to get away from Stephanie, but I don't blame her. A woman with curly auburn hair calls Shea over to her; I'm guessing it's his mother. My three-month-old sister, Olivia, starts crying, which causes Mom to go in search of a bottle. John leaves to go find Madison, which leaves me alone with Stephanie Kester. This group dissolved faster than a room does after someone passes gas. Can anyone tell me why this is the second time in a week that I've been left alone with this woman?

"It seems like you're adjusting very well to life in Knox Hollow!" she says enthusiastically.

"Yeah, I've made some new friends. I'm starting to get used to it," I reply.

"I'm glad you're fitting in so well. With a gorgeous face like yours it shouldn't be too hard!"

What is this woman's obsession with calling me beautiful? I appreciate the compliment, but it's starting to make me uncomfortable.

I force a smile on my face and say, "Thank you."

For a moment, it's quiet, which is odd because I don't think Stephanie has stopped talking since I met her. She looks like she's thinking hard, which is also weird because she seems like someone who just says whatever pops into her head.

Finally, she speaks up, "Well, I'm going to get a refill of this." She points to her empty wine glass. "I'll catch up with you later! Enjoy yourself!"

Grateful for this encounter to be over, I say, "Okay, I'll see you later."

She goes to walk away, but turns around, and our eyes lock. I swear something in her face shifts. Her usual fake enthusiasm turns into a cold stare, like she's been possessed. It's the weirdest thing; It makes me feel like her hazel eyes are staring straight into my soul.

"One quick thing, Izzie," she starts as she walks back towards me, close enough to whisper in my ear. "Next time you want to listen in on one of my phone conversations, don't leave behind any evidence. And just for future reference, I have 24 hour surveillance cameras . . . everywhere."

"I didn't mean to —" I'm interrupted by her high-pitched voice.

"It was so great talking to you!"

To say that I was flabbergasted would be a major understatement. I feel a chill spread throughout my body even though it's 80 degrees outside. So, Stephanie did see me that day. Oh God! I made a stupid mistake, listening to that conversation and then completely giving myself up. I feel like I'm already knee deep in Stephanie's mess. Was she serious about having cameras? That would explain why I felt like I was being watched as I stood on the porch. But why would a person need 24 hour cameras *inside* their house? Or was she just trying to scare me because I infringed on her privacy? Either way, I may have landed myself a permanent spot on Stephanie's bad side.

*****

I'm trying really hard to just be a normal teenager and enjoy the night, but I can't escape my thoughts. I guess I'm not as good at pretending everything is fine as I thought I was. The sun has set and darkness has settled over the street. The streetlights illuminate the cul-de-sac, and everyone is huddled around a blazing bonfire. All of the children have been put to bed, so the real party is just beginning. But I can't erase Stephanie's words from my head. She hasn't said anything else to me since, but I can't shake the feeling that something is not right. Stephanie hasn't stopped moving all night. Every time I see her, she's in a totally different spot with a new group of people. It's like playing Where's Waldo, except it's where's the crazy lady who lives next door. I met some more new people who I can't even remember now, and I hung out with Hazel and the others for a while. But I just feel so drained. I stand down at the bonfire, off in the back, trapped in my own head. I notice Stephanie sitting awfully close with her arm around a man who I quickly realize is not Richard. Now, that's strange. I need to stop trying to get involved in other people's problems when I can't even handle my own.

The air is thickly coated with the smoky smell of the raging bonfire. As I walk away, the warm air from the flames fades into the slight chill from the night air. I head up the rolling hill of the Kester's front lawn towards their porch. I'm not really even sure where I'm walking to. I just don't feel like being around all those people right now, yet I don't want to go home and be alone. I find Shea sitting on the front porch. I spent so much of today worrying about everything else that I didn't really even have a chance to talk to him all that much.

I take a seat next to him as he looks up and says, "Long day?"

"You don't even know."

"What's going on up there?" he points to my head.

"You don't want to know."

"Try me."

I'm so emotionally shut down that I think why not tell him? It's not like I have anything else to lose.

"I found out my dad's an alcoholic, today. Apparently that's why my parents got divorced. He chose drinking over his own kids. I've spent the last seven years defending him and hating my mom for pushing him out of our lives. Oh, and I found out on Tuesday he crashed his car into a tree, and now he's still in a coma in the hospital. I don't even know if he's going to make it. Life is great," I say to him while looking straight out into the glowing stars.

"My dad died back in May. He committed suicide. Didn't even leave a note," Shea says quietly.

My heart drops into my stomach. Oh my God. I can't even imagine what he's going through. Here I am complaining about my dad, who despite his shortcomings, is still alive, barely, but alive. I glance over to meet his eyes so our faces are turned to face each other. His eyes seem to glow like the stars in the night sky. Sadness is written all over my face, and I feel once again that Shea and I have an understanding of each other that is far beyond words.

"It's okay," he says softly. "It's all okay."

Slowly, he places his hand on top of mine, delicately wrapping our fingers together. I feel his hand shaking in mine, most likely from speaking about his dad's suicide. The comforting silence settles over us once more as I turn my hand palm side up to take his hand. This is the first time in the last few days that I've felt something other than nothing. Other than numb. Other than empty. Our eyes stay together, each of us totally lost in the other. The thoughts that were so loud before are drowned out by the sound of my heart beating. Everything around us is becoming hazy, like the feeling when you're first waking up, drifting between dreams and reality.

He leans in. Slowly. Quietly. It's like the rest of the world has stopped moving. Even time can't break through our moment. I bend my head forward, meeting him halfway. Suddenly, my lips are pressed up against his. The world is spinning around us, but we are perfectly still. Loneliness, anger, fear? I don't know what those are anymore. We pull apart for a moment, reading each other's faces for a cue. But I don't feel like waiting any longer. Before I know what I'm doing, my lips are locked against his, and my hands press against his strong jaw line, feeling his soft, tan skin. It seems as if there is some greater magnetic force pulling us together.

"CRASH!" I hear a loud banging thud that jerks the two of us apart. I look behind me to see Graeson, like a bull in a china shop, stumbling back from the glass door with two bottles of Tequila in his hands.

"Graeson!" I hear Hazel's voice coming from behind him, "Did you just walk into the door?!"

"I did, in fact, walk into it. They really shouldn't make clear doors."

Hazel rolls her eyes and helps him outside. Lucky for us, I think Graeson doesn't realize that he literally barged in on our moment. He either hit his head too hard or has had a little too much alcohol to understand what's going on around him.

"I seem to have obtained a few bottles of Tequila." The words roll rapidly and loudly off his tongue. "I say we have ourselves a bit of fun."

Hazel shakes her head and says, "Absolutely not. I think you in particular have had quite enough."

I've shut off the logical part of my brain, and the emotional distress I've dealt with this week is compelling me to make a terrible decision. I keep thinking, what do I have to lose? Why not have a little fun?

"I'm in," I say confidently.

"Alright," Shea looks up at Graeson. "I'm down."

"This is a terrible idea," Hazel begins. "I'm not sticking around for this."

"Come on, Hazel. It's okay to break a rule every once in a while," Graeson encourages her.

"Let's live on the edge tonight," I push her.

She seems stuck between letting loose for once in her life and following the rules as she always does.

A small smile spreads over her face, "Why not?"

I take the bottle from Graeson and take a swig, the liquid burning as it flows down my throat.

That's the last clear memory I have of that night. Little did I know, evil intentions were developing and unfolding right under my nose. By morning, the sun would rise, the effects of alcohol would fade, and I would find myself in yet another mess.

*****

I wake up in a cloud of dizziness and confusion. My eyes can't focus in on anything, and the room appears to be spinning in slow, hazy circles. I can feel my brain throbbing in my head; it feels as if there are thousands of hammers pounding through my skull. This is by far the worst headache I've ever had. All at once, I am hit with a wave of nausea that sends a stream of hot bile up my throat. I need to go find Advil and water and coffee *now*. Right now. I slowly make my way out of bed, feeling like I'm in one of those spinning tubes in a Fun House at a fair. I guess this is what I get for how I acted last night. Not that I even really remember what went on. I can kind of make out blurry bits and pieces, but nothing all that coherent. I'm sure nothing *bad* happened. Embarrassing? Most definitely. But not bad.

I creep down the stairs, hanging onto the railing for dear life. I'm trying to be as quiet as I possibly can be. My mom will literally kill me if she finds out, and John will make me listen to one of his "make good choices" speeches.

When I reach the kitchen, I head straight over to the coffee pot and pour the black liquid into the mug, listening to the sound of it streaming into the ceramic cup. I watch the half and half swirl around, creating a creamy kaleidoscope. I grab an Advil from the counter and shove it down my throat with one large gulp of water. Maybe if I get some fresh air, I'll feel a little better. Although, I can't tell if the sickening feeling in my stomach is from the alcohol or the guilt. With my mug in tow, I make my way to the sliding glass door facing the backyard. The morning sun gleams through the glass, creating shadows of light that dance across my face. The mix of sunlight and caffeine is giving me some much needed life.

I open the door and feel the cool breeze blowing gently against my skin. I inhale deeply, trying to take in the fresh air. Instantly, I am hit with the smell of freshly watered flowers, last night's lingering bonfire, and a strange odor. When I step further outside, the odor hits me like a train. The rancid smell makes me gag, and I find myself simultaneously swallowing vomit and covering my nose with the neckline of my shirt. What on God's green earth *is* that putrid scent?

As my stomach is churning, I suddenly feel something wet and sticky rubbing against my foot. My feet are submerged in some strange substance. Please don't tell me I'm stepping on throw up or dog poop. That would really be sickening.

I look down slowly, slightly scared about what my bare feet are touching.

My heart stops. The blood in my veins runs bitterly cold. My eyes bulge as my body goes completely numb, paralyzed with a sickening fear. This can't be real. This can't be real. I must be hallucinating. But the smell. The overpowering odor. It's growing stronger and stronger. I close my eyes for a moment, hoping when I open them this will all be just a weird dream. I look down again at my feet, stuck in a sticky puddle of half dried blood the color of red wine. And when I move my eyes further, I am hit with my worst fear. In front of me lies a limp, discolored body. Oh no. Oh no. Oh no. It's the only thought my brain can come up with. I'm standing in a pool of crusty blood with a dead body in front of me. Not exactly how I saw this morning going. The body is as grey as smoke combined with a bluish tint with long, dark hair matted down by dried blood. My eyes are instinctively drawn to the face, a bullet hole lodged into the center of the forehead. Before I see it, I already have a terrible, sinking feeling in my gut. They say to always trust your instincts. I don't want to trust them right now. Because if I'm right about this . . . I don't even know.

My eyes analyze the face: the long, skinny nose, the delicate fanning eyelashes, the bright hazel eyes clinging onto the last seconds of life.

In front of me lies Stephanie Kester, dead and bloody on my back porch with her cold, dead eyes staring straight into my soul. I let out a deafening scream of bloody murder.

CHAPTER 6 - The Bloody Shoe

It's always the husband or the boyfriend. Isn't that what they all say? Sometimes, it's a case of passion, where affection burns too bright too fast and love quickly turns into a creepy obsession. Sometimes, it's a case of jealousy, where a situation of disloyalty results in a fit of rage. And sometimes, it's a case of both, where an intense passion turns deadly when the person sees the one they love with someone else or being unfaithful. At least that's what I've learned from all the true crime novels I've read.

I knew something wasn't right about this town. I knew something wasn't right about this street. I knew something wasn't right about *her*. A few hours ago Stephanie and her yellow sundress were the center of attention, prancing her way around the party, laughing with her friends, drinking wine out of crystal glasses, and causing drama among her neighbors. And now? Now, she's nothing more than a limp, discolored body sprawled out in the backyard of a family she barely even knew. What a way to bite the dust. The image of her horrified face is burned into my eyes. When I close them, all I can see is the bullet hole forcefully lodged into her forehead, the pool of half dried blood that gathered beneath her, and the utter desperation in her hazel eyes. There was still so much life in her eyes. It was like her entire existence was now confined to those two gaping holes above her nose.

I sit in the corner of the new sectional in our living room with my knees curled up to my chest. I stare straight ahead of me, focusing on one point on the wall. My hands haven't stopped violently shaking since I found the body. Her body. Stephanie's body.

For the past hour, there's been a swarm of police officers, paramedics, and concerned neighbors hovering in our backyard. Mom sent me inside while she and John called 911 and figured out the situation. I haven't moved once in the last hour.

Mom opens the slider door, which has the curtains pulled over it so I can't see outside, and sits down next to me on the couch. She wraps her arms around me, and I let myself fall into her hug.

"It's okay. It's all going to be okay, honey," her voice soft and smooth, like a drop of honey.

My head is resting on her shoulder, and my body is curled up against her. This time, I don't fight her reassuring words or her comfort. It makes me feel like I'm a little kid again. When I was little, I used to be terrified of the dark. I hated feeling alone and helpless, unable to see anything. I used to think that there were monsters under the bed and in the closet and behind the curtains. After mom and dad put me in my bed, I would lie there crying. I was too scared to yell out to them or move because I thought the monsters would get me if I did. So, I would cry quietly, shaking under the covers. But every night, my mom would come in. I still don't know how she heard me. Maybe it was some sort of sixth motherly sense. She would sit next to me on the bed, and I would curl up next to her, feeling safe and unafraid. She would sing this song she made up that I can't remember the words to anymore, and eventually, I would fall asleep until the sun came up in the morning and the monsters were gone. I think the monsters are back now. But this time, it might take more than a lullaby and the morning sun to make them go away.

"I'm so sorry you had to see that. You shouldn't have had to," she says, her voice flowing like the crests on a wave. "You don't have to say anything now. I'll be here whenever you're ready to talk, sweetheart."

I look up at her, her icy blue eyes glowing with comfort, "I think I'm going to go upstairs and take a shower."

"Okay, honey, okay. I'm going to make you something to eat."

I don't fight her on it like I normally would. Instead, I just nod my head and walk upstairs, letting her take care of me. I head to my room to find some clothes to wear today before I hop into the shower. My knees feel weak and shaky as I make my way to my bedroom, and I'm not sure if it's from the hangover or the shock. On the bright side, my mom and John are going to be too preoccupied to figure out that I was drinking. I'm sorry. I shouldn't have said that. I'm really such a terrible person. I open my closet door and see last night's outfit thrown in a pile on the ground. Seeing it probably reeks of Tequila, I pick the clothes up to throw them in the laundry. I wish I hadn't. Underneath my clothes are the sandals I wore last night, and underneath those sandals, the off-white carpet is stained red. Bloody red. I drop to my knees, and my worst thoughts are confirmed when I turn the sandal over. One shoe is coated in a thick layer of dried blood that has seeped through the carpet. I feel my breathing become jagged and rapid, until it's so fast and shallow that I'm hyperventilating. Why is there blood on my shoes? I had nothing to do with Stephanie's death. And then it hits me like a train hits a car that has crossed the tracks a moment too late. I don't remember anything after Graeson passed me the bottle. I don't even remember getting home or in bed. I was angry last night. I was upset and mad at the world and emotional. What if I —? No! I can't go there. I wouldn't do something like that. Right? Right? No, no, no. Burning tears start pouring down my cheeks, as I hyperventilate faster and faster, louder and louder.

All of a sudden, someone bursts my door open. No, no, no! Luke comes barreling in, and his eyes bulge when he sees me kneeling and sobbing on the floor.

"What's wrong?" he asks with a sense of urgency.

I can't speak because the lump in my throat has grown so big. His face turns to total shock when he looks down to the bloody shoe I'm grasping in my furiously shaking hands.

"I don't know! I don't know how that got here. I don't know why there's blood on it," I'm sobbing. "I don't know, Luke! I don't remember anything about last night." My voice comes out shaky and partially incoherent. I feel the panic rising in my chest and the world closing in on me. I feel like there's a swarm of yellow jackets buzzing around in my brain and an angry bunch of crows jabbing at my insides causing the vomit to make the journey back up my throat. Luke crouches down to my level and grabs my shaking hands.

"Stop!" His voice is loud and strong. It makes me stop rambling instantly.

The sound of my heart beating echoes loudly in my ears, making me feel like I'm listening to a stethoscope.

"I walked you home last night. I brought you inside and got you settled in your room," he says quietly.

"I d-don't remember a-anything. Wh-Why is th-there b-blood on m-my shoe?" My crying comes out like a whiney, drawn out moan.

"Izzie, listen to me," he speaks slowly and clearly. "I walked you home last night. I brought you inside and got you settled in your room."

His hands are steady and his face is relaxed and calm, but I can tell he's worried on the inside. Luke is a protector. Even when he's angry, he tries to protect my feelings and mental state. He's always the one to step up in a situation and take charge in his own quiet way to make everything alright for everyone else.

"Why is there blood on my shoes from last night? Luke, I
—" My voice is faster now and filled with sobs.

"You didn't do *anything*, Izzie. I know you, and you
wouldn't hurt anyone, even if you don't remember what
happened," he reassures me.

"But why is there blood on my shoe?" I ask again because
he seems to be avoiding the question. My voice comes out hoarse
and low, like a whisper.

"She was found on our back porch. Maybe you stepped in it
at some point last night before I brought you home. It was dark
out. This doesn't mean you did anything wrong."

I want to believe his words, but something about it does not
settle well in my brain. I was so emotional last night. Could I have
done anything? The thought is like a weight pushing on my chest
and making it hard to breathe.

"What about the carpet?" I cry.

"Go take a long, hot shower. You still reek of alcohol. I'll
take care of this."

"Are you sure?"

"Yes. You need to pull it together. Nobody hears a word
about this," he commands.

"I thought you said I didn't do anything."

"You didn't, but it won't look good to people on the
outside. Just go and shower and try to get it out of your mind."

I wrap my arms tightly around Luke, holding onto him for
dear life.

"I'm so sorry, Luke," I whisper. "I'm so sorry."

"I'm sorry too."

"I need you in my life, Luke. I can't stand to have you mad
at me."

"We're okay, Izzie. I have your back."

I stand in the shower with the water as hot as it can go. The
rising steam makes my headache disappear and my mind relax.

Slowly, I focus on the sound and pattern of my breathing. Inhale and exhale. Inhale and exhale. Inhale and exhale. I imagine my breath like a wave of the ocean. Inhaling is like the wave rising to the formation of a crest and exhaling is like the gradual falling of the water onto the shore. John taught me this exercise a few years ago. I'm trying to stop the hyperventilating, and this seems like one of the only things that's helping. I don't know how to begin sorting through my feelings about finding Stephanie's body. I want so badly to go back to that numb state, but the images won't leave my mind. I have to deal with this.

A while later, I step out of the shower, dry off, and change into a pair of sweatpants and an oversized sweatshirt. I know it's hot, but I can't stop shivering and feeling bitterly cold. The mirror is all cloudy and fogged up. I wipe off a small section in the middle with the towel. The broken girl is still staring back at me, with her tear-filled eyes and blotchy face. When will she go away? I miss the girl with the bright eyes and carefree smile and happy demeanor. Where did she go?

*****

Mom hands me a cup of coffee, a bagel, and a bowl of fruit when I come downstairs. She, John, and Luke are sitting around the counter looking both tired and distraught. An awkward silence settles over us. No one knows what to say about this. Everyone thinks I'm a doll made out of glass. They all think I'm so fragile, and they're so scared to break me into a million pieces. But this elephant in the room is one that we cannot get around.

"Why was she on our back porch?" I say casually as if I'm asking about the weather.

Everyone seems a little taken aback by my straightforwardness and my willingness to talk about the situation. I surprise myself when the words come out, but I'm sick of everyone looking at me as if I'm about to shatter like a piece of glass at any given moment.

John clears his throat and replies, "I think that's what we'd all like to know. The police are handling it. They can't do much until the autopsy, but it's not going to be good."

"You know, most people bring flowers or wine or cookies, but I guess a dead body is a great housewarming present. Nothing says "welcome home" like a dead person does," my mom says sarcastically.

John's eyes widen and his face looks a little shocked at my mother's remark. I can't help but agree with him. Mom's typically sensitive and empathetic, and this doesn't really seem like a laughing matter.

"Mom!" I say surprised.

"I'm sorry, I'm sorry," she shakes her head. "But we moved in a week ago. We came here for a fresh start and this is what we get. Honestly, it would be easier to deal with the mess your father's gotten himself into."

"Let's not talk about Dad," Luke says like the true mediator he is. "One issue at a time."

"I'm just wondering when we're ever going to catch a break," Mom says with a slightly raised voice. "I'm so tired of constantly fighting these uphill battles."

I look to John, waiting for him to pipe up with some positive words of encouragement like he always does, but he says nothing.

"John," I start. "Please say something positive."

"I thought you hated my positivity," he responds.

"I think we all really need it right now."

John gives me a small smile, and I swear something clicked into place. I didn't feel any awful or angry feeling towards him. In fact, I was almost grateful that he was here to keep us all from flying off the handle. Maybe it was seeing a dead body on my back patio that made me realize my problems are so minute in the grand scheme of things. Or maybe it's the thought that there might be a killer on the loose that made me realize who the real enemy is. Or maybe it was seeing Mom looking so utterly defeated that made me understand how much we needed John to push us through this. Trying to love me is no crime, at least not one that can be prosecuted in a federal court of law. I still don't like John at all, but I don't think I totally hate him anymore. My heart aches for Mom, partly because I know how she's feeling and partly because I'm part of her problems. I can see that she's tired of fighting. Since she and my dad got divorced, she hasn't stopped fighting these major battles. From his alcoholism, to supporting two kids as a single mom, to my constant berating and arguing over her every move, to finding a dead body on her porch. She never gets a break.

"We're still going to get our fresh start, Brenna. All of us are going to get our fresh start. I don't know what to say about Stephanie. I wish I did, but I really don't know. It doesn't look good, but we just have to help each other get through this," his voice is calm and genuine. John makes people feel good for a living, and I hate to admit, he's pretty decent at it. His deep voice is always calm and steady and evenly paced. This whole thing has made me realize I have much bigger fish to fry than hating him.

The image of the blood on my shoe is nagging my brain. It's playing on repeat, like an annoying commercial jingle you can't get out of your head. Every time it flashes in my mind, it is followed by the image of Stephanie's lifeless hazel eyes, sending a chill down my spine. I'm doing my best to ignore it — to tune it out — but the feeling that I did something wrong has made a permanent residence in my brain. But there's no way I did anything. Stephanie had a bullet lodged into her forehead. I don't even have access to a gun. There aren't even any guns in our house. So, there's no way I could've had anything to do with it, right?

Suddenly, John's phone starts ringing, breaking the silence and making me jump a little. I'm still shocked and in overdrive from this morning.

"Hello," I hear John say.

I can't tell who he's talking to, but then he says, "Okay, we'll be down shortly. Thank you."

"Who was that?" mom asks.

"That was an officer from the police station. They want Izzie to go down and tell them what she saw this morning," I can tell he's a little nervous to tell this to me.

"What?!" My eyes bulge, and I feel my heart drop into my stomach. What if I did something? What if they know?

"Why do they need her to do that?" mom asks with a level of annoyance.

"She found a dead body on our porch this morning," John answers. "Of course they're going to have questions."

My mom rolls her eyes, "This is ridiculous."

I can tell she's completely fed up, but I understand why. I understand that she was trying to get away from a difficult life at home and ended up finding a bigger issue. However, she's normally much more sensitive. Then again, I completely flip out all the time over absolutely nothing, so maybe this reaction is completely warranted. I'm eerily underreacting, Mr. Positivity is always looking on the bright side, and Luke always keeps his reactions to himself. I guess Mom is just reacting in the way a normal adult would. I've never understood emotions. They're just far too confusing for my liking.

"I really don't want to go," I complain.

"I know, Iz, but we want them to figure out what's going on. They need your help for that. They're not questioning you or anything like that. They're just trying to learn information," John replies.

"Can you please just tell them I don't want to talk about it?" I beg.

Luke pipes up, "You have to go, Izzie. There could be a murderer running around here."

Nervous energy fills the room after Luke says that. We were all thinking it, but no one wanted to say it out loud. Saying it out loud makes it become real, and no one wants this to become real.

"We'll go to the police station, and we'll take it from there. It's going to be okay," Mom says, but I can hear the uncertainty in her voice. She has no clue if it's going to be okay, but she's trying her best to put her feelings aside and be strong for Luke and me. Or really just me, because we all know Luke is strong enough on his own.

*****

"Mom's waiting in the car," Luke stands in the doorway of my room.

I'm sitting on my bed in some sort of trance with my eyes attached to the site of the bloody shoe. My room smells of lemon scented carpet cleaner from Luke scrubbing the blood out of the floor. The carpet is back to creamy white; You can't even tell there was blood there less than an hour ago.

"I don't know what I'm supposed to say to them," I say.

"They just want to know what you saw," he responds.

"I saw a dead body on our porch. What else is there to explain?"

"Quite a bit."

"What if they ask about last night?" I ask.

"Then you'll tell them the truth — you hung out with your friends, you walked home with me around midnight, and you slept until eight when you found Stephanie on the back porch."

103

"But what about the shoe?" I say with tears starting to brim in the corners of my eyes.

"You aren't going to say anything about the shoe."

"But you said I needed to tell the truth."

"The truth is that you didn't do anything. This will just complicate everything. I know you're innocent, Izzie."

"I'm not so sure about that."

*****

The police station is hot and stuffy, making the air feel thick and heavy in my lungs. The ceilings are low and everything seems to be made of brown wood, with the exception of the occasional metal desk. Everything is pretty bleak, even the shades are pulled over the windows. An officer leads mom and me to a small waiting area and tells us someone named Detective Heights will meet with us shortly. I hear the low buzzing of the air conditioner and the sound of my shoe hitting the wooden floor. A few drawn out minutes later, the heavy wooden door creaks open and an exceptionally short woman strolls in. Her yellow blonde hair is pulled back into a ponytail, and a thin, black headwrap rests on her head. She wears light blue skinny jeans, a plain grey t-shirt, and black Nikes.

"I'm Detective Heights. Sorry to keep you waiting, I've had a crazy morning," she apologizes.

I'm taken aback by her petite figure and squeaky voice. I've always pictured detectives as seven foot tall, muscular men who could kill you with their crazy intimidating looks. But in walks this tiny blonde girl who can't be much older than me.

"It's alright." Mom stands up and stretches out her hand, "I'm Brenna Mason, and this is my daughter, Izzie."

Detective Heights shakes our hands and says, "It's wonderful to meet you both. I think you both know why you're here. I'm just going to ask Izzie a few questions about the scene she witnessed this morning so the police department can start taking the necessary measures. It's really important to remind you that I'm just trying to learn some basic information about the situation and this is in no way a questioning of any sort. With that being said, would you follow me to my office, Izzie?"

The bitter chill that has stuck with me throughout the morning fades away as I begin to sweat from the inside out and realize how ridiculous I must look in this bulky sweatshirt and fleece lined sweatpants.

"You want her to go in there alone?" my mom asks with a raised eyebrow.

"Well, you're welcome to join us Mrs. Mason, but we prefer to interview witnesses without the pressure of outside factors. We don't want anything to skew the witness's responses."

I'm not sure if I'm more afraid to be alone in there or to have my mom watching me answer her questions. This sounds like a lose lose situation for me.

"Okay, I understand. I'll be right out here if you need me, Izzie," she takes my hand and gives me a reassuring nod.

"Follow me, Izzie! I'll take good care of her, Mrs. Mason," she says eagerly and cheerfully.

Detective Heights's office can't be more than 200 square feet, and is very underwhelming. I always pictured there to be something exciting and intriguing about detective's offices. I mean, it's the place where massive crimes and murders get solved. This looks like a normal everyday office where one might pay their bills, not serve justice to criminals. It just seems ordinary. She has a small desk in the middle of the room that holds a computer and is cluttered with various papers and manilla file folders. In the back right corner, there is a small table with a coffee maker and a couple of mismatched mugs. In the back left corner, there is a bookshelf filled with a mixture of ancient looking and brand new books.

"You can take a seat right here," she points to the chair in front of the disorganized desk behind which she takes her seat.

She places an empty file folder and a legal pad on the desk in front of her, which is covered with various scraps of paper, file folders, and pens, and takes a pair of square, black rimmed glasses out from a desk drawer. I still can't believe *this* is Detective Heights.

"So, you're Detective Heights?" I ask, confused by the image of this lady.

"Yes, that's me. Go ahead, laugh," she smiles slightly, clearly used to this reaction.

"I'm sorry, that wasn't nice. It's just that I pictured you differently and your name is just not matching up with your . . . sorry . . ."

"It's not matching up with my height. I know, I get it all the time. But I am four eleven and proud," she jokes.

My brain is still swirling around in my head. I feel like I'm trapped in one of my favorite mystery novels.

"Alright honey, let's cut straight to the chase," she motions for me to take a seat again.

I sit down slowly, trying to steady my shaking legs and hands. Beads of sweat begin to roll down my forehead, and my cheeks feel like they're burning up.

Detective Heights seems to sense my intense nerves because she says, "Please don't be nervous. I know how much of a scare you probably had this morning. The only reason you're here is to tell me what you saw so we can make sure everyone in Knox Hollow is safe. You're not being questioned or accused. Plus, I'm the least intimidating person in this entire place."

I awkwardly smile at her attempt at humor because I can't manage to speak. Someone is dead and I'm sitting in a police station. Someone is dead and I'm sitting in a police station. Someone is dead and I'm sitting in a police station. The thought runs in circles around my brain. The more I say it, the more it scares me. I can't bring myself to look at her in the eyes. Sitting here just makes me feel like I'm guilty.

"I only have a couple questions for you. We want to figure this all out as quickly as possible. Obviously, we don't have the autopsy just yet, but we want to start our interviews as soon as possible while the information is still fresh in your brain."

"Okay," I say.

"Can you tell me what led you to finding the body?" she asks casually.

"I woke up and went downstairs for some coffee. I went to go sit outside, and when I opened the slider door, it . . . she . . . Stephanie was lying on my back porch."

She makes a couple notes on her pad before asking another question, "Can you describe the scene to me in as much detail as you remember?"

"At first I didn't see anything, I just smelled this odor, which was the dead body. I was walking, and I felt my foot step in something sticky. When I looked down, I was stepping in dried blood. And . . . uh . . . that's when I saw the body." My stomach feels nauseous just recounting the story to Detective Heights.

She makes more notes, "Alright. Was the victim already dead when you discovered her?"

"Y-Yes," I stutter. I feel the sweat seeping through my excessive layers of clothes, and my hands are clammy.

"I know this is difficult, Miss Mason, but —"

I cut her off without even meaning to, "Actually, my last name is Andrews . . . I'm sorry, that was rude. I didn't mean to just cut you off. I'm a bit of a disaster these days."

"There's no need to apologize. I shouldn't have assumed," she smiles cheerfully and continues on with the questions, "How long did you know the victim?"

"About a week. I just moved in last Friday."

"I see, you're new to Knox Hollow. This is a terrible first impression," she laughs. "So I take it you didn't know her too well? How many times would you guess that you interacted with her?"

"I barely knew her. I met her twice."

"Can you describe those encounters?"

"The Friday we moved in, she and her husband came over to our house and introduced themselves. They stayed for a glass of wine with my parents, and I talked to her a little bit. And then last night was her annual summer party. I talked to her for a few minutes, but she was mostly just saying hello and welcoming me and my family to the party. I never got to know her or anything like that."

"Was there anything suspicious or strange that you noticed about the victim or the people around her? Anything that seemed strange to you?"

Strange doesn't even begin to define my impression of Stephanie. Should I tell Detective Heights about the secret she whispered in my ear or the strange phone call or the threat she delivered to me on the night of the party? It's not like I even have concrete proof of any of these things. They could all be logically explained. They're all only based on my overemotional speculation. And if I tell her those things, I have to explain why I ran out of Stephanie's house and the bloody shoe I found in my closet. By telling her all these things, I may implicate myself.

"No," I say unsteadily. "No."

"Are you sure?" she questions.

The beads of sweat start to trickle down my forehead. I feel like I'm being accused, like I'm guilty.

"Yes, I'm sure. I honestly didn't know Mrs. Kester well at all. I don't know what normal looks like for her. I can't tell you if she seemed off because I don't know," my voice comes out more annoyed than I want. I'm making effective use of my best defense mechanism — anger.

"I see," she says calmly, but I can tell she knows I'm not telling her the full truth. "So there's nothing that seemed odd to you at all?"

My eyes are darting around her office, as if I'm searching for the answer and waiting for it to appear scrawled upon the walls.

"N-No," I stutter. "I didn't even know her."

"But somehow she ended up on *your* back porch," her voice is soft, but strong, cutting through the nervous energy between us and sucking the air out of my lungs. What the hell did she mean by *that*?

Detective Heights comes across as innocent, docile even. I think I may have severely underestimated her. I can tell by that line she snuck in with ease that Detective Heights is sharp and quick minded. She appears to be friendly and unintimidating, but she's a seasoned pro. The way her pearl grey eyes are staring into me makes me feel like she already knows I'm leaving out valuable information. It's like her sharp grey eyes are calling me out and saying "try me".

"I have no idea how that happened," I plead because in all honesty, I haven't the least bit of a clue.

"You seem like a smart girl, Izzie, so I'm not going to push and pry just yet. I trust that when the timing's right, you and I will be able to help each other out."

I feel like that was her nice way of calling me a big, fat liar. And technically, I'm not lying, I'm just withholding some ideas and speculative thoughts that I have about what are most likely meaningless events. She pushes that topic to the side for the moment. She knows she's in my head. She's baiting me, like a quiet fisherman waiting for a big catch. She thinks if she gives me space, the guilt will force me to tell her what I saw. But let me tell you, Detective Heights has met her match because I, for one, do not give in to anyone.

Detective Heights asks me a couple more basic questions regarding the party and Stephanie and my discovery of the body this morning. I keep all my answers brief and vague in hopes of getting out of the sweltering room as quickly as possible. All I want to do is curl up in a ball on my bed and pretend the rest of the world doesn't exist. Detective Heights maintains a cheerful demeanor the whole time, but I can tell she's waiting to pounce on me. To her, it's just a game of time. It's like she has me figured out. It makes me feel like her brain already has a plan for how to get me to crack.

"Well, Miss Andrews, you are free to go," she scribbles a few more notes and hands me a business card. "If you think of anything that might be important, give me a call. I'll be in touch."

Detective Heights walks me back out to my mom and thanks me for my help, even though I've been far from helpful. The time on my watch reads 2:00 p.m. and I realize I've eaten nothing but a few bites of a bagel all day. I'm suddenly starving. All I want is to go back into my room and forget the world, but the thought of going back to the house is making me shiver.

I decide to send Hazel a text and see if she wants to go grab something to eat. She and I have quite a bit of catching up to do. She responds almost immediately, saying that she would love nothing more than to meet me at the Roadside Diner in twenty minutes. Mom agrees to drop me off there with the promise I do not leave alone. A few minutes later, I am walking into the Roadside Diner feeling unsteady on my feet from the shock, nerves, and hangover.

Hazel waves to me from a booth in the back, and as I walk closer she says sarcastically, "You look great."

I hang my head, slip into the booth, and reply jokingly, "Are you referring to the bags under my eyes, the sweatshirt I've sweated through, or the fact that I haven't brushed my hair today?"

I don't understand how Hazel can look so put together after last night. She wears a pair of jean shorts and a frilly white tank top, and her hair is thrown into a ponytail with a red bandana as a headband.

We go quiet for a minute, and I feel Hazel's happy demeanor change into nervous energy.

"I'm sure you heard about Stephanie," I say.

She nods her head slowly, "Yeah. I don't . . . I can't believe it."

I hear my heart beating loudly in my ears, "She was having fun with her friends and then she was on my back patio dead. How does that happen?"

"I don't know. It makes me sick. Is it true what everyone's saying? About the . . . bullet hole in her head."

"Yeah. She was shot."

I tell Hazel about finding Mrs. Kester and my visit to the police station. Her mouth permanently hangs open, and every so often she shakes her head in disbelief.

"I will never drink that much again," Hazel vows. "That was so unlike me, and I . . . I will never do that again."

"Me either. Never again," I agree. "Can I ask you something?"

"Of course," Hazel's voice is quiet.

"Do you remember anything about last night?"

"Bits and pieces. Everything is a little blurry. I remember hanging out, and I remember walking home, but somehow I ended up waking up on the basement couch. Drinking last night made me feel out of control. I didn't like that feeling."

"Me neither. I'm worried, Hazel. That I did something last night. I can't remember anything. It's like there's this big, black hole over those hours."

"I don't think you did anything bad. We all just hung out and then went home. Your brother Luke, I think, walked you home a little before I walked Graeson home. He was much further gone than I was. I wonder how he's feeling today?"

So, Hazel watched Luke walk me home? That means I was with them all night. How did that blood get on my shoe then?

Hazel senses my nerves and says, "You shouldn't stress yourself out about this, Izzie. We made a mistake, but it's over now. I think this feeling is coming from finding Stephanie."

What Hazel says makes sense. Finding Stephanie has definitely taken a toll on my mental state. Combine that with the cruddy feeling from last night's drinking, and everything adds up. What Luke said also made sense. I probably just stepped in blood at some point before Luke walked me home. I'm trying hard to convince myself of this, but something doesn't add up and is making me feel paranoid.

"I'm just nervous," I say.

"It's been a really weird day."

"I feel like something's off about all of this. I keep getting this eerie feeling."

"Me too. It's probably just the shock of it all. This is the second death Mayflower Circle's had in the past two months."

My heart sinks as I remember what Shea told me about his dad last night.

"Shea told me about his dad last night," I say as Hazel shakes her head in disbelief. "Before he kissed me, he —"

"BEFORE HE WHAT?!" Hazel yells, causing multiple heads to turn our way.

Everything that happened this morning has caused me to forget all about my little moment with Shea.

I feel myself smiling for the first time today, "Yeah, we kissed."

"Why am I just hearing about this!?" she exclaims.

"I've been a little preoccupied," I answer sarcastically.

It's funny to think that if I had gone home instead of walking up the Kester's hilly lawn like I had contemplated, I never would have kissed Shea. I never would have drank, and maybe Stephanie Kester would not have died on my back porch. Thinking about it now sends an uncomfortable feeling through my body. I had been so busy worrying about Stephanie this morning that I had forgotten about Shea, and now that I'm thinking about it, I'm heavily overthinking about it. I'm so embarrassed about how I acted in front of him. What did he think when he heard that her body was found in my yard? I wonder if he thinks I'm guilty of something. And does he even like me? Or was that just a one time thing in the heat of the moment? There's so many questions and awkwardness now surrounding all of it. Why can't life just go back to being simple?

Hazel shoots questions at me like one throws darts at a target, eager and excited to hear the story. It's weird, but for a moment it's like we're just two normal girls whose biggest problems revolve around a first kiss, not a murder. Once she's satisfied with my account of the moment, the two of us quietly enjoy our foods, lost in our own thoughts. When I look up from my sweet potato fries, I say to Hazel quietly and with a little uncertainty as to how she'll take the question, "If it's true that she was murdered, who do you think did it?"

She looks a little stunned, but then turns her face into pensive thought, "I'm not sure. It's hard to think that anyone would do something like that. Who do you think did it?"

While that is a difficult question for Hazel who sees the best in everyone, my true crime warped brain is filled with hundreds of theories, each one more fascinating than the next.

113

They say it's always the husband, which makes placing the blame on Richard exceptionally easy and plausible. The defeated look in his eyes and the way he angrily tugged on Stephanie's arm serves as easy evidence, but there's something about him that makes me believe — or at least want to believe —that he's innocent. They say it's always the husband, unless it's the boyfriend. The secret side love. The guilty affair. Which in this case, would provide solid reasoning for Stephanie dashing down Mayflower Circle in the dead of night in a flashy dress. It's only speculation, but oftentimes the lines of speculation and reality can blend until they're one in the same.

CHAPTER 7- Bad Decisions

"The police are going live in ten minutes," Luke comes into my room and almost trips over the stacks of boxes I have yet to unpack. "Seriously, Izzie, you need to start unpacking."

I thought there might be a chance after . . . you know . . . finding a dead body in our yard that maybe we'd move back to Portland. Instead, Luke and John installed a new security system and Mom put up a sign that read *Home Sweet Home*.

"Hazel should be here any minute," I say to him.

"Hazel?"

"Yeah, Hazel. You met her at the party."

"I know who Hazel is," he sounds all flustered and rushed.

"Are you good, Luke?" I laugh.

"I . . . I'm fine. When is she coming?" he says as his face turns redder by the moment.

Oh. My. God. I think Luke has a thing for Hazel.

My eyes go bright and a sly smile spreads across my face.

"Do you like Hazel?" I inquire.

He stares down at his feet and contemplates how to answer my question, "Uh no . . . I barely even know her."

"So what?"

"I'm walking away now," Luke awkwardly laughs.

I start teasing him, "You like Hazel! You like Hazel!"

I know I sound like a crazy-eyed middle school girl, but I don't really care. I shouldn't meddle, it never ends well, but maybe I can work something out for the two of them. They'd be pretty great together.

115

Hazel texts me that she's here, so I go downstairs to meet her. The police are making a public statement tonight at six. I'm so nervous to watch that I asked Hazel to come over for moral support. The last few days I've felt much better. The hangover and the initial shock faded, and I was back to feeling more like myself. But there's still a small little nagging thought in the back of my brain that sends an eerie feeling into the pit of my stomach. So when they announced that the police were coming out with a statement, the nervous feeling grew quite a bit bigger. The logical part of my brain knows that there's no way I could have done it. There's so many inconsistencies if that were the case. If I was with my friends all night, wouldn't someone have noticed that I was missing? Where would I have gotten a gun? And for the love of God, wouldn't you remember if you murdered someone in cold blood? There's no way I did it. That was just an emotionally shell-shocked reaction, and once I started thinking clearly, I realized that it's going to be alright. Now, if I could only get that strange feeling to go away, I may actually have a chance of getting back to the happy girl I knew so long ago.

After a bit of small talk with my parents, I take Hazel down to the small living room in my basement to await the news from the police, but not before I begin a bit of meddling.

"Luke," I call upstairs. "Come down and watch with us!"

He appears at the top of the stairs and says, "I'm going to watch upstairs with Mom and John."

I shoot him a look and yell back, "Oh perfect, come on down!"

"That's not what I said," Luke mutters confusingly.

I glare at him and harshly motion for him to come downstairs. Reluctantly, he makes his way down while rolling his eyes at me. His mocha colored hair that was a ruffled mess five minutes before is now spiked up in front with gel. I'll have to remember to tease him about that later. His bright green eyes can't seem to leave the floor, but his smile is still sweet and heartfelt. Luke and Hazel are two of the only people I actually like in the world, so this could work out for them.

"Hazel, you remember my brother, Luke," I say, reintroducing them to each other.

Hazel's bright energy is in full force as she smiles at Luke and says, "It's nice to see you again."

His face blushes a vibrant shade of red, "You too."

We settle in on the couches downstairs, making ourselves comfortable before whatever this big announcement may be.

"What do you think they're going to say?" Hazel asks, her thin legs crisscrossed on our sofa.

Luke replies, "They're probably going to tell us they're officially opening up a murder investigation. I can't see them giving us too much information."

"I just feel so bad for Richard and her kids," Hazel sympathizes. "I can't even imagine what they're going through."

"How old are her kids?" I ask.

"Twelve, nine, and seven," she replies.

"They're so young," Luke shakes his head.

"I wonder how Richard's taking it?" I say.

"I bet he's heartbroken. It was his wife, and it's not like he even had a chance to say goodbye," Hazel responds.

"Do you think a small part of him is relieved?" I suddenly remember that there's this thing inside of your head called a filter that your thoughts are supposed to slide through so you don't sound like a complete sociopath to the people around you. I guess this one slipped through the cracks. Hazel and Luke's faces are a mixture of shock and disgust.

"What did you just say?" Luke gawks at me.

"I don't know, there was just something about the defeated look in his eyes and the way she treated him. It was just a thought."

"You have a sick brain," Luke taunts.

117

"Say you have a spouse who is constantly berating you and causing chaos everywhere he or she goes. At some point, you just become so defeated you can't even try to stop it anymore. Wouldn't there be a small part of you that was relieved that you didn't have to put up with that anymore? You'd never admit it out loud, but . . . I don't know . . . it's just a thought."

Luke shakes his head, while Hazel seems to take my words into consideration. She says, "How could anyone possibly be relieved about death?"

"You're going to scare all your friends away, Izzie, if you keep talking —" I cut Luke off because the commercial ends, and the TV screen lights up with the image of Detective Heights and another man at a podium.

Detective Heights stands comfortably in front of the cameras with her pin straight blonde hair neatly combed down to her elbows. Next to her is a man towering over her, with a full head of reddish brown hair. He has a tall, but lanky build, and lush green eyes. He seems to be sweating through his clothes and stands awkwardly by the podium, clearly uncomfortable with the cameras. Luke, Hazel, and I go completely silent in anticipation of the news.

The male detective clears his throat and stutters, "Good evening ladies and gentlemen. My name is Detective Joseph Burnside."

"My name is Detective Lauren Heights, and we're the lead detectives on the Stephanie Kester case," her voice is confident. "According to the autopsy report, the evidence we've acquired from the scene of the incident, and firsthand witness accounts, we have ruled the death of Stephanie Kester a homicide."

Even though I knew that was coming, the words shock my ears. We were all thinking it, but hearing Detective Heights confirm all of our suspicions is so surreal.

Sweat-stained Detective Burnside steps up to take over speaking, "We want to assure you that we are exhausting all of our leads and diligently using our resources to solve this case. The safety of Knox Hollow's residents is of the utmost importance to all of us, so we ask for your patience and cooperation as we work."

Detective Heights adds, "Our condolences extend to the family and friends of Mrs. Stephanie Kester, and we ask that you grant her family privacy as they grieve. If anyone has any information they believe could be helpful to the Knox Hollow police department concerning this ongoing investigation, please contact us. Your identity will be kept confidential. Thank you."

With that, Detective Heights and Detective Burnside step down from the podium and out through the brown wooden doors, fighting off a swarm of obnoxious reporters with microphones and cameramen.

Hazel's face is as pale as the moon, "Wow."

"They couldn't have given us any more information?" Luke shakes his head.

All of us sit wide-eyed, staring at the screen as if we were waiting for them to blurt out, "Just kidding."

"Let's go for a walk," I say. "I need some air."

The three of us make our way upstairs and outside into the fresh air. The evening air is cool, and the day's humidity has broken leaving a slight breeze.

"Who do you think did it?" I ask, unable to hold back the question any longer. Yes, I understand that it was a very unsympathetic thing to say, but the urge was too strong.

"Seriously, Izzie," Luke sighs. "Someone died and that's the first question you ask."

"I'm sorry, but tell me you're not wondering the exact same thing," I retort.

Luke just shrugs the remark off because he knows there's no point in arguing with me about this. Although it's fairly warm out, the sky is colored an eerie grey, which makes me shiver a little bit.

We're walking along in silence, all of us trying to organize and process our thoughts. I'm not really organizing my thoughts, more so filtering them to make sure I don't say anything else that's either insensitive or psychotic sounding. I've read enough crime novels to have hundreds of suspicions swirling around in my brain. Suddenly, I hear a loud bang from behind. I whip myself around and see Richard thundering out of the Kester's house, slamming the front door as he takes large, booming steps. He reaches his sleek, black car, launches himself inside, and bashes the door shut. He backs the car out of the driveway at full speed, and rams into their mailbox, sending it flying into the middle of the street, creating a shower of metal pieces, and crushing the flowers surrounding it. He doesn't seem to notice or care since he speeds away at at least 100 miles per hour, not bothering to notice what's around him. I watch Richard's car fade into the distance until I can no longer hear the rev of his engine. Hazel, Luke, and I must look pretty strange to anyone walking by. The three of us are frozen in the middle of the sidewalk with gaping eyes and wide open mouths, staring into the street.

"What was *that*?" Luke's quiet voice breaks the silence.

"I've known Richard for ten years, and I've never seen him even raise his monotone voice. I don't know *what* that was," Hazel answers, her voice almost raspy from the shock.

Before I even realize what my body is doing, I start walking towards the broken mailbox and crushed flowers. I'm not exactly sure why, but I feel terrible for Richard. He lost his wife, and if this investigation goes the way most do, the finger is going to be pointed directly at him. Even if there's not enough evidence for him to be prosecuted or accused, the public will blame him. He'll constantly live under that umbrella of public shame and scrutiny, even if he's innocent. I've always had a soft spot for underdogs and lost causes and the misunderstood, probably because I'm all of those things myself. Richard seemed to be a broken man with a big heart. I just can't picture him and his doe like eyes holding a gun to his wife's head.

"What are you doing?" Hazel calls out.

"I'm picking up the pieces of his mailbox. He doesn't need the entire world to know he's losing it."

Luke is hesitant at first, but Hazel rushes right over, and all of us begin to clean up the mess from Richard's wreckage. We gather pieces of sharp metal and smushed flowers and place them aside as we attempt to salvage what we can of the main structure. A few minutes later, I hear the front door creek open and a gangly boy about the age of twelve steps out.

Hazel notices him and calls out in her sweet tone of voice, "Hi Alex. The mailbox fell over so we're just cleaning it up."

The boy doesn't speak, but walks down the rolling hill and over to where we're hunched over by the mailbox. I notice he's tall and lanky and seems to have a muscular build that he's yet to fill in. Alex has sandy blonde hair that is buzzed in the back but long on top and brushed into a little swoop. Instantly, I see a younger version of Stephanie in him. He has her long, skinny nose that curls into a gentle point and her coal black, fanning eyelashes. He has her sun kissed skin and the same freckles over the bridge of his nose. The only difference is his eyes. Alex's eyes are a deep blue like Richard's as opposed to Stephanie's hazel ones. I always felt that all of Stephanie's enchantment and passion and craziness came from her eyes. Alex's blue eyes give his face an entirely different look and bring about a different vibe, however, it's a vibe I can't quite put my finger on. He's the perfect mix of Stephanie and Richard, like a perfectly crafted stained glass window.

"My dad backed over the mailbox," his voice is raspy and straightforward.

Hazel looks up at him, "It's okay."

"The police report sent him over the edge. He's been a wreck all week," Alex adds.

"That's understandable," Hazel's voice is soft and soothing. "I'm sorry about your mom, Alex. I don't even know how hard it must be."

"The police are going to take him in for questioning tomorrow, I think," Alex says ignoring Hazel's sympathy.

An awkward silence settles over us. What are you supposed to say to a boy whose mother was just murdered and whose father is about to become the prime suspect in the case? Alex's eyes have been staring off into the distance the entire time. He hasn't made eye contact or altered his glance once since he's been down here.

"He didn't do it. No one's going to believe it, but I know he didn't do it," Alex adds as you can hear the fear seeping into his voice.

It hits me like a bullet to the heart because I know that feeling. I've felt that yearning in the pit of my stomach. That feeling of just closing your eyes and praying with everything in you that your beliefs are true. That feeling of placing all of your blind faith onto a mere hope. That feeling of holding onto the image of the one person you thought you knew. I felt that when my mom told me about my dad. I didn't want to believe that he could have walked away from us for alcohol. I still don't want to.

"I believe you," my voice catches Alex off guard because he suddenly breaks his stare and turns to meet my eyes.

He nods his head, and the smallest inkling of a smile pierces his cheek. Alex doesn't say anything, but I can tell he feels what I said. Sometimes you don't have to fix a situation to make someone feel better. Sometimes, all a person needs to know is that there's someone on their side.

"You do?" he questions.

"Yeah, I do. I believe you, and I believe your dad."

"Most people don't."

122

"Well, I'm not most people."

We finish cleaning up as best we can as the sun sets behind us, signaling the official arrival of dusk.

"Do you want me to stay with you until your dad gets back?" Hazel asks.

"No, it's okay. He should be back soon," Alex replies.

"I really don't want to leave you and your sisters alone," Hazel pushes. "Have you eaten dinner yet?"

"No, but we're fine," Alex replies.

"Alex, please just let me get you settled inside. It's getting dark out," Hazel pleads.

After a little bit of pushing, Alex agrees to let Hazel watch over him and his sisters for a little bit. I will say, as much as I'm rooting for Richard, I'm a little shocked he left his young kids alone right after his wife was murdered a few yards away. But grief works differently for everyone, and I'm in no place to judge him or his actions. Luke and I say goodbye to Hazel and Alex and make our way back home. As we turn to walk away, I catch a pair of eyes peeking out from behind the downstairs curtain. Pale blue ovals are staring out at me, and I catch the shadow of a little girl I recognize to be Ella Kester. I would say she was strange, but I feel like that would be insensitive at the moment.

As we walk back up the driveway with the stars just beginning to break through the grey sky, I say to Luke slyly with a wide smile spread across my face, "So, you like Hazel?"

"I do not!" Luke says defensively.

"Tell that to the gel you put in your hair," I tease.

Luke rolls his eyes jokingly and begins laughing, "You're really the worst sometimes."

I smile brightly, "I know."

*****

123

Detective Heights was right about me after all. The guilt from leaving out what could be crucial pieces of Stephanie's story started to eat me alive. The morning after the police made their announcement about the death being declared an official homicide, I couldn't shake the feeling that some bear-like creature was gnawing at my insides. Turns out this bear-like creature was a little something called guilt. I felt so guilty that I dashed into Luke's room while he was still sleeping, aggressively woke him up, and spilled every little detail about everything that went on since we've moved here. I think it was a lot for his sleep deprived brain to process, but it felt good to finally get it all off my chest and to have Luke on my side once again. Luke convinced me I had to tell Detective Heights about everything . . . well everything but the shoe. We both agreed that that would complicate everything when there's a logical explanation for it. I must have just stepped in blood at some point before Luke walked me home, and because it was dark, I didn't notice it. That's logical. Right?

I'm sitting in the waiting area outside Detective Heights's office, unsure if I'm having trouble breathing from the stuffiness of the room or the weight of the words I'm about to reveal. The air is so sweltering that my thighs stick to the plastic of the chair anytime I try to move. My jean shorts feel permanently glued to my body, and my hair is becoming frizzier and frizzier due to the humidity. Detective Heights better get out here soon or else I'll lose all the nerve I have. A few minutes later, a man approaches me and extends his arm. My first instinct is to scream, but then I recognize the man as the sweaty detective from the public announcement.

"Excuse me . . . Miss . . . I'm Detective Burnside," he stutters. "Detective Heights is running late . . . uh . . . she asked me to get started."

There's something about his nervousness that makes me feel much more at ease with him than I did with Detective Heights.

My superstitious mind had felt like she was trying to trap me in a lie — and rightfully so — but this guy makes me feel safe to share my observations.

I stand up, and you can hear the crackling noise as my sweaty legs unstick from the plastic of the chair.

I shake his outstretched hand and say, "My name is Isabelle Andrews."

I follow Detective Burnside through the main area of the police station. We walk in between two rows of metal desks with secretaries and officers busy at work. When we come to the front of the station by the main entrance I catch sight of Detective Heights. She's standing with her arms crossed and her eyes intently fixed on the person she's talking to. My glance shifts to the person at the same time his head turns to me. Our eyes lock, and I find myself in an intense stare with a pair of deep blue eyes that tell the story of a broken man. Richard. Detective Heights is running late because she's questioning Richard. My body continues walking as my eyes continue communicating in some weird way with Richard's. He's probably so embarrassed that I saw him here, but on that note, should I be embarrassed that he saw me here? Soon enough, Detective Burnside has led me down a short hallway, and our stare has broken. Detective Burnside fumbles with a key chain, unlocks the door, and leads me into what I'm assuming is his office. I notice the area is identical to Detective Heights's office — same grey walls, same small desk, and same wooden blinds pulled halfway down the window. The only difference is that his office appears to be pristinely organized with not one thing out of place. There's a stack of manilla file folders stacked exactly one on top of the other and a row of pencils lined up with the points perfectly matched.

"You can have a seat," he starts. "Can I get you any water or coffee?"

"No thank you," I reply. "Will Detective Heights be meeting us here?"

He takes a swig of water from a metal bottle and then says, "Yes, she'll be here shortly. She wanted me to listen to what you have to say to her."

"Detective Burnside, would you mind if I asked you a question?" I say.

He clears his throat and takes a seat at the desk, "No, I wouldn't mind."

I think deeply about how to word the question, "Do you think it's going to take a long time to solve this case?"

Detective Burnside looks pensive, deeply considering my question, "It's hard to say. Investigations are always very unexpected. It'll depend on a lot of factors."

I nod, "I read a lot of true crime novels. I never thought I'd be living one."

"I hear you were the one who found the body. I know how traumatic it must've been."

"It was terrifying. Every time I shut my eyes, all I can see is her face."

His lush green eyes are filled with sympathy, "That's not surprising. I've been in your shoes. It comes with the job, but it still doesn't get easier watching people suffer."

"I'm just scared. Something like this happened on my street."

"Miss Andrews, I promise you we are doing everything we can to make Knox Hollow safe. We have police cars patrolling your street all night. You don't have to worry."

"Do you think the person who did it lives on my street?"

The first question was just to test the waters, to see if he was willing to talk to me. And the whole "I'm scared" performance was mostly to see if I could get a little insider information out of him. For some odd reason, I'm not all that terrified. I feel like I should be more scared, but then again, when do my emotions ever appear as they should? Plus, Detective Burnside's nerves seemed to have relaxed drastically since he started talking about his job.

He furrows his eyebrows and replies, "I can't release that type of information, Miss Andrews. I wish I could help ease your mind, but we're still looking at suspects."

I nod, but decide to pry more, "I understand, but you really can't even tell me if you think that the person lives on my street? I'm scared for my life."

That may have been a bit too dramatic, but also effective because Detective Burnside seems to squirm in his chair. His eyes continuously dart around the room, looking for a way out of this conversation. And due to his body movements and the way he keeps apologizing for my fear, I believe I have my answer. Mayflower Circle is a dead end street with a cul-de-sac. Everyone was hanging out right in the middle of the circle, which means no car would've been able to pass by unnoticed. I guess the person could've come on foot, but that doesn't seem probable, especially since Mayflower Circle is kind of off the beaten path. Stephanie was still in her party clothes when she was murdered, and the dried blood made it look like she had been dead for quite some time. Wouldn't it be easy for someone she knew to lead her into a quiet place away from the party and pull the trigger? It has to be someone on our street. There's no other explanation. Plus, Detective Burnside's anxiety is making that pretty clear to me.

"Do you know what time she died?" I ask another question because he doesn't seem to be able to answer my first one.

"That I can tell you. We suspect she died around 2:20 a.m."

Just as I'm about to open my mouth again, the door opens and in walks Detective Heights.

"Well hello there, Isabelle. Why does it look like you're torturing my partner?" she laughs at Detective Burnside's obvious nervousness.

I smile at her and uncomfortably laugh, feeling all my confidence drain away.

"I had a feeling I'd be getting a call from you," she pulls up a chair next to Detective Burnside.

There she goes again with her passive aggressive remarks, trying to make me feel like she knows me and what my next move is before I even make it. It's really so obnoxious.

"I remembered something about Stephanie. It slipped my mind last time we talked."

She nods her head nonchalantly, using her glasses to see straight through my lie. "Slipped your mind, huh? I'm glad you remembered. Please, Isabelle, enlighten us."

Detective Burnside takes out a legal pad and a pen, while Detective Heights sits back in her chair with a subtle smirk on her face.

"I told you about how Stephanie and Richard came over the first night we moved in. They talked to my parents and me for a while. Stephanie kept making comments about knowing all the gossip. She seemed to be a couple of glasses deep into her wine so I didn't bother asking her what she was talking about, but then when she turned to leave, she grabbed me by the arm and whispered something like "We all have secrets, and he knows all of them."

Immediately, I exhale because I think I had been holding my breath the whole time I was talking. Detective Burnside is furiously scribbling notes on his pad, and Detective Heights seems to be deep within her own thoughts, carefully considering my words.

"Anything else?" Detective Heights asks a few moments later.

"Actually, yes."

I quickly fill them both in on the phone call I overheard, making sure they knew that I did not break into her house. I also tell them about seeing her running down the street in the middle of the night, and the threat she served me at the party. I can't remember exactly what she said. I just remember her telling me not to listen in on others' phone conversations, but I feel like there was another comment she made. Anyway, both detectives fire questions at me, and I try to explain the different scenarios to the best of my abilities. I'm still unsure if they believe me or think I'm some stupid kid making up stories.

"That's very interesting," Detective Heights says, and I can't tell if she actually believes me or is just humoring me. "Can I ask why you didn't tell me this last time?"

I debate lying to her again and telling her that I forgot, but that seems like a terrible excuse that she didn't even believe the first time I used it.

"To be honest, I was scared," I say, playing the emotional card. "I had just found a dead body on my back porch, and then I was in the police station being questioned about it. I broke under the pressure. I had a really hard time when we moved across the country. I have a lot going on. It was just all too much."

Detective Heights nods sympathetically and her cold eyes seem to be genuine.

"Thank you for deciding to tell us. You made the right choice, Isabelle. I just have one question for you before you go." I nod my head, eager to hear her question. "Why do you think Mrs. Kester was running down your street at that hour?"

I try to keep my face from giving too much away. I've spent many days and nights thinking about it, and there's really only one situation that seems likely.

"Why are you asking me?" I ask.

Detective Heights smiles and says calmly, "Because I think you're a very smart girl. One who knows a lot more than she lets on. I want to know what you think."

I take a deep breath, "Can you promise me that what I say won't leave this room? I've already had enough trouble fitting in. I don't need my neighbors to think I'm spreading rumors about them."

"I promise that what you say will stay between us."

"Okay," I take in another deep breath. "I think Stephanie was cheating on her husband . . . with someone on our street."

Detective Heights seems very amused by the whole situation. She smirks smugly and says, "It seems like you've done a bit of detective work yourself."

I'm over this conversation and Detective Heights's attitude. I feel like she doesn't believe what I'm telling her and is making a mockery out of me. But in all honesty, I don't even know if I would believe me.

"I observe a lot," I begin. "You notice a lot when you sit back and just listen and watch."

"You're a very bright girl, Isabelle. That's a big part of our job — observing. We listen to people and observe their mannerisms. We analyze crime scenes and tangible evidence. I've always thought if you observe enough, you can solve the case. Thank you for your *stories* and your *theory*. I'll be in touch."

That line makes the blood in my veins boil to an extraordinarily hot rate. I knew it! She doesn't believe a freaking thing I said. I hate the way she looks down on me and chuckles at my accounts. I tried to be helpful, but I'm done with her. I understand why she may question my words, but she didn't have to make it so obvious that she thought I was foolish.

I make an impulsive decision to passive aggressively show Detective Heights how I feel. I look to Detective Burnside, extend my hand, and give him a bright smile. I say cheerfully, "It was really nice to meet you!" Then, my face goes stone cold as I turn to Detective Heights and say, "I hope you're a better detective than you are person.

"I can't believe you said that to her," Hazel sits wide-eyed on her bed, half laughing and half shocked at me as I recount my entire visit to the police station to her.

"I know, I know. It was a last minute decision. It kind of just came out of my mouth before I could stop it."

"Do you think they're going to arrest Richard?" she asks.

"I don't know. It was so weird, Hazel, the way he looked at me. I don't think he wanted anyone to see him there, especially not the girl who found his dead wife," I respond.

Hazel shakes her head and seems lost in her thoughts. I've been trying to put all of the pieces together of everything I know, but the night of the party is so blurry. It's as if all of my memories were wiped clean, like chalk from a blackboard at the end of the school day. I feel like I'm missing something. I remember Stephanie saying something to me that made me uncomfortable, but I just can't remember what exactly that was.

Hazel pulls me out of my absent memories when she says, "Let's walk again and this time not clean up the Kester's front lawn."

"Sounds like a plan," I laugh.

We make our way downstairs and through the kitchen, and that's when I see Hazel's dad for the first time, sitting at their kitchen counter with a beer and a clipboard in his hands. I must admit that I'm a little taken aback by the sight of a professional NFL player casually sitting in Hazel's kitchen. Carson Huntington is a rough looking man with arms and legs of steel. However, age has definitely caught up with him, and time has not been on his side. Even though he still has a muscular and fit build, his stomach protrudes from what I assume is years of being held back by his knee injury and drinking. His forehead is creased with lines of worries, and his grey blue eyes seem shallow and dull, instead of determined. His once flowing blonde hair is buzzed short in the back and the front is hidden by a baseball cap, most likely to cover his receding hairline. He looks more like the shell of the NFL player than the actual guy.

"Dad, I've told you about my friend Izzie, right?" Hazel addresses him.

"Nice to meet you," he extends his monstrous hand and grunts. "I'm Carson Huntington."

"Nice to meet you," I say, unsure if I'm supposed to acknowledge the fact that I've seen him on TV.

Carson Huntington goes back to staring at his clipboard, seemingly unamused by Hazel's presence.

"We're just going for a walk," Hazel says. "I'll be back before dinner."

He makes a grunting noise and nods his head while keeping his eyes on his clipboard. Hazel rolls her eyes, and the two of us start walking out of the door.

Hazel looks over to me, "I told you, if it's not football, he doesn't care."

"I'm sorry," I say because I don't know how else to respond.

"It's fine. I can get away with a lot because he never pays any attention."

"When do you ever do anything wrong?" I laugh at her remark.

"I said I *can* get away with a lot, not that I *do* get away with a lot. And besides, I can be rebellious sometimes!"

I roll my eyes at her jokingly, "Oh please, Hazel."

The two of us play off each other back and forth until we hit the sidewalk, and . . . oh no! I catch Graeson and Shea out of the corner of my eye and have to fight the urge to whip myself around and run away as fast as I can. I'm so embarrassed about how I acted in front of him, and I have no idea what that kiss meant. And as we all know, I suck at emotionally centered things. I haven't thought about what I'm going to say to him. Dear God, I'm about to make such a fool of myself.

Hazel, seemingly unaware of my discomfort, walks over to them in her typical bright and cheery fashion.

"Well hello there, ladies. I haven't seen you in quite a bit, Miss Isabelle," Graeson says with his usual charm.

"There's been . . . a lot . . . going on lately," I half smile.

His usually cool and casual face melts into a sympathetic glance, "I understand. Finding dead bodies in your backyard is not something you get over too quickly."

I smile at him as he and Hazel begin discussing something I'm not paying very close attention to because my eyes turn to Shea. For a moment, I let myself fall into his familiar smile, and everything feels safe again.

"Hey," I say quietly.

"Hey," he says back.

It's like it's the only word in both of our vocabularies because neither one of us says anything for the next minute.

"I'm sorry you were the one to find the body," he says sensitively.

"It's okay," I reply.

With the mention of the body, I feel the walls building themselves back up, and the awkward feelings settle over me again. I feel myself pulling away from him because I'm embarrassed and confused.

The four of us start walking down the street as Hazel and Graeson seem to be in an intense debate, completely oblivious to me and Shea.

He turns to me and says with a slightly nervous voice, "We should talk about that night . . . when you're ready of course."

After his sweet remark, I say probably the most insensitive thing I could have possibly spewed out of my mouth. I look down at my black flip flops and say, "There's nothing to talk about."

My response catches Shea completely off guard. He almost stumbles over his own feet and his face does a double take. I look up and see his blue eyes filled to the brim with hurt and shock. As soon as I say it, I immediately regret ever letting those words roll off my tongue. I need to stop letting my embarrassment and awkwardness speak for me.

Shea doesn't reply, and the two of us walk in silence until I overhear Graeson say something to Hazel, "You know I cracked the camera on my phone the other day and —"

Something about his sentence stands out to me, so I cut him off, "What did you say?"

Graeson looks back to me slightly confused, "I said that I cracked the camera on my phone the other day."

Suddenly, a memory forces through my brain, sending a harsh pain through my forehead. I squeeze my eyes shut, trying to focus in on the scene. I see Stephanie and her yellow sundress with her hazel eyes glaring at me. She struts closer, and I can almost feel her limber fingers pressing against my shoulder. She whispers, "Next time you want to listen in on one of my phone conversations, don't leave behind any evidence." But there was one more thing, I'm sure of it! What did Graeson say that sparked this memory? That's it! Cameras. He was talking about his camera! And that's when I remember the exact words she uttered in my ears. She said to me, "And just for future reference, I have twenty-four hour surveillance cameras . . . everywhere." If Stephanie was being truthful when she threatened me with her intense level of security cameras, there might be real video evidence of her killer.

Everyone looks at me like I'm a patient who recently escaped from the psych ward of the hospital. My eyes are bulging with this newfound information, my heart is beating a million miles a minute, and my breathing sounds jagged.

"We need to go break into Stephanie's house."

CHAPTER 8 - For Whom the Bell Tolls

Stephanie's house is quiet, except for the faint hum of the air conditioner, which is causing me to shiver. I'm overly cautious of every step, careful not to make a sound. I hear Shea's jagged breathing next to me.

"Could you breathe quieter?" I shoot him a look.

He glances over at me and rolls his eyes, making me realize how ridiculous this all is.

"We really shouldn't be in here," he whispers.

"You didn't have to come with me. Leave if you want," I whisper back harshly because I feel like Shea's holding me back.

"There was no way I was letting you come in here alone," he says as his voice echoes off the high ceilings. "This house is like Satan's den."

I want to argue back, but I know he's right, and the fact that he's still trying to protect me even after I treated him so terribly is keeping my mouth shut. We tiptoe down the main hallway with the smell of Febreze and some sort of burnt food filling my nose. There's something exhilarating about doing something you're not supposed to do and being somewhere you're not supposed to be. Graeson is checking for outside cameras and a very reluctant Hazel is standing guard out front. She only agreed because she knew she couldn't stop us from carrying this out.

"What exactly are we looking for?" Shea whispers.

"Cameras," I reply, keeping my answers short.

I catch him shaking his head out of the corner of my eye, and it hits me that I most definitely blew up whatever the two of us had. I liked him. I really liked him, but I ruined it by pushing him away. Right now, I can't think about this. I need to focus on finding these infamous cameras Stephanie threatened me with. Shea and I make our way through the main foyer, down the long, dark wooded hallway, and into their luxurious kitchen where the smell of burnt food is most prominent. By the looks of the kitchen, I take it Richard doesn't have too much experience cooking. Dishes with crusted over remnants of food are stacked one on top of the other, filling every inch of the sink and spilling out onto the neighboring counter. Dirty pots and pans still hang out on the stove and random ingredients are spewed throughout the counter as if the pantry and refrigerator exploded. When we've searched the kitchen best we can, making sure not to touch anything, we walk into the dining room. The room has a vintage beauty about it, but that's not what catches my eye. In the middle of the gorgeous dining table is a centerpiece of dead sunflowers, decaying and drooping into an ominous sight. The last time I was in this house, it was overflowing with beauty and style. Now it's eerie, and it feels almost dangerous to be here. Shea was right. I feel like I'm walking into the middle of Satan's den.

A little while later, Shea and I have searched the entire first floor with no luck. Maybe Stephanie's threat was just that — a threat with no truth behind it.

"I think we should just go, Izzie. We didn't find anything," Shea says.

I don't want to walk away with nothing, and I have this strange feeling in the pit of my stomach telling me to stay, telling me there's something I'm missing.

"Upstairs!" I say to Shea louder than I mean to. "We have to check upstairs!"

Before he has time to reply, I'm racing up the stairs in search of God only knows what. I don't know where these mysterious cameras are or if they even exist, but I have a strong feeling that there's something upstairs that may help me.

"Izzie!" Shea's voice echoes up and bounces off the high ceilings. "Stop!"

My momentum is carrying me so fast I do a complete 360 when I try to turn around to talk to him.

"We need to go. What are you even looking for?" he asks.

"Something that will tell us who murdered her!" I reply passionately.

"This isn't our job. The police will handle it."

"I don't care. I'm going to look around. Are you coming or not?"

Shea looks back and forth between me and the front door, contemplating his next move, trapped between the safety of being outside of these four walls and the thought of leaving me alone in here. I start walking further up the elegant staircase and he follows me. He's too scared to leave me alone in the house because let's face it — I'm a loose cannon. We creep down the dimly lit hallway until we reach the master bedroom with the door ajar.

"You know we can get arrested for this, right?" Shea says, clearly nervous.

"We'll only get arrested if we get caught," I say casually, doing nothing to help calm his nerves.

Shea's phone buzzes loudly. The noise echoes throughout the room and makes me jump.

"Hazel said Graeson's done and they'll explain later. I'm not sure what that means," Shea reads the message.

"Okay," I say. "I'll be quick."

I start roaming around the room, taking in as many details as my brain can process. Clothes are thrown in a heaping pile in the corner of the room, and given the faint odor they're putting off, I suspect they haven't been washed in awhile. The bed is unmade, and the sleek grey headboard has a brownish colored stain on it. A vintage looking vanity catches my eyes. It seems to be one of the only things in this house that is still intact. The pristine glass reflects three different images of myself, and a velvet chair holds its position as if waiting for someone to sit in it. Two picture frames rest upon the glossy surface of the vanity: one of a youthful version of Stephanie and Richard and one of two small children holding a newborn baby. I can't get over how young and genuinely happy Stephanie and Richard look. It makes me think that maybe their relationship was more than just eyerolls and arguments at one time. She wears an oversized crew neck and sits on a concrete wall overlooking the beach. Richard is behind her with his far less sculpted arms wrapped around her. Her hair is blown to the side, tangled from the ocean air. Their smiles are wider than the ocean itself, and I feel like I can imagine that moment perfectly. It also makes me feel slightly melancholy. Time had faded them so far away from this image. Do relationships always end up like this?

All of a sudden I feel Shea grab my arm and harshly pull me towards their pitch black closet. My knee jerk reaction is to scream and ask him what the hell he's doing, but he puts his hand over my mouth. His hand is gripped so tightly around my arm I can feel it shaking. What in God's name is he doing?! Shea dives into the dark pit that is Stephanie's closet and pulls me until I feel the cool surface of the wall against my back. Her long dresses hang in my face, and I feel his body pressed up against mine.

"What —"

"Shh," he whispers in my ear, his voice raspy and shaky. "Someone's in the house."

I feel my heart drop into my stomach, sucking the wind right out of me. Shea's released his grip on my arm, but I'm so scared I instinctively latch back onto him and hold on so tight I'm most likely cutting off all of his circulation. My head is pressed up against his chest, trying to sink low enough to conceal my face behind the hanging clothes, and I can hear his heart beating through his shirt.

"Is it Richard?" I whisper as quietly as I can.

"Probably," he says trying to steady his breathing. "I heard footsteps on the stairs, and then I saw a black shoe."

"Did he see you?"

"No."

The two of us fall silent, waiting for what is next. And then I hear footsteps. Slow, heavy footsteps. Footsteps that gently slap the hardwood floors. Footsteps that fall in an even, measured pattern. Footsteps that are coming closer with every passing second. The creator of the footsteps, who I'm assuming must be Richard, roams around the room. This will officially go down as the worst idea I've ever had. Most of my ideas are bad, so this is saying a lot. Even if Richard leaves the bedroom, how are we supposed to escape this nut house? And if Richard finds us, how would we explain why we were hanging out in his bedroom closet? I realize my hands are wrapped so strongly around Shea's arm that my fingernails are digging into his skin.

The footsteps sound increasingly louder, and I can't tell if they're actually coming closer or if I'm just paranoid. Suddenly, the lights flick on, burning my eyes and sending a rush of fear throughout my body. I clutch Shea and lean as far back as I can against the wall. My body is violently shaking, and I squeeze my eyes shut. When I was little, I used to think if I couldn't see someone then they couldn't see me. I'm using that logic now because I have absolutely nothing else. I'm praying Stephanie's long dresses will conceal us.

Richard steps into the walk-in closet and rummages around on the side opposite of where Shea and I are hiding. I notice his dark jeans and his black Nikes, but the clothes block my view of anything above his knees, and I'm still trying to keep my eyes shut.

If he catches a glimpse of my blue eyes, we're dead. Probably, not literally, but I guess you never know.

Richard moves around, ruffling through clothes and shoes and whatever else is in here. What is he looking for? He pushes himself up on his tiptoes and moves objects around on the top shelf. Then he starts moving the hangers as if searching for something to wear. The more hangers he moves, the less cover we have. Suddenly, he squats down and reaches his arm out in my direction. I see his hand, tucked into a black leather glove, feeling around the floor next to me. His long, gloved fingers are dancing across the dark wooded floor. Why is Richard wearing black leather gloves in the middle of summer? Maybe he's a lot shadier than I thought. But then again, I'm the one breaking and entering and hiding in his dead wife's closet, so I really don't have any ground to stand on with this. His fingers wiggle around, feeling the ground for some absent object. His hand reaches out farther, less than a centimeter away from my leg. I hold my breath, terrified to make even the slightest move or sound, and ever so carefully straighten my leg out and force it up against the wall. No longer pressed into a ball position, I sit awkwardly with one leg extended and the other bony knee bent up to my chest. The only sense of reassurance that is keeping me from completely breaking down is Shea's arm. Richard's hand continues to feel around, narrowly missing mine and Shea's bodies. He knocks over a tall rain boot that tips over onto me. I see his figure stand back up, and the light flickers off, sending a wave of darkness over the closet. The sound of the footsteps becomes fainter and fainter until I hear a downstairs door shut. I release the breath I had been holding and can feel Shea's body relax because we're squeezed so close together. My limbs feel stiff, and my fear has me paralyzed in the corner of a dead woman's closet. When I shift my body, the rainboot comes crashing down onto the hardwood and something falls out of it, making a thud sound as it hits the floor. I pick up the object, which is an old model of an iPhone. Who keeps their phone in a rainboot in the back of their closet? Well, if you know me at all, you know exactly what irrational move I plan on carrying out next. I quickly throw the phone into the pocket of my jean shorts. There's no way I'm coming out of this terrifying situation with nothing. Shea slowly stands up, but I don't follow his lead because my legs feel numb and weak.

"It's okay, Izzie," he extends his hand and helps me to my feet. "Let's get out of here."

My mouth is so dry I can't speak, but I nod my head and take his clammy hand. When I'm up on my feet and we start walking out of the closet, I don't release my grip on his hand. He turns to meet my eyes and gives me a confused look, seeing that I have given him so many mixed signals today it's not even funny. I let my eyes do the talking, trying to convey how sorry I am and how thankful I am to have him even though the words are escaping me right now. He nods, seeming to understand my message, and the two of us quickly make our way out of the Kester house.

Hazel and Graeson are waiting for us in my driveway, which neighbors Stephanie and Richard's house, looking quite anxious. Hazel paces in rapid circles around the blacktop, and Graeson stands with his hands in his pockets breathing in heavy sighs.

As soon as they catch sight of the two of us, Hazel rushes over and hugs me while Graeson notices our hand holding and makes a confused face.

"Promise me you will never do that again!" Hazel cries. "I almost had a heart attack."

"Why didn't you tell us Richard came home?" I ask her, my voice sounding raspy from holding my breath for so long in the closet.

Graeson and Hazel have identical lost stares in their worried faces. Graeson says, "Richard didn't come home."

"Yes, he did," replies Shea. "He came into their house, and we had to hide in their closet while he walked around in the same room."

Hazel shakes her head, "I've been out here the whole time, and Richard never came home. No cars pulled in the driveway, no people even walked by."

"What does that mean?" Shea's eyes are bulging as he tries to grasp what is going on.

I'm trying to connect the dots myself, but my brain can't quite wrap itself around the idea. If it wasn't Richard who came home, then that must mean that someone else was breaking into Stephanie's house in search of something. The thoughts start sprinting in circles around my head, like horses running around a racetrack. If my gut feeling is right, Shea and I may have just been centimeters away from Stephanie Kester's killer.

*****

The four of us are sprawled out in various positions in my basement trying to piece together the events of the last hour.

"Tell me again what happened," Hazel says, deeply concentrating on the information.

"We searched the entire downstairs and didn't find anything except a mess in the kitchen," I started.

Shea picks up the story, "Then Izzie had the genius idea to check out the upstairs."

He glares over at me, and I just nod because I am solely responsible for getting us trapped in the closet.

I glance over at him, "I'm sorry! I'm sorry! How was I supposed to know Richard was going to come home?"

"I'm telling you," Hazel says. "Richard never came home. I watched their driveway the entire time."

"Then who was in their house? And how did they get there?" Shea asks.

143

"They got in there the same way you bozos did. The back door was unlocked," Graeson answers.

"Did you find anything outside?" I ask Graeson, whose job was to scout out the backyard, deck, and front for cameras.

"No luck. There was nothing, but Stephanie was highly intelligent. If she had cameras, they'd be hidden well enough that some idiot like myself wouldn't stumble upon them. I wouldn't count that out yet."

Silence settles over the room like a thick blanket as we all try to make sense of this information. The dots are starting to connect in my brain, and the pieces are falling into place.

"I found this in Stephanie's closet," I throw the iPhone I found out in the middle of us.

Everyone's eyes pop from their sockets as they look from me to the phone in awe.

"It was in her rainboot," I look over to Shea. "I knew there was something up there."

"What does all this mean?" Hazel says with her eyebrows furrowed making her face radiate nervousness.

"That's definitely a burner phone," Graeson starts. "When I was little I used to hide my Halloween candy among other things in my shoes in the back of my closet. My parents never found anything."

"When you were little?" Hazel says, not passing up the chance to call Graeson out. "You still hide things in the back of your closet. I've seen the bottle of Tequila in there."

Graeson flashes his charming smile, "We're not talking about me. I'm just saying that if this is Stephanie's phone, she didn't want people to find it. Most people don't keep their phones in their closet."

"What if Richard hid it?" Shea raises the question. "What if it is Stephanie's phone, and there's something on there he didn't want anyone to find."

"The police are going to search his house. He'd have to be smart enough not to hide it in there," Graeson replies.

My brain is on the verge of a theory. I can feel the wheels turning, almost grasping the floating idea. Then it hits me, and everything clicks into place.

"It's simple," I say, confident in my revelation. "We all know Stephanie was shady. If she was involved in something that she didn't want anyone to know about, she would use a burner phone. Richard would never stumble across the phone in her rain boots, so it was the perfect hiding spot. Except, she was killed. The person in the closet snuck in from the back and was wearing leather gloves in the middle of summer. They have to be the killer. I'd bet you my entire life savings that the person was after whatever is on that phone."

Hazel nods her head, "That makes perfect sense! Whoever it was wanted to get rid of their link to Stephanie or any evidence this phone has."

"So if we have the phone, then we're one step ahead of them!" I add excitedly.

"And we can figure out what Stephanie was hiding!" Hazel responds.

Graeson seems lost as the two of us go back and forth, developing this theory and plunging head first into the murder case. I'm starting to think that I can figure this case out myself. I've spent so many years reading and watching and being totally obsessed with true crime, and now, I'm living in an actual case. Detective Heights can suck it. I'm going to prove to her that I was telling the truth this whole time.

"We've got one problem," Shea holds the phone in his hand and his lips turn down to a slight frown. "It's locked."

For a minute, I feel the adrenaline and high hopes plummet, but then a crucial piece of information fills my head and I'm soaring again. I smirk slyly at them. I know just how to unlock the burner phone.

*****

What are you supposed to say to a man who just lost his wife and children who just lost their mother? I don't know, but I feel like "I'm sorry for your loss" just isn't enough. Their entire life has been blown to shreds and me standing there with an awkward frown telling them I'm sorry isn't going to fix that. Funerals have always made me uncomfortable and nervous. You sit in this room full of people crying and hugging each other, while a dead body lays before you in a coffin. I never know what to do, so I end up sitting in the back of the room thinking that we spend all this time worrying and struggling and living just to end up a dead body on display in the front of a room of people we barely even knew. It makes the whole concept of life seem like a waste of time.

I brush my long hair, working to smooth out all the tangled knots. As I'm brushing, I read over the notes I scrawled in a journal about Stephanie. Everything I know, all of my information is here. Hazel, Graeson, and Shea helped me to put more of the pieces together, but there's still so much we don't know about her. Along with my weird encounters and observations of Stephanie before her death, I've written about the mystery person in Stephanie's house and the burner phone we found in the back of the closet. I gave the burner phone to Luke, who is a complete technology whiz. If anyone can hack into the phone, it would be him. I refused to tell him where I found it or what it was, which unsettled him, but he's on a need to know basis only. Before Hazel, Graeson, and Shea left late last night, we spent hours combing through details. Right before they left, Shea made a comment that I can't get out of my head. He said, "The person who did it lives on this street. There's no other way it could've gone off without anyone knowing or becoming suspicious." It made me think of an Agatha Christie book I read called *And Then There Were None*. It was one of my favorites of hers because of the shocking twists the book provided. Ten random people are invited to an island, all unknowing that there were others arriving with them. They all get there, meet each other, and have a luxurious dinner together. During dinner, a guest chokes and dies. The others think nothing of it, until one by one all the characters start to die off. That's when Justice Wargrave, one of the characters, makes his infamous comment that defines the entire book. He tells the group that the killer is one of them. The book was pure genius, but it's quite ominous that I can apply it to my real life. The killer is among us. For the murder to have taken place in the middle of an outdoor party, it has to be someone who lives here and knows their way around. I just hope this doesn't end like the novel. The book ended up with ten corpses.

I hear a knock on my door, which pulls me out of my slightly disturbing line of thinking. Luke walks in and I catch him subtly rolling his eyes at my still unpacked boxes. His hair is styled neatly, and he wears a pale blue button up shirt that brings out his emerald green eyes.

He holds up Stephanie's phone, "This phone . . ." he trails off as if he doesn't know how to finish the sentence.

"What about it?" I prompt him to continue talking.

"I don't know where you got it," his face looks like he's going to be sick. "But . . . this is bad."

"I told you not to look at anything!" I raise my voice.

"I didn't, stuff just popped up when I unlocked it," he replies quietly.

I rush over to him to go rip the phone out of his hand, but as I approach, he flings his hand away, maintaining a tight grip on the phone.

"Give it to me, Luke!"

"Not until you tell me what's going on," his voice is calm and steady.

"I can't tell you," I lower my volume. "You'll be mad at me."

"I'm not giving it to you until you tell me what's going on. I just hacked into a phone for you, no questions asked. Now, you need to tell me what this is."

"I don't want to pull you into it."

"You've already pulled me into it, Izzie. Whatever you've done, I promise I can help you."

His sweet tone of voice and his desire to help me makes me melt. Luke is always looking out for me. He doesn't even know what I've done and he's already on my side. And if I tell him, he might be able to help us figure out who killed Stephanie.

I take a deep breath, "Okay, I'll tell you."

Luke leans against my bed and crosses his arm across his chest, a curious sparkle gleaming in his eyes. He thinks he's ready to hear this. I assure you he is not.

"The phone is Stephanie's. I found it in her closet," I grit my teeth and turn my face sideways, as if bracing for an impact.

"Why were you in Stephanie's house?" His eyebrows are raised so high they basically blend into his hairline.

I feel myself quivering, shrinking into a corner, "I was looking for cameras."

Luke stands there with his mouth hanging wide open, staring at me like I'm a violent patient who recently escaped a mental asylum. The silence makes me uncomfortable, so I start speed talking, trying to make my story sound less . . . well . . . crazy.

"I remembered something from Saturday night. Stephanie threatened me with cameras from the first time I was in her house uninvited and told me she had twenty-four hour surveillance cameras around and that she knew I listened in on her phone call.

So I convinced my friends to search her house for cameras and then this person showed up and . . ."

Luke cuts me off while I take in a much needed gulp of air. "So what you're saying is that you broke into Stephanie's house and stole her phone?" His tone is accusatory and his voice is riddled with concern.

"No. The back door was unlocked, so technically I did not break in."

"Were you invited into her house?" he accuses, doing a much better job of proving his point than I am.

"Well . . . not exactly."

"Then you broke in," Luke shakes his head. "What were you doing in her closet?"

"I told you, we were looking for cameras. Shea and I couldn't find any downstairs, so I went upstairs. But someone else was in the house, Luke. Shea and I hid in the closet while the person searched the master bedroom. They even looked through the closet. The person's hand almost touched me. But that's where I found the phone — in the back of the closet."

"It was probably Richard coming home."

"No. Hazel stood guard out front the entire time. Nobody came home, no people walked by, no cars drove down the street. The person snuck in through the back, and they were wearing black leather gloves."

The color drains from Luke's face as he tries to process all the information I just laid on him.

"So someone else was breaking in the same time you were, and —"

I interrupt him, "I was not breaking in!!!"

He throws his hands up in the air, "Nobody was home and you weren't invited. You broke in! But that's not the point. That person must have been . . ." he trails off.

"That person was the same one who killed Stephanie, and they were after the burner phone."

Luke takes a deep breath, completely taken aback by my information. After a few moments, he sighs and says, "Why would you go to her house?"

"I was trying to be logical!" I spit back at him without really thinking about my words.

Luke stands up from the bed and throws his hands up over his face. He raises his voice, "Logical?! A logical person does not break into the house of a murder victim! A logical person does not steal possible evidence! A logical person does not get themselves voluntarily involved in a murder investigation!"

My actions sound completely ridiculous hearing them come out of Luke's mouth. This is insane. I'm insane.

"I'm going to figure out who did this, Luke. I'm going to figure out who killed Stephanie."

Luke's eyes bulge, "This isn't one of your crime novels you can try to solve. This is real life, Izzie. This is dangerous."

"This is the only way I can know for sure I had nothing to do with her death," the words roll off my tongue before I even realize what they mean. I didn't know I was still holding onto the fear that I did something unspeakable that night, but I guess deep down it's been the driving force behind my desire to solve this case.

The energy in the room shifts into a kinder and softer environment.

"You didn't do anything," Luke says softly. "I know you didn't."

"I need to do this, Luke. Whether you want to help or not."

Luke's gaze wanders around the room, stuck between his options.

"Okay, I'll help you, but only to make sure you stay safe and don't get arrested."

I throw my arms around him and hug him tightly, grateful to have him on my side.

"Thank you so much, Luke."

"Don't thank me yet. You're going to want to see what's on this phone first."

Luke unlocks the phone and pulls up a screen. I take one look at it, and my entire body goes numb.

*****

The line of people waiting to pay their respects for Stephanie snakes around the brick building, and more people are arriving by the second. It's no surprise that Stephanie was this popular, but the amount of people is a little overwhelming. As we move closer to the door, I feel my insides twisting and turning, sending a wave of nausea throughout my body. The thought of standing in front of Stephanie's family is making me sick. I was the one to find her body. I kicked off this entire nightmare for them. And after taking a brief look at Stephanie's burner phone, I don't think I can walk in there and mourn her. Richard has no clue, and I can't stand in front of him and act like I don't know anything. I feel my heart pulsate faster and faster and sweat droplets start to gather at the top of my forehead. Olivia's been fussy this whole time, and as we are quickly approaching the door, she begins to scream a high-pitched, squeaky noise that grants us some stares from judgy snobs. Mom tries to console her, but Olivia doesn't seem to be letting up.

"I'll take her," I say, while reaching for the baby. "I'll take her for a little walk, and I'll meet you guys in there."

John and Mom look at me oddly because I've never offered to hold or help out with Olivia before.

"Are you sure?" mom questions.

I smile slightly to show her I'm being genuine, even though I'm not. "Yes, let me take her."

Mom hands Olivia over to me, and I awkwardly walk back through the line of people and into the parking lot. I have never been more thankful for this baby in my entire life. Her crying gave me the perfect excuse to not go into the funeral home. On the side of the building, there's a small bench surrounded by blooming tulips. I sit down and turn Olivia so she's facing me.

"Thank you so much," I coo in a high-pitched voice.

Olivia's crying subsides, and she smiles one of those involuntary mouth movements babies make. She makes little high-pitched sounds and squirms around in my arms.

"You didn't want to go in there either, huh?" I say to her in the same high-pitched voice, "That's okay. I didn't want to either."

This is what I've come to. Talking about my problems to a three-month-old in a baby voice. I guess it's not the weirdest thing I've done this week. Olivia smiles again, and I realize that this may be one of the first times I've ever spent time with her. Now that I am, I actually kind of like her. Sure, she cries and screams a lot, but then again so do I. At the end of the day, we both just want to be loved. Holding her makes me feel peaceful and calm. The way she sits squirming in my arms with her bright blue eyes trying to absorb the world around her makes me think of how innocent she is. How she has no clue how cruel this world can be. No one's ever wronged her or hurt her. No one's ever broken her heart. These thoughts make me want to protect her. To keep her this innocent forever.

"We're going to be okay, Olivia. You and me, we're going to be fine," I pull her closer and rock her gently until her eyes flutter closed.

I know I should probably go inside now that the baby calmed down, but it's so peaceful and quiet out here. I don't want to sit inside a hot and stuffy room full of people crying. I'm sitting back and contemplating what to do when I hear footsteps approaching me. I crane my neck behind me, careful not to wake Olivia up. Hannah's walking towards the bench with her adorable, red headed baby fussing in her arms.

"Hi," she says softly. "He was not having it in there."

I smile brightly at her, "Neither was she. You can sit if you'd like."

There was something about Hannah that I really liked when I first met her, and if she's sitting out here, that means I don't need to rush inside. Hannah takes a seat next to me on the bench while Boston fusses in her lap. Her chestnut colored hair is thrown into a ponytail and her eyes have dark circles under them. Last time I saw her she was bursting with kind, quirky, and bright energy. Now she seems tired and defeated, as if she's aged years in the past week.

"How is it in there?" I ask.

"It's," she pauses, "so strange. This woman berated and belittled me for years, and now I'm supposed to sit in there and listen to everybody talk about her like she was some sort of saint. I know, I sound terrible. She didn't deserve to die, but it's hard to sit in there."

As strange as it sounds, I know exactly how Hannah feels. I understand it completely. People die and all of sudden everyone cares. Everyone's talking about how wonderful and amazing they were. People you haven't talked to in years and who never bothered to reach out are worshipping you. People who hated you are saying how great of a person you were. It's like you die and all your wrongdoings are forgotten. The person becomes a saint, the picture of greatness, an idolized image. Hannah's right. I only saw Stephanie berate her once, but I can't imagine it's easy to stand in there and hear people say all these great things about the person who spent years trying to tear you down.

"You don't sound terrible. I understand," I say.

She turns to me and I can see there are tears brimming in her hazel eyes, "I don't know why I'm telling you all of this. You barely even know me and probably don't care."

"I just moved here, and you are one of the only people I know and like, so I don't mind."

She laughs while wiping a loose tear off her blush coated cheek, "That's sweet. I'm sorry, I've just had one of those weeks."

"I've been there quite a few times this past month."

The sun beats down on us, its rays bouncing off my skin.

"Is your husband here?" I ask.

"He's inside still. I just took Boston out for some air. Beckett was *closer* with Stephanie than I was," she says casually, but I swear I see her roll her eyes.

I nod my head and make a little "hmm" noise.

*****

I hold a sleeping Olivia in my arms as I stand in the back of the packed funeral home. The stuffy room is overflowing with people, making the air heavy. The smell of flowers, mint lifesavers, and incense fills my nose. People are quietly mingling and mourning with each other, while the line of new guests waiting to pay their respects to Stephanie continuously flows in the room. After chatting with Hannah briefly, I made my way inside so I could at least make an appearance. I feel like it would look bad if the neighbor who found the body didn't show up at the wake. But I told my mom that I would hold Olivia because that gives me an excuse to stand up in the back of the room, as far away from the body as I can be. The thought of seeing her dead corpse for a second time is making me sick to my stomach. Even now at the back of the room, my eyes still catch a glimpse of her graying flesh and coffee colored hair laying perfectly still. Is it weird that I'm waiting for her to pop up at any moment and tell us all it was just a big joke? That it was all an act and the show's over now. Richard

154

is trembling as he stands at the front of the room with a constant line of guests hugging him and showing him their sympathy. He looks like he's about to fall apart at any moment, like he might literally break into a million little pieces in front of my eyes. Watching him try to stand and greet these people is like watching a baby horse stumble and fall every few minutes as it tries to walk on its weak legs. I notice three children lined up next to him, also recipients of false sympathy from people who once knew their mother. I recognize Alex, who looks straight out ahead of him without moving his glance and seems uncomfortable with all the people, and Ella, who appears to be oblivious to the whole scene. In the middle of them, is a second girl who appears to be about nine years old. She's the spitting image of Stephanie, with the same hazel eyes, tanned skin, and long arms. Even from back here, I can tell she radiates the same sass and attitude Stephanie once did. She stands there with her lips in a pout, running her fingers through her wavy, mousy brown hair. This little girl has a bad case of RBF, a permanent scowl sprawled across her face. I'm observing the broken Kester family when I feel someone come up next to me. I look over and see Graeson looking very dapper and charming in his suit, but with his hair still an adorable spiked up mess.

He glances at Olivia nuzzled against my shoulder and whispers in my ear, "You look a lot less intimidating with a baby in your arms."

I turn my head to face him, tilting it forward in annoyance and rolling my eyes.

"Lighten up," he taps my shoulder playfully.

"Did you just tell me to lighten up at a wake?" I say in an accusatory tone.

He purses his lips, "I realize now that was not the correct thing to say at this moment. Are you scouting out suspects?"

"Huh?" I ask, confused.

"Everyone from our neighborhood is here, and you're standing in the back, staring around the room. I thought you might be doing some research," he replies.

"I hadn't even thought about that," my eyes go wide in excitement. "I don't really recognize anyone, point them out to me."

"Alright, so," he points his finger blatantly into the center of the room.

With my free hand, I yank his hand and force it down. I look at him, "Don't actually point!"

"You said point them out!"

"Point with your eyes and your words!"

He shakes his head and smiles, "You women are so confusing. Okay, so you see that lady with the obnoxious hat with the flowers on it?" I nod. "To the left of her. See the women standing with the baby and the guy with the blue tie? That's Dr. Sawyer Hastings and Dr. Rachel Hastings."

Dr. Sawyer Hastings is chatting intently with his wife and another couple. He keeps making motions with his hands to emphasize his words. He has a mop of dark espresso colored hair that curls under his ears and sits spiked and ruffled on top of his head. Even from back here, his eyes jump out from his face, a sharp gunmetal grey that makes him look bold and confident. His oval shaped face is decorated with a hooked nose and eyelashes that look like they are covered in mascara. He stands at around six feet with light muscle tone and a thin build. When he smiles dimples pierce his cheeks, making him seem friendly and personable. The casual and confident way he carries himself reminds me of an older version of Graeson. Next to him, his wife stands holding a round faced, bald headed, blue eyed baby. Dr. Rachel Hastings has straight, burgundy tinted hair that falls slightly past her shoulders and an angular face with a harsh jaw line and a pointed chin. Doe-like, warm brown eyes adorn her smooth and clear complexion. She wears black high heels that cause her to be a few inches taller than her husband, which makes me wonder what that does to his ego. She's beautiful in an endearing sort of way. She nods her head as she listens to the conversation, her face coated with a gentle and loving sympathy. Still, there's something about her that tells me that she is bursting with vibrant energy and is strong-willed.

"What kind of doctors are they?" I ask Graeson.

"He's a plastic surgeon and she's some sort of surgeon for babies."

So these people are the real deal. Fancy surgeons who live in one of the richest neighborhoods in all of Massachusetts. Once I've made enough mental notes to write down later, I say to him, "Okay, who's next?"

Graeson points out a girl who appears to be in her early twenties, "Mrs. Isla Grimaldi."

I don't know how else to describe her other than stunning. Isla Grimaldi is like a porcelain doll with delicate features and a petite frame. Thick, platinum black curls drastically contrast her pale, snow white skin in a way that makes her stand out in the crowd. She wears a navy blue dress that dips a bit too far down for a wake and brings out her kaleidoscope like icy blue eyes.

"The man next to her is her husband."

I assume Graeson is referring to the young, attractive blonde guy standing to her left. I say to him, "The blonde guy?"

He snickers, "Nope, the one walking towards her with the dark hair."

My mouth drops open, "That old guy?!"

Graeson smirks, "Yes, that would be Thomas Grimaldi. He's nearly forty, and she's not quite twenty-five. No one really knows how they ended up together. They're pretty private, so no one sees much of them."

"Wow," I say smirking at Graeson. "This day keeps getting more and more interesting."

When Thomas reaches Isla, they begin making out in the center of the room as if no other people are around. It seems highly inappropriate, not only because we're in public, but because we're at a wake. There's something seriously wrong with the people in this neighborhood.

Graeson's busy pointing out another neighbor when Hazel approaches us.

"Sorry I just came over. My parents had me on Jack duty. The kid doesn't sit still," she says. "Did Luke get into the phone yet?"

"He just got in. I didn't have much time to look at it, but it's bad. You have to see what's on it," I reply.

"What'd you find? Graeson asks.

"I can't talk about it here. I'll show you later. Luke just unlocked it before we left, so I didn't see too much, but what I saw was bad."

Hazel runs her fingers through her golden curls and then crosses her arms across her chest, "I really can't believe she's dead."

Graeson turns to Hazel, "Well, believe it. We're scouting out suspects. Now, where were we?"

Hazel raises her eyebrows and shakes her head, "You're trying to find the murderer at the wake?"

Graeson nods his head, "Exactly."

Hazel gets on board with the idea and starts pointing out people to me. She says, "See the man with the glasses and the dark hair? That's Forrest Shepard. He owns a major bioengineering lab up in Paine's Creek.

Forrest Shepard is a lanky man with black rimmed glasses that cover his electric green eyes and rest atop his pointed nose. His face is clean shaven with high cheekbones and a long, oval shape, as if someone had stretched out his face. He stands at about 5'10" and has an awkward look to him, like a teenage boy who hasn't quite filled in his body yet. He appears to be swimming in his suit. I watch him run his fingers throughout his root beer colored hair that's clipped short as he stands seemingly withdrawn from the conversation he's in. Forrest seems to be jumpy and anxious, completely lost in his own thoughts as if his brain were moving a mile a minute. Something about him reminds me of a little mouse.

"The man's brilliant," Graeson starts. "But completely oblivious to social cues. He married up big time. I still don't know how he swung it."

Graeson motions to the lady standing to his left. "That's his wife, Mrs. Cora Shepard."

"Holy crap! You're not kidding," I stare bug-eyed at the couple. Cora Shepard could be a model, and here she is married to some geeky little scientist. Cora Shepard has thick, dark chocolate colored hair that cascades down her back. Her heart shaped face is home to two copper colored eyes that look like shiny pennies and full, deep red lips that give way to a mysterious smile. Something about her face makes her seem disconnected and cold, like she has no interest in making small talk with the people around her. She appears to be about 5'8" with long legs and a thin waist. I feel both stunned, perplexed, and utterly confused about how this relationship ever got started.

"They have three little girls," Hazel says. "Sophie, Genevieve, and Macie."

"How did they ever get together?" I laugh.

Graeson smirks, "That might be a bigger mystery than who killed Stephanie."

"You're so judgy," Hazel says to Graeson. "I think there's only a few people left that you don't know." Hazel leads my eyes to a woman who appears to be in her early sixties with coal black hair that has faded into a pepper grey. Her face is made up perfectly with makeup that attempts to hide her wrinkles, and I must say, it masks enough of them to make her appear younger. She wears a deep purple dress that compliments her grey blue eyes. You can tell she used to be quite the catch back in her day. She talks in soft, measured words to a young boy, who appears to be in his mid-twenties. The boy's slate grey eyes roam around the room, apathetic to the woman's words, and every few seconds the woman places her hands on his shoulders to steer his attention back to her. He repeatedly taps his large hand against his pale face, creating red marks up and down his cheek. I watch the boy try to yank his neatly styled, coal black hair, but the lady gently pulls his hand down and attempts to regain his attention.

"That's Lillian Black and her son Easton," Hazel explains.

"The boy's psychotic, all the screws are loose up there," Graeson says as Hazel slaps his arm as hard as she can. "OW! What in the bloody hell was that for?"

"That was for your comment. Easton has a mental disability, and you have no right to make fun of him or call him names," she replies with a stone cold face.

"Jesus Hazel, that killed!"

Hazel ignores his remark and turns to me, "They keep to themselves for the most part. Easton has schizophrenia, so Lillian takes care of him full-time."

I nod and feel my lips turn down to a frown. I can't even imagine how hard that is for the both of them. All the people who stare and call him names behind his back, they don't understand him. No one does, and no one tries to. Everyone probably treats him like he's less than human, like he doesn't have any real feelings, like he's some sort of monster.

At that moment, Shea makes his way over to us, walking away from a woman with auburn hair. He says hi to Graeson and Hazel before awkwardly half waving at me, which reminds me of how much I screwed things up. Hazel clearly senses the tension and shoots me an inquisitive stare. I just shrug my shoulders, implying that I will fill her in later on my social awkwardness.

"Is Saige's family here?" Shea asks.

"I haven't seen them. The calling hours end in a few minutes, so they must not be coming," Hazel replies.

"That's really weird," says Shea with an odd expression on his face. "You would think all of Stephanie's neighbors would be here. Whether you like her or not, they should be showing their respect."

I can sense Shea becoming slightly worked up over the matter, which makes me wonder if this has something to do with his dad's death back in May.

"Who's Saige?" I ask.

Shea and Hazel look at Graeson with accusatory faces and don't stop staring until he feels awkward enough to start talking. "It's a long story that I would rather not explain here." He places his palm over his face and shakes his head, "You know, it was not my fault!"

"Yes it was!" Shea retorts, "It was absolutely your fault."

I'm very interested to hear about this Saige girl and to learn about her family's absence from the wake.

"Oh, oh! Look over there!" Hazel slyly motions to a man with two young children walking towards Richard and his kids, "That's Beckett St. James and his kids, Vivienne and Brennan."

"That's Hannah's husband, right?" I question.

Hazel nods as I observe him and his kids. Beckett St. James is a tall, burly man with a muscular build and a sandy blonde beard that covers the whole bottom half of his face. His piercing blue eyes and thick, ruffled hair makes him outwardly attractive. A little girl with bronze curls and a toddler with tiny glasses follow behind him as he makes his way to talk to Richard. Now that I've matched the name with the face, I realize this is the man I saw Stephanie cozying up to at the fire the night of the party. The picture on the phone. The face and the name. Holy crap.

I turn to say something to my friends, when all of a sudden I see Richard swing his arm behind him and shove his fist full force into Beckett's face. Beckett St. James crashes to the ground with a thud, clutching his nose and knocking down his toddler son on the way. The entire room goes silent as everyone in the room stares directly at the unfolding brawl. The only sound is Vivienne and Brennan shrieking and crying as they watch their dad stumble to his feet with blood dripping from his nose. As Beckett steps up to challenge Richard, Hannah walks in holding her sleeping baby. She lets out a gasp and grabs her children's hands, then turns right back around and walks out the door.

CHAPTER 9 - Watch Your Back

Everyone stands stunned, unsure of how to react. The four of us are in the back, me clutching a little tighter on to Olivia who's still sleeping in my arms. It's like someone has pressed the pause button on the scene and we're all frozen in time, as still as Stephanie's body in the casket. Hazel's dad calmly walks over to Richard, places his hand on his shoulder, and leads him outside while Dr. Sawyer Hastings tends to Beckett, whose nose is gushing blood. This is by far the most action packed wake I've ever been to. I can't help but think Stephanie's laughing at us all from above, proud of the scene she's caused. A part of me can't wait for this to be over, can't wait to be back at my house and at my bay window, safe from the overarching shadow of Stephanie's body. Yet a part of me doesn't want this to stop because I feel like I'm gathering more and more information by the second. This wake is like a reality TV show, all that's missing is the dramatic table flip.

I look to my friends whose faces are a mix of shock and concern.

"This can't wait, I have to show you what's on the phone."

"You brought the phone here?" Shea whispers.

"I was too scared to leave it at my house," I reply. "I didn't want anyone to come looking for it."

I quickly walk over to my mom, pass off the baby, and motion for Luke to follow me so we can show them what he found on the phone. The four of us follow Graeson into a small room behind the space where the service is being held, or I guess *was* being held. The room is dimly lit with dingy scarlet carpets and mismatched furniture pieces. In between a couch with purple flowers and a beige armchair is a pale green vase that I'm praying to God is not some cremated body. The room smells strongly of spearmint, and a gold cross hangs on the wall closest to me.

I reintroduce Luke to everyone as the four of us huddle around him and the burner phone.

"You're brilliant, man. How did you unlock it?" Graeson asks.

"So basically you . . ." Luke starts, but then I cut him off.

"No one cares about the techy stuff, show them what's on the phone!" Luke shoots me a look, which makes me realize that was a bit harsh. "I'm sorry! I'm just really anxious!"

Luke unlocks the phone, the bright screen illuminating his face in the murky room. Immediately, the image that sent chills down my spine flashes in front of our eyes. Even though I've already seen the picture, it sucks the air straight out of my lungs and sends a burning sensation throughout my chest. I watch as Shea's bright blue eyes bulge so much they nearly pop out of their sockets and as Graeson covers his wide open mouth with his hands. Hazel lets out a loud gasp and clutches Luke's shoulder in shock. If my mind weren't so preoccupied, I'd comment on the fact that she reached out to him, but there are more pressing issues than meddling in Luke's love life. Shea shakes his head and opens his mouth to speak, but no words come out. On the iridescent phone screen is a picture of Stephanie Kester with her lips locked on Beckett St. James, her hands tangled in his ruffled, sandy blonde hair. It was shocking enough the first time I saw it, but at the time I didn't know who the mystery man was. Now that I've put a name to the face, it's all the more appalling.

I hear Hazel's shaky voice, "This can't be real. They're both married with little kids. How could they do this?"

"There's more," Luke starts. "I didn't look through it yet, but there are a string of texts between the two of them that go back and forth for months."

"We need to go through this phone as soon as possible," Hazel says. "I don't think this can wait."

All of a sudden, I hear a high-pitched, but bold voice speak up from behind us, "What do you think you're doing with my mother's phone?"

I flip my body around to face the speaker as my heart beats rapidly in my chest. The voice is coming from the little girl with the scowl I saw standing with Richard. It's no shock that she's Stephanie's child, or shall I say the Spawn of Satan. Her lips are pursed, making her look angry, but there's something in her eyes that tells me she's enjoying this.

"Alison," Graeson steps up to her, putting a charming smile on his face. "Shouldn't you be in there with your family?"

She fires right back, "I could say the same thing about you five." Her eyebrows slant downwards, accusing us with her facial expressions. I'm wondering why I'm so intimidated by this nine-year-old girl.

Seeing that Graeson's British charm didn't work, Hazel and her genuine kindness step up to the task. "Why don't I walk you back to your dad?"

Alison shakes her head and smirks, "I'm going to make myself clear: you have something that belongs to my mother, and I have information that may help you."

"How long were you listening in on our conversation?" Graeson asks.

"Long enough to know that you guys broke into my mom's old phone and found a picture of her kissing someone who's not my dad," she says with a stone cold face.

"I'm sorry you heard us. I'm really sorry," Hazel apologizes.

165

Alison rolls her eyes playfully, "I'm not surprised about that. I had a feeling. I have to be back out there in a minute, so I'll cut right to the chase. I have information that could help you play your little detective game. Information you need." She pulls a slip of paper out of the hidden pocket in her dress and hands it to Shea. "Follow these directions and I'll give you my information and my silence. If you don't, I'll tell everyone how you stole the phone."

"What do you get out of it?" I ask, catching her off guard.

A malicious smile spreads across her face, "Everything you need to know is on the paper."

Having successfully threatened a group of high schoolers, Alison struts out of the back room, flipping her wavy hair over her shoulder. Before she makes her grand exit, she looks behind her and says in a sing-songy voice, "Bye, Shea," and winks at him. I watch his face turn a vibrant shade of red as Graeson fights off a chuckle. I'm not sure if I'm more stunned that we're being blackmailed by a nine-year-old girl or that this nine-year-old girl is doing a much better job flirting with the boy I like. Life is great, just great.

*****

The four of us sit in my basement, surrounded by bowls of popcorn, with Stephanie's burner phone and Alison's note in front of us. On the perfectly creased white paper, Alison's fourth grade handwriting reads, *"7p.m., Roadside Diner, Wednesday night, bring 300 dollars in an envelope."*

"Are we really going to be blackmailed by a nine-year-old?" Shea says.

"A nine-year-old who has the hots for you," Graeson laughs, clearly proud of his joke.

"I can't do this," Shea rolls his eyes and smiles. "This is so weird."

166

"I think we should meet her," I speak up. "What if she really does know something that could help us?"

"Or what if she's just trying to con us into giving her three hundred bucks," Shea responds.

"I'm willing to take that risk," I reply. "She lived with Stephanie, I'm sure she knows a lot that we don't."

"Yeah, but you don't know Alison. She plays these little mind games with people to get them to do what she wants. It's all a game to her, and I don't really feel like playing," Shea argues back.

I'm as stubborn as a piece of gum stuck in someone's hair, so I decide to push my point harder. "Her mom just died. Why would she be playing games about that? What do you think, Hazel?"

Hazel looks awkward, not wanting to get in the middle of this argument that has a lot of underlying tension. Eventually she replies, "I'm sorry, Shea, but if we want to figure this out, we have to take a risk. You're right, Alison plays mind games, but she also loved her mom. Maybe she wants to help us figure this out, so she can find some closure with all of this. So she can feel safe in her own home."

Hazel makes everything sound so sweet and kind, but Shea's still not buying it. "This is ridiculous."

Shea, Hazel, and I continue to argue back and forth about how to handle the situation. Then Graeson's voice slices through the argument. "Does anyone want to know what I think?"

We all look at him, shocked he even understands what's going on because we had to explain the whole situation to him three different times. I kind of forgot he was here. We stare at him with furrowed brows, unsure of what is about to spill out of his unfiltered mouth.

"You're all missing the point. Alison knows we stole the phone and said if we don't show, she'll tell. We don't really have another option."

"Wow," Hazel says slowly. "You actually said something smart."

Graeson smirks and nods his head, "I'm quite brilliant."

"I wouldn't go that far," Hazel replies with a smile.

"So we have to show up. There's no other way," I say while looking directly at Shea who just rolls his eyes.

After we've settled the debate about Alison, the four of us decide to start looking through Stephanie's burner phone. Unfortunately for us, Stephanie was no idiot when it came to hiding her secrets. The camera roll is wiped clean and so is her cloud, leaving us with nothing but three text strings to sort through. The first text string is the one between her and Beckett with the picture of them kissing. According to the messages, it's a selfie Beckett took of them and later sent to Stephanie with the caption, "Our first and only picture together." It makes sense that he sent it to her. I knew Stephanie was too smart to have something as blatantly incriminating as that on her phone. We read through the messages — the first one dating back to March of last year — but find nothing all that surprising. Just a lot of words that were pretty uncomfortable to read in a group setting.

"So Stephanie was involved . . . romantically . . . with Beckett, which is why Richard punched him?" Graeson asks for the third time in the last half hour.

"Yes," says Hazel in an annoyed tone. "I don't know how many more times I can explain it to you."

"Okay," I say to steer us back on track. "We know from this that their affair started around mid-March of last year, but how did Richard find out about it if we have the phone?"

Graeson pipes up, "Wait, you're right. There's no other reason he would have pummeled him at his wife's wake."

168

"That was pretty arrogant of Beckett to walk right up to Richard. He deserved the hit, even though Richard's timing was far off. Izzie, didn't you say Hannah made a comment about Beckett and Stephanie?" Hazel asks.

"Yeah, Hannah said something about them being close, and she looked like a wreck. Her eyes were all puffy and swollen. She reminded me of what my mom looked like when she and my dad got divorced. And she didn't even try to help Beckett after Richard leveled him."

"Do you think Beckett told Richard?" Hazel asks.

"What a way to kick a man while he's down," Shea says.

"I don't know, but I feel like this makes Beckett look really bad," I say.

"Not just Beckett," Hazel adds. "It makes Richard and Hannah look really guilty. It gives both of them a motive."

I hadn't even thought about that. This little love triangle is incriminating everyone involved. People do crazy things for love. Richard could've killed her in a fit of rage when he found out about the affair. Years of being devoted to her and dealing with her crap all culminated in one fatal gunshot. Beckett could've had an unhealthy obsession with Stephanie and allowed his emotions to get the best of him. Maybe he got mad that Stephanie wouldn't leave Richard to be with him or maybe she threatened to come clean about their relationship and he killed her to preserve his family. Hannah has more reason than anyone to have pulled the trigger on the woman who spent years berating her and then tried to steal her husband right out from under her. Yet I can't picture any of them actually killing Stephanie. I can't see any of them holding a gun to her head, pulling the trigger, and walking away like nothing happened. But people surprise you. Desperation changes normally functioning people into savages. As much as I don't want it to be any of them, especially Hannah, it's a real possibility we have to consider.

Once we've exhausted all the possibilities around Stephanie and Beckett, we begin to dig through the second chat. The earliest messages date back to only a few days before Stephanie died, which makes me think Stephanie deleted the conversations every so often so no one could look back on them if they ever got a hold of her phone. The exchange reads as follows.

Stephanie: *"I meant what I said. Be there with everything."*

Mystery Number: *"I'm out. This is wrong. I could lose my job and so could you."*

Stephanie: *"I swear I'll tell her everything."*

Mystery Number: *"Go ahead. I'm out. The deal is off."*

Stephanie: *"You're going to regret this."*

There are no messages after the Wednesday before the party. No replies from the mystery number. Then it hits me! That was the day I dropped the boxcutter in Stephanie's house when I was listening in on her phone call. This has to be the same person she threatened to kill if they didn't deliver whatever it was she wanted.

"This is the person on the phone!" I exclaim. "From the first time I was in Stephanie's house!"

"Oh my gosh!" Hazel yells, remembering what I had told her earlier about the incident.

"You broke into her house more than once?" Shea asks, perplexed by our enthusiasm.

"No, that time I was sort of invited in, but that's not the point! I overheard her on the phone, and she was telling someone they better have whatever she wanted by Thursday or she'd kill them," I say brushing off the question.

Graeson's icy blue eyes widen, while Shea puts his hand to his chin as if he's deeply contemplating. The string doesn't tell us much, but it's a start.

"What do you think their deal was?" I ask.

"Drugs, money, blackmail, maybe another secret affair? God only knows," Graeson replies jokingly.

Drugs, money, blackmail or love. Is that what this all is going to come down to? I know Graeson's kidding, but something stands out to me. Something about it turns some lightbulb on in my head. I just can't quite figure out what it means.

"Let's look at the last text string!" Hazel says enthusiastically as her body shakes like an over caffeinated middle school girl.

We pull up the screen with the messages between Stephanie and a blocked ID, which is weird because all the other people Stephanie was chatting with had phone numbers. All the other mystery people had phone numbers, no names, but at least some form of identification. We read the message, and silence settles over the room like a dark storm cloud. Even though the humidity was almost unbearable today, I feel goosebumps popping up on my arms and legs. My heart is pulsating as if someone were currently squeezing it. I try to swallow the spit that's gathered in my open mouth, but the lump in my throat won't allow anything to pass down. I feel like I'm choking on my own words, unable to release them. I glance at Hazel, whose ocean eyes are brimming with tears.

"The date," Hazel says with a quiet and shaky voice.

My eyes move back to the screen and scan over the date of the message. Friday June 23rd. Oh God. I bring my hands up and bury my face in them. Oh God, this is bad.

The message in front of us from the blocked ID reads, "*See how easy it is for me to get you alone. Next time, I'll shut you up for good. You're dead.*"

"We need to give this to the police," Shea says loudly.

"We can't!" I reply. "How would we explain where we got it?!"

"It doesn't matter. Someone is dead and there's a murderer

171

on the loose! We need to give this to the people who actually know what they're doing," he snaps back.

Graeson says, "We could try to call the number."

"No!" Shea responds, "We need to go to the police."

"There is no number to call, it's blocked. I don't think we should do anything yet," Hazel starts. "I think we should meet with Alison, see what she has to say, and then take it from there."

"I agree. Can we make a deal? No one says anything until we meet with Alison tomorrow?" I add.

Graeson and Hazel, who are both on board, nod their heads in agreement. All of us turn to look at Shea, whose face is growing more concerned and annoyed with every passing second.

"This is ridiculous," he says as he stands up and leaves the room, running up the stairs.

"I'll get him," I say to Hazel and Graeson.

I feel responsible for bringing Shea into this whole mess, and I still feel awful about what I said to him the other day. I really did want a chance with him. There was just so much emotion and chaos associated with that night. I don't know why I pushed him away.

I race up the stairs and out the front door where Shea is walking down the driveway.

"Hey!" I yell, "Wait!"

He whips his body around, "What!?"

"Can't we talk about this?"

"Oh, so now you want to talk?"

I go to argue back, but his words sink in before I have the chance to speak. After thinking for a minute, I reply, "I'm sorry! Okay, I'm sorry."

Shea continues walking away, so I have to run to catch up to him. When I reach him I put my hand on his shoulder to slow him down.

"What do you want me to say?" he says. "One minute you're kissing me and the next you're saying you want nothing to do with me. You're holding my hand and then you're ignoring me. I don't know what you want from me."

"Shea, I'm sorry. I want . . . I . . . you can't tell anyone about the phone!"

His face drops, hurt written all over it, as I immediately regret the words I just spewed out of my mouth. It's like he was waiting for me to say something reassuring, something to tell him I felt the same way he did, but instead I just took his hopes and crumbled them up like a fresh sheet of white paper. He sighs and says, "I'm not going to say anything about the phone. Just leave me alone."

The words hit me like a bullet to the chest. They sound so cold and cruel rolling off his tongue, but then again, I deserve it. His honesty sends a stinging sensation throughout my heart, and I suddenly feel a wave of regret wash over me. I can't even argue with him. All I've done is screw up over and over again. I'm like a tornado rolling through other people's lives, destroying everything in my path including them. Nothing I can say can fix that. Maybe I'm just too messed up.

He starts walking down the street towards his house as I call out his name one more time, desperately grasping at words that won't come. My friend back in Portland used to tell me that if the person looks back at you as they're walking away, they like you too. Whether or not that has any truth to it, Shea doesn't look back.

*****

I spend the rest of the late afternoon and night holed up in my room crying over everything that's happened. I feel all of the unrelenting emotions moving through me like the violent waves of the ocean during a storm. Everything from the past few weeks is gnawing holes in my heart, causing my body to just cry and cry and cry. Why is it that a humans' natural reaction to any problem is to simply cry? Do we really think that expelling water through our eyes is going to solve anything? But like any irrational teenage girl, I throw myself on my bed and let the tears fall until there is physically no more water left inside of me. I am crying about missing home. I am crying about my dad because even though he pulled out of his coma and is going to be physically okay, he's on his way to rehab. It's like my entire childhood is warped when I look back on it. All those memories have been replaced with darker ones, making me rethink everything I thought I knew was true. He tried calling once, but I can't even talk to him. Hell, I don't even like thinking about him right now. But honestly, I can't tell if I'm more mad at him or at myself. I am crying about Stephanie and the horrifying image of her dead body. I am crying because I feel terrible for Hannah and Richard and Alex and Ella. But mostly, I am crying about Shea. We had something special. There was some sort of unexplainable connection between the two of us. I felt it. He felt it. I know he did. When I was with him, I had felt happier than I had been in a long time. And I screwed it all up. I was a wrecking ball, crashing right into our relationship with no regard for anything. He was so good to me. Shea is kind and compassionate and considerate, and I pushed him away. I do what I always do — push away all the good things and people who come into my life. I don't know why I do it. It's not a conscious decision. Just look at what I did to John. Shea hates me now, and he's probably never going to talk to me again. I almost told him that I wanted something with him — today out on the street — that I liked him so much it hurt. But then my brain panicked at the thought of being vulnerable and suddenly I was talking to him about the phone, which was probably about the worst thing I could have done. I cry myself to sleep from the weight of it all.

When morning comes, the sun peeks through my windows casting light through the blinds. I hear a faint knock on my door and mumble for whoever it is to come in. The person knocking is my mom, who walks in with a mug of coffee in one hand and a laundry basket in the other. She places the laundry basket down and sits on the edge of the bed while handing me the cup of coffee.

"How are you holding up, bud?" she asks, her voice sweet and soft like warm maple syrup.

"I'm fine," I lie. I've never been good at talking about my feelings or things that are going on in my life. It's like there's a wall between my emotions and the real world that keeps me from being vulnerable.

"Your mouth is saying you're fine, but your face is telling me a different story. I know when something's wrong, Izzie. I'm your mom, you can't slip anything past me."

This is why I love my mom. The way she just automatically knows there's something off makes me feel like maybe my place in this world isn't so lost after all. It makes me feel like someone sees me and understands me or at least tries to. I'm not even understanding myself much these days. Maybe I should just give it a try — being vulnerable. Maybe I should tell her my problems and gain some sort of insight because clearly I can't handle it all on my own. But of course I can't tell her about my involvement in solving Stephanie's murder.

She reaches for my hand, "You've been through so much in the past few weeks."

"I screwed up, Mom. I screwed up big time."

"What happened?"

"Besides the fact that we were just at the wake for the dead neighbor I found in our backyard and Dad's lying in a hospital bed, I completely ruined everything with Shea."

"Shea? I knew there was something going on between the two of you! That's so great, honey," she says excitedly.

"No, Mom. You're not hearing me correctly. I ruined it. Destroyed it. Crushed it."

"Oh no, I'm sure whatever you did was not that bad. What happened?"

"We kissed on the night of Stephanie's party," I say as her eyes light up with excitement and she lets out a little squeal. "Then a few days later, he asked if I wanted to talk about everything, and I told him no. Do you hear me?! I told him no! What kind of a person says that?"

"Oh gosh!" she says a slight smile spreads across her face. "Do you like him, Izzie?"

"Yes! Of course I like him. He is perfect, but I screwed it all up."

"If you really like him, Izzie, you can fight for him. We all say things we're not proud of. We all say things we don't mean. You were going through a lot, and if Shea is as amazing as you say he is, he'll understand. On one of the first dates I went on with your dad back when we were sophomores in high school, he went to hold my hand and I pulled it away. Literally flung my hand as far away as it could get from his, like it was some sort of muscle spasm. And the weird part, I liked him. I liked him so much, but I was scared. Putting yourself out there is scary. You can fix this, Izzie."

I've always thought that I was exactly like my dad, but hearing my mom talk makes me think I'm more like her than I thought.

"But there's more. I felt awkward about everything so I just ignored him, and then when I went to talk to him he told me he didn't know what I wanted from him and to leave him alone."

"Hmm, okay," I bet she's wondering how I became so emotionally inept. "He's confused, and I don't blame him. I don't think he meant that though. He's just as scared as you are. He doesn't want to be rejected. You just have to go and apologize and be honest with him. Tell him what's been going on and tell him how you feel. He'll understand."

She smiles at me, and for a moment, I feel like everything is going to be okay. Maybe she's right, maybe I can fix this. Either way, I have a mom who loves me more than she loves to breathe, so I would say I'm pretty lucky.

*****

I sit at the kitchen counter reading my book when my phone is bombarded with messages, creating a continuous ping sound. Most of the messages are from Hazel telling me to check Instagram and Facebook NOW. Yikes!

I open Facebook on my phone and the first image that pops up in my feed gives me that familiar sinking feeling in my stomach. I scroll down further and see that the same picture has been reposted over and over again. The photo of Beckett and Stephanie kissing has been reposted by everyone in Knox Hollow, complete with nasty comments about both the Kester and St. James families. My mind instantly goes to Hannah. Now every judgy snob in town knows her private business. How did this picture even get out into the world of social media? This afternoon is not off to a great start.

"Izzie!" I hear my three-year-old sister Madison's squeaky voice from behind me.

I turn around in the chair to find her in a princess dress with a sparkly tiara and plastic high heels.

"Wow, don't you look beautiful Princess Madison," I say.

She blushes, "Thank you."

I turn back to my phone, furiously texting Hazel back, but Madison tugs on my tank top.

"What is it?" I say.

"We have to talk!" she says confidently.

"Oh yeah?" I play along

"I *need* to go to the park!"

"You do?"

"Yes! I need to go!" she urges.

"When daddy gets back, you can ask him to take you."

She shakes her head as her lips form into a pout, "No, no, no. I want *you* to take me."

I evaluate my options: I can either take her to the park and get silently judged by some prissy, rich mothers, or I can stay here reading and continue to stress out about the ongoing murder investigation. Neither sounds all that appealing, but I think getting some fresh air and moving around would do me some good.

"Okay, you win. I'll take you to the park, but you can't wear those shoes."

She smiles a wide smile that shows off her tiny teeth. "Deal."

I quickly yell up to my mom to tell her where we're going, and a few minutes later Madison and I are on our way to the park that's about a five minute walk from our house. The day is warm but not sweltering, and the sunlight feels good on my skin. The news about Stephanie and Beckett's affair is spreading like wildfire through social media, and I can't stop wondering about who got a hold of it and how they did. It was originally posted by an anonymous account, which seems a little sketchy. Madison sings as she skips along, although most of her singing consists of mumbled words that don't make sense. When we arrive at the park she immediately starts running around and races to the slide.

"Wait Madison!" I yell as she comes running back to me. "I'll be right here if you need me, okay? Be careful." She nods her head like an obedient little puppy and dashes away. The park is fairly empty for such a warm day, but then again, it is a Wednesday afternoon. I forget that just because I have the summer off, it doesn't mean everyone else does too. I notice two mothers sitting on a park bench, each holding a baby and chatting away. One lady's back is to me and the other one who's facing me intently listens and nods her head along. It takes me a minute but I realize that the lady facing me with the brownish red hair is Dr. Rachel Hastings. The other lady shifts positions, turning her head in my direction, and I quickly realize that it's Hannah. If I were her I'd be too scared to even leave my house. Hannah catches a glimpse of me, waves, and motions for me to come over. I feel the awkward tingling rapidly rising in my body. I don't know if she knows that I know about everything.

"Hi," Hannah says cheerfully. "How are you today, Izzie?"

Isn't it funny how we always ask how other people are, but never actually give honest answers or care about the other person's response? It would be uncomfortable to tell someone that you're not doing well, that life is giving you a run for your money. So we smile and we say we're doing great and move on with the conversation. Anyways, I feel like I should be the one asking Hannah if she's okay. My life may be spiraling a bit but that's nothing compared to Hannah's, whose world has just been blown apart.

"I'm pretty good," I reply awkwardly before I reach my hand out to greet Rachel. "Hi, I'm Izzie."

Rachel smiles a bright smile that shows off her teeth, which are slightly too large for her mouth, "It's nice to meet you, Izzie. I'm Rachel. I met your parents at the block party. They seem like such good people."

"Thank you," I say back, unsure about how to continue the conversation.

Hannah's face looks red and blotchy, and the bags under her eyes seem to have doubled in size since I last saw her. I want so badly to blurt out and tell her how sorry I am and that I believe she's innocent. Everyone on Facebook is calling her a murderer, some even went as far as to call her a homicidal maniac, but they don't even have a clue. You're supposed to be innocent until proven guilty. Since when did assumptions and speculation and rumors determine a person's innocence?

"Will you be going to Knox Hollow High?" Rachel inquires.

"Yeah, I'll be a senior," I reply.

"Wow! That's so exciting. I feel like we were seniors only a few days ago," she says, turning to Hannah. "I'd give anything to be in high school again."

"You guys went to high school together?" I ask.

Hannah nods and smiles, "Ages ago. We both grew up in Albany and somehow ended up back together here in Knox Hollow."

Rachel nods, "We used to tear it up in high school. Remember that party you threw when your parents went to Chicago for the weekend?"

Hannah's laughing now, "You mean the party you basically forced me into having?"

"It was so worth it! That was the night I finally got George Avery to notice me. He was such a good kisser. That was one of the best parties," Rachel gushes.

"It was until you drank too much and fell through the downstairs window," Hannah replies.

"I forgot about that!"

"How could you forget about falling through a window?" Hannah jokingly shakes her head.

"There was a lot of Tequila in my cup," Rachel laughs.

I've always wanted this type of relationship with someone. A person who knows all your secrets and stories. A person whose been with you through all the embarrassments and the wild nights, all the tears and stupid mistakes, all the setbacks and the laughs. Someone who's been there with you through everything. Someone you have so many inside jokes with it's hard to keep track. I've never really had that. I had friends back in Portland, best friends even, but I've never had this type of bond. I've never had that one person who knows you even better than you know yourself. I guess you could say Luke is that person, but it doesn't really count if you're related. I feel like friend is such a loosely used word nowadays anyway. It just doesn't mean that much anymore. I feel like Hazel might be that person for me. She's been the best thing about moving here. Maybe I have finally found my person.

When Rachel and Hannah finish talking about their old high school days, they start talking to me about my own high school career. Hannah is telling me about the different English and creative writing classes I can take. She tells me about this one class that sounds particularly interesting about mystery writing. That topic somehow leads us into my love of Agatha Christie, who, come to find out, is one of Hannah's favorites as well.

"Have you read the ABC Murders by her?" Hannah asks.

"I haven't read that one yet," I reply.

"That's one of my favorites! I have it at the house, you'll have to stop by later and take it. I'm telling you, you'll love it."

"You wouldn't mind?"

"No, not at all. I'm an English teacher, I have more books than I know what to do with. Come by later today or tomorrow, whenever you get a chance!"

After about thirty more minutes at the park, it's time for Madison and I to make our way back home. I'm not entirely ready for my meeting with Alison later tonight. However, I am not sure if I am more nervous to talk with Alison or to see Shea. My day is going to consist of talking to the woman whose husband was having an affair with their murdered neighbor, paying off a nine-year-old for information about that murder, while simultaneously trying to ignore the boy I messed things up with during my attempt to solve the murder. Nothing about this is normal.

*****

Hazel picks me up at six forty-five in her grey Altima before we head over to get Graeson. She wears black leggings and a black Nike sweatshirt with her real housewives cheetah print sunglasses. Shawn Mendes's latest album hums through the speaker as we roll down the street.

"Why are you in all black?" I ask, a small smile spreading across my face.

Her face lights up as she says, "I'm incognito! Flying under the radar."

"You do realize we're not robbing the place?"

Hazel starts to answer, but then her face goes blank as she considers what I said, "Oh, that's right. Way to kill my excitement."

"Do you know if Shea's coming?" I ask her.

She shrugs her shoulders, "I wouldn't get your hopes up. When Shea sets his mind on something, he doesn't really change it. I think you should just talk to him, Izzie. He only told you to leave him alone because he thought you were rejecting him."

"You sound like my mom," I throw my head back against the seat. "This sucks. I had a chance, and I threw it away."

"Shea's an easy person to talk to, just tell him how you feel," Hazel encourages.

"I don't like talking about my feelings."

"I know, but you're running out of options. Communication is good. Shea will absolutely forgive you if you're just honest with him. He's been hurt a lot in the past few months, he just didn't want to end up burned again. But I saw something in him when you moved here. You brought something out of him, it was like we had an even brighter version of the old Shea back."

"Uhh!" I roll my eyes and slam my head against the seat again. "This whole growing up thing is hard."

We pull up in front of Graeson's house as he comes stumbling out with one shoe half on and the other one in his hand. He launches himself into the car, trying to fight off the pelting rain that's been falling since earlier this evening.

"Jesus, it's pouring!" he yells when he gets into the car shaking like a wet dog. "Shea texted me and said he's not coming."

I can't tell if I'm relieved or disappointed that I don't have to see him. Whatever. Right now I need to focus on Alison and the information she has for us.

"Hazel," Graeson snickers. "May I ask why you're dressed like you're about to rob a bank?"

"I was trying to dress incognito!" she fires back.

Graeson turns to me, "What's wrong with you?"

"I screwed up," I groan.

"Are you talking about Shea?" he questions.

"Shea told you what happened???" My eyes bulge as my cheeks flush in embarrassment.

"No, he didn't say anything about whatever's going on here," he motions to me sitting with my head flung back with a bright red face. "But I do know how to read a room." Hazel shoots him a look so he adds, "Okay, sometimes I know how to read a room. The guy's desperately in love with you. I don't know what went down, but literally all you have to do is tell him you like him. He talks about you all the time!"

"Shea talks about me?"

"Shea doesn't stop talking about you. But I was specifically told not to tell you that, so if he finds out you heard it from me, I will deny it."

Well this gives me quite a bit to think about. I decide to push it to the back of my brain and deal with it later, which has been a very popular solution lately.

"So what's our plan when we get in there?" I question.

"I don't have much experience negotiating blackmail, so I don't know! Is anyone else's heart racing? Because my heart is racing! My heart is definitely racing!" Hazel replies, her voice sounding louder and more anxious with every word.

"Whoa! Slow down, Hazel. How much coffee have you had today?" Graeson laughs.

She takes a sip of coffee from the cup in the holster before she says, "Only like four cups. It's not that much!"

She goes to take another sip, but I grab the cup before her jittery fingers can. "This is for your own good. I'm cutting you off."

We glide along the coal black glossy surface of the rain covered pavement. I stare out at the window watching the rain pelt the streets until Hazel pulls into the parking lot. Here we go. Let's hope Alison has something good for us.

The three of us walk into the quiet diner, the bell jingling as we open the door. The smell of roasting coffee beans, charcoal, and french fries fills my nose. There's something charming about being in a little dinky diner while the world is both literally and figuratively storming. It makes me feel safe and secure, like I'm in a little bubble away from my troubles.

Out of the corner of my eye I see Alison who waves slyly, wiggling each of her little fingers. That comforting feeling fades as soon as I see her scowl. She sits there with a strawberry milkshake poised in front of her, her neon pink painted fingernails wrapped around the cup. Her hair is pulled into a high side ponytail, which somehow makes her all the more evil looking. I know that's really not that nice to say about a little girl, but it's true. We make the awkward trek over to Alison's booth. I slide in first, and then Graeson jumps past Hazel and throws himself in so fast after me he practically crushes me. I guess he really didn't want to be stuck sitting next to Alison. Hazel gives him a death stare as she takes her seat next to Stephanie's mini me.

"I'm so glad you could all make it!" Her face is coated with a thick layer of fake enthusiasm. "The strawberry milkshakes here are my fav —"

I cut her off with a harsh tone, "This is cute and all, but we're not here to play games. Tell us what you know and we'll give you your money. It's that simple."

Alison seems to be caught slightly off guard, but she rebounds quickly. You can see the wheels spinning in her head, like gears on a well-oiled machine. She fires back, "Looks like someone forgot their table manners. I'll give you a pass this time because you're new around here, but next time I won't be so patient. This is my show, and it will be run *my* way. This is how it works: you give me my money and I'll tell you what I know."

"No," I reply. "I don't trust you one bit."

"I'm not here to be ordered around by *you*."

"And I'm not here to be conned by a nine-year-old."

"It's funny, my brother said you were nice. He's so naive," she talks as if she were an adult commenting on her stupid kid's mistake. She sounds exactly like Stephanie with her condescending voice.

Graeson holds up the crisp white envelope of money, which makes Alison's hazel eyes light up like a wild cat's.

"This is yours," he unseals the envelope and slyly shows her the contents. "It's all here. Tell us what you know, and we'll hand over the money."

"Fine, just this once I'll play it your way," she says and I can't tell if we've rattled her or if the money's made her forget about her ridiculous antics. She takes a long sip of her strawberry milkshake before saying, "My mom met with Sawyer Hastings every Wednesday afternoon at exactly four-thirty. He always handed her a brown paper bag, and she would give him a white envelope just like that one you have there. He never stayed long, which I thought was strange because my mom was always up for good chat and a glass of wine."

I'm not sure what I was expecting to hear, but this wasn't it. I'm not exactly sure what to do with this information. "How do we know you're not making this up?" I question, giving her the stare my mom always gives me to catch me in a lie.

She rolls her eyes, "I'm not an idiot. Here's your proof." She pulls two printed photographs from her small, sparkly backpack and places them delicately on the table. Both pictures are clear images of Stephanie and Sawyer exchanging a brown bag and white envelope. Alison may be manipulative but she's not a liar. The pictures seem to be taken from above — maybe an upstairs window or the back deck — and show that their discreet meetings took place in Stephanie's backyard within the privacy of her massive oak trees.

"How did you get these pictures?" Hazel asks with a confused expression.

"I took them," Alison says proudly. "And I have tons more where that came from. Everyone around here has something to hide, but what do I care? It makes me *a lot* of money."

This instantly makes me think of what Stephanie said that first night: *We are plagued with secrets, and he knows all of them.* I feel like we're going about this investigation in the wrong way. We need to stop thinking about who could've killed Stephanie. We should start thinking about what everyone's trying to hide. Alison is a lot of things, but an idiot isn't one of them. On the other hand, I'm slightly disturbed that this little girl seems to blackmail people into paying her money. I can't tell if that makes her a genius or a psychopath. Maybe both.

"You blackmailed your own mother?" Hazel says, sounding almost disgusted.

"You never know when certain information is going to be useful. Besides, if my mom taught me anything before she died it was that you're not going to get anywhere special by playing nice. You do what you have to do."

"Do you know who killed your mom?" I ask point blank.

186

"No, but she wronged a lot of people. I know a lot of people's secrets, but other than these pictures I didn't really know anything about her. My mom was good at hiding things. I'd bet you there's tons of little things hidden in our house, underneath the floorboards, hidden in the walls. There's so many secrets she brought with her to the grave. She was good at the games she played. Where do you think I learned it all from?"

The Kester family is sounding more and more messed up by the second. What kind of mother teaches her daughter about manipulating people before she teaches her how to say please and thank you? It makes me feel really lucky to have my mom and John and even my dad.

Suddenly, a thought hits me like a bird hits a window. "Alison," I say. "You need to be careful. Whoever hurt your mom is still out there. If they find out you have all this blackmail they might come after you. You have to stop this for now. I need you to protect yourself."

She smirks smugly, "No offense, but I can fend for myself."

"This is serious," Hazel adds. "You need to be careful, Ali."

"I appreciate your concern, but I'm not here for life advice. I gave you my information, now where's my money?" she says coldly.

Graeson hands her the envelope, and her greedy fingers clutch it instantly and slip it into her backpack. A Cheshire cat smile spreads across her face as the three of us quickly say our goodbyes and leave the diner as fast as we can. On the way out, I look back over my shoulder at Alison. From here, she's just a young kid sitting in a booth all alone. Her confidence seems to have faded now that she's by herself. It makes me think that maybe Alison is just a scared little girl who's trying to put up a tough front. Because as we're walking away, she just seems so small.

CHAPTER 10 - Silent

When I was around six years old my parents took Luke and me to Disney World. On the plane, I told my dad that I was going to ride every single roller coaster they had. When we got there I remember standing in front of Thunder Mountain, red-faced with my little blonde pig tails shaking, absolutely terrified. I remember feeling a shivering sensation spreading through my body, and it felt like aggressive butterflies were jabbing at my insides. My knees felt weak like limp spaghetti noodles, and my heart pounded the way a mallet smacks meat. But being the stubborn person I am, I decided I had to go on the ride or all that talking on the plane I did would make me look pretty stupid. I was terrified, but I sat down in the seat, buckled myself in, and prayed to God I wouldn't throw up everywhere or fall out of the cart. I have the same exact feeling right now. My phone is laid out in front of me with Shea's number on the screen. All I have to do is press the call button. For the past hour I've been sitting here watching the rain pour down from the sky and slap the streets with the phone poised in front of me. I've written down three versions of things I could possibly say to him if he even answers, but knowing me I'll end up blubbering some stupid words that push him farther away. After hearing what Graeson said in the car, I realized I can't keep waiting to fix my mistakes. Sometimes you wait too long, and before you know it, your chance has passed. But, God, this is hard! It seems so simple in theory: dial the number, call, and apologize. I feel just like I did as I stepped on that roller coaster, scared and anxious. I guess relationships are no different than roller coasters. Even though you're afraid, you jump in, buckle up really tight, and hope that when everything stops moving, you're still hanging in there.

While I'm lost in my thoughts, I accidentally knock my phone off the bay window. My hands grasp at it and catch it before it falls to the floor, but when my eyes take a glimpse at the screen, I realize I accidentally hit call. My thoughts are all jumbled and panicked as I jump off the seat and start frantically pacing around my room. I can't hang up now because he'll see that I called. The only coherent thought I have is "please don't pick up." I repeat it over and over again while the ringing phone pierces my ears.

"Hi," I hear a voice on the other line.

No! No! No! My brain scrambles around trying to find the words, but everything is going blank. What am I even supposed to say to him!? This was a stupid stupid stupid plan!

"Izzie? Hello?" he says again.

"Hey," I say awkwardly. "Uh . . . what's up?"

"I'm not sure, you called me."

"Oh, that's right."

The line falls silent as I try to quickly skim through all the different versions of what I could say. All of them sound so ridiculously stupid and rehearsed and robotic.

"If you're calling about the phone, I told you I'm not going to say anything," Shea pipes up.

"No, no, that's not why. I need to talk to you. I . . . I didn't mean any of what I said . . . I . . . I just need to talk to you."

He doesn't say anything for a moment, which sends goosebumps down my arms and legs. "I understand if you don't want to," I add as the panic of rejection rises in my chest.

"No, of course I want to talk to you."

"I know it's bad timing, but I'll be out on my front porch if you want to come by. I know it's raining and everything, but I'd rather do this in person."

"Okay . . . okay," he repeats the word as if he's trying to reassure himself, trying to boost his confidence.

"Okay, okay," I say it twice for good measure.

I hang up the phone and breathe in a massive sigh of relief. So far I haven't completely screwed this up, but the night is young and I can still cause a lot of damage. My emotions start running, my mouth misfires, and then all bets are off.

A few minutes later, I'm sitting on our front porch watching the rain dance across the pavement. Mom and John are already in bed, so I was able to easily slip out. Goosebumps cover my arms and legs, and I can't tell if it's because of the chilly air or the nerves. I see a black car pull down the street in my direction. It parks in front of my house, and I see Shea head out and jog up the driveway.

I start laughing, "Did you seriously drive over here?"

"It's pouring," he says as he takes a seat next to me.

Silence settles over us again, which makes me realize that I'm supposed to be the one talking. Words are failing me. My brain is grasping at letters, trying to form sensible thoughts.

"I'm a pusher!" I blurt out.

He looks at me with a confused expression, his eyes squinted and his mouth slightly open, "You're a what?"

I take a deep breath, "I'm a pusher. I push people away because I get awkward and scared that they're going to leave me or hurt me or honestly, I don't even know what. I say things I don't mean as a defense when I feel myself getting close to people. I screw up good things. I've liked you since the first day I met you and that scares me senseless. But I don't want to screw this up, I don't want to push you away." I feel the tears welling in my eyes, and I have to stop talking to ground myself. I feel myself spiraling, falling down a dark and twisty rabbit hole. The minute I say the heavy words to him, I feel a weight lifted off my shoulder, but I don't feel relieved. I suddenly feel like I'm spinning in circles,

190

unable to bring myself back into reality. It's as if those vulnerable words were the only things tethering me to the ground. Burning hot tears roll down my cheeks as I shake my head in embarrassment. I promised myself I wouldn't cry, that I wouldn't make myself look like a disaster. I don't even know what I'm crying about at this point. I'm crying about everything and nothing all at the same time.

"Hey," he places his hands on either side of my face, the length of his little finger resting on my jawline. He gently turns my face so my gaze is fixed at him instead of the ground. I feel his hands steadying my shaking body, tethering me back to the ground. His hands are soft and warm, shielding my face from the biting air. His eyes are wide, like glossy orbs. I can tell he's nervous, as if he's unsure if this is the right move. "It's okay. Don't cry, it's okay." His words are simple, but they hold so much meaning. Slowly, he removes his hands from my face and wraps his arm around me, pulling my shaking body into his. Without thinking, I rest my head on his bony shoulder, feeling the cotton of his shirt against the side of my face. I feel myself shrinking into his arms, letting my thoughts and worries fade into the background. The chill that covered my body like a blanket fades as his hand gently rubs my arm. I hear his heart beating through his shirt, jumping through the cottony fabric. I can tell he's nervous, that he's bolder than he thought he could be. His hand makes its way upwards to my hair, fingers combing through my baby blonde locks until my heart rate slows and the water draining out of my eyes dries up. Even with all of our dysfunction and awkwardness, it feels like the perfect moment. I'm a cringey mess just like I thought I'd be, but it doesn't seem to matter now. We're as close as we were in Stephanie's closet, but this time there's no fear of dying or going to jail, so it's even better. We sit there for a while, just enjoying each other's company. We don't talk, but we don't need to. No words could possibly do these feelings justice. I feel like I could sit here with him forever, watching the rain dance with his arm gently around me. The sky fades from grey to black as the hours melt into each other, and far too soon for my liking, Shea leaves to head back home. This time, he looks back.

*****

"So, this is the plan?" Shea says.

The four of us have spent the past few hours diving back through the information we have and deciding on how to proceed with our investigation. Right now we need to figure out who the blocked ID threatening Stephanie is, what Dr. Hastings's deal is, and, as Alison indirectly told us, what everyone else is hiding. We decided that Luke would try to figure out who the blocked ID is, seeing he's the only one who knows everything about technology. Graeson and Shea are going to start digging around our other neighbors, especially Beckett and Richard who are shaping up to be the prime suspects even though I don't really feel like either of them could've pulled the trigger. Hazel and I are dealing with Dr. Hastings. We're going to meet back up in three days to share our findings and hopefully make some headway. I feel like there's a clock watching over us, making a "tick-tock" noise with every passing second. Every time I think of this constantly ticking clock, all I can see is the bloody shoe that created a deep red pool on my carpet. I'm still waiting for more memories to pop into my head. I read something online that said that sometimes after a black out the memories will reappear randomly. I'm still waiting for something to trigger the memories the Tequila so graciously made disappear because I feel like I'm running out of time to prove to myself once and for all that I had nothing to do with this.

"Graeson, you need to be subtle when you're trying to pull information out of people," says Hazel who was extremely skeptical of letting him take the lead on this part of the investigation.

"I am the king of subtlety. I eat, sleep, and breathe subtlety," he smirks.

"You have about as much subtlety as a grenade. Last time you told me you let a girl down subtly it was Saige," she gives him an accusatory stare. "And we all know how that ended up."

"You people don't let anything go! The past is in the past. I almost hit Izzie with a car but she's not holding on to that," he replies.

"Actually, I haven't forgotten about that," I remark. "Who is Saige and what happened?"

Graeson flings his head back, smacking it against the wood of Hazel's back patio chairs. Hazel and Shea just laugh at him, which causes his cheeks to turn a vibrant shade of red.

"Fine! Fine! I'll tell you, but then we're done talking about this. Before I start this story, may I remind you that all people make mistakes," Graeson says.

"Someone's getting all fired up," Hazel laughs as Graeson gives her the evil eye.

"So Saige Vanderwaal lives next door to Hazel. She's in our grade, and she's a basket case. She's literally psychotic. Her sister on the other hand, she's gorgeous, but that's not the point. One night, my mates and I were playing a game of truth or dare."

"Hold up, you and your friends play truth or dare? What are you a bunch of little girls at a sleepover?" I ask while trying to fight back a laugh.

"Your little boy toy was there too!" Graeson points at Shea, which makes both of us turn fire engine red. That sure shut my big mouth up real fast. I hope Shea didn't say anything to him about how much of a disaster I was the other night. Graeson continues on with his story, "Long story short, I was dared to ask Saige out on a date. I felt awful, but I had no choice."

"What do you mean you had no choice! It was a game of freaking truth or dare!" Hazel says loudly. "No one was holding you at gunpoint."

"You can't back away from a dare, Hazel! That's like walking into a room full of explosives and lighting a match."

All three of us look at him with utter confusion and Hazel says, "What does that even mean?"

Graeson just shakes his head and continues on with his story, "As I was saying," he jokingly glares at Hazel as he speaks. "I asked Saige on a date, and she texted back right away saying yes. The girl was desperate. Apparently she had a thing for me, but I didn't know."

"How could you not know?" Hazel asks. "She was literally obsessed with you since sixth grade. The most oblivious person could have figured it out. Even Shea knew!"

Shea stares at Hazel with his eyebrows furrowed, "Hey! I'm not oblivious."

She gives him one of those stares my mom gives my when she knows I'm lying. "Oh please. But Saige was basically in love with Graeson, and whether you knew it or not, you used her to amuse your stupid friends."

"Easy, Hazel," Shea says. "I'm one of his stupid friends."

Graeson smirks, amused at how easily he's worked Hazel up. "I asked her on a date and she said yes. I felt too awful to cancel on her, so I was hoping it would kind of fizzle out on its own. But she wouldn't let up! She was like a piece of gum that gets stuck in your hair. A stage five clinger! The first date was awful, literally the worst date I've ever been on. I would've had a better time with a rabid porcupine. All she talked about was her pet rabbit and her eyes were all googly. She kept trying to hold my hand, and she chewed with her mouth wide open! A bomb going off would've been quieter. It was like a beaver gnawing through a

194

tree. Then she asked me on a second date and I couldn't figure out how to say no."

"You never should've asked her out in the first place," Hazel interjects.

"Hazel!" Graeson says sharply. "I thought this was my story.

She crosses her arms across her chest and leans back in her seat, signaling for him to go on. So far, this Saige girl is making me feel a little less of a disaster when it comes to relationships. At least I'm a likeable disaster.

"So," Graeson starts again. "We went out for dinner, and I did something bad."

Shea tries to fight off a laugh, but suddenly, it bursts through his pursed lips. This makes Hazel start giggling, until Graeson shoots them both a dirty look.

"It was awful, the whole thing, but her chewing. I couldn't handle it. I was about to lose it! I told her I had to go to the bathroom, and then I snuck out of the restaurant and never came back," his lips curl up into an awkward attempt at a smile.

"Oh my God!" I stare at him with my lips pinched tight together, trying to fight back a laugh because this really isn't funny. But I can't help it, and before I know it the laugh escapes my mouth. "You're an ass. You couldn't just sit through the date and tell the poor girl the next day?"

Graeson runs his fingers through his ruffled hair, "I didn't know what to do. The sound of it was making me want to stab my eyes out with a fork! Her lips were smacking, and I could see the food in her mouth. You should not be able to see the food inside someone's mouth!" His voice becomes so worked up that his face turns red and the veins in his forehead begin to pop.

"It couldn't have been that bad," Shea says.

"You never should've asked her out in the first place. You used her. I mean, Saige is a little out there . . . but she didn't deserve that," Hazel comments.

"I can't believe you just left her," I add.

Graeson shakes his head, his blue eyes gleaming against the sunlight. "She hates me now. Literally hates me. Every time I see her, she gets all in my face and yells at me. Sometimes she even kicks me. It hurts!"

"I don't blame her," I reply. "Did you apologize?"

"Yes, I sent her a text to tell her I was sorry."

"How many times do I have to tell you that a three word text message does not count as an apology!" Hazel says, using her hands to emphasize the point.

To be fair, if her chewing was that loud, I would've done the same thing. I don't know why, but the sound of people chewing makes me want to rip my ears right off, toss them down the garbage disposal, and grind them up until there's nothing left. Okay, that might be a bit extreme, but it's the most God awful sound I've ever heard. I just can't handle it. I met this guy back in Portland, and we went out on a date. He was adorable, but he chewed with his mouth wide open, and long story short, there never was a second date.

A little while later, and after Graeson and Hazel's bickering has settled down, we leave Hazel's back patio. I swear the two of them are like an old married couple. Graeson's off to some fancy gala with his parents, and Hazel has to pick her little brother up from football camp. The four of us make our way out of her backyard. We reach the sidewalk, and suddenly Graeson mutters under his breath, "Oh, God."

"What's wrong?" I ask him.

He motions slyly at the house next door where a girl who appears to be a little older than us is getting into the passenger seat of a running car. She's about 5'5" and perfectly skinny with long, dirty blonde hair held back with a black headband. She swings a designer purse over her bony shoulder and gracefully slips into the car, concealing herself behind the black doors.

"Saige," he says rolling his eyes.

"That's Saige?" I ask, highly confused. From everything I gathered, Saige was a psychotic mess. This girl is obviously gorgeous and very put together. There's something about her that makes her seem welcoming and warm.

"No," Graeson says and points to the front of the house where a second girl is coming out the door. "That's Saige."

Well, that makes more sense. Saige seems to be about the same height as the other girl with the same bony build, but that's where the similarities end. Her sunflower blonde hair is cut in a bob right above her shoulders, and she whispers something under her breath as she stumbles towards the car. I think she's talking to herself. She catches sight of us and quickly changes her direction to come our way. Graeson nervously runs his hands through his hair, although I think he's more annoyed than he is nervous. As Saige gets closer, her eyes shift from dull and boring to evil looking. It seems like all of her crazy is held in her brown eyes. They seem to light up with a devilish spark as she approaches.

"Hey," she says, her mouth twitching. "Is this your new skank of the week?" Her voice is cold as she looks from me to Graeson.

I make a disgusted face as Graeson says, "No, this is the girl who moved into the Peterson's old house."

"Oh," she raises her dark black eyebrows and looks me up and down. I feel like I'm in some police line up as she seems to take in every detail of my appearance. "You're underwhelming," she snarls.

"Stop, Saige. Be nice," Shea pipes up.

The dirty look I'm giving Saige fades away as Shea speaks. It's sweet that he's defending me to this lunatic of a girl.

"You're the girl who found Stephanie's body," she stares me down.

"Nice to meet you too," I stare back and cross my arms, standing my ground.

"Did you kill her?" she questions.

"What?" I fire back, completely caught off guard.

"Saige, stop. You're not funny," Shea defends me.

"I just think it's funny. We live in this perfect little neighborhood and then you show up, and suddenly someone ends up dead. Just a funny little *coincidence*," Saige smirks.

I'm about ready to throat punch her. I fold my hands to fists, harshly digging my fingers into my palms and forming little half moons on the surface of my hand.

"Saige!" I hear a loud, shrieking voice calling her name from behind her.

We look up and a woman who appears to be in her early forties steps out of the front door and down the brick steps. She's tall and skinny like her daughters, but she wears a perfectly pressed white collared shirt underneath a bubblegum pink cashmere sweater that makes her look both classy and uptight. Her dirty blonde hair is chopped above her shoulders and falls in curling iron swoops. Her grey blue eyes are shaded by a pair of black rimmed glasses and her cheeks are coated with so much blush you would think she was running a dangerously high fever. Her face is thin and hollow looking. Her cheekbones are high and prominent, but her actual cheeks don't fill out, causing her face to jut inwards. This lady's face shape reminds me of a horse, a pretty horse, but a horse nonetheless. The way she struts out of the house is a dead give way of her personality. She seems controlling and high strung.

"Let's go, Saige," she repeats the command again. "Now!"

Before walking away to her preppy mother, Saige shoots me one more conniving look and says, "I wouldn't blame you if you did it. Stephanie deserved to die."

With those words lingering in the air like smoke after a fire, Saige clumsily walks away and into the car, but not before winking at me.

We all stand there in silence, watching the Vanderwaal's car drive away. This girl is a whole new level of crazy that I didn't even know existed. And I thought I had issues.

"Well, on that note, I've got to go get ready for this gala my mum is forcing me to go to," Graeson says to break the silence.

"Do you think she . . .." I start, but can't finish the thought.

"No," Graeson says. "She says these crazy things all the time to get attention. There's no way she killed Stephanie. Rumor has it that she's on all sorts of meds."

Graeson might be right, but something about her leaves an unsettled feeling in the pit of my stomach.

Hazel bites her lip nervously and then says, "I think we should look into this as soon as possible. I don't think she did anything, but we can't take that lightly. I have to go pick up Jack, but we'll talk later."

Hazel walks into her house and Graeson heads down the street, leaving Shea and I standing like statues on the sidewalk.

I look to him and say with a small smile on my face, "You stood up for me when Saige said all those things."

"It was mean what she said. I know you're capable of standing up for yourself, and I hope you don't mind, but I wasn't going to let her talk to you like that," he stumbles over his words nervously.

"It was cute," I smile, which makes him relax. It feels good to have someone on my side, someone to defend me even when other people are trying to tear me down. "You wanna go for a walk?" I ask him because I don't really feel like going home. Shea's presence is so comforting that I just want to be with him for as long as I can.

He smiles, two identical dimples peeking out from his cheeks, and we start walking away from Mayflower Circle. I don't know where we're going, but I really don't care. Honestly, I would walk into the mouth of a volcano if I were walking with Shea.

"So," he starts. "I don't know what we are, and we don't have to put any sort of label on it, but I want to take you out on a date." His cheeks blush a bright shade of red, contrasting his sun kissed skin. He takes a deep breath and then says, "Would you like to go out with me?"

I'm grinning from ear to ear, happiness emanating from my body. I feel like the two of us are glowing in the sunlight, living in a world completely separate from everyone else.

"It's about time you asked," I laugh.

He glances at me, and I can't help but notice the way he smiles with his eyes, innocent and genuine. There's something almost childlike about it. I reach for his hand, no longer caring about making the wrong move or saying the wrong thing. I'm a disaster, and Shea accepts me for that. He and I walk off with the sunlight bouncing off our skin, hand in hand. For a moment, the world around me has stopped and everything feels okay.

*****

Hazel and I are sprawled out in lawn chairs on my back patio, coming up with a plan of attack for our search into Dr. Hastings and his role in all of this madness. So far we've come up with nothing. Hazel twirls her golden curls around her fingers, while she stares out at the tree line. She looks at me through her Real Housewife-like cheetah print sunglasses while talking to me about what could've been in the bag and envelope Sawyer and Stephanie exchanged.

"It's got to be drugs," I say to her.

"I don't know. I just can't see either of them taking or selling drugs. It just doesn't seem right," she replies.

Hazel can't believe it because she always sees the best in everyone. She wants to believe people are good and innocent. Me on the other hand, I'm a terrible person. I think the world is a sucky place full of sucky people. Hazel's viewpoint is a nice change of pace, but it's not reality. I've learned the hard way that when you try to see the best in people, they end up proving you wrong and hurting you.

"What else would be in that brown bag?" I question.

"I don't know," she shakes her head and twirls her hair a little faster. "Chocolates?" I jokingly roll my eyes at her naive sense of people. She continues, "I'm pretty sure there was money in that envelope she gave him. They must've had some sort of deal worked out where she paid him for whatever was in that brown bag. Alison said they met every Wednesday, so it was definitely a pre-planned deal. I just can't figure out what he would need money for. Sawyer and Rachel are both surgeons at one of the best hospitals in Massachusetts. I don't think they're hard up for cash."

"I bet Rachel doesn't know. Their meetings seemed pretty secret. What if he needed money for something he couldn't tell Rachel about?"

"If he needed money for something he didn't want Rachel to know about, he may not be able to just take it out of their account, especially if she takes care of the finances. She would know something was wrong."

"Yeah! He needs money so he goes to Stephanie, who has more of it than anyone on this street. Were the two of them friends?"

"They went to high school together, and they seemed pretty close. Rachel didn't seem like a huge fan of Stephanie, but then again, no one really was. Sawyer and Stephanie were definitely friends. So he goes to her, and she's willing to help him, but for a price. They work out this deal, and everything's fine until a few days before her death."

"I bet you that phone call I heard and those text messages were from him. Their deal must've gone south," I add.

"But it still doesn't add up. Why did he need money? And why did everything fall apart?"

I start biting my fingernails, mulling all of this over. He and Stephanie worked out some sort of deal. I'm willing to bet she gave him money in turn for drugs, but that doesn't explain how he got his hands on them or why she needed them. I feel like we need to talk to him. I want to be able to see who he is and have a better idea of his character.

"We should meet with him, Hazel," I say.

"What do you mean?" she raises an eyebrow.

"We should go talk to him. We can subtly ask around and see if we can pull any information out of him without him knowing."

"How would we explain why two seventeen-year-old girls want to go hang out with *him*?"

I think for a moment and then say, "You could pretend you want to be a surgeon after high school. You can ask him if you can talk to him about med school and all that stuff. I'll just tag along."

Her eyes light up at the thought of it, "That sounds a little crazy."

"Wanna' hear a crazier idea?" she nods, but I don't think she's ready for what I'm about to suggest. "If we get Shea or Graeson to help, you can have your conversation with him while we see if we can find any clues inside his house."

Hazel's eyes bulge, and she shakes her head, "We can't break into another person's house!"

"Just think about," I say. "We can regroup tomorrow."

It's quiet for a few minutes, only the sound of the wind ruffling the bushes and a neighbor mowing his lawn fills my ears.

"Did you patch things up with Shea?" she asks quietly.

I forgot I hadn't had a chance to tell Hazel about this yet. I fill her in on all of the little details as she gushes and blushes like it were her own story I was telling.

"Oh my God!" she exclaims. "That's so great! I'm so happy for you! I feel like the old Shea is back. We lost him for a little while, but you brought him back."

I smile, "He brought me back. I've been going through a rough patch, but everything seems to be okay now. It's not just Shea, it's you too, Hazel. All of you, even Graeson. I've never had friends like this."

Hazel opens her mouth to reply, but our sappy conversation is suddenly interrupted by a shrieking, panicked voice.

"Stop! Stop chasing me! Leave me alone! Stop! Stop!" the voice screeches.

I spring up from the lawn chair, instinctively searching for the source of the noise. Whoever is making this sound sounds like they're struggling. Hazel and I both start running around the side of the house in the direction of the screaming.

"Stop chasing me! Stop! Leave me alone! Leave me alone!" the person howls.

As we curl around my house, I catch sight of a dark haired man running up the sidewalk and into my yard. He screams, a screeching, strained noise pouring from the depths of his throat. He runs clumsily, but with an urgent purpose, thrashing his arms as he glances behind him every few seconds. "Stop chasing me! Stop!" he continues to shriek. There's no one behind him. There's no one in sight as far down the street as I can see.

"Easton," Hazel sighs. When she says his name, I can place who he is. This is the boy I saw at Stephanie's wake who stood with his mother. Easton Black. I remember the way his slate grey eyes darted around the room as his mother tried to pull his attention towards her, instead of his thoughts. I can't imagine what it's like for him, constantly being trapped inside his mind with no escape.

Hazel walks over to him, and at first I'm unsure what she plans on doing. She approaches him, blocking his path of travel. For a minute, I'm almost positive he's going to run her down.

"Easton," she raises her voice so she can be heard over his screaming. "Easton!"

He stops suddenly in his tracks, seemingly stunned by Hazel's presence. He slows his body down, but continues to ferociously whip his head around behind him, searching for the invisible aggressor.

"They're after me!" His voice is panicked and shrill.

"Easton," Hazel's voice is loud, but kind. "You're okay. They're not chasing you."

"Yes they are! They're out to get me!"

I feel helpless as I stand here, and something about the whole situation leaves an eerie feeling in my stomach. These monsters chasing him aren't real, they're in his head. I can't tell what's more terrifying.

"Easton, I promise they're not behind you. They're not chasing you. Just come here," she motions for him to walk closer to her.

He obeys, taking slow hesitant steps towards Hazel. He mutters under his breath. "They're out to get me."

"Have you learned any new songs on the piano?" she asks to distract him.

He paces in a circle around Hazel, whispering under his breath, "I saw him. I saw him with the gun."

This sends a tingling chill down my spine that spreads into my shoulders and down my arms. Goosebumps erupt on my limbs, causing the hairs on my arms to stand up. Who did he see with the gun? Is it conjecture from his imagination or is there a layer of truth behind it? I walk closer to Hazel and Easton, slowly inching my way forward so I don't scare him.

"Tell me about the song you learned on the piano. What's it called?" she asks him again.

He stopped pacing, but his body seems to be in a state of constant motion. He bounces up and down on his toes, and his fingers shake at his sides.

"The song — it was by Elton John. It's called "I'm Still Standing," he replies, focusing on Hazel's question.

Easton spends the next few minutes telling Hazel all about his piano, but I'm not really paying attention to what he's saying. All I can think of is what he said about the gun. I know he has schizophrenia, but there's something about this that stands out. Something I can't quite put my finger on. It's like a polaroid picture that hasn't finished developing.

"Who are you?" Easton turns his attention to me.

"I'm Hazel's friend," I say as calmly as I can manage. "My name is Izzie." I reach out to shake his hand, but he rips his arm away from me and stumbles back a few steps.

"Are you one of them?" he quivers.

"No," Hazel chimes in. "Easton, this is my best friend. She moved into this house a few weeks ago."

"I don't like this house. I don't like this house. I don't like this house," he repeats.

"You know I wouldn't lie to you, Easton. This is my best friend. She's not out to get you." Hazel's explanation seems satisfactory enough for Easton. He releases the tension in his shoulders and stops bouncing up and down. His black hair is plastered with sweat to the side of his face and parts of his forehead, most likely from running for his life.

"Let's walk you home to your mom," Hazel says gently. "I bet she misses you."

He starts fiddling with his fingers again, but follows Hazel's lead down to the sidewalk. He says in a casual tone, "My mom doesn't believe me. She's not taking it seriously, says it's my mind tricking me. But I saw him. The man. He had a gun. He was hurting her."

Hazel and I exchange a look that screams *what the hell?* I can see the anxiety swimming in her eyes.

I ask him quietly, "Who was this man? Where did you see him?"

He just shakes his head, "He's watching. He's always watching."

"Easton," I say louder. "Who was this man?"

"They're out to get me," he says in an unusually calm and monotone voice.

We've lost him. Just like that, he's slipped from the grasp of reality and is once again lost within his own head.

We reach the Black household, and before we even get to the front steps, the door flings open. The woman dashes down the steps to Easton and wraps him in her arms, holding on to him for dear life. Her pepper grey hair is askew, and her makeup looks only half done. It's like she started getting ready, but never had a chance to finish. At the wake she looked so distinguished, but here she looks small and weak.

"Easton," her voice is strong. "You cannot run off like that. You made me very scared."

I'm surprised with how calm her voice is. She appears to be a bit of a nervous wreck, but manages to conceal that while she's talking to her son. However, her words are useless as Easton falls deeper into his mind. Lilian walks him over to a rocking chair on the front porch, and once she gets him settled she makes her way back over to us.

"I can't thank you two girls enough. I was getting ready in the bathroom, and he was playing his piano. A few minutes later I go to check on him, and he's gone. He's quick. We've been having a hard time lately, he's been particularly stressed out. Yesterday I found a stack of his Seroquels under his pillow. He's been hiding his meds because he's worried they're poisoned. I'm so sorry for any trouble we've caused you," she says with a hint of worry in her voice.

"It was no trouble Mrs. Black," Hazel replies. "I'm sorry you guys are going through a rough patch."

"You're too kind, dear," Lillian says before thanking us again and turning back to tend to Easton.

Hazel and I start walking away, and when we're out of ear shot, I say to her, "I know this is going to sound insane, but what if Easton saw the person who killed Stephanie?"

"I don't know," Hazel's voice shakes. "That whole thing is making me feel . . . anxious. I tried to get him to talk about the piano. He really likes the piano. It helps distract him from his thoughts." As she talks I notice her face looks as if she's just bitten into a lemon.

I know trusting the guy with schizophrenia and taking his words to be fact may sound a bit, well, irrational, but there was something about the way he spoke to us that made me feel like Easton knew what he was talking about. When he was running and saying people were out to get him, he was disconnected and panicked. But when he was talking about the man with the gun, he was calm and seemed to be in touch with reality. He knew what he was talking about. He had to. I feel like I'm grasping at straws. Maybe I'm becoming so paranoid that I'm jumping on invisible leads, following threads of evidence that don't lead anywhere. But when Easton said "he's watching," it pulled me back to that first night I met Stephanie, when she told me that "he knew all their secrets." If there's any truth in Easton's words, I bet the "he" in each of their stories is the same person.

207

"I guess it's possible that Easton saw the person, especially if he's been running off and not taking his meds. We should try to talk to him again. We'll have to be subtle about it though because it seems wrong to force information out of someone who is mentally unstable," Hazel says.

We pass the St. James house, which makes me realize I never stopped by Hannah's house to get that book. I'm out of things to read, and if I have any hope of getting some sleep tonight, I need to get that book.

"Hannah said she has a book for me. Would you mind going with me to get it quick?" I ask Hazel who says that she wouldn't mind at all.

We trudge up the sloping driveway, which has chalk scribbles over most of the black concrete. Beckett and Hannah's lush green lawn is scattered with various bikes, scooters, and balls. Their house looks like a loving and comforting place, somewhere their kids would grow up feeling safe and secure and happy. You look at their house and you have no idea about the issues and the pain they're going through. You see this beautiful house, but you don't see the cracked foundation. A family's entire life is lived inside those four walls, but we see nothing more than the bricks and the flowers on the outside.

We step up to the red brick house and knock on the door. A few moments later I hear faint footsteps on the inside, and Hannah opens with the red headed baby attached to her hip.

"Hi, girls," she greets the two of us with a bright smile. "Come on in. Are you coming for the book?"

I nod my head, and for a minute feel bad that I'm only here to take a book and go home. As soon as I walk inside, the house hits me with a feeling of comfort and warmth. It gives me the same feeling that my old yellow house in Portland once did. Family photos fill the walls and a large, brick fireplace sits center stage in the living room. Children's toys are thrown about, but the mess only brings out the house's character. It's so different from Stephanie's, which was so eerily perfect it felt more like a creepy set of a horror movie than a home. The toddler with glasses is deeply asleep on the couch with a pale blue blanket laying over him.

She catches me looking over at him and says, "Brennan played a little too hard today."

"Thank you so much for letting me borrow the book," I say to make conversation.

"Of course," Hannah replies. "I'm just happy that people your age still read."

She leads us into the kitchen where her daughter stands on a stool in front of the kitchen island stirring a bowl of brownie batter. Her bronze curls are styled in pigtails and chocolate coats her cheeks and lips. Music hums from a small speaker that hangs out on the copper and white swirled granite countertops.

"Hazel!" she cheers as she jumps off her stool and runs over to hug Hazel.

"Hi, Vivienne!" Hazel smiles and hugs the little girl.

Hannah, Hazel, and I talk for a little while about high school and summer vacations. I want so badly to blurt out that I know about Beckett and to ask if she's okay, but I feel like that might make everything worse.

"I have that book right upstairs," Hannah starts. "I'll be right back."

Hannah leaves the kitchen with Boston in her arms, while Hazel and I listen to Vivienne tell us some story I'm not really paying attention to. Suddenly I hear sirens wailing, the sound of it pierces my ears. The shrieking noise becomes increasingly louder with every passing second. Curiosity takes over, so I walk to the front door and peek out. Three police cars zoom down the street, their flashing lights blur together, filling my eyes with red and blue streaks. This can't be good. The wail of the sirens sucks me out of reality and suddenly a memory forces into my head. The image is so clear, so vivid, it's terrifying.

My phone on my nightstand rings, a shrieking, wailing sound. The noise drills into my ears, causing the pounding in my head to increase. I reluctantly turn over. It's some number from Arizona, just someone trying to sell me something. Everything feels blurry. My throat is dry, so dry I can't swallow. I need water. I push myself up in bed and step out of the covers. I'm still in my clothes and my shoes from the party. My body feels heavy, like I'm carrying around bags of flour. I have to stop and steady myself on my bed. I creep downstairs, forcing my way through the darkness that fills the hallways and the rooms of my house. I reach the kitchen and pour myself a glass of water. The liquid whirls around in the glass as it drips from the pitcher. I struggle to keep my sluggish eyes open. And then I hear a sound. I can't process it at first, but it's coming from outside. I hear it again, this time the noise is clearer, crisper. It's a woman laughing. I walk closer. No, she's not laughing. She's screaming. She's howling. She's screeching. I reach the slider, and the noise stops suddenly. I hear gasping, as if someone is just catching their breath. Or losing it. I place my hand on the slider, the glass feels cold against my skin. What is going on? Everything is hazy and blurry. Is this a dream? I stick my head out, I'm not sure why I don't feel scared. The darkness is so thick it covers my eyes like a mask. But I see the woman. On the cold concrete. She's laying down, still trying to catch her breath. I hear rustling. I look up and catch a glimpse of a shadowy figure. It's gone before I have a chance to get a good look, but I catch a black shoe shuffling through the grass. I glance back at the woman. Her eyes meet mine, and for a moment the two of us stare intently at each other. She was screaming, but she doesn't look scared anymore. I think she needs help. I step outside. The air feels cold on my skin. I take a step. And then another. The woman. She's silent, laying rigid and motionless on the ground. Shadows dance across the patio. Everything goes black.

I don't have time to be horrified by the memory because the sound of the sirens ceases and is replaced by an eerie silence. A silence that tells you something bad is coming. I hear a harsh knock at the door. Something inside of me knows, but my brain can't grasp the situation. Hannah moves to answer the door. I hadn't even realized she was back downstairs. She opens the door a sliver and a stream of daylight pours into the house. The person on the other side pushes the door open further, but my view is blocked by Hannah's body.

"Hannah St. James," the voice says. "You are under arrest for the murder of Stephanie Kester. You have the right to remain silent."

CHAPTER 11 - Yesterday

Take me back to yesterday.

The haunting melody of Yesterday by the Beatles echoes from the speaker and tiptoes around the house, lingering in the silence like an unwanted guest. I remember this song from a long time ago. My dad used to play it on his guitar when I was little. He'd play when I couldn't sleep or when I was scared. Something about the melody always made me feel calm. But now it sounds ominous, making me feel like there's someone lurking in the shadows, watching all of this unfold. For a few seconds, no one moves. Hannah stands as still as a statue, still blocking my vision of the people at the door. The panic swirling in my stomach is making me sick, and I feel like I'm about to throw up.

Yesterday slipped from my grip the way summer gives way to autumn.

The initial shock fades and so does the silence. Suddenly, everything starts moving even faster than before, like a machine on overdrive. It's like time is trying to make up for the last few seconds we spent paralyzed in the gut-wrenching news. Hannah moves away from the door, daylight pouring through and stinging my eyes. I realize there is more than one person at the door. There's a stocky bald man in a police uniform, and next to him is a familiar face I have no interest in seeing. Detective Heights. Oh God. Behind her is Detective Burnside, who fidgets with his sleeve, while Detective Heights rattles off some rehearsed script you always hear in movies when someone is arrested. She sounds like a chihuahua on caffeine as she talks a mile a minute, not even giving Hannah a second to process the news. I stand there with my mouth gaping and my eyes like a deer in the headlights. I want to do something, but my body won't move.

Yesterday shattered in my hands like broken glass, leaving behind scars on my palms.

Hannah turns her back to the door slowly. The color has drained from her face, making her look sickly and ghost like. She bites her lip hard, drops of blood starting to pool at the surface. She walks a few steps closer to me and Hazel. "Will you watch them until Beckett comes home?" Her voice is oddly monotone, but fragile, as if it's about to break at any second. I try to answer, but all of the words have been sucked from my throat. I nod as she places the baby in my arms. I notice her hands are violently shaking, like one of those massage chairs they have in the mall. I grasp the baby, clinging onto him for dear life, but I'm not sure if I'm trying to protect him or comfort myself. He starts fussing as Hannah places him in my arms, his squeaky wail making tears brim in my eyes. She kisses him gently on the head, like she's saying goodbye. "Mommy!" Vivienne cries. She's holding on to Hazel's shirt, clinging to the fabric with every bone in her body. Vivienne dashes up to her mom, tears slowly rolling down her cheeks. "Mommy, don't go!" She throws herself into Hannah's body, wrapping her tiny arms around her neck and burying her face in Hannah's shoulder. "Mommy has to go away for a little while, but I'll be back soon. Daddy's going to take good care of you. I love you, honey." She pulls Vivienne away from her shoulder so she can look her in the eye. Hannah lovingly wipes away the tears from her face. "No, mommy, you can't go!" Vivienne is screaming. Hannah tries to turn back to the officers, but Vivienne won't let her go. Like a toddler hanging onto a toy she doesn't want to share, she hangs on to Hannah with everything she has. Hazel, with tears trickling down her cheeks, steps in. She pulls Vivienne back and holds on to the little girl's trembling body.

213

Vivienne thrashes around, desperately trying to break out of Hazel's grip and screaming. I hear Hannah's heavy and hollow breathing. She bends over and kisses the little boy sleeping on the couch. He's lost in his own dream world and has no clue that when he wakes up, his mother will be gone. My hands are shaking as I hold on to the baby, bouncing him gently to stop his crying.

Yesterday disappeared like a missing child, lost to the shadows.

She walks up to the officers, and presents her hands. Detective Heights orders her to turn around. For someone so small, her presence seems to consume the whole room. Hannah's face is blank, stripped of all emotion. She doesn't cry or scream or proclaim her innocence. Instead, she does as she's told, like a lamb on its way to the slaughter. It would be so much easier to watch if she put up a fight, if she cried and screamed. I wish she'd cry or try to tell them she's innocent. But she doesn't fight. She's defeated. Completely and utterly defeated.

Yesterday faded away like a moment becoming a memory.

Stephanie stole her husband, and now she's stealing her life. Is this what love turns into? One day you're happily in love and the next you're on your way to jail for the murder of your husband's mistress. But she didn't do it. I know she didn't do it. There's a strong burning in my chest, making me feel like there's fire in my lungs. The officers escort Hannah out of the house in silence. Why is this so easy for them? She's an innocent, young mother of three, and they're destroying her life like it's nothing. It's easy for them to squash a family between their fingers.

Yesterday whispered into the wind the forgotten lyrics, the anthem of the broken and the hopeless and the lost.

"Stop!" The sound of my voice surprises me. "No! You can't take her! She didn't do it! She's innocent!"

I feel like a little kid, throwing a tantrum, and I suddenly realize why Hannah remained emotionless. It's easier to make a clean break, to walk away with any shred of dignity you have left. It's not like crying and screaming is going to change their minds. It's just going to make you look stupid. I don't know why I feel like this will help. I guess putting up a fight makes me feel like I tried, makes me feel like I'm less helpless than I actually am.

Detective Heights gazes over at me, her posture rigid and stiff. The panic looming in my eyes is reflected in her pearl grey irises. In that moment, I realize that she's just as scared as I am. She knows that arresting Hannah isn't right. She knows that she didn't kill Stephanie. But there's some evidence that's pointing in Hannah's direction. Evidence that Detective Heights, despite her fierce determination, cannot refute. The question is, what do they have on her? The bigger question: if Hannah didn't do it, does that mean the killer's still lurking around town?

My body is shaking as Detective Heights nods her head at me. Maybe it's me reading into it, but I swear that that was her way of telling me she was going to do everything she could to help Hannah.

All too soon, the police escort Hannah out of the house, the door closing with a bang as they leave. Suddenly, Hannah is gone and a ghostly silence settles over the brick house.

Yesterday washed away with the tide, like forgotten objects carried out to sea.

The sirens begin shrieking again, the blue and red flashing lights seem to be screaming "guilty, guilty, guilty." The sound fades into the distance, but the events of the last few minutes still hang in the air like smoke from a burning building. Yesterday, Hannah had no idea she was about to be locked behind bars for a crime she didn't commit. Yesterday, Beckett had no clue that his little love affair would paint his wife as a criminal in everyone's eyes. Yesterday, their kids didn't know that they were going to lose their mother. Yesterday, life seemed a little brighter, a little clearer. Yesterday. Take me back to yesterday.

Yesterday left too soon, like a goodbye a moment too late.

*****

"They arrested the wrong person. I don't care what evidence they have. There's no way Hannah did it. She's being framed," I say passionately to Shea.

The two of us are hanging out in my living room, waiting to meet up with the others later today to go talk to Dr. Hastings. He sits with his back against the linen colored couch cushions and his arm around me, and I lean up against him, feet curled onto the seat. I know I'm supposed to be worried about Hannah and that concerning memory I recovered, but right now, I'm just so happy to be here with him. It took us a while to get to this place, but now that we're here I don't ever want to leave.

"I can't believe you saw her get arrested. What did Beckett say when he got home?" Shea asks.

"Nothing," I complain. "Hazel and I had to explain what happened, and he just stood there completely stunned. He looked like he had tears in his eyes, but he wouldn't talk or even move. He didn't even thank us for watching his kids. But he seemed really shaken up."

"I just feel bad for their kids," he says.

"I can't even think about this right now," I sigh. "It's hurting my brain."

He smiles slightly, "Then let's talk about something else, and we'll worry about that when Hazel and Graeson get here."

"Should we talk about the schizophrenic who went for a jog in my backyard or the break-in we're about to commit?" I say sarcastically.

"You know, before you came here I had never broken into a house. I hadn't even gotten detention at school. Now, I'm on my second break-in in less than a week," he laughs.

216

"I seem to have that effect on people," I smile brightly as he pulls me closer and unexpectedly kisses me square on the lips. I kiss him back, running my fingers through the thick mop of caramel colored hair on his head, engulfed in the smell of his cologne. I could get used to this.

"Get a room!" I hear Graeson's loud, sarcastic voice.

Shea and I separate, and Shea looks at him and says, "Seriously, dude?"

Graeson smirks as I roll my eyes at him. Shea and I have kissed twice, and Graeson has ruined both. His timing seriously sucks.

"Why didn't you knock?" I roll my eyes. "You don't just walk into other people's houses."

He shrugs his shoulders, "You're about to break into a house, and you're upset that I didn't knock."

"Where's Hazel?" I ask him.

"She's on her way over. She should be here any minute," he replies.

I'm a little nervous to put this plan in action. After Hannah was arrested, Hazel said that she was willing to go talk to Dr. Hastings if it meant that we would have a chance to help her. So, she called him, told him she wanted to be a plastic surgeon when she grew up, and asked him if they could meet to talk about his career. Lucky for us, he was excited about the chance to talk to Hazel about his job. While Hazel talks to him, Shea, Graeson, and I are going to sneak in through his backdoor and rummage around his house to see if we can find anything that ties him to Stephanie's murder. Or at the very least tells us what his deal with Stephanie was about.

Luke comes running down the stairs and into the kitchen, the burner phone in his hand, with a big smile on his face.

"What are you so excited about?" I ask jokingly.

"I traced the blocked ID and found the number of the phone it's tied to!" he says excitedly.

He starts rambling, trying to articulate to us how he figured it all out. I don't have the heart to tell him I'm too much of an idiot to understand anything he's saying.

"Wait, Luke, slow down! What are you saying in dumb people words?" I ask him.

"I was able to trace the blocked ID and find an actual phone number. We can call the number and figure out who it is!" His eyes light up like a little kid in Disney World for the first time. Excitement and adrenaline start rushing through my body. This is huge. Whoever this is was threatening to murder Stephanie. Whether or not they were the one to actually pull the trigger, I'm not sure. It seems like a lot of people wanted Stephanie dead. Richard, Beckett, Hannah, Sawyer, and those are just the people I know about. But whoever the blocked ID is may have killed her or at the very least have information we could use.

"Oh my God!" I hug Luke, who seems a little concerned with my excitement. "That's amazing!"

"We should call it!" Graeson says, his eyes lit up like a Christmas tree. "I should be the one to call. I used to prank call people all the time."

"I don't think that has anything to do with this," Shea says jokingly shaking his head at Graeson's stupidity. "But this is really good news."

At that moment, Hazel knocks on the door, and I race to answer it so we can fill her in, but not before I say to Graeson, "See, that's what you're supposed to do before you barge in."

When Hazel comes inside we all rush to tell her what Luke found, each of us spewing words at her as fast as we can.

Hazel squints at us and starts twirling her golden curls around her finger, "Slow down, I'm not getting any of this."

Graeson, Shea, and I shut up and let Luke explain it to her because in all honesty, we have no clue how he figured it out.

"You're a genius!" she exclaims, smiling at Luke. "Seriously, I don't know how you figured that out, but it's amazing!"

Luke turns crimson, his face blushing like there's no tomorrow, and I eye him suspiciously.

"It's no big deal," he tries to play it cool.

"Yes it is! We have to call . . . now," Hazel says enthusiastically.

"Like right now?" Graeson asks, "I was really looking forward to another break-in."

"We can't wait around anymore. Every minute we waste is another minute Hannah spends rotting away in a jail cell for a murder she didn't commit," Hazel replies.

"Jeez, Hazel, that was harsh," Shea says.

"Let's call now, and then we'll go meet with Sawyer," I speak up. "Hazel's right, we don't have time to wait around."

"What are we supposed to say if this person answers?" Shea asks.

"Anything really, you just have to keep them talking long enough so we can see if we know whose voice it is," Luke replies.

"Let's just pretend to sell something," I say, "I can do the talking."

"Are you sure about that?" Luke questions, "You jumble up your words sometimes."

"I do not! I'm great with my words," I say looking at my feet because I'm too embarrassed to meet his eyes. Everyone knows I suck at using words, but I'm too proud to admit it. "Come on, I know I can do this."

Luke and the others agree to let me do the talking, much to Graeson's dismay, who was hoping he would get a chance to show off his prank calling skills. The phone is poised in the middle of us

219

on the granite countertops. I take a deep breath, inhaling all the confidence I can, and hit the call button. The whole house falls silent. The only noise comes from the quiet hum of the refrigerator. Five rings and the phone goes to voicemail. Each of us simultaneously release the breath we had been holding while waiting. Well that was anticlimactic.

"One more time," Hazel says to Luke who nods his head.

The phone begins to ring again as I take another deep breath, trapping the air in my lungs and holding it there until my chest feels like it's about to burst. It rings once, twice, three times, four, five, and then as I'm about to give up, I hear a quiet rustling sound.

"Hello?" asks a silvery, feminine voice.

Uh-oh. I start fumbling for my words, my mind drawing a complete and total blank. I glance over at Luke, who's standing wide-eyed, wondering what on God's green Earth I'm waiting for. He shoots me an exasperated look, daggers flying out of his eyes and into my soul.

"Hello," I reply slowly, unsure of what I'm about to say next. "I work for the Knox Hollow Gas and Electric Company, and I'm calling to see if you'd be willing to answer a few questions for a survey the city is conducting?"

"You work for the gas and electric company?" she sounds suspicious. "You sound a little young."

Feeling self-conscious, I make my voice deeper, "I get that a lot, but yes, I work for the gas and electric company. I just have a few questions if you could spare five minutes of your time." My attempt at a deeper voice sends Graeson over the edge. He tries to stop the snickering, placing his hand over his mouth, but that only makes more noise. Hazel pushes him, motioning for him to go into the other room so we don't blow our cover.

"Alright, fine," she sounds annoyed, like she's far too important to be listening to me.

I hadn't thought this far into this plan, but then again when do I ever actually think things through? So far no one seems to recognize the mystery caller's voice. And what was I thinking with gas and electricity? What the hell kind of questions am I supposed to ask?

"Okay, here we go. Do you use gas or electric appliances?"

There's more rustling on the other line, making it sound like she's moving around. She says, "I'm not sure about that. My husband deals with all that kind of stuff, you might be better off talking to him."

All of a sudden, Hazel springs up from the chair she was sitting in, eyes wide like a kid who's downed one too many pixie sticks. She starts mouthing something to me, her mouth making incomprehensible movements that I can't decipher into words. Her hands start flailing and she mouths the word "paper." Luke scrambles to get a piece of paper and a pen for Hazel, who's silently freaking out. Shea points to the phone and motions for me to keep the conversation going.

Meanwhile, the mystery lady is waiting for me to respond. She says, "Are you still there?"

I force my attention away from the spectacle unfolding in my kitchen and say, "Okay, thank you, I will make note of that. Question two, what is the average temperature you keep your house at in the summer and the winter?"

"I think we keep it around seventy-four in the winter and seventy-two in the summer. I'm always cold so our temperature is a little high," her voice seems to have softened, the annoyance faded into a sweet and subtle tone.

Luke goes on a rampage through the kitchen drawers as Hazel is literally shaking, eyes lit up like New York City, while Graeson is bent over hysterically laughing. I hear a bang on the other line and then the rev of a car engine just starting up.

I try to keep her talking, waiting for Hazel's revelation. I ask, "Are you satisfied with the price you're paying for gas and electric?"

"I assume so. I'd have to ask my husband. He deals with all of our finances. I could give you his number. He'd be able to give you more accurate information," she replies.

I look to Shea who nods at me, and I say, "That would be great."

"His number in 413-555-7817," she recites the phone number, her voice sounding far more at ease than it was when she first answered. I repeat the number in my head until it's burned into my brain. It makes me laugh at how stupid people can be. She was more than willing to give her husband's phone number to someone impersonating a gas and electric company worker. If I asked for her social security number she'd probably give me that too.

I look up to see that Luke has finally found paper, and Hazel is scribbling something on the white sheet. She quickly writes and then shoves the paper in the middle of the table so Graeson, Shea, and I can see.

In tiny, neat handwriting the name *Isla Grimaldi* is printed across the paper in black ink. It takes a minute, but then I remember the porcelain doll like young girl who basically made out with her old husband at Stephanie's very eventful wake. The soft, silvery voice definitely matches her petite figure and mysterious personality.

"Are you sure?" I mouth to her.

She mouths back, "I think so."

An idea pops into my head. It's a long shot, but it just might work. If she really is as naive as she seems, we might be one step closer to finding Stephanie's murderer and saving Hannah.

"Our company is planning to add some new gas lines to different areas in town. If you don't mind me asking, what's your address?"

The line is quiet for a moment, and then she says, "Twenty-four Mayflower Circle."

I race over to the window and look down the street. Sure enough, there's a black car pulling out of the driveway of the house marked 24 Mayflower Circle.

*****

"What does this mean!?" I ask, excitement running rampant in my body.

"I don't even know!" Hazel exclaims.

"How did you recognize her voice?" Shea asks. "We barely ever see her."

"It sounded familiar. She and Thomas were in front of me and my family when we were in line for Stephanie's wake. She sounded annoyed when she first started talking to you, but as you went on she became friendlier, and it reminded me of the way she talked to him. There was a . . . softness . . . in her voice."

"I can't believe she gave us her address," Luke says. "That was almost too easy."

"But why was Isla threatening Stephanie? I don't know her too well, but she seems nice enough, not like someone who would threaten to brutally murder someone," Shea adds.

"Stephanie brought out the worst in people," Hazel replies.

"What's the deal with her husband?" I ask, "Isn't he . . . like . . . ancient?"

Hazel begins to fill us in, "He's about forty, and she's around twenty-four. He moved in here with his first wife maybe ten or so years ago. They got divorced a few years back and somehow he kept the house. About a year and a half ago, Isla moved in. No one really knows how they ended up together, but it's pretty weird. Not to mention, they're big fans of PDA."

"How do you remember all of this?" Graeson asks, perplexed at Hazel's precise retelling of their ages and timeline.

"I have a really good memory. Little details just stick in my brain," she replies.

"Do you know what he does for a living?" Luke asks, his eyes squinted the way he does when he's thinking really hard about something. I can tell he's onto something, but I'm just not sure what. His brain is spinning, an idea developing and forming in his head.

"He's an English professor at Williams College," Hazel replies confidently.

"And how old did you say she was?" Luke adds.

"Twenty-four," Hazel replies, as I sit back wondering what Luke is piecing together.

"That means she would've graduated two years ago," he thinks out loud.

"That's kind of how math works, genius," I say sarcastically.

Luke rolls his eyes at me and then says, "You wouldn't happen to know what college she went to?"

Hazel shakes her head, and I suddenly realize where Luke's train of thought is headed. I have to admit, it's pretty clever and makes perfect sense. I raise an eyebrow at Luke, urging him to go on and fill us in on what he's thinking.

He takes a breath in, "It's kind of a long shot, but if she went to Williams, he could've been her teacher. The timing of everything would match up. Say they met sometime during her first two years at school. They caught some feelings, but knew it was dangerous and inappropriate. So they kept it a secret until she graduated, and after that, they could do whatever they wanted."

Wow. My brain is reeling, trying to take in all of the information Luke is laying down. But that still doesn't explain why Isla was threatening to strangle Stephanie. Unless . . .

"Oh my God!" I blurt out to the alarm of everyone else in the room, "What if Stephanie found out about them and threatened to go to the Board at Williams. That would've destroyed Thomas's career and their relationship. Maybe Isla was trying to protect them."

"Why would Stephanie want to expose them? Hazel asks curiously.

"Why did Stephanie do anything she did?" Shea asks rhetorically.

"I'm not sure," Graeson cuts in. "But if we don't leave now, we're going to be late to meet with Dr. Hastings."

*****

Hazel and Sawyer sit in wood rocking chairs on the Hastings' front porch, while Luke stands guard on our front porch, watching across the street to make sure Dr. Hastings doesn't go inside and our cover isn't blown. Graeson, Shea, and I have successfully snuck through to their backyard and are now climbing up the wooden stairs to the deck above. Hazel babysits for the Hastings so she remembered that Rachel works late on Wednesdays. As long as she keeps him talking, we should be able to search through the house without any trouble. After the last break-in, I don't want any more close calls.

We climb up the wooden stairs, the late afternoon sun fading behind the clouds and giving way to the cooler night air. The Hastings' deck is something straight out of a Pottery Barn catalogue. Massive teal pots of brightly colored flowers stand at the corners of the frame adding a vibrant character to the space. In the middle of the deck, there are two love seats with cream cushions and navy blue pillows facing each other with an orangey

225

wood table in between them. Vases of red and yellow petunias and green succulents sit on top of the coffee table and twinkle lights are strung along the railings. I can picture Rachel and Sawyer sitting out here on quiet Sunday mornings, sipping their coffee and on Thursday nights after a long day at work, enjoying a bottle of wine while talking about the surgeries they performed.

Graeson steps up to the slider door and tries to tug it open, but it doesn't budge. He glances back at me and Shea, furrowing his brow. He yanks at it a couple more times with no luck. I step up to the door and start pulling at it myself. Not that I thought the door would magically open because *I* was yanking at it, but Graeson's not always the brightest bulb, so I had to check for myself.

"Are you freaking kidding me?" I run my fingers forcefully through my hair. We had covered everything from keeping Sawyer distracted to checking Rachel's work schedule to even having a lookout watching over the whole scene. But we did not account for the door being locked. The one time I actually think something through and it still goes wrong. I throw my head back, looking up at the sky as if I'm waiting for the universe to give me some sort of sign. And then I see it. A little bit above the rail of the deck is an open window. It's only about five feet up. If I stood on the moderately steady rail, I'm pretty sure I could reach the window and pull myself up using my nonexistent arm muscles.

"That window is open," I say casually, pointing to it.

Shea and Graeson's jaws drop as they stare at me like I've completely lost it. Well . . . maybe I have. Graeson starts laughing and then says, "Good one."

"No, I'm serious. If you guys help me onto the rail, I can reach the edge of the window, pull myself up, and then let you guys in," I respond while they continue looking at me like I have three heads.

"Okay, Spiderman. Go ahead and scale the wall," Graeson replies sarcastically.

"Izzie, this is a terrible idea. What if you fall?" Shea asks, concern coating his voice.

"Then hopefully I'll land on my feet," I respond. "It's the only way in. We're wasting time. Hannah's sitting in a jail cell right now and being crucified by the entire town. If I have to climb through a window to get her out of there then so be it."

Graeson jokingly whispers to Shea, "I don't think we can stop her."

"Okay," Shea says, "but I'll climb through the window. I don't want you to get hurt."

"That's sweet, but there's no way either of you will fit through it."

"Oh, I'm not offering to climb in for you," Graeson smirks.

Shea and I both glare at him, and I say sarcastically, "I don't know what we would do without your help."

I'm done wasting time — who knows how long Hazel can keep Dr. Hastings talking — so I step up to the rail.

"Wait," Shea calls out. "At least let me help you. Graeson, go down below the window so if she slips, you can catch her or at least break her fall."

Graeson scrunches up his face in protest, but Shea tells him to go. Shea takes my hand and helps me onto the rail. My knees feel wobbly on the thin piece of wood. I clutch onto his hand, using him to steady my body. When I've found enough balance, I reach my hands up, searching for a good grip on the windowsill. My legs are shaking, feeling like globs of jiggly jello. I press my hands as hard as I can into the ledge, pulling my body up with the strength of my noodle arms. I push myself up until my chest is almost even with the ledge. Sweat starts to gather in my palms, loosening my grip on the windowsill. Suddenly, my left hand slips. Adrenaline starts racing through my veins, and my heart falls into my stomach as I hang on by a couple sweaty fingers. I hear Shea yell something, and then he reaches to me, trying to save me from falling. With everything I have in me I cling to the window and try to get my left hand back on the windowsill. Somehow I manage to do it. I grab the ledge, clutching onto it for dear life. As quickly as I can, I once again push my body upwards, feeling the muscles in my arms rippling in fatigue. When my ribcage is level with the window, I slide my head and stomach in and hover over their kitchen counter. I swing my legs in, and soon enough, I'm safe inside. That was one of the most terrifying experiences of my life. My heart is still pounding through my chest and my legs feel like thin, limp spaghetti noodles. I crouch down, touching the floor with my hands and thanking my lucky stars that I'm on solid ground.

After taking a moment to ground myself — literally and figuratively — I dash to the slider to unlock the door. Shea and Graeson come running in. Shea rushes over to me, nervousness written all over his face, and he wraps his arms around me, pulling me tight into his chest.

"Never scare me like that again," his grip is tight in my arms, but he releases when Graeson clears his throat to remind us that we'd better get moving.

Our plan is to split up: Shea will take the upstairs, I'll take the ground floor, and Graeson will take the basement. That way we can check the whole house in less time than if we were searching together.

I take a deep breath in, still shocked from almost falling from the window, and say, "Let's go. Keep your phones on and meet back here in 15 minutes."

The three of us go off in our separate directions, unsure of exactly what we're looking for. The Hastings' house is designed with bright splashes of color and unique decorations that somehow work together. I wander around aimlessly for a few seconds, trying to take everything in and figure out where to start. If I were Sawyer, where would I hide something so Rachel wouldn't know? I walk through the kitchen and past the living room where there is a wall of black and white photographs of their family in various colored frames. A picture of Sawyer and Rachel in their scrubs smiling together at the hospital catches my eye, along with one of Rachel and their baby on the beach. I can't imagine there'd be much in there, so I pass through the dining room. There's something strange about an empty house. Next to the dining room is a white painted door. With curiosity filling my brain, I quietly creak open the door, feeling the cool metal of the door handle in my sweaty palms. The door conceals a large office space. The walls are painted a deep grey, and there's a heavy, dark wooden desk in the middle of the room facing the wall with neat stacks of papers and files, jars of pens and pencils, and few photographs. On the wall to my left is a massive bookshelf filled with what seems like hundreds of medical related books, and on the wall to my right Sawyer's degrees are displayed. Now this is the perfect place for him to hide something from his wife.

I start pushing papers around on his desk and opening drawers, each of them filled with ordinary and boring contents. My heartbeat echoes in my ears, sounding like the hands of a ticking clock. I kneel down to open the last wooden door, and it won't budge. It's locked. I look around the room for a key, searching back through the drawers, desk top, and anywhere else a key might be. I can't find anything, but I remember reading once in a book about how some detective used a paperclip to crack a lock. I find a paper clip holding together a stack of papers and carefully slip it off. I unwind the paperclip until it's as straight as an arrow, and then force it into the lock, twisting it every which way. Suddenly, the lock makes a clicking noise, and the drawer slides open ever so slightly. I can't believe that actually worked.

I pull the wooden drawer open, and . . . holy crap. The wind is sucked out of my lungs, the way a vacuum cleaner sucks up dirt particles. Sweat gathers in droplets at the top of my forehead as adrenaline pumps through my veins, sending a rush of nervous energy throughout my body. Even though it was a possibility lingering in my head, I hadn't really expected it to be true.

In the drawer lies two large, gallon sized plastic bags filled to the brim with orange bottles of pills labeled with various names of alarming, addictive drugs. What the hell is he doing with all these drugs? This has to be what he was secretly handing off to Stephanie, but the real question is why did she need them? And what did he do with the money he got in return?

I realize that there's something else in the drawer. I turn my focus to the small, rectangular object in the back corner. Gently, I reach my hand in, cautiously pulling out the item. I feel the cool, smooth surface of the object against my fingers. I see that the item is a cell phone, the newest model of the iPhone with a sleek white case. Who keeps their cell phone in a locked drawer? I hit the home button, and the iridescent light of the screen flashes in my eyes. One look of the lock screen and my mouth drops open in horror. Oh no.

CHAPTER 12 - Puzzle Pieces

"Richard?" Luke asks.

I shake my head, my high ponytail swinging back and forth, "He's like a giant teddy bear."

"Beckett?"

The name hangs in the air for a moment, "I just don't see it. No offense to him, but he doesn't seem clever enough to commit a murder and frame his wife for it."

"Hannah?"

I pucker my lips, thinking back over all of the information from the past few weeks, "No, I can't believe that."

"The police obviously have something on her, Iz. That's the key. We have to figure out what evidence they have. But I don't think we should count her out. She seems really nice, but you can't tell me it doesn't seem possible. Her husband was cheating on her with a woman whose favorite pastime was bullying her."

I shake my head again, but this time with more force, "It seems like everyone here is hiding something. Think about it: Beckett was cheating on his wife with Stephanie who was cheating on her husband. Isla was sending death threats to Stephanie who may have known about her and Thomas's inappropriate relationship. There's a schizophrenic who swears he saw a man with a gun, and I have no idea if I'm supposed to believe him. Sawyer's hiding drugs in his desk drawer and was secretly meeting with Stephanie to give them to her. We still have no clue why she needed them. Oh, and Alison blackmails people on the daily for money."

Luke starts laughing because this sounds so insanely ridiculous. I feel like normal people don't have to deal with these things. I still don't know what to make of that memory I seemed to have retrieved at Hannah's. I remember walking from my room and downstairs to get some water. I remember hearing a noise outside, a noise I couldn't really distinguish. Was it laughing? Or crying? I remember opening the slider and seeing the woman lying below, but that's all. The memory stops there. Like a book with the last chapter missing. I can't shake the anxiety that rises in my chest and compresses my lungs every time I try to think back and concentrate on the moment. In the back of my mind, there's a little whining voice that repeats "guilty, guilty, guilty" over and over again. If I could just remember what happened next I could gain a little clarity, perhaps a sense of relief. Was Stephanie already dead when I saw her? Or did I . . . kill her? I don't think I would ever do something like that, but I don't know if I trust myself.

"What about Sawyer?" Luke pulls me out of my thoughts.

"I could see that. From everything Hazel tells me, he's an older version of Graeson. Charming, but kind of an ass. Hazel said he likes to showboat and eats up compliments like candy. He probably thought that there was no way he'd get caught, and then things turned ugly. He tried to back out, but she wouldn't let him, threatened to ruin his life. The only way he could save his job and his family was by finishing her off. I still don't know why he needed money. Like Hazel said, he and his wife are pretty well off."

Luke's gaze lingers somewhere off in the distance, and I can tell he's not exactly paying attention to what I'm saying. Suddenly, his eyes perk up and he says, "Last night when the four of us were talking we couldn't figure out how he was getting his hands on all of those drugs."

I wrinkle my eyebrows, "Yeah, so?"

Yesterday, the five of us snuck into Sawyer and Rachel's house to see if we could find anything that tied him to Stephanie's murder. In one of his desk drawers, I found a stash of pills and a cell phone. When I clicked on the home button, the screen lit up with a picture of Stephanie's three kids. So, unless Sawyer has a freakish obsession with Stephanie's kids, he was hiding her phone in his desk, which does not fare too well for him. I took pictures of the contents of the drawer, but I couldn't take the actual phone because if I did, he would know someone was on to him. The one advantage we have is that he has no idea that we know about what he's hiding. Keeping this advantage is my top priority. But not having access to the phone leaves so many questions, the most important being why the hell does he have it? After all of that excitement, we spent hours combing through facts and trying to connect all of the dots. Hazel and Luke are going to start looking into Isla and Thomas, while the rest of us deal with coming up with a plan of attack for dealing with Sawyer. I may have meddled just a bit and purposefully made Hazel and Luke work together. This whole thing is like putting together a puzzle with missing pieces and no picture to go off of.

"He works at a hospital," Luke starts explaining his thinking. "We're so stupid. It was in front of us all along. Sawyer's a surgeon. He probably has access to every drug under the sun."

"I feel like an idiot. That makes a lot of sense. But why did Stephanie need drugs?"

"Why did Sawyer need money?" he answers me with a question.

I throw my head back dramatically and groan, "I miss Portland."

"I know, me too," Luke's expression softens. The room falls silent, each of us thinking about home. Even though I'm starting to feel like I belong here, there's still a part of me that misses the way life used to be, the days when the world seemed like a brighter place. The divorce was so long ago and those happy moments before everything crumbled are so far gone, the memories packed away in boxes in the attic collecting dust.

"What about Isla?" Luke asks, his voice cutting through the nostalgia that settled over the room.

"I could see it. People do crazy things for love. If Stephanie threatened to break them up, she may have threatened to kill her. Maybe it was just threats at first, but then her emotions got the best of her. But that's for you and Hazel to worry about. She's coming over to help me get ready in a little bit, but after I'm gone, maybe you two can get to know each other," I smirk.

Luke sighs and shakes his head, "Can you please leave this alone?"

"Come on," I tease. "You obviously have a thing for her."

"No, I don't," he stares at me, his emerald eyes hard and serious.

"You guys would be so cute together. Just tell me if you like her or not!"

"I don't want to talk about this with you," he laughs awkwardly as his face turns pink.

"Oh, so do you want to talk about it with Hazel?" I add in slyly.

"You're so annoying," he says, but then pauses. "Say, hypothetically, that I did like Hazel. I could ask her out without any help from you."

I go to reply, but then I hear footsteps down the stairs, and my mom appears in the basement. She wears a pair of jeans, a fancy cheetah print tank top, and black heels, which reminds me that she and John are going out to dinner tonight. Which also reminds me that Shea and I are going on our first date tonight. Thinking about Stephanie's murder is the only thing keeping me from completely psyching myself out and overthinking this. I've messed things up with Shea so many times, so I only have one shot at pulling this off. I'm particularly good at screwing relationships up, so tonight should be interesting. But then again, I've never been with someone like Shea, someone who truly cares about me.

"What are you two up to?" she asks. Her voice is calm and sweet, but there's something in her green eyes that makes her seem worried.

"Just hanging out," I answer. "Hazel's coming over soon to help me get ready."

She smiles, dimples creasing her cheeks, "Tonight's the big night! You'll have to tell me everything when you get home! Luke, are you still good to watch the girls? John and I are leaving around seven, after we send Izzie off."

Luke nods, "Yeah, I'm good."

Everything's quiet for a moment, "Your dad just called. We've talked a few times, and he's doing much better. They moved him to a rehabilitation center. He would love to hear from you guys. I understand and he understands if you don't want to talk to him, but he misses you two."

Luke nonchalantly nods, pretending the words hold no weight. I feel like there's tiny claws pulling at my heartstrings. I feel stuck between missing him and the anger that rises in my chest when I think of everything he's done. I think about saying no, telling mom I'm not ready. But if I do that, who's to say I won't keep pushing the call off. Pushing him off? When am I ever going to really be ready to speak to him? I read something once that said ready isn't a feeling, it's a decision. I just need to decide. Decide if I want him in my life. Decide if I want to forgive him. Decide if I want to finally stop holding onto the divorce like a baby blanket I can't bring myself to get rid of. When I think of him I think of the man who played the guitar for me when I couldn't sleep at night. The man who always caught me when I fell off the monkey bars. The man who defended me even when I was wrong. I don't want to sever ties with him. I don't want to lose that part of me, the part of me that's him. He's made a lot of mistakes, but he's still my dad. The urge to simply hear his voice takes over all other thoughts, and I'm suddenly hit with the need to make the call.

"I'll talk to him," I blurt out, "I'll talk to him, now."

"You don't have to talk to him now, sweetheart. I promised you I would be honest from now on, so I just wanted you to know what was going on," she replies.

"I need to talk to him now or I'll lose my nerve," I say, my voice stern and unwavering.

"If that's what you want," my mom replies, not wanting to argue with me.

Mom takes her phone out of her back pocket and pulls up the number of the rehabilitation center he's staying in. Luke slides upstairs quietly, trying not to draw any attention to himself and not wanting any involvement in this.

"Are you sure?" mom questions. I nod, knowing that if I don't talk to him now, I may not talk to him ever. I just need to take the first step. Plus, I need to deal with this at some point so I can move on. I need a clear head for my date tonight. There's no way I can have another meltdown in front of Shea. Everyone says there's no time like the present.

She holds the phone to her ear, and I hear it ring a few times before a muffled voice answers. "I'd like to speak to one of your patients," she says to the lady on the other end. There's a few moments of quiet before she says, "Tommy Andrews."

She hands the phone over to me and places her hand lovingly on my shoulder and says, "I'll be right upstairs if you need anything."

I wait for a few seconds, deeply thinking about what I'm going to say to him and quickly realizing that I did not think this through. I'm nothing if not impulsive. But then I hear a faint rustling on the other line and the familiar voice my heart had been aching to hear, "Hey, kiddo."

236

"Hi," I say eagerly.

"How have you been?" His voice is raspy, but patient.

"I'm okay, but how are you? Are you feeling okay?" I reply, the words coming much easier than I thought they would. Suddenly, I feel like the two of us aren't thousands of miles apart.

"I'm getting better, but you don't have to worry about me, Iz. Your mom and I have been talking, and I'm so sorry you found out about everything like that. I —"

I interrupt him, "You don't have to apologize."

"Yes, I do. I absolutely need to apologize to you. I made so many mistakes, Izzie. I made some bad decisions, and I have no one else to blame but myself. I want you to know that it was nothing you, your mom, or your brother did. It was all me. I'm so sorry. I should've been better for you, Iz. You deserve the world. I should've been there for you, and I wasn't. I'm sorry, so so sorry. I don't expect you to forgive me now or ever. You don't have to talk to me. If you want me to stop calling, I will. But I want you to know that I'm getting help now. That accident was a wakeup call, and I'm going to turn this around. It's late, I know, but I need you to know that I love you. I love you more than anything else in this world. I just want you to be happy, bud."

Tears trickle down my face, and I feel the pent up anger that filled my chest slowly dissipate. All of the negative feelings and emotions start to leak out of my body as the tears roll down from my eyes like rain rolling down a window sill. I take a deep breath in, the air feeling lighter than it did before. Finally, all of the feelings I had stored in my body, like fireflies in jars, have escaped. The numbness, the refusal to deal with my issues is what has been making me feel so awful and act so ridiculously. But now, I've released it all, like a balloon floating up into the clouds.

*****

237

We step up to Shea's car, and he opens the passenger door for me, which makes me blush just a little bit. I feel a flutter in my stomach, the butterflies making me feel both excited and anxious. My palms are sweating, which makes me really self-conscious and nervous if he tries to hold my hand. After my conversation with my dad, I feel so much lighter, like my mind is suddenly freed from the trap of all those feelings that sat on it. Hazel came by shortly after to help me get ready. She did my makeup much better than I ever could've done and helped me find something to wear, which was almost an impossible feat seeing that I still haven't unpacked the boxes in my room. Eventually I settled on a casual, light blue dress that hits right above the knee and that Hazel said brings out my eyes. I'm still not sure if I'm ready for this, my first official date with him. I just don't want to do anything to mess this up again. Key word being *again*.

He slides into the car, filling my nose with the faint smell of his cologne. His caramel colored hair is spiked up a little in the front, the sunlight pouring through the car windows highlighting his blonde undertones. This feels like something out of a movie, him picking me up and opening up the car door and taking me out to dinner. I know it's basic, but it makes my heart want to explode.

The car glides along the black concrete, rolling along the surface the way a paint roller rolls over a wall in need of a fresh coat of paint. I find myself stealing glances at him every so often, staring at his sparkling blue eyes and the dimples that crease his cheeks.

"Are you going to try out for the basketball team?" he asks looking over at me, meeting my eyes and causing my face to turn all sorts of red because he knows I was staring at him.

"I don't know," I reply, fighting back the embarrassment. "I played back in Portland."

"Was it weird having to move going into senior year?" he asks genuinely.

I think for a minute about how to respond and then say, "I'm really stubborn, as you probably already know, so I did everything I could to stop us from moving. I wouldn't pack or talk to either of my parents, and when it was time to actually go, my mom had to basically force me into the car. I was angry. Everything was in Portland. My friends, my dad, my home. You know, I still haven't unpacked any of my boxes. My floor is literally overtaken by cardboard."

"You haven't unpacked yet? How do you find anything?" he smiles.

"Let's just say getting ready is a process," I laugh.

"You look beautiful, so I would have never known."

An involuntary smile spreads across my face, his words causing the butterflies in my stomach to start moving around at double the speed. I say to him, "I didn't think I would belong here, I didn't think that anyone would accept me and all of my . . . issues. But then I met you. I think I like it here, now."

He blushes, his tanned skin changing to a shade of maroon. All at once, everything seems to look a little brighter. Maybe I'm not as lost as I thought I was. Maybe I've finally found my place in this world. Maybe, just maybe.

Dinner was exciting and perfect. We spent the whole time talking, and the words came so easily. It was like I had known him forever. The best part was that I wasn't awkward or a cringey mess or sobbing disaster, which is a pretty big deal seeing that I've been at least one of the three every time I've ever interacted with Shea. After dinner, we get into his car as dusk is beginning to encroach on Knox Hollow.

"Can I show you something?" he asks when we're in the car.

"Sure," I reply. "What is it?"

"Just wait," he says.

239

The car winds along the twists and turns of the road. A few minutes later Shea pulls into a fairly empty parking lot of a tall store building. Daylight is still clinging onto the sky, its grasp on the town slowly slipping.

"Where are we?" I ask curiously.

"I'll show you," he gets out of the car and comes around to my side, opening my door. He takes my hand and leads me behind the building. We walk around back, humidity still seeping through the air. Behind the building is another, smaller parking lot, which makes me wonder where we're going.

"Up here," he says casually, pointing to a ladder attached to the brick building.

"Up where?" I say, eyes wide.

"Up there," he points to the ladder again. "Come on, it's an easy climb, and the view is amazing."

"Are we supposed to go up there?" I ask him. Ever since I basically scaled the side of the Hastings' house, heights have kind of freaked me out.

"I don't know, Graeson and I have done it a couple times," he answers.

"Oh, that makes me feel so much better," I say sarcastically.

"You climbed up the railing of a deck and into the kitchen window of a house the other day. This should be easy compared to that," he smiles.

His smile instantly makes me feel giddy, and I think to myself: screw it! I'll climb up the stupid ladder if it means I can spend more time with him.

"Alright," I say with a twinkle in my eyes. "Let's do it."

Shea helps me onto the ladder, and I start to climb up, my knees feeling a little unsteady. When both of us are safe and secure on the roof, or at least as safe and secure as you can possibly be on the top of a roof, we walk to the middle of the flat surface. I gaze outwards, and instantly, the beauty of the view almost knocks me off my feet. The pale blue sky is fading into a swirl of peach and coral, cherry red and strawberry pink. All of the clouds have dissipated, the vibrant colors making the sky look like it's on fire. In the distance, I can make out the blurred outlines of the looming mountain peaks that seem to blend into the horizon. I've always had a thing for sunsets. I've always felt like they were such a simple and underappreciated thing. Watching this one fills me with a sense of peace, a sense of hope that maybe tomorrow will be a little bit better. And being here with Shea, well that makes it all the more perfect.

He takes a seat in the middle, and I follow his lead. I ask him jokingly, "Do you take all the girls up here?"

He smiles, dimples piercing his cheeks, "No, just Graeson, but he's not the best date."

We go quiet for a few minutes, just taking in the view. There's something so comforting, yet exhilarating about Shea's presence. He has the strange ability of making me feel like the world has slowed down, yet is simultaneously spinning in circles at a million miles an hour. The pinks and oranges of the sky are fading into streaks of navy blue decorated with tiny specks of gold.

"Can I ask you something?" I ask him.

"Yeah," he looks over to me, his blue eyes glowing as darkness starts to surround us.

"What was it like when your dad died? You don't have to answer, I probably shouldn't have asked that. I'm sorry," I ramble.

"No, no, it's fine," he replies. "I don't mind. People never ask me about him. No one wants to talk about it, not my mom or my siblings or my friends. Everyone walks around it, like it's some sort of forbidden subject, an embarrassment. Something that shouldn't be talked about. You're one of the first people to ask me about him."

I slide myself closer to him, pressing against his body and resting my head on his shoulder. Something about being up here and talking just makes me want to be close to him. He takes his arm and wraps it around my shoulder, drawing me close to him.

"He had a lot of demons. He was going through so much more than anyone ever knew. I still don't know why he did it, but I know he was struggling, that he couldn't see the light at the end of the tunnel. The first week after he died it was like I was living in slow motion. I still expected him to be there. I would wake up in the morning and expect to see him sitting at the kitchen counter drinking his coffee. I would get home from school and wait to see his car coming down the street on his way home from work. After it happened, when he wasn't there, it was like having to relive it all over again. I had to remind myself he wasn't coming home, he wasn't *ever* coming home. But that feeling fades after awhile. The worst part of it was the way everyone looked at me, like I was an animal in a cage. Like I was so fragile I could break at any moment. No one knew what to say, so they tiptoed around me. I can't blame them, it's not an easy situation. But it gets easier. If you surround yourself with good people, I don't know, I feel like it helps."

His eyes are fixed outwards, staring at the stars, but I feel like he's looking beyond them, looking at whatever else might be out there. The chill of the night air penetrates the humidity that had hung in the air throughout the day. I press closer into him, feeling safe and calm in his arms. He turns to me and the corners of his mouth turn upwards into a small, but genuine and kind smile.

I get home that night, stars filling my head and hearts filling my eyes. I make it up to my room in a hazy daze. I take a look around the room at the cardboard sea and start to unpack the first box.

*****

I walk into the diner, awkwardly tugging at the silver bracelet on my wrist. I catch sight of Alison in the same booth as the first time we met her here, and an odd sense of deja vu comes over me. She notices me in the entryway and waves a condescending little wave, wiggling each finger. I walk towards her and discreetly slide into the booth. Her mousy brown hair is up in a high ponytail, tied with a pale pink scrunchie that perfectly matches the t-shirt under her denim overalls.

"I was surprised to hear from you," she says, tapping her neon pink painted fingernails on the table.

"Oh trust me, I was surprised myself," I reply. "But I need your help."

I hate to say it, but Alison sent us down the right path with Sawyer. I figured she would be my best bet for more information. She made it seem like she had blackmail on the entire neighborhood, and even though it may just be another one of her games, I'm starting to learn not to doubt this little girl.

"Do you have my money," she asks directly, raising her eyebrows and forcing her lips into a pout.

"You know how this works," I fire back. "You talk, and I'll give you the money. I told you last time, I'm not playing your games."

"I still don't understand what Shea sees in you. He's so nice, and you're a little . . . aggressive."

I bite down on my lip hard, trying to keep myself from throat punching her. I take a deep breath, reminding myself that beating up a nine-year-old girl is really not okay, even if she completely deserves it.

"I guess opposites attract," I say back, fake kindness coating my voice. "How do you even know about us?"

She giggles sarcastically as if asked her just about the stupidest question in the world. She snarls, "I have my ways. Let's just say the two of you hang out on your front porch quite a bit."

God, I can't stand her! I've never met a child I've disliked more than this one. She irks me in ways I didn't even realize were possible. I say to her, "Can we just cut straight to the point?"

"You're really taking all of the fun out of this, but fine. What do you want to know?"

"I'm going to tell you something that you can't repeat. Okay?" She nods her head and pretends to lock her lips with an invisible key. "We found pills in Sawyer's house, lots of them. We think he was giving your mom the drugs in exchange for money. Do you know why she needed them? Or why he needed the money?"

A sly grin spreads across her face, "I don't know why he needed the money, but I do know what my mom did with the bag he gave her each week."

"You do?!" My eyes pop out of my sockets as I realize this is becoming a little easier than I thought it would be. Alison is chock full of information, you just have to figure out how to get her to sing. She nods with her high ponytail swinging from side to side, but doesn't speak, making effective use of the dramatic pause. "So," I urge. "What did she do with the bag?"

The familiar Cheshire cat grin creeps across her face, "Now I've got your attention. We're going to play this *my* way this time. You want your information? Hand over my money."

Life is like one big game to Alison, where each day, each decision, each move is worth points. Everything is about winning or losing, nothing is given away for free. Each move she made is calculated, a part of some bigger strategy. Life is a game to Alison, and right now, she's beating me.

"Don't push me," I grit my teeth. "I don't trust you as far as I can throw you."

"I'll put it simply because you don't seem to understand me. If you don't want to play by my rules, then leave. Remember that I don't need you, you need me. The choice is yours," her voice is stern and full of sass. I sit there stunned as this little girl is kicking my ass at whatever game we're playing. She leans back against the red leather of the booth, crosses her arms across her chest, and begins to stare me down with her cold, haunting hazel eyes that remind me so much of Stephanie. I don't give in, especially not to nine-year-old puppet masters, but I feel like I have no other option. If I don't play it her way, I may never find out who killed Stephanie, or at least I won't be able to find out in time to save Hannah.

"Fine," I say as calmly as I can manage while I place the white envelope filled with Alison's money on the table between us. Her greedy, perfectly manicured fingers scoop up the money and shove it into her sparkly backpack, which makes me wonder how many similar envelopes she has in there, stuffed with money in return for her silence or her information.

Her scowl instantly fades into a manipulative smile, the face of a girl who just got exactly what she wanted. She says to me, "I told you my mom met with Sawyer every Wednesday, and they would exchange their envelopes. Well, she would take that paper bag, and she would give it to Forrest Shepard. He lives next door to you on the left. About an hour after Sawyer left, she would run over to his house. She was never gone for more than five minutes. I know she wasn't meeting with his wife, Cora, because she took their daughters up to her mother's house in Stratton Woods about an hour away on Wednesdays. It was funny because she'd get home, and she'd sit the three of us down — me, Alex, and Ella — and she'd tell us not to tell Dad that she had left. It was this whole rehearsed speech. She'd tell us exactly what to say and make us repeat it until we had it perfect, and we'd recite it to my dad when he got home. It went something like 'We came home from school, mommy made us a snack, and helped us with our homework until you got home.' After, she would give us all a packet of M&M's, like we were dogs being rewarded for obedience. She taught me a lot about how to lie, how to get people to do what you want."

I feel a nauseous pain in the pit of my stomach. Alison's story about Stephanie coaching her kids to lie leaves a disturbing taste in my mouth. I feel like I can't even blame this tiny manipulator for her actions. She was raised this way, raised to lie, raised to play games, raised to use people, raised to fend for herself and to trust nobody. You can't blame the monster, you have to blame the people who created it.

"Why didn't you tell me this before?" I ask because I'm unsure of how to respond to her unsettling childhood.

"You didn't ask," she retorts. The empathy I just felt for her disappears as she falls back into her sassy habits. "All I know is that when she came home, the paper bag didn't come with her. Whatever it was, she left it with him."

My brain is reeling, trying to process this new information and fit it in with what I already know. I feel like someone has delivered me a package of computer parts, and now I have to put together the actual computer. Except, in this case, there's no directions or a picture of what it's supposed to look like. Instead of focusing on everything about Forrest Shepard, all I can think about is the image of Stephanie sitting her kids down at the kitchen table and forcing them to lie for her.

"Ali," I say calmly. "How are you holding up with everything that's going on?"

For a minute her expression softens, and I swear I see tears brimming her hazel eyes. The brick walls she puts up, the games she mastered, all of that seems to fade. But that vulnerability diminishes almost as quickly as it arises.

"I'm fine," she says, and she seems disconnected from the situation, from her emotions, her whole play it cool persona disappearing and leaving her flustered. "She made a lot of bad

246

decisions, and now she's dead because of it. There's nothing else to talk about."

I fix my gaze on Alison, taking in everything about her: the mousy brown hair, the deep red puckered lips, the coal black eyelashes, the hazel eyes. I take a good, long look, but for some freakish reason, all I can see is myself.

*****

"John!" I call out as I walk in through the garage after a strange meeting with Alison Kester. "John! Are you home?"

"In here," I hear John's voice echoing from the kitchen.

I rush in at a million miles an hour, my brain moving much faster than my body. When I was driving home, an idea popped into my head. Once I have my mind fixed on something, I can't let it go. But for this plan to go off, I need John.

"Woah, slow down," John looks slightly alarmed as I come in total hell on wheels. "What's up?"

He stands at the kitchen counter, bouncing Olivia in one arm, so she'll fall asleep, and holding a black gel pen in the other. He reads a stack of papers that are busting out of a file folder, and looks up when I barge in. His cornflower blue eyes seem to be brighter beneath the glossy surface of his glasses, which he only needs to read. In a few weeks, John will be starting his new job as a clinical psychiatrist at a hospital nearby. He was offered the position as a supervisor of clinical psych at the hospital, which is part of the reason we moved. He's been reading up on current patient files and has been drowning in paperwork since we first got here, in preparation for the job.

"Did you know the people next door have a daughter Madison's age and another one Olivia's age?" I ask with far too much drama and enthusiasm.

"No, I didn't know that," he looks at me with a confused expression. "That's good to know."

"We should invite them over!" I say trying to tone down my energy level, but with little success.

He closes the file folder and steps away from the counter to place a sleeping Olivia down in the bassinet. John stands at around 6' 2", so he has to bend down awkwardly to place her in. He says to me, "If they have kids Madison and Olivia's age then I'm sure we'll get to know them at some point."

"No, we should invite them over tonight," I respond.

"Can I ask why you want them to come over so much?"

"Uh . . ." I stutter. "I just think it would be the neighborly thing to do. I've heard that they're great people, and it's time for us to get out there and be social! Plus, it'll help the girls make new friends!"

John looks at me inquisitively, as if he's not sure if I'm just suddenly enthusiastic or if I've completely lost it. Unfortunately, I would have to go with the latter.

"I'm happy you're so excited about this. I'm just not sure where it's coming from," he smiles.

"I just feel like I'm finally starting to belong here, like I have friends. This move has been so hard, I really think it's time to plant our roots, you know?"

He smiles again, the familiar comforting grin that I've seen so many times before, "You're right, Iz. I'll talk to your mom when she gets home. I just want to tell you how proud I am of you. You've been through so much, but you've come out on the other side so much stronger. I know the two of us haven't always gotten along, and you probably don't want to hear this from me, but I'm proud of you."

His words catch me off guard and send a shivering sensation through my body. Normally I would say some awful, snarky remark, but all I feel right now is grateful. John stepped up so many years ago, and he's tried so hard to help me. I've made loving me a difficult task, but he's never stopped trying. I used to think that loving John was betraying my dad, but now I know I can love them both. Now, I realize that maybe all of the bumps in the road were really my blessings in disguise. I think about it for a moment: without everything I've been through, I never would've met John, my mom never would've had my sisters, I would've never met Hazel or Graeson or Shea.

I don't know what possesses me to do this, but I walk up to John and hug him tightly, which makes me realize that I don't think I've ever actually hugged him before. At first he seems a little shocked, but then he puts his arms around me.

"What was that for?" he asks.

"For always being here," I smile.

A while later, John has invited the Shepards over for drinks. At first, my mom was a little bit uncomfortable with inviting them over seeing that we didn't know them and were known as the house where Stephanie's body was found. But I think John convinced her by saying how great it was that I wanted to reach out and get to know people in our town. I kind of feel bad for exaggerating and purposefully pulling on his emotions to get my way, but not bad enough to do anything about it. I'd like to say I'm no longer a terrible person, but then I think back to the amount of house break-ins and secret blackmail meetings I've taken part in.

I sit outside on our back patio with my mom and John, while Madison runs around in the yard barefooted. Sitting out here still gives me such a strange and haunting feeling. All I can see is the spot on the patio where Stephanie's corpse was sprawled out and the pool of blood stained the ground beneath her. The body's gone and the blood stains have disappeared, but the memory of it is at the forefront of my thoughts.

I see the Shepards walking over, the mysterious couple and their children making their way over to our patio. I'm hoping to get a better sense of who they are tonight. If I know more about them,

I might be able to figure out what their involvement in Stephanie's death is, if anything.

"Hi," John says enthusiastically. "We're so happy you guys could stop by!"

"Thank you for inviting us," Cora says in a way that is polite, but not warm. A common courtesy with no meaning behind it.

The two of them sit down, Cora holding their youngest daughter and Forrest looking quite uncomfortable. He seems to squirm in his chair, unable to sit still. He looks down at his hands and fixates on his fingers that tap the sides of the chair. Cora glances at him and clears her throat quietly, which seems like her friendly reminder for him to stop being such a weirdo. We make the necessary introductions, but the conversation falls flat after that. John, an expert at making awkward situations feel a little less uncomfortable makes small talk with the couple, trying to create a conversation. I don't pay attention to anything they're saying because all I can focus on is Forrest's mannerisms. He strains to keep eye contact with whoever is talking, and continuously looks to the side of him, as if someone were watching him. He responds in short little phrases, jumbled words rolling awkwardly off his tongue. I still don't understand how the two of them are together. I glance over at Cora noticing the way her dark chocolate hair rolls down her back in thick waves and how her copper eyes seem to glow in the evening sunlight. She radiates beauty and elegance, meanwhile her husband reminds me of a slimy, little mouse. At least it seems like their kids got Cora's genes instead of his.

"So, what do you do for work?" John asks Forrest.

Forrest fiddles with his black rimmed glasses before replying, "I own a bioengineering lab in Paine's Creek about an hour away." His voice is nasally and almost robotic.

"That's really cool," my mom answers. "What kinds of things do you do up there?"

"We develop equipment and devices to solve prominent medical and clinical problems. We determine the best methods, protocols, and usage of our technology and work with additional researchers and medical professionals to make advancements in our field." The man sounds like he's reciting something he read in one of those science textbooks at school I never pay much attention to. You can almost see his brain moving inside his head, the wheels turning at maximum speed.

Mom and John both nod awkwardly, unsure of what to say. Cora rolls her eyes, but I can't tell if it's directed at our stunned, judgy faces or Forrest's social awkwardness. She says, "He always talks like that. He loves his work." Forrest nods his head rapidly like a little kid agreeing with their parents because they're too scared to speak for themselves. I would love to hear the story of how they met.

"What grade are you going into?" Cora turns her attention to me.

"I'll be a senior in the fall," I reply. I want to ask them something, something to stir up a response that points me in the right direction.

"It must have been so strange to find a dead body in your backyard," Forrest pipes up out of the blue.

He catches me off guard, but I'm happy to be on this subject, hopeful it will spark something inside of him. I say, "It was awful, not exactly the best housewarming present."

My mom shoots me the evil eye, telling me without words that my sarcasm about Stephanie's corpse was probably not the most appropriate thing to say.

Forrest chuckles, "Your humor, I find it refreshing."

"Thank you," I respond. "Were you close with Stephanie?"

And with that question, Forrest suddenly stops all of his squirming, all of his fidgeting. He looks up at me, his jaw clenched tightly and his electric green eyes cold and wide like an owl, pupils darting around in every direction as if he was possessed by some evil spirit. He doesn't blink, he doesn't move, he doesn't speak. But his stare, it's enough to tell me that my question was not welcome.

CHAPTER 13 - Pull the Trigger

How far does a person have to be pushed before they snap? What lines have to be crossed before they lose total control? What makes an ordinary person become a murderer?

Richard, Beckett, Hannah, Sawyer, Isla, Forrest. I repeat the list over and over again in my head. Richard, Beckett, Hannah, Sawyer, Isla, Forrest. One of these people was pushed too far. One of these people was shoved so far over the edge that they snapped. But why? What got them to that point? I go through the list a couple more times, thinking hard on each name that appears in my head. Richard, Beckett, Hannah, Sawyer, Isla, Forrest. There's so many questions, but no answers to be found.

I think back to what Graeson said about how most murders come down to one of four things: drugs, money, blackmail, or love. Richard could've killed because of love. The woman he married was cheating on him. Maybe that, combined with dealing with all of her issues, games, drama, and manipulation, made him lose control. Richard doesn't strike me as a guy who'd commit a murder in a fit of rage, as a guy who would lose his temper in such an extreme fashion. He just seemed so defeated, his blue eyes sunken back deep in their sockets. I feel like if it was Richard, he would've planned the killing, down to the very last detail. But I know I can't count him out just yet.

Beckett also could have killed for love. If Stephanie threatened to tell everyone about their affair, he may have shot her to shut her up. Or maybe he tried to break it off and she wouldn't let go, so he thought he had to get rid of her. I'm not sure, but I have this strong feeling in the pit of my stomach that he didn't commit the murder, that he's just a guy who made a very stupid mistake that ended up backfiring on him big time.

Hannah. It hurts me to even think about Hannah. Every time I do, all I can see is her ghost-like face as Detective Heights handcuffed her. She didn't even fight back, just threw her hands up as if she knew she were a lost cause, as if there was no hope left inside her. We have to find what the police have on her. They can't just arrest someone based on speculation. There has to be substantial concrete proof of her guilt in Stephanie's murder.

Sawyer could have killed her because of drugs and money. From the burner phone messages and the phone call I overheard between the two of them, Dr. Hastings wanted to pull out of this deal because he knew providing her with a steady supply of pills would ruin his entire life. But Stephanie had a firm grip on his arm, and she threatened to expose him. She also said she'd kill him if he did something, I'm not sure what because I couldn't hear him talking. Maybe Stephanie attacked him, and he shot her in self-defense. Or maybe he killed her to preserve his reputation. Either way, he had her cell phone in his locked desk drawer. Even if he wasn't the one to kill her, he has some sort of involvement.

If Isla murdered Stephanie, it was because of love and blackmail. People always say love can make you do crazy things. If Stephanie threatened to expose Isla's relationship to her college English professor, he could have ended up in prison. Not that I have any experience with this, but I'd have to imagine it's very difficult to be in a relationship with someone who's locked behind bars. Love and blackmail. Is that what pushed Isla over the edge? She strikes me as bold and fierce, someone whose petite and innocent appearance makes people doubt what she's truly capable of. Sometimes a threat is just a threat, but what if this time it's more? What if she murdered Stephanie?

Forrest. That last suspect on my list. He sure has the brain to be a killer, but wouldn't that mean he would have carefully planned out the details? Stephanie's death didn't seem to be meticulously thought out. I feel like someone with his brilliance would've hid the body better and wouldn't have left crucial pieces of evidence like her burner phone just lying around for anyone to find. But the look he gave me. I still can't shake the bitter chill that crept up my spine and crawled down my arms like a spider. I have to figure out the relationship between Sawyer, Stephanie, and Forrest. Why was she sending her pills from Sawyer to Forrest? She obviously didn't want Richard to know about it. When it comes down to it, he also could have killed Stephanie.

This is my thought process at 3 a.m. Nice, isn't it? If I'm not going to sleep, I might as well keep digging into this murder. Clearly, staring into the darkness of my room is not helping, so I decide to just get the day rolling. I throw on an old hoodie over my t-shirt and walk as quietly as I can down the stairs. I brew a pot of coffee — God knows I'm going to need a lot of caffeine to make it through this day — and open my laptop, the fluorescent screen illuminating the darkness around me.

Where to start? I decide to begin with creepy Forrest because, right now, he's on the top of my list. I search his name, but can't find any records of him. I remember something Luke told me: to find information on someone, you may have to try different angles, use indirect routes to get to the person. I start researching labs in Paine's Creek, and lucky for me, there's only one in the small town. I click on the link and start reading all about the bioengineering lab and hmm . . . well this is weird. It says on the website that the lab is owned by a man named Daniel Wilkinson. There's a picture of him too, a middle aged blonde man who looks about as similar to Forrest as I do to Beyonce. There's a page dedicated to all of their employees, so I go through all of the names and pictures to see if I can find Forrest. I read every single word on each page of the website, finding a lot of information my brain cannot handle at 3 a.m. There's no mention of Forrest Shepard, not once on the entire site.

I fall down the rabbit hole, googling and researching until my eyes are so blurry it physically hurts to stare at my computer. I glance over to the clock on the oven and realize it's already 7 o'clock. I've been at this for four hours! I guess time really flies when you're trying to find the person who murdered your neighbor in your backyard.

I hear footsteps coming down the stairs and see Luke making his way into the kitchen.

"How long have you been awake?" he asks groggily, rubbing the sleep out of his eyes.

"Since 3 a.m.," I yawn. He glances from me to the empty coffee pot on the counter and shakes his head.

"How much coffee have you had?" he laughs.

"A lot. Probably too much. But how much is too much? I mean, there's no such thing as too much coffee!" I reply, feeling the buzz of the caffeine starting to take effect. "Okay, maybe I've had too much. I couldn't sleep. I just kept thinking about everything with Stephanie's murder, so I decided to do some research. You're not going to believe what I found."

He comes and sits down next to me at the counter, squinting his eyes to make sense of the screen. "This page is for the bioengineering lab in Paine's Creek that Forrest said he owns, but if you read their website, it says the owner is some guy named Daniel Wilkinson. So then I looked through all the employees. See this section? It lists each employees' name, what they do at the lab, and a picture of them. There's no mention of Forrest Shepard. I read through every tab on this website, Luke, and there's not one mention of his name."

I look to Luke's face, waiting to see it fill with pride because of my sleuthing. "Wow," he says. "I'm impressed."

"I was channeling my inner Luke when I was researching."

"I've never been more proud of you," he laughs jokingly. "But that's really strange. Why would he lie about owning the lab?"

"I'm not sure," I comb my fingers through my hair. "But I looked it up, and it's only a little over an hour away. I was thinking we could all drive up there and see if we can find any information."

"I don't know, Iz. I don't want to cause any problems."

"Come on, Luke. We have to do everything we can to save Hannah. The police think she's guilty. If we don't figure out who did this, she's going to sit in a prison cell for the rest of her life," I hear my volume getting increasingly louder, and my hands are furiously shaking from the caffeine.

"Okay, we'll talk about it later today when we meet up with everybody," he says as I reach for the coffee pot to keep feeding my addiction. He places his hand firmly on my arm before the pot's in my grasp and says, "Izzie, I think you've had enough." I hang my head, but realize that he's probably right.

Luke takes the remote and starts flipping through channels on our tiny kitchen TV. In the background I hear a news reporter say, "Last Wednesday, Hannah St. James was arrested for the murder of Stephanie Kester."

"What is that!?" I exclaim.

"I don't know. I was just flipping through, I —" I cut him off. I say, "Shh! Shut up!"

"St. James's arraignment will take place tomorrow. Her lawyer, Deborah Gordon, has made a statement on her behalf." The screen cuts to an image of a middle-aged lady with cinnamon brown hair cut in a bob. Her eyes appear to be laser focused, set on whatever's in front of her. She wears a crisp, black pantsuit, and speaks confidently. She says, "My client categorically denies the accusations against her and looks forward to proving her innocence. At this time, we have no further comment." Short and straight to the point, but not helpful at all.

"What's an arraignment?" I ask Luke.

"It's the first step in the whole trial process. Basically, the judge will read the charges against her, and then Hannah will make her plea. It sounds like she's pleading not guilty, so the judge will decide her bail," he responds.

"I need to go see her," I say point blank.

"What?" Luke's face drops. I'm surprised he still gets so shocked at the insane ideas that spew out of my mouth.

"I need to go see her, Luke. I don't know why or what I'm looking for, but I just feel like I need to see her."

"I really don't think you should, Izzie," he warns.

He keeps on talking, informing me about all of the possible things that could go wrong and why this is such a terrible idea. But I'm not listening. All of his words float around in the air, but don't quite make it into my ears. When I make up my mind about something, I'll go through with it at all costs. I've made up my mind about seeing Hannah. Nothing anyone can say will stop me now.

*****

The guard is silent as he leads me into the room. My hands feel shaky, but I'm not sure if it's from my nerves or the sheer amount of caffeine I consumed. I stare down at my feel, fixated on the shoelaces of my Converse, counting each measured step I take. Why am I here? There's a few other people here too, scattered about and talking to their person on the other side of the glass. The guard points at a chair, telling me to sit and wait for Hannah. He steps back, standing against the wall behind me, which freaks me out a little bit. I feel like I'm being watched, like I'm guilty. I have to continuously remind myself that I'm not on the other side of the glass, but I can't help but think that I could be.

A few minutes later a door on the other side opens and a guard ushers Hannah in. At first I'm not even sure it's her. She sits down slowly, and when she sees my face her lips fold upwards slightly into the smallest indication of a smile. Hannah picks up the phone with her hand and presses it against her ear. I do the same, feeling the cold metal against the side of the face.

"Izzie, I didn't expect to see you," her voice is raspy, but I can still faintly hear the warmth in it.

"I wanted to see how you were. I hope you don't mind me coming," I sound quiet and unsure of myself.

"Of course I don't mind you coming. I didn't get the chance to thank you for staying with my little ones. I appreciate you and Hazel being there for them when I couldn't. How are they?"

"They're good. They miss you so much, but they're doing alright. Hazel and I have gone by a couple of times to see them."

I take a good look at Hannah. The life seems to have been pulled out of her hazel eyes, leaving them to look like dull and dark gaping holes. The color that drained from her face the day she was arrested still hasn't returned, her skin appearing to be tinted gray. The dark circles under her eyes seem to be the focal point of her face, like storm clouds that overtake a sunny day. She looks like she's already dead, like a corpse. It's like she's lived hundreds of years in the past few days. I feel a sickening pain in the pit of my stomach. What happened to her?

"Beckett's come a few times to see me. He feels like this is his fault. It's tearing him apart," Hannah says with a certain emptiness in her voice.

Of course he feels like it's his fault. It is his fault. It *should* be tearing him apart. I have no sympathy for Beckett St. James. Maybe that makes me cold, but I just don't understand how Hannah can feel bad for him.

"I see the look you're giving me," she looks directly at me.

"I just don't see how you can feel bad for him. How can you forgive him after everything he's done?"

"Oh, I'm not forgiving him. We made a vow to each other, and he cheated on me with the lady next door. I'm mad that he cheated, but I'm more upset that he lied about it. I don't think I'll ever forgive him for that. If I ever get out of here, I won't go back to him. But it's not his fault that I'm in here. How could he anticipate her murder? I can't blame that on him. I didn't kill Stephanie, and I will go to my grave saying that, but it's not his fault. He didn't know or want any of this to happen."

I consider her points for a minute, but can't see past all of the lying and cheating. In my book, it is his fault. I see it as black and white. Guilty or innocent. To me, guilty should be written in permanent marker across his forehead.

"You're going to get out of here, Hannah. I promise, we're going to find out who really did this."

"They all think I'm guilty. It makes perfect sense, doesn't it? I found out my husband was cheating on me with the woman next door, so I killed her. It makes their case easy, ties it all up in a neat, little bow."

"What do they have on you, Hannah? Why do they think you did it?" I question.

"After that picture of Stephanie and Beckett kissing was released on social media, the police sent me and Beckett in for questioning. Beckett had come clean to me and Richard before the wake. They got a warrant to search our house and took samples of our DNA. I didn't think they'd find anything. I had nothing to hide. They found a few guns in the safe, but Beckett hunts, so I didn't think I'd have anything to worry about. Then they arrested me. This woman tried to steal my husband, and now she's trying to steal my life. Even in death she has a hold on me. The gun in the safe matched the one used to kill Stephanie, it still had remnants of her blood on it. My DNA matched the DNA found at the scene.

They said strands of my hair were found where the body was. And I don't have a clear alibi. I went home early and put the kids to bed, but I have no one to testify that I stayed home."

I shake my head, the anger rising in my chest, "You're being framed. Someone is going out of their way to make you look guilty."

She hangs her head and tugs at her chestnut colored hair. I want so badly to kick down this piece of glass between us, to give her a hug and tell her that everything is going to be alright. Even from here, I can tell how much weight she's lost, how defeated she is. But there's still something inside of her, the smallest bit of hope she's gripping onto.

"Do you have any idea who might be trying to frame you? Who would've wanted Stephanie dead?" I ask, trying to pull more information out of her.

She looks up again, and our eyes lock. She says, "I remembered something I saw, and at the time I didn't know what it meant. But I've had a lot of time to think," she laughs a little, making me wonder how she's able to joke at a time like this. "I think I have an idea of who it might be. I'm meeting with my lawyer later today to talk about it before my arraignment. I just want to see my kids. I want to hold them and tell them I love them. I'm so tired, but the thought of them makes me want to fight."

I feel my lungs stop working as I grapple with what she just said. I can feel both the adrenaline and the caffeine cursing through my veins. "Who?! Who do you think is doing this to you?" My eyes are laser focused on Hannah, and my ears are ready to catch what she says. I don't want to miss a single word of this.

She inhales a deep breath, "I think —" She's cut short when the guard comes out of nowhere. "Time's up," he says sternly. NO! I feel my heart drop to the floor.

"Hannah! Who do you think it is!? Hannah!" I yell.

She glances at me, fear filling her eyes to the brim as the guard takes the phone from her and ushers her out of the room.

"NO!!!! Please! Just five more minutes!" I scream hopelessly at the guard like a kid begging their mother for a few more minutes of sleep before school.

He shakes his head firmly, his bushy eyebrows furrowed. He repeats the same merciless line as the other officer, "Time's up."

"Please! I only need a few more minutes!"

"I said time's up! Stop making a scene or I'll ban you from visiting again."

I sigh and walk out the door bubbling with anger because I'd rather not test this guy's patience. He could take me out with the force of his little finger. Besides, he has a taser so I'm not really in a position to egg him on.

I get into my car, feeling extremely frazzled. I was so close to knowing who might be framing Hannah, one major piece of the puzzle was almost in my hands. Almost. *Almost* might just be the saddest word in the dictionary. Almost means that you nearly had something, and you lost it. The thing you wanted was so close your fingertips could touch it, but your grasp slipped. *Almost* is worse than *never*. At least if you never had something, you wouldn't know what you were missing. It wouldn't hurt as much. But almost having something and then feeling it slip away, well that feeling sucker punches you right in the gut.

Now I'm in an extra terrible mood, so going home is probably not my best bet. I need to do something productive, need to feel like I'm a little less helpless. I start driving, hoping that I'll think of something to do along the way. The sun reflects off the black leather seats of my car, sending a burning sensation through my legs. It feels like the sun's rays are actually balls of fire, coating the air with a sweltering heat. On top of the heat, hunger jabs at my insides, making me realize I haven't eaten all day. Is this what being up since three a.m. does to you? Because right now I'm hungry and tired and hot and feel like I'm quickly losing my mind! And then I see it. Out of the corner of my eye, I see the police station and immediately think of Detective Heights. I think it's time I paid her another visit.

I walk into the station and up to the front desk, trying to retain as much composure as I possibly can. The air in the station is thick and humid, making it difficult to breathe. I tell the curly haired lady at the front desk that I need to see Detective Heights, that it's an urgent matter, even though it's not. I actually have zero clue what I'm going to say to her or why I'm here. You could say this was impulsive, but I prefer the term spontaneous.

The woman picks up the phone on the desk and says to the person on the other line, who I'm assuming is Detective Heights, that there's someone here to see her. A few minutes later, Detective Heights comes strolling out, her yellow blonde hair thrown up in a ponytail and her grey eyes already analyzing me.

"Isabelle," she smiles. "We have to stop meeting like this?"

Ugh. I see she hasn't lost her obnoxious sense of humor. She leads me down the hallway and into her disorganized office.

"You can sit here" she points to a chair opposite her desk. "What can I do for you? Gladys said it was urgent."

She sits down at her desk and takes a long swig of her water. Detective Heights is already on my nerves. I mean look at her, just sitting back and watching me crack under the pressure. I anxiously search my brain for something to say to make me look like less of an idiot. An awkward silence settles over the room and I feel the sweat drip from my forehead as Detective Heights stares at me with her all-knowing pearl grey eyes. I keep opening my mouth to talk, but no words come out. God, I'm making a fool of myself.

"I'm just going to be completely honest: I don't know why I'm here. I . . . I . . . don't know. I'm looking for something, I guess. I just don't know what," I say.

"Well, maybe I can help you find what you're looking for. A lot of times, people who are wrapped up in an investigation come around here to find answers. Something tragic happens, and they feel scared or confused. They feel like if they know all the facts or learn what's going on, it'll help them move on. Something traumatic happened to you. You found a dead body in your backyard. Maybe you're just looking for closure."

I mull her words over in my head. What she's saying makes sense, but it's not the whole reason that I'm feeling this way. I need reassurance that I had nothing to do with this murder, but Detective Heights can't give that to me.

"You arrested Hannah St. James," I say, my voice shaking slightly. "Do you think she did it? Because I *know* that she didn't, there's no way she could have." I know I'm going off of blind faith, but there's no chance Hannah could have killed Stephanie.

"It doesn't matter what I think. I have to be objective. I look at the facts and the evidence. I look for motives and backstories. If I let my own personal feelings or opinions cloud my judgement, I wouldn't be very good at my job."

"I'm just worried. If Hannah didn't do it, the real murderer is still out there."

"I assure you, we haven't stopped working on the case. We take homicide investigations very seriously. I promise, we won't stop looking. I know how scary this is. Do you want to know why I became a detective?" I nod my head, so she continues on with her story. "I was eleven when someone broke into my house and pulled a gun on my father. I still remember standing at the end of the hallway, looking out from my bedroom, and him screaming at me to go in and lock the door. My father died, and they never found the man who did it. We never got any sense of closure. I

264

became a detective so that I could help people find that closure I missed. So they could sleep in their beds at night knowing they were safe. So they didn't have to go through life always checking over their shoulder. So I could feel a little less helpless than I did then. That's why I became a detective. I take this *very* seriously, Isabelle. I can promise you that."

"I'm sorry about your dad. You know that first day I met you I basically attacked you for calling me Miss Mason? That's my stepdad's last name, and up until a few days ago I hated him. My dad lives in Portland, Oregon and is in rehab. I thought I should apologize for how I've acted towards you."

She smiles, showing off her perfectly white teeth, "No need to apologize. I've dealt with much worse than that. I'm sorry about your dad, but you know, that's what makes you as strong-willed and as passionate as you are. I appreciate your concern."

"Can I ask you one more thing before I go? I don't want to waste any more of your time than I already have," I ask.

"Of course," she replies. "Fire away."

"Normally the first person arrested is the husband, at least that seems to be the pattern in everything I've read. Why didn't you arrest Richard?"

"I can't say much about our investigation, but I will tell you that we did bring Richard in for questioning. He had an airtight alibi. That's really all I can say."

"Can you tell me what his alibi was?" I question.

"You really like to push it, don't you?" she smirks. I start to roll my eyes, but then remember that my face does not need to show what I'm feeling on the inside. She adds, "But it's not really a big deal if I tell you. Richard's the CEO of a major life insurance company. He had an emergency at work. He left the party early to go into the office. He was seen on tollbooth cameras on the highway heading to his office. Three different security guards at his company confirmed that he was there from 10 p.m. to 5 a.m.

Stephanie was dead by then. Cameras in his office saw him, and it was confirmed that his badge was used to check in and out at those times."

The file on the counter catches my eye. In tiny, but sloppy letters Kester, Richard is written. I bet there's a bunch more files just like that one. Each one with a different name of a different suspect, their life stories and darkest secrets scrawled onto the pages. I'm itching to get my hands on those files. But how? Detective Heights's attitude toward me has definitely softened since we had a little heart to heart about our fathers, but there's no way she'll turn a blind eye so I can look at those files. I need a distraction. Just something quick, so I can snap a picture of the pages in Richard's file. It looks pretty thin, so it won't take long to get snapshots.

"I see you staring this file down," she gives me an all knowing stare.

"I'm not!" I quickly defend myself.

"I know what you're thinking, so I'll stop you before it goes too far. Don't try to take this file or any of the others. You know you can face serious charges for stealing pieces of evidence in an ongoing murder investigation?" she raises an eyebrow at me.

You can also face serious charges for breaking into people's homes and stealing burner cell phones you find in the back of dead people's closets. For a second there I thought I was actually starting to like Detective Heights. She just rubs me the wrong way, thinking she knows everything about me and the way I think. Well, I guess in this case she was right, but that's not the point!

"Why are you really here, Isabelle? I told you the first time we met that I thought you were a very smart young lady. I don't feel like you'd come here randomly."

"I want you to know that Hannah's not guilty! You're wasting so much time and energy while the murderer is still out there! What if he strikes again?" I fire back. I don't know why I came here, but, subconsciously, I think I wanted to find something to prove to myself that I wasn't guilty of anything. I don't know why I expected to find it at the police station, but maybe I thought that being here would provide me with some reassurance. Maybe I thought it would give me some control over the situation. Maybe I thought it would make me feel less helpless. Honestly, I don't know why I do most of the things I do but it did tell me two things. One — Richard has a solid and indisputable alibi. Two — I cannot stand Detective Heights!

Detective Heights replies to my question, "We are doing everything we possibly can, as I told you before. Detective Burnside and I are very good at our jobs. I don't think you have to worry about the killer striking again."

Oh how wrong Detective Heights is.

*****

Later that night, Graeson, Hazel, Luke, Shea, and I meet at Graeson's house to discuss any new information we've learned in the last few days. Hazel and Luke did some digging and found out that Isla Grimaldi did, in fact, attend Williams College where Thomas Grimaldi was her professor. They got married right after she graduated, showing that all of the dates line up. This makes it totally plausible that Stephanie threatened to expose their relationship, causing Isla to send her threats. Isla and Thomas's relationship sends a weird and disturbing feeling throughout my body. I can see what she liked about him. From all of the pictures I've seen, he's very handsome and charming. He has hair the color of leather and eyes the color of topaz with a strong jawline and a charismatic smile. But still, it just seems so wrong.

Hazel and Luke are still coming up with a plan of attack for dealing with Isla, a way of proving either her innocence or her guilt. Shea, Graeson, and I have come up with very little in terms of Sawyer. I researched the guy for hours, and nothing but excellent achievements, prestigious awards, and amazing reviews has come up. Graeson's idea was to walk over to his house and confront him, but everyone pretty much shot that down.

I fill everyone in on my strange interaction with Forrest, how I think he's lying about his job, and my meeting with Alison. I also tell them about my visit with Hannah, my impromptu meeting with Detective Heights, and Richard's airtight alibi. Saying it all out loud makes me realize how much I've accomplished in the past few days. I paid off a nine-year-old for blackmail, visited an inmate in jail, almost had a throwdown with a guard, investigated my strange rat-like neighbor, and tried to steal files from a police station. Look at me go!

"This is a lot of information for my brain to process," Graeson whines. "I really think we should just go confront Sawyer."

"Like I said before, you have about as much subtlety as a grenade," Hazel retorts. "I think we should drive up to Forrest's lab and see what we can figure out. I don't understand why he would lie about his job."

"I feel like the more we dive into this, the more I realize how much everyone is hiding. All of these people look so normal and innocent on the outside, but everyone's hiding something," Shea says and then he turns to me. "I can't believe you figured all of this out. Did you sleep at all?"

"Nope. I've been up since 3 a.m., and I've drank about seven cups of coffee!" I respond, sounding and feeling completely wired.

"Out of all of these people, who would've wanted her dead?" Luke asks.

Suddenly, I hear a banging noise right outside Graeson's bonus room door. I feel myself jump and instinctively reach for

Shea's hand. A middle-aged blonde lady stumbles in holding a half empty wine glass.

"That's my mum," he whispers to us before turning his attention to her. "Why are you up here?"

She walks a few more wobbly steps closer to us, her feet as unsteady as a baby first learning to walk. She has bleach blonde, pin straight hair that falls slightly above her shoulders. She has a heart shaped face with spray tanned skin a little too orange to look natural. Her icy blue eyes are identical to Graeson's, and she's dressed to the nines, her outfit including a lavish pearl necklace.

"I overheard your conversation," she says, her British accent even thicker than Graeson's. "You think you can solve the murder of my best friend." Her teeth are stained with red wine. She takes another sip, or really more of a chug of her wine, the glass clinking against her teeth.

"My mum and Stephanie were best friends," Graeson explains to us. "They were quite close. She likes her wine a lot, it makes her a little snippy. Please excuse this scene. Mum, I think you should go back downstairs with Dad and Charlotte."

"Oh, shut your trap young man! Listen to me, kids," she slurs as she motions for us to come closer and leans her head farther in our direction. "Stephanie was my best friend in the entire world, but she had a lot of enemies. So many enemies. Oh so many enemies, but aside from the lying and the cheating, she was a good person." She starts hysterically laughing, sounding like a hyena. "Who am I kidding? She was a bitch! But I loved her. She was my best friend. You know I don't trust those bigshot detectives one bit!"

"Mrs. Ambrose?" I speak up, surprised with the nerve I've suddenly acquired. "Do you know who would've wanted Stephanie dead?"

She snorts, "Oh darling! You children are like little foxes chasing your tails. You're asking the wrong questions! You keep

269

asking who would've wanted Stephanie dead, when all you need to be asking is who pulled the trigger."

Suddenly, Hazel's phone makes a pinging noise, the sound breaking through the ominous quiet following Mrs. Ambrose's theatrical comment.

"Oh my God!" Hazel's phone drops from her hand to the floor with a thud as her face turns alarmingly pale. "Hannah's dead."

CHAPTER 14 - Catching Fireflies . . . and Killers

I feel like I'm free falling, like I'm suspended in time itself. I'm paralyzed in the moment, trapped in a horrifying nightmare I can't wake up from. My heart skips a beat and all the air has been sucked out of my lungs. Everything seems to be spinning in blurry circles around me, making me feel like there's billions of bees buzzing in my head. My body goes rigid, all of my joints and muscles constricting and tightening, making it so I can't move. I'm trying to breathe, but I feel like there's a weight crushing my chest and lungs, restraining the air from passing through. It feels like someone just kicked a soccer ball full force into my stomach. A bitter chill spreads through my body, causing goosebumps to erupt on my arms and legs. I hear voices in the background, the sounds echoing and fading in my ears. This can't be true. I was with her a few hours ago. I was just there. Oh my God. I'm going to be sick. I launch myself upwards and take off running towards Graeson's bathroom. I fall to my knees as a stream of beige vomit emerges from my mouth and into the toilet water. The acidic puke stings my throat as I sit there heaving, still unable to breathe.

Shea rushes in after me and crouches down to my level. He places his hand gently on my back and says, "It's okay. It's okay. Izzie, look at me." I look up at him, focusing my gaze in his bright blue eyes. "You're okay. You're going to be okay," he says calmly.

I don't understand how he can be so calm at a time like this. Maybe his dad's death has made him good at handling tragic situations.

I start hyperventilating, panicking, because I can't catch my breath. "I can't breathe! I can't breathe!" I gasp. Utter fear fills my eyes as he wraps his arms around me and pulls me into his body. I sob into the soft cotton of his t-shirt and cling to him. I feel the warmth of his body and the pressure from his arms tightly around me, which helps me start feeling grounded. "It's all my fault," I cry.

"No it's not," he holds me tighter. "You didn't do anything. Just try to take a deep breath, Izzie. This is all going to be okay."

"No, it *is* my fault. She was about to tell me who the killer was! Someone wanted to get rid of her before she talked. If I never went to visit her, she wouldn't be dead!"

"There was nothing you could've done to cause this. I know it's a lot right now, but I promise you that it's not your fault. Just try to breathe. Come on, breathe with me. In and out."

I follow what he says, trying to just focus on my breathing. In and out. In and out. In and out. The tears keep pouring down my face, stinging my cheeks, but I feel like my lungs are finally working again.

"I'm sorry I'm such a mess," I say to him when I've finally gained a little composure.

"Why are you sorry? No matter what, I'll be here for you. You have to know that this wasn't your fault, Izzie. You can't blame yourself for this. Whoever killed her is seriously messed up, and it has nothing to do with you."

When I'm slightly less of a disaster, Shea and I walk back to the bonus room where everyone else is. Hazel sits with tears streaming down her face while she stares into the distance, eyes fixed on a random point on the wall. Graeson paces the room with his hand covering his mouth while Luke reads the breaking news intently on his phone. Mrs. Ambrose has disappeared, leaving the room silent, like a muted TV. Everyone is still moving, but there's no sound.

My footsteps echo as I walk into the room, while the quiet buzzes in my ears. Everyone looks up at us as Shea and I step into the room.

"Is she really dead?" I ask quietly.

Luke nods his head slowly and says, "It says that they think she died at around two p.m. She was scheduled to meet with her lawyer at three. When the guards went to her cell to take her to meet with the lawyer, she was dead."

I feel my knees becoming weak and my pulse rapidly increasing, but I know I have to keep a clear head right now. I can't freak out and panic again.

"Is there any other information? I need to know everything," I say.

"Are you sure?" Luke asks, his voice riddled with concern. "I think it's just going to make you more upset."

"I need to know, Luke. Hannah was about to tell me who she thought the killer was, and now she's dead. Whoever killed her is going out of their way to make sure that Stephanie's murder doesn't get solved. But I was there. I sat across from her. I saw the emptiness in her eyes and heard the hopelessness in her voice. If I hadn't gone, maybe she would still be alive. I just need to know exactly what happened," my voice is unsteady, but surprisingly loud and confident.

"Okay," Luke starts. "When the guards went to get her, they found her lying in her cell with one stab wound to the throat. They aren't sure if she committed suicide or if . . . if . . . she was murdered. All they said is they're not releasing any other information at the time, but that no one should worry," he laughs sarcastically. "I guess that's supposed to be reassuring."

"The person who killed Stephanie has to be the same person who killed Hannah," Hazel speaks up. "Hannah was about to tell her lawyer something that could link someone to the murder.

273

Wouldn't it make sense that Stephanie's killer took Hannah out before she exposed him or her?"

"You can't sneak into the jail and kill someone. It's locked up and guarded at all times," Shea adds. "Maybe Stephanie's killer paid off an inmate to get rid of Hannah."

Shea and Hazel both make solid points. My head goes straight to Stephanie's killer when I think about the person responsible for Hannah's death. There's no chance this was a random act. Hannah seemed so hopeless when I visited her, but still, I can't imagine her giving up that easy. She loved her kids with every bone in her body. She said she was going to fight for them, that she would do anything to hold them again. I don't think she'd end her life if she thought there was any chance of her getting to see them again. I don't believe in coincidences. The person who killed Stephanie has to be the same one who killed or ordered the kill of Hannah just as she was about to reveal an important piece of evidence. This is going to sound insanely strange, but I feel a small sense of relief. If these two murders are connected, then that means I didn't kill Stephanie. That means I'm not guilty. All I know is that I need to stay focused. I have to figure out who did this to Hannah. I need to give her the justice she deserves.

"We can't give up on this," I say. "We have to find the murderer."

"I don't know," Luke responds. "This is starting to feel really dangerous, Izzie. I don't know if we want to cross paths with this person. If we keep digging, what's to say this person won't come after us."

"We have to do this for Hannah. I'm not giving up until we find out who did this," I fire back. "She deserves justice. We can't give up on her."

"I'm in," Graeson stands up next to me. "We came this far. Plus, I'm really enjoying breaking into houses."

Hazel glares at him, "This is not the time for jokes. But I'm in too. For Hannah."

"Me too, for Hannah," Luke agrees, but I'm pretty sure he's only willing to help because Hazel is.

"Alright," Shea says. "For Hannah."

We sit awhile longer in silence, each of us too tired to keep working, but a little too on edge to head home. Even though the lights are on, I can't help but feel like some mysterious darkness has descended upon us. My thoughts continuously drift to Hannah. Her hollow, defeated face is burned into my brain. She's gone, she's really gone. A few hours ago I was talking to her, and now she's dead. I feel like the human brain wasn't meant to comprehend such loss. I just don't understand how a person can be here one minute and gone the next. It's the worst feeling — a mixture of disbelief, guilt, and sadness. It feels like there's this emptiness hanging around in my heart and a heaviness in the air I'm breathing. You know what the worst part is? The world keeps spinning and everyone will keep moving on with their lives just the same. When you think about it that way, it makes it feel like her life was so insignificant. The world won't even feel the impact of this loss. But I feel it. A few days from now, Hannah will be nothing more than an old newspaper headline. It makes me wonder who's going to remember me when I'm gone. Will I be nothing more than a name in the obituary section of the newspaper?

For Hannah. I keep repeating it in my head, trying to keep myself from spiraling down a dark and twisty tunnel. We have to figure this out for Hannah. For Hannah. For Hannah.

*****

"I have to ask you something," Hazel says to me nervously while the two of us sit on the front porch, in the new rocking chairs my parents just bought.

"Okay," I respond. "Is everything alright?"

"Everything's fine . . . I think," she says. This is making me extremely anxious. I'm not sure how much more shocking news I can take this week.

"Hazel, you're starting to freak me out. What is it?"

"Would it be weird if I went on a date with your brother?" she asks anxiously.

My face instantly lights up, my eyes popping with excitement and my mouth turning up into a wide smile. Finally, my constant pestering of Luke and meddling with his love life has paid off!

"Oh my gosh, Hazel! I've been waiting for this to happen for forever! Did he ask you out?"

"Not officially, but when you went out with Shea, I stayed and talked to Luke for a while. He asked me if I would want to go out with him sometime, but we didn't plan anything. I wanted to ask you sooner, but then everything with Hannah happened."

"Hazel, of course you can go out with him! I've been waiting for him to ask you out for weeks."

"Wait, are you saying that he's wanted to ask me out for a while?" Her cheeks blush and her ocean eyes start shining a bit brighter.

I smile slyly, "He's liked you for a few weeks. He wouldn't admit it to me because he gets annoyed when I'm all up in his business, but I just knew. I am totally fine with the two of you going out."

Hazel is beaming as she says, "Thank you. I really like him, but I didn't want to go for it without asking you. He's a really nice guy."

"He's my best friend," I say. "You should totally go for it."

The early afternoon sun hangs in the cloudless, pale blue sky, and the air smells of mowed grass and the blooming peonies my mom just planted in the front yard. Out of the corner of my eyes, I notice Easton Black walking down the street. He mutters to himself, using his hands to help him communicate to this invisible person. I'm not sure what he's talking about, but he seems to speak with a high intensity.

"Easton," I whisper to Hazel. "We have to go question him about the man with the gun."

"We can't interrogate a schizophrenic!" Hazel says harshly.

"Why not?" I fire back.

Hazel looks at me like I've lost my mind, "Because! He's mentally unstable!"

"So? He knows something about a man with a gun!"

"He also thinks there are invisible people watching him and chasing him all the time!"

"Come on, Hazel. It can't hurt just to talk to him for a few minutes."

"I don't know."

"Hazel, please! You're so good with him. We can talk to him together!"

"Fine. You can be very pushy," she laughs.

As Easton is about to walk past my driveway, Hazel and I rush down to meet him. At first he seems startled by our presence and considering the fact that the two of us basically charged at him like bulls, I understand the reaction.

"Hi, Easton," Hazel says calmly and gently. "How are you today?"

"I'm good," his voice is slow and robotic. "I think I'm supposed to ask you how you are."

"I'm doing good, thank you for asking," Hazel responds.

Easton's slate grey eyes dart from the sidewalk to Hazel and then over to me. He squints at me, staring me down until I feel so uncomfortable that my toes are curled far under my feet. I feel the air around me go cold, causing the hairs on my arms to stand up.

277

"Are you hurt?" he finally says to me.

I don't say anything for a moment because I'm trying to process the question. Am I hurt? Why would I be hurt?

"I'm not hurt," I answer. "I'm fine."

"You were hurt," he says again as he steps closer to me, "You were hurt."

"When was I hurt?" I ask him.

He takes another step closer while he continues to squint his eyes, as if he's analyzing my face. Easton's so close I can smell the spearmint toothpaste on his breath.

"That night. I saw it. You were hurt," his voice is eerily monotone.

"What happened?" I ask, trying to coax the story out of him.

He starts muttering under his breath again, mumbling some incoherent words. He shakes his head furiously and stares down at the sidewalk. He's lost his grip on reality once more, retreating to the world inside his head.

"Easton," I say impatiently. "Easton. I need to know what happened!"

Hazel eyes me, signaling not to push too hard. She asks softly and quietly, "Can you tell us what happened that night?"

He removes his gaze from the sidewalk and meets Hazel's eyes, "The man. He had a gun. He hurt *them*."

Hazel and I look at each other, communicating our shock and fear with our facial expressions. He clearly said *them*, meaning more than one.

"Tell me about the man. What was he doing?" Hazel questions. She's taken over the questioning because she's obviously a lot more patient than I am.

He takes another step closer to us and whispers, "He's watching us right now." Chills spread through my entire body, a shivery cold feeling that pricks my skin. Easton points out

278

somewhere in the distance. I feel my stomach clench as I look in the direction he's pointing. It makes me feel like there's someone lurking in the shadows unnoticed. Someone who knows the truth about Stephanie and Hannah.

All of a sudden Easton lets out a deafening shriek. The noise pierces my ear, sending a wave of terror through my body. Easton continues to scream bloody murder as Hazel and I stand there unsure of what to do. He takes off running down the sidewalk, his legs pumping with a burning passion behind him. His shrill howl continues all the way down the street, until he reaches his front door.

I glance over to Hazel, and she looks over at me. Both of our eyes are wide with shock and our mouths hang open. We stand there in silence for a few minutes, trying to find the words to describe this.

After a while, I say the only words I can come up with to Hazel. I ask her, "What the hell was that?"

*****

"Are you sure you're going to be alright here alone?" my mom asks me for the millionth time today.

"Yes, I'm positive. I was sure about it the first time you asked, I was sure about it five minutes ago when you asked, and I'm sure about it now," I reply.

"I just don't like the thought of leaving you two here alone all night, especially with everything going on."

"We'll be fine! It's less than twenty-four hours and we have the new alarm system."

"Are you sure you don't want to come with me and the girls?"

"No offense, but I'd rather stick my head through a meat grinder than go to Sesame Street live," I laugh.

"It's not that bad," she jokingly rolls her eyes at my overdramatic comments. "Make sure you have that alarm on at all times and the door locked when you're inside. Call me or John if you need anything."

She continues on with this speech for another ten minutes, warning me of all the hazards I could possibly encounter ranging from house fires to lunatic burglars breaking in. I've completely tuned it out. It's the hundredth time I've heard this lecture and frankly, I probably wouldn't follow most of what she said even if I was listening. She and John bought Madison tickets to see Sesame Street Live for her birthday in Boston. The four of them — Mom, John, Madison, and Olivia — were supposed to be heading up together, but John's mom recently fell and broke her hip, so he's heading up to Harwich Port in Cape Cod to see her. After Hannah died, my mom's been extremely hesitant to let Luke and I stay home. I have plans for my night with no parents around, so I've been trying my best to get her to go.

"I might just stay home," she says worriedly.

"Mom, Madison will be so disappointed if you don't go. She's been looking forward to this for weeks! You can't let her down because of me and Luke. We'll be fine. We'll keep the alarm on at all times," I try to convince her.

While she's debating, John comes down the stairs with his overnight bag and Madison in tow.

"Alright," he says cheerfully. "We should all be ready to go. Everything's packed. I double checked the outlets to make sure everything's unplugged. I think we're good to go."

"She doesn't want to go anymore because she's nervous to leave Luke and I alone. Please, please, please talk some sense into her. We're going to be fine!" I say to John.

Madison walks over to my mom in the kitchen, her tangled mocha brown hair topped with a princess tiara and her cheeks rosy red. She looks at my mom and pouts, "Mommy! We have to go see

Elmo!"

"Brenna, it's going to be fine. I'm only about an hour away. If they need anything, I can be here fast. Plus, there are neighbors all around if they need anything. We can't let this murderer run our lives. You and the girls have been looking forward to this," John says calmly. His voice is so reassuring, he could convince you of anything.

"Please, Mommy!" Madison begs.

I pick up Madison, which makes her giggle, and say, "How could you say no to that face?" Madison delivers her best puppy dog face, making my mom melt at the sight of it.

"I feel like I'm being ambushed," she laughs. "But okay, we'll go. You need to promise me Izzie that the alarm will be on and you'll answer when I text to check-in."

"I promise," I agree.

"What are your plans for tonight?" she asks.

"Oh, nothing much," I lie. "I'm just going to hang out around here, maybe see Hazel."

"Just stay safe and make sure your home and inside by ten. And please keep me updated on where you are," she says.

"No problem," I smile. "Have fun in Boston. Luke and I are going to be fine."

Luke comes down from his room, and we all say our goodbyes. With the amount of hugging going on, you would think they weren't going to be back for weeks.

"Did she buy it?" Luke asks.

"It was like taking candy from a baby. She thinks we're staying home all night. This is going to be fun," I reply.

Graeson told us about this spot in the woods that he and some of his friends from his soccer team used to hang out and throw parties at. He had an idea — a surprisingly good one — for all five of us to go up there and hang out by the makeshift fire pit. I understand that if there's a killer on the loose, walking around in the woods in the middle of the night is probably really stupid. But hey, you're only young and dumb once! Besides, the thought of sitting by a fire in the woods with Shea is making me and the butterflies in my stomach feel giddy.

When Luke and I are back inside, I say to him with a smirk on my face, "So I was talking to Hazel yesterday . . ."

His face instantly turns an alarming shade of crimson as he looks at me bug eyed, "What did she say?"

I smile slyly, "Wouldn't you like to know?"

"Izzie!" he yells. "What did she tell you?"

I laugh at how easy it is to rattle him, "She just said that you asked her out. She wanted to make sure I was okay with it. She sounded really excited."

"She did?" he asks intensely as he continues to blush.

"Ooh, someone's turning all red," I tease.

He rolls his eyes at me, "You're the worst."

"You're so easy, Luke, it's hard not to," I laugh. "But seriously, she sounded really happy. I think you guys are perfect for each other. And tonight's the perfect night to get *closer* with her."

"That was almost nice," he shakes his head jokingly. "You can't say anything to embarrass me in front of her."

"I make no promises for the things that come out of my mouth," I joke.

"Izzie! I mean it!" he says with annoyance seeping into his voice.

"Dude, relax," I respond. "It's going to be a great night."

Later that night, we all pile into Graeson's baby blue Cadillac and brace for the ride ahead of us. I pull my seatbelt extra tight as he pulls out of Mayflower Circle on two wheels, just barely missing the Black's grass. With the top down, I feel the wind rushing through my blonde hair and the evening air brushing against my skin. My stomach lurches every time Graeson hits the gas pedal or nearly hits multiple mailboxes and telephone poles on the side of the road.

"So what should we do about what Easton said?" Hazel asks.

Our strange interaction with Easton has been nagging my brain, leaving a sour feeling in the pit of my stomach. The last two times I've talked to Easton I was left with an eerie and unsettling feeling. The line between reality and imagination is so blurred with Easton. But I swear, something changed in his voice when he was talking about the man with the gun. How am I supposed to know if there's any truth to what he's saying? And why was he so convinced that I was hurt?

"Hazel Huntington, there will be no talk of Stephanie's murder or anyone connected to it tonight! We are going to have ourselves a grand old time," Graeson pipes up.

"It was so strange," I say, responding to Hazel's question. "Maybe we talk to him again?"

"Why are you guys putting so much weight into what Easton Black says? He has schizophrenia. He's mentally unstable. He doesn't know what he's talking about," Graeson whines.

Graeson makes a solid point. Maybe Hazel and I are just reading too much into Easton's words. Maybe we're making more out of what he says than it really is. When Luke and I were little, we would lie in our backyard, look up at the clouds, and try to figure out what shapes they made. We'd spend hours arguing over what each one was. Was it a bunny rabbit or a flower or a dragon? We'd come up with the strangest and most outlandish shapes we could think of, but when it came down to it, all it really was was a cloud. There were no dragons or rabbits in the sky. Only clouds. Maybe we're doing the same thing with what Easton said — trying to mold his words to fit some crazy theory.

Hazel and Graeson bicker back and forth about what Easton said until Graeson finally erupts, "Tonight is about having fun! We can talk all about this tomorrow. Please Hazel, for the love of all things holy, can we just have a good time tonight?"

Hazel thinks pensively for a few moments before saying, "Okay, fine. But just for tonight."

Graeson swerves into the parking lot of a park at about five hundred miles an hour. For a second I feel like I'm going to be literally thrown out of the car. The parking lot is completely empty and the playground is deserted. It's weird to look at the structure and not see any little kids swinging or running or sliding. Dusk is settling over Knox Hollow. That, combined with the vacant playground, sends a grim feeling through my body — almost like a premonition of something going wrong. I need to just get out of my own head. I'm here with my best friends to have a great night.

"The trails are down this way," Graeson points behind where the car is parked to the thick layer of trees. "We'll take that one down, and it'll lead us to the clearing where the fire pit is."

Graeson leads the way into the trails as the brightness from the day quickly fades into a gloomy grey haze that settles over the wooded area. Hazel and Luke follow behind him, flirting with each other as they go. I hesitate to step into the trails, feeling like there's some invisible force pulling me back.

"Are you okay?" Shea asks, noticing my hesitation.

"Yeah," I stutter. "I'm fine. Just lost in thought."

He takes my hand, and the two of us follow the others into the woods. I let the odd feeling go, knowing that it's probably my overactive imagination stirring up problems. Large trees line both sides of the trail, standing so tall their leaves seem to touch the sky. The dirt path is rocky and filled with tree roots that will knock you right off your feet if you're not paying attention. Graeson holds a flashlight out in front of him, the yellow beam of light illuminating the space in front of us. Wind rustles the tree branches, causing them to sway and creating shadows on the path. Small animals run around in the bushes and trees, their movements making noises.

Every time I hear the sound I jump and squeeze Shea's hand. I feel like someone's following us, like there's somebody lurking in the shadows and behind the trees, waiting for the right moment to pounce on us.

"Are you sure this is safe?" Hazel asks worriedly.

"Of course this is safe. Don't be silly, Hazel," Graeson replies. "Do you think something's going to jump out and grab you?" At that moment he reaches out and shakes Hazel, much to her surprise, who lets out an ear piercing scream.

"Graeson! I swear to God!" she yells at him and punches him in the arm.

He starts hysterically laughing, "Come on, loosen up. It's all in good fun."

They go on with their banter, Graeson cracking himself up while Hazel mutters at how he almost scared the living daylights out of her and how immature he is.

After we've been walking for a while, I say to Graeson, "Are you sure you know where we're going? I feel like we've passed this spot already."

"I could walk here in my sleep," Graeson responds confidently. "It's just up a bit this way."

I start to doubt Graeson's abilities and wonder why I trusted him to lead me into the woods late at night. How stupid am I? However, a few minutes later we arrive at a small clearing with a fire pit made out of stones and rocks in the middle.

"I told you I knew where I was going. No one believed me," Graeson says.

"You don't have the best track record," Shea comments jokingly.

The boys get to work starting the fire while Hazel and I set up the folding chairs that we carried down here. Now that we're here with the light of the fire, the nervous feeling has faded and I start to relax. There's something magical about being down in the woods by the fire. The smoky smell fills my nose as I push myself closer to the blazing flames in order to prevent the cold night air from catching my skin. The moon hangs in the sky like a shiny, round pearl, casting pale beams of light onto the woods. Little pieces of ash from the fire fall onto my bare legs like snowflakes. Crickets chirp in the background and I can hear everyone around me talking and laughing and making jokes. This is what summer feels like. Just living for the thrill of one exciting night without any fear of time or tomorrow. Just enjoying the moment we're in now.

"Did you ever hear about the old car that's in these woods?" Graeson asks. We all shake our heads and ask him what he's talking about. "There's this really old model of a 1950's Chevrolet Styleline Coupe a little down that way off the path. It's beaten up pretty badly and parked in the middle of a thick patch of trees and bushes. No one knows how it got here."

"How far down is it?" Luke asks inquisitively, his interest peaked at Graeson's story.

"A little over a quarter of a mile," Graeson answers. "Want to go see it?"

"Sure!" Luke says excitedly.

"Anyone else want to come?" Graeson asks.

"I'll go," Hazel says.

The thought of leaving the fire and heading deeper into the woods and the darkness makes me shiver. There's no chance I'm letting Graeson lead me on another adventure through the forest.

"I'm good," I speak up. "It's cold, and I'd rather stay near the fire."

"I'll stay with you," Shea says, his words sending the cold away.

The three of them go off further down the path in search of this mysterious car, and it's too dark to be sure, but I swear I see Hazel take Luke's hand. I guess the sparks from the fire aren't the only ones flying. I inch my chair closer to the fire and closer to

Shea. Smoke sears my eyes, burning the gaping blue pools above my nose until they water. I scrunch up my nose and squint, trying to shield them from the stinging smoke. I notice fireflies blinking off in the distance, yellow green dots flickering on and off.

"Look at all those fireflies," I say to Shea.

He smiles and says, "My sister and I used to catch them all the time in the summer. We'd run out in the backyard with mason jars and catch as many as we could."

"I was never patient enough to catch them. My dad would try to help me, but I would give up within five minutes. They move too fast, and it's hard to see them when their light keeps flickering off," I laugh at myself.

I stand up from my chair, not exactly sure what I'm doing, but just knowing that I want to live in the moment. I want to be bold and young and not worry about all the little things I spend so much time thinking about. I walk a few steps over to his chair and crouch down so our faces are level. Before my brain can catch up with what I'm doing, I lean in and kiss him, feeling the rush of all my emotions. He kisses me back, pulling me onto his lap and then running his fingers through my hair. Finally, a perfect moment between the two of us that Graeson can't ruin. I'd much rather him third wheel with Hazel and Luke than with me and Shea. We pull away for a moment, and I'm unable to open my eyes for a few seconds. Just feeling his warm, tanned skin against mine blocks out the cold night air around us.

Suddenly, I hear an excruciatingly loud noise that rattles me from the inside out. What the *hell* was that? I look to Shea, my face a mixture of confusion and fright. We stand up and look around, trying to identify the source of the noise. I feel a small wave of fear rising in my body as my heart starts to beat faster. I feel like the premonition of danger I had before we came down the trail is starting to come true. Everything is eerily quiet for a moment, even the crickets have stopped chirping. Another few seconds pass. Silence. Out of nowhere, another popping noise pierces my eardrums, this one sounding much closer. My heart begins to race, and I can hear myself breathing heavily. I'm terrified to move even the slightest bit. Another moment of quiet. Quickly after, another popping noise is set off. It sounds like firecrackers, but louder and far more intense. Another popping noise echoes through the forest, causing me to drop to the ground in fear. Suddenly, I hear footsteps rushing towards us, slapping the dirt and rustling the leaves on the ground.

Shea looks at me with utter panic in his bright blue eyes and screams, "RUN!!!"

My adrenaline begins to kick in, rushing through my veins and propelling my body up from the ground. I start to sprint, moving my legs as fast as I possibly can. I feel my muscles rippling and my feet throbbing as I dive deeper into the darkness, unable to see two feet in front of me. I'm blindly trying to avoid roots and rocks along the path, praying to God I can somehow keep myself from falling. I have absolutely no clue where I'm running to, but that doesn't seem to matter now. All I can think about is pumping my legs as fast and as far as they can go. Those popping noises were gunshots. Someone is after us, someone with a lethal weapon. That lingering feeling that someone was watching may not have been that far off. But there's no time to be scared. My lungs burn as if they were on fire, and it feels like there are thousands of knives being jabbed into my stomach.

"BANG!" Another gunshot fires off as I instinctively duck and cover my head. Shea runs behind me. I know he could go a lot faster than this, but he won't leave me alone. All of a sudden, my foot smacks straight into a tree root, and I go flying. I land face first into the dirt, my left ankle crushed under my body. I clench my jaw and bite down hard, puncturing my tongue with my teeth. Metallic tasting blood and coarse dirt fill my mouth, and I desperately try to spit to get some air into my lungs. Pain sears my ankle, and I feel the urge to scream. It feels as if someone has chopped the whole thing off, sawed right through the bone. I try to stand up, but immediately fall, the weight of my body crushing my ankle with a snapping sound and hitting me with an agonizing ache. This is where it ends for me. I can't run, I can't even move. This is it. I'm going to die.

I feel Shea bending over me. I say to him in a panic, "Go! Run! Just leave me! Go Shea!"

"I'm not leaving you here!" He says back passionately. I start to argue, but he quickly helps me to my feet. I put all of my weight onto him, using him as a human crutch.

"Get on my back," he says as he bends down. I follow what he says without hesitating and hoist myself up onto his back. I hang on around his neck, holding onto him with everything I've got left in me. The person with the gun is hot on our trails, their footsteps become increasingly louder with every passing second. Sweat pours down my forehead as Shea carries me and sprints through the woods. I'm tossed around on his back as he dodges roots and rocks in his way. He veers off the path suddenly, diving into a thick sea of trees. I notice the old car Graeson was talking about a few feet away from us partly hidden by branches and tree trunks. The black paint is scratched and rusted over, and certain parts of the car are bashed in. Even though our lives are in danger, I'm still wondering what the story behind this car is. I can't tell if this car is a saving grace or a bad omen.

"We're getting into the car," Shea whispers to me. He stops running and opens the back door as quietly as he can. He lowers me down onto the leather seat and climbs in after me. We crouch down on the floor so we're out of sight from the windows, squishing ourselves between the front and back seats. Both of us are completely silent, the only sound is our heavy breathing. Sweat plasters my hair to the sides of my face, and my ankle stings and throbs with unbearable pain.

I hear the footsteps of the shooter run by, his or her shoes booming against the dirt. Another shot rings out, which makes my entire body go rigid. I feel a tear roll down my cheek as the noise echoes and bounces off the trees. The footsteps pass, and silence settles over us. Shea and I stay scrunched up between the car seats for what feels like an hour, both of us completely silent and still.

"Are you okay?" Shea whispers. "What did you hurt?"

"I fell on my ankle. I think I broke it," I whisper back, terror creeping through my voice.

"I think he or she's gone. I'll carry you up, and then we'll get out of here as fast as we can."

"What about Hazel and Graeson and Luke?" I ask, my voice is hoarse. I had forgotten while we were running for our lives, the three of them had gone off to see the car we were currently hiding in. "What if something happened to them?"

"They probably heard the noise and ran up to the car," Shea reassures me, but I can tell he's terrified on the inside. "We have to get out of here."

I feel frozen in the backseat, horror filling my entire body to the brim. I want to get out of here, but I can't find the courage to break away from this paralyzing fear.

"It's okay," Shea says softly, but with a sense of urgency in his voice. "We need to get out of here."

I take a deep breath in, suppressing the searing pain in my ankle and the horror building in my chest. I push myself up from the floor and Shea helps me to my feet. My legs are violently shaking as I stand up.

Shea piggybacks me all the way up to Graeson's baby blue Cadillac. He runs the entire way at top speed, while I continuously look behind us and brace myself for the sound of gunshots. I feel a bitter chill filling my insides from the core, even though my face is sweating. I don't even know how to feel. All I can think about is getting into the car and getting home.

When we reach the car, we find Hazel, Graeson, and Luke anxiously pacing around. I thank my lucky stars that I'm out of the woods and away from the horrifying darkness.

Hazel rushes up to us, "What happened? We heard this sound and thought it was gunshots. We didn't know what to do, so we ran up! We kept trying to call you! Oh, please tell me you're alright!"

"We need to leave *now*," Shea demands.

Everyone obeys what he says without question and rushes into the car. This is the one and only time that I'm grateful for how fast Graeson drives. As we drive, Shea recounts the story to the others, but I don't hear much of what he says. There's this obnoxiously loud ringing in my ears that blocks out all other sounds. My mind feels empty, physically unable to form any thoughts.

We pull on to Mayflower Circle, the car engine revving loudly past all the dark and silent houses. Graeson drops Hazel off first with Luke walking her inside to make sure she's safe. Then Graeson drops me off with Shea to help me inside. Not only is my ankle throbbing, my body feels completely paralyzed. I feel like I can't move a single muscle or joint. Shea helps me out of the car, as Graeson says, "Make sure she's safe."

He walks me up the driveway, into the house, and up the stairs into my room. I balance all of my weight on him, unable to put any pressure on my ankle. I don't even have any words to talk about tonight. Everything just feels so numb like I'm living in someone else's body, someone else's story.

Shea helps me into bed and kisses the top of my head before saying, "Are you sure you're okay here?"

I nod, unable to force any words out of my mouth. He turns to walk out, but the second he touches the door I feel a sinking feeling in my stomach.

"Shea," I blurt out, my voice raspy.

He turns around, "Yeah?"

"Can you stay with me?" I pause. "I don't want to be alone right now."

He walks back over to me and sits on my bed with his back against the headboard. I instantly curl up as close as I can to him, burying my head into his side as he wraps his arms around me and holds me tight.

I never thought I'd fall asleep that night, but I soon drift off into a restless place. Eventually, morning comes and sunlight pours through my bedroom windows. I wake up in a daze, unsure if all of this was a nightmare or a reality. But when I wake up, Shea is still in the exact same place as he was last night, his arms still around me and my face still pressed against his side. After everything we've been through, this is all I need.

CHAPTER 15 - Second Chances

I stand in the shower for at least an hour, scrubbing the dirt caked on my legs and the sweat out of my hair. My ankle is swollen to the size of a softball, with blue and purple bruises covering my skin. It's taking everything I have in me just to stand up and take a shower. I wince every time I put even the least bit of pressure on my ankle. A constant searing pain shoots through the bone. I wash the dirt out from under my fingernails and the dried blood on my lips. I step out of the shower and throw on a pair on black leggings to hide the bruises on my ankle. I'm not sure how I'm supposed to explain how I acquired them to my mom, so I'm hoping if I just take it easy for a few days, the pain and bruises will go away. There's no way I can let her find out about last night. The woman was terrified of me just being home alone for a few hours. How is that conversation supposed to go? *Hey Mom, I let Graeson drive me out to the woods in the middle of the night, and while I was making out with the guy I'm not sure if I'm officially dating, we almost died because some person took a couple shots at us. But don't worry, we hid in some sketchy old abandoned car until he or she was gone. Oh, and I tripped over a root and may have broken my ankle.* Yeah, no way she can find out.

I brush out my hair, trying to rid it of all the tangles and knots. I examine myself in the mirror, wondering how to make myself at least semi presentable for when Mom and John get home. My face looks pale and hollow, and my eyes seem tired and empty. I feel like so much life and energy was pulled out of me last night. I start putting on some blush to bring some color back to my face and a little bit of mascara to make my eyes seem less exhausted. About halfway through my makeup I realize I don't have the patience to do this right now. Instead, I make my way into the kitchen and grab the first coffee mug I lay eyes on. Hopefully, the caffeine will jog my brain and get it to start functioning on a normal level.

Luke's already downstairs when I come down, sitting at the kitchen counter nervously tapping his leg and watching the news.

"Hey, how are you feeling?" he asks.

"I'm okay," I say, but I'm not sure if I mean it. "My ankle hurts, but it should be fine. Don't say anything to Mom or John about what happened last night."

"What exactly happened last night?" Luke looks at me with worry written all over his face. "I'm still so confused."

I pour a cup of coffee and sit down next to him at the counter. I take a sip of the steamy liquid and a deep breath. I say with a raspy voice, "I don't really know. Shea and I were sitting by the fire and we heard this popping noise. We kind of just sat there for a few minutes and then there were three or four more shots. It was definitely gunshots that we heard. And then the person came after us. We just started running. I didn't even know where I was going, but we just kept running. I tripped over a root and fell on my ankle. It hurt so bad I couldn't even move, so Shea piggybacked me. He veered off the path, and we hid in that old car. The shooter didn't see us and kept running by. Once we were sure he or she was far enough away, we ran up to Graeson's car."

Recounting the story sends a chill through my body. It sounds like something out of a movie or a book but this, this was reality. I could've died last night. I shudder as that thought passes through my head. I don't want to think about it.

"What happened to you guys?" I ask Luke.

"We hadn't quite made it to the old car and we heard a bang, that popping noise you were talking about. We kept walking a little bit, but then we heard a couple more gunshots that sounded a lot closer. We ran up to the car and called you guys," he answers.

"This can't be a coincidence, Luke. With everything going on, there's no shot that this was random. No pun intended."

"We're close to finding the killer. Just hear me out, this might sound a little . . . crazy. We're figuring a lot out about everyone and the things they're trying to hide. One of these people may have killed Stephanie, and then killed Hannah when she tried to say who she thought it was. What if we're onto something? If we're so close to figuring out who this person is, they probably panicked. They took a couple shots at us to scare us off, to stop us from digging further."

"That's what I was thinking. We're getting too close for comfort to someone. My money's on Sawyer or Forrest. They thought they could scare us off with a couple shots, but I'm not giving up on this. I need to know that I didn't do anything, and I need to get justice for Hannah."

"Speaking of Hannah . . ." Luke starts. "The news broke the story this morning before you came down. They ruled her death a suicide."

"That's a load of crap!" I raise my voice. "There's no way. It doesn't add up. If she thought she knew who the killer was why would she commit suicide before she had a chance to meet with her   lawyer?"

"I know," Luke says quietly. "It doesn't make sense. Detective Heights and Detective Burnside are making a public announcement tonight."

"This is ridiculous! They're going to stop looking into this case! They think Hannah killed Stephanie and then killed herself so she wouldn't have to go to jail for the rest of her life. Hannah didn't do it! We can't let the entire world think she's a murderer!"

"We're not going to let that happen. We're close to finding

this person. I can feel it. Take that anger and channel it into solving this."

Luke always knows the right things to say to keep me from falling off the edge. I take a deep breath in and try to exhale all of the anger. Panicking doesn't solve anything. I need to stay focused.

Suddenly, I hear a knock at the door. The sound catches me off guard and makes me jump. I eye Luke, scared to answer after everything that went down last night. He understands that my concerned look means that there's no way in hell I'm going to be the one to open the door to whatever serial killer or lunatic murderer is out there. He stands up from the chair and makes his way over to the front door. He opens it slowly, while I stay in the kitchen bracing myself for whoever this may be.

"It's Hazel," he calls out.

I release my breath, feeling relieved. Okay, so maybe I'm not as fine as I told Luke I was.

Luke leads Hazel into our kitchen. She looks anxious, something about her just seems off. Her hair is thrown up into a messy bun, and she wears a pair of Nike running shorts and a t-shirt.

"How are you feeling?" she asks nervously. "I've been worried sick about everything going on. I couldn't sleep last night."

"I'm okay," I say confidently, even though that's so far from the truth. "Are you good?"

"I'm fine," she replies. "Just a little shaken up. Is your ankle okay?"

I pull up my pant leg and show her my alarmingly swollen and bruised ankle. Hazel gasps and says, "Yikes! You have to get that checked out! Those bruises are almost black, which means that this is a serious injury."

"I'm fine, it's just a little bruising. I'm not going to the doctor because that would take a lot of explaining."

"Okay, but if you're not going to go to the doctor, you need to stay off your ankle. You should ice it and keep it elevated."

"I will, Doctor Hazel," I joke.

She rolls her eyes jokingly, "I'm just looking out for you."

"I know," I half smile. "It's what I love about you."

"Did you hear about Hannah?" Luke juts into our conversation.

Hazel shakes her head in disgust, "They're ruling it a suicide. That just doesn't sound like Hannah at all. She's not a murderer. I don't think she'd give up that easy."

"She didn't commit suicide," I say. "She was murdered because she knew something. And I don't think last night was random."

"What do you mean?" she asks.

Luke and I spend the next few minutes filling Hazel in on our superstitions about how last night is somehow wrapped up in both Hannah's and Stephanie's deaths.

"That makes sense in some weird, twisted way," she agrees. "So that means we're on to something. Who are we close to exposing? Sawyer, Forrest, Isla, maybe even Beckett. We're on to all of them."

"That's what I'm thinking," says Luke. "I feel like it's Isla. Stephanie's murder seemed like a crime of passion, not a premeditated plan."

"You should keep looking into her," Hazel responds. "In the meantime, Beckett asked me to babysit this morning. I'm on my way over there now. I'm going to snoop around a little and see what I can find."

"That's perfect!" I say. "You'll have full access to his house, and you won't even have to break-in. Can I come?"

"I don't see why not," she answers. "I'll just tell Beckett you're here to help. It's not like he'll care. And then the two of us can do some digging."

A little while later, Hazel and I are on our way over to the St. James residence while Luke dives back into the mysteries revolving around Isla Grimaldi. Stepping up to the brick house instantly takes me back to the day Hannah was arrested. I still vividly remember the knock on the door and the way time seemed to freeze. It's an odd sense of déjà vu I can't seem to shake.

Beckett answers the door, and I can't help but notice how different he looks from the first time I saw him at Stephanie's wake. His beard is an unmanicured mess; it looks mangy and overgrown. His warm brown eyes are dull and cold, and the skin underneath them is red, as if he's been crying. His lips are turned down into a permanent frown, and he seems at least fifteen pounds lighter than the last time I saw him. Even though he still stands at 6'4", he seems to have shrunk. He doesn't say anything, just lets us in and goes back to his cup of black coffee in the kitchen. The silence in the room stabs my stomach.

"We heard about Hannah," Hazel says quietly. "I'm so sorry."

He nods his head, but keeps his eyes on the cup in front of him and his mouth shut. It seems like it's taking everything he has in him not to break down in tears. That must be one interesting cup of coffee though, seeing it's the only thing he's looked at for the past five minutes. Awkward silence fills the room, making my insides twist. I start nervously tapping my non-throbbing foot against the ground, trying to ignore how uncomfortable I feel.

"Did you kill Stephanie?" I blurt out.

I instantly cover my mouth and turn to Hazel with my eyes as wide as saucers. Holy crap! That was not supposed to come out of my mouth. The filter in my brain is clearly broken. Shoot. This is bad. It just slipped out! Hazel shoots me a look of horror and shock and confusion. Oh God! I couldn't think of anything else to fill the uncomfortable silence? I have an incredible knack for making awkward situations more awkward than necessary.

Beckett quickly turns his attention from his coffee cup over to me. He doesn't look angry, but the sadness that consumed his face is gone. His eyebrows are furrowed, and his nose is scrunched up, like he's trying to figure out if that actually just came out of my mouth. I think I'm more shocked than everyone else in the room by what I said.

"Are you asking me if I murdered Stephanie?" he says, annunciating each syllable in each word.

This guy isn't too bright. I'm pretty sure I clearly blurted that out in the middle of his kitchen.

"I . . . I . . . I did not mean to say that out loud," I respond, trying to save myself, even though what I did is far beyond help at this point.

He takes a sip of his coffee and then says, "I did not kill Stephanie."

"I really shouldn't have asked that. I'm sorry," I apologize awkwardly.

"Why the hell would I kill Stephanie?" His eyes start to water and he seems to be genuinely wondering where I'm coming from. I thought his motive was pretty clear.

"You were having an affair with her," I say point blank. "A lot of times it's the husband or the boyfriend. I don't think you're a murderer but it just makes you look guilty."

"That's all it is in this damn town. If you look guilty, you must be guilty. I did not kill Stephanie. I don't give a rat's ass what anyone else thinks," he slams his fist down onto the table. I instinctively take a step back and shudder at the loud noise. The house goes quiet again, while Beckett stares down at the counter seemingly frozen.

A few moments later he looks back up at us with tears in his eyes and says quietly, "I'm sorry. That was . . . I'm sorry . . . I didn't mean to snap. These past few weeks have been a living hell. My wife went to jail and now she's dead. I loved Hannah. I loved her more than anything." All at once, the tears he'd been suppressing start to stream down his face, as if his eyes were clouds and his tears were a downpour.

Hazel inches closer to me and whispers, "I think you broke him."

With one of his big hands he wipes the tears away from his eyes, but as soon as he does more take their place. "I made a mistake," he cries. "I made a horrible, horrible mistake. I cheated on her, and I can't change that. I never should have. It was stupid. But I never thought it would spiral into this."

It's a surprising sight, this burly, muscular man sobbing about his dead mistress and dead wife. I'm not exactly sure what I should do. Should I comfort him or just be quiet?

He starts talking again, "I'm the reason Hannah ended up in jail. If I never had the affair, we wouldn't have been in this situation. I know why you asked me that question but you have to understand, I loved Hannah. I loved Hannah more than anything in this world. She was my wife, the mother of my kids. What am I supposed to do now? I don't know the first thing about raising these kids on my own. I was stupid. I didn't love Stephanie. It was a stupid, awful mistake, and it ruined my entire life. We dated for a little while back in high school. It was an old flame I never should have reignited. I never loved Stephanie. I didn't kill Stephanie, but I'm the reason Hannah's dead. I had everything I wanted, and then I blew it all up by getting involved with Stephanie." He covers his face with his hands and shakes his head.

He had everything, and then he ruined it for himself. I do that all the time: sabotage all the good things that come my way. Seeing where that got Beckett scares me.

"Do you think Hannah killed Stephanie?" I ask him.

"I don't know. I don't think she would, but I wasn't with her for that entire night. She went home to put the kids to bed and I hung out until the early hours of Saturday morning. I don't know what to believe. All I know is that my wife is dead because of me. I will live with that for the rest of my life. Every day, I have to look my kids in the eye knowing that I'm the reason they don't have their mother."

"We don't think Hannah committed suicide," Hazel speaks up from behind me.

Beckett looks extremely confused and says, "What do you mean?"

"We think she was killed," Hazel replies. "By the same person who murdered Stephanie."

His brain seems to be having trouble processing the information. He stares at us for a few moments with his mouth hanging open and his eyes squinted.

"I went to see Hannah the day she died. She seemed tired but not hopeless. She told me that she knew something, something about who the killer was. She said she was meeting with her lawyer later that day to talk about it. She was going to tell me who it was but our time ran out. We think whoever killed Stephanie knew Hannah had figured it out and got rid of her to cover it up. They made it look like a suicide to keep themselves from being exposed."

Beckett's face widens, a mixture of shock and confusion. He looks like he's just seen a ghost, with his mouth open wide and his eyebrows raised. But there's something in his eyes that's changed. Maybe it's me just imagining things, but it seems as if the smallest bit of life has returned to his brown eyes. "I went to see her the day before she died and she was not hopeless at all. She kept talking about how confident her lawyer was and how she couldn't wait to see the kids again. She didn't sound like someone who was about to commit suicide. So if you're right, Hannah didn't kill herself?"

"*If* we're right, Hannah didn't commit suicide or kill Stephanie," Hazel reiterates, stressing our uncertainty.

He takes a deep breath in and out and says, "The police want to close the case, but if you're right that would change everything. If you need any help or information about Hannah let me know. I would be more than happy to help you clear her name."

I smile at him, but I feel a small sense of guilt in the back of my mind. If we're wrong about this, we're giving him false hope. We're letting him believe in something that may not be true. I feel bad, but the small smile on his face makes me think that maybe Beckett St. James needed a little bit of hope, even if it's false. Maybe he needed something to hold onto, something to ease the pain. I guess false hope is better than no hope.

"You two are young, you have a lot of life ahead of you. But I want you to know something," Beckett says. "You're going to make plenty of mistakes. You're supposed to mess up and fall on your face a few times. But you have to understand that all mistakes have consequences. And life . . . life doesn't always hand you second chances. You don't always get a chance to fix your mistakes. Some mistakes are permanent, there's no coming back from them. I will never be able to fix mine. I don't get a second chance to make things right. At the end of the day you have to be able to look yourself in the mirror and live with your choices. So just remember that. Don't make a mistake that will damage your entire life or somebody else's because you can't count on a second chance."

I feel a tear stream down my face and something in my brain seems to click. And even though I have no evidence to prove it, I take Beckett St. James off my list of suspects. He's a broken man who made a horrible mistake, but that doesn't make him a murderer.

*****

302

"Graeson," I say as the five of us are crammed into a booth at the diner, "I'm going to say something, and I want you to promise me that you won't let it go to your head or your ego."

He smirks, his dimples piercing his cheeks in the most adorable yet obnoxious way, and replies, "I'm listening."

After our visit with Beckett this morning, I'm feeling extra motivated and extra bold. Maybe it's because of Beckett's motivational speech or the fact that I looked death in the eye and survived. Either way, I'd like to keep this momentum going.

"Oh God!" Hazel rolls her eyes. "If his head gets any bigger, it'll explode."

Graeson looks at her with a goofy smile, "I take that as a compliment."

"Graeson, listen! Remember your idea about confronting Dr. Hastings? You said we should just go in there with the pictures we have and make him confess. Basically pull an Alison and blackmail him into telling us what's going on," I inform everyone.

"Are you serious?" Shea asks while he looks at me like I have three heads. "If he really is the murderer, that would make him the same person who tried to kill us last night. I don't know about you guys, but I'm not too sure I want to just walk into this guy's kitchen and make him angry."

"And do you really think if he is the killer, he'll just admit to it? No! He'll probably kill us right in the middle of his kitchen like Shea said!" Hazel raises her voice.

"Hazel, be quiet! People are staring. You guys just don't want to admit that I had a brilliant idea," Graeson says, his ego swelling as much as my ankle.

"No, Graeson! I just don't want to die!" she fires back loudly.

"Okay everyone, let's calm down," says Shea, trying to keep the peace. "We need to do something about Dr. Hastings. I'm not saying that confronting him is a good idea, but we have to come up with some sort of plan. He had Stephanie's phone and a massive bag of drugs. He may not be guilty of murder, but he's guilty of something."

"Going in there is a bit of a risk, but he won't kill us. Think about it: if he takes all five of us out in his kitchen, everyone will know it was him. We just have to be calm and not aggressive," Luke speaks up and looks directly at me.

"I am not aggressive!" I shoot back at him.

Everyone eyes me the way my mom always does when I'm lying. I roll my eyes as Shea says, "You're aggressive, and we love you for it." This makes me blush and forget why I was annoyed.

"I think it's our best way to get answers. There's no way he can deny it if we have proof," Graeson adds.

"I say we go for it," I respond. "Detective Heights is going to close this case soon and everyone's going to think Hannah was guilty. If we can prove that she was framed, we'll be able to clear her name."

"This could end horribly for us," Hazel disagrees. "I would like to make it to my senior year of high school."

"You sat outside with the man on his front porch while we broke into his house, but you're saying no to just going over and talking to him?" Graeson comments.

"I did that before someone tried to kill us last night! Before I really thought he might be a murderer!" she tells him.

"Hazel, you're not going to die. If anything starts to go wrong our houses are only a few yards away," Shea adds.

"Oh, now you're all in on this too?" she says shaking her head.

"Look at it this way, whether or not we decide to help it's going to happen," he replies.

Eventually, Hazel reluctantly agrees to help us confront Dr. Hastings. And thank God that she did because she's really the only one who's mastered the whole being gentle and subtle and not awkward thing. Later that night — around 5:00 — I watch Sawyer's car pull into his driveway. I text everyone to tell them we're ready to go.

With the pictures Alison gave us, along with the pictures I printed out from my phone of his desk contents in tow, I meet up with my friends at the bottom of my driveway, hoping to find some much needed answers. Although he only lives a few houses down, the walk feels long and gives me plenty of time to doubt what I'm doing. Confronting a possible murderer may not be one of my best ideas, but at least it's not as bad as walking through the woods in the middle of the night. We reach their front porch and I nervously step up to knock on the door. I take a deep breath, trying to inhale all the courage and nerve that I can. I just have to stick to our plan. Show him the pictures and let him explain or threaten to go to the police. Whatever happens in there I have to stay calm and focused. I can't blurt out random accusations because I feel awkward.

I step back from the door and wait. And wait. And wait. The anticipation is killing me. I know he's home. I stand there restlessly and transfer all of my weight to my right ankle. My left ankle is still throbbing and swollen and this whole wearing long pants in the summer things is pretty sucky.

I'm focusing on the pain in my ankle when the teal painted door swings open. Sawyer Hastings stands there rolling up the sleeves of his baby blue collared shirt. His dark hair sits in a ruffled mop on top of his head, and his expression is slightly puzzled but welcoming.

"Well, hello there," he smiles. "What can I do for you guys?"

"We need to talk to you," Graeson speaks up. "There's something you need to see."

He tilts his head to the side like a dog begging for food and asks skeptically, "Would you like to come in?"

Graeson nods and Sawyer guides us into his eccentric and unique house. I hobble in, unable to put any pressure on my left ankle. Sawyer leads us into his kitchen where a glass of whiskey over ice rests on the counter.

"What do you need to talk to me about?" he asks, his face scrunched up in confusion.

I place the three printed pictures in a straight line on the counter. They say a picture is worth a thousand words, but according to the look on Sawyer's face, these may be worth a billion. His eyes scan over the pictures as his mouth drops open slowly. His face pales, and he keeps his gaze on the pictures for at least five minutes. When he looks up his face is pinched together, and his eyes are hard. However, he doesn't seem to be very frazzled and stays very composed.

"How'd you get these?" His tone is surprisingly light.

"That's not important," Graeson replies. "We're taking these to the police unless you can explain them."

He walks over to his glass of whiskey and downs the whole thing in one gulp. "You think I killed Stephanie?" He looks at us inquisitively.

"We don't know," Hazel speaks up. "That's why we're here and not at the police station."

He opens a cabinet in his kitchen and takes out the bottle of whiskey. He pours the liquid into his glass, filling it to the brim. Sawyer takes another swig and rubs his chin with his hands like he's contemplating something. I hear a clicking noise, high heels against the hardwood floors. Sawyer sighs and takes another long sip of his drink as Rachel appears from the staircase and in the kitchen.

"He just spit up all over my dress, I had to—" she stops mid- sentence when she sees the group of us. She furrows her eyebrows and looks from Sawyer to the five of us, waiting for someone to explain what's going on.

Sawyer shakes his head and points to the pictures, "See for yourself."

Slowly, she walks over to the counter, the sound of her black heels echoing throughout the kitchen. She picks up the picture of Sawyer and Stephanie with her long, thin fingers. At first, Rachel doesn't react. She picks up the next picture — the one of the bag of pills — and covers her mouth with her other hand. Panic swims in her wide, doe-like eyes as she gently takes the third and final photograph, which clearly depicts Stephanie's cell phone in Sawyer's desk.

She places the pictures down on the granite countertop in a neat stack and then slides her hands down the sides of her dress, smoothing the fabric out. She takes a long breath in, but I don't ever see her exhale. Her eyes are filled with tears, but her face is pinched into a hard and cold stare at Sawyer.

"What the hell did you do?" she says sternly.

"I know how bad this looks," he surveys the room and then laughs a little. "Believe it or not I have an explanation." He seems amused but I can't tell if he's just using his laughter as a defense mechanism. "Go ahead and sit down," he says to us. "You too Rach, this is going to take a bit of explaining."

I take a seat at the kitchen counter, grateful to be off my ankle. I wonder if this is the part where he gives us his dramatic speech on why he became the killer and then tries to murder us all. Maybe I've been reading a few too many mystery novels lately.

"I'm going to start out by saying that I did not kill Stephanie," he speaks slowly and clearly, carefully choosing his words.

"Then how can you explain these pictures? Why was her phone in your desk?" Rachel asks, sounding like she's on the verge of either tears or screaming.

"I started gambling again," he says point blank. He looks up from his drink to Rachel with his teeth clenched, as if he were bracing for impact. She doesn't say anything, just stares him down with rage written all over her angular face.

Rachel's silence seems to hurt Sawyer worse than her yelling would have. After a few moments of unbearably awkward silence, he says, "Come on Rach, say something."

"I don't know what to say to you right now! You promised me, Sawyer. You promised me you would never do it again," she raises her voice.

"Rachel," he looks at her charmingly, the same way Graeson did when he almost ran me over with his car. "I know I promised you, and I meant it at the time. I didn't set out to break that promise. It just happened."

"That's not an excuse! That's not even a good explanation!"

"Rachel," he uses his hands to tell her to calm down. "Just hear me out. I know it's not an excuse. I regret it more than you know."

I still have yet to hear the words "I'm sorry" come out of his mouth. Talk about pride.

"I don't mean to break up this *lovely* conversation," Graeson starts. "But if you could just give us the simple explanation about what's going on, we'll let you two be."

Sawyer seems thankful for Graeson's interruption because it pulls him away from the brewing argument with his wife.

"Yes, I was getting to that," he says coolly, making me even more shocked at how calmly he's handling this situation. He seems to be unaware of the mounting pressure. "I guess the cat's out of the bag now, so I might as well come out and say it," he clears his throat and continues. "I have a gambling problem. Well, it's not really a problem, more like a minor flaw."

Rachel throws her hands up in the air, "No, it's not a minor flaw! It's a problem! It's an addiction!"

"Okay, I hear you," he says, talking with his hands. "A few years ago — about a year and a half after we got married — I gambled away so much money we almost lost the house. I drained most of the money in our savings accounts. I'll admit, it was pretty bad."

"Pretty bad?" Rachel pipes up. "It was horrible! We almost lost everything! That's when you promised you would never gamble again."

"Yes, you're right, Rach," Sawyer half smiles. "I promised I would never gamble again. And for six years, I didn't. I earned back the money I lost and replenished our savings accounts. We were back on track and everything was perfect. But then we had the baby and I got promoted at work. The stress just piled up, and I started gambling again. Some people run or meditate, I gamble. It helps relieve the pressure."

"You don't think I was stressed out? I didn't start gambling our lives away!" Rachel buts in.

"Well when you put it that way," he shakes his head and then looks back to us. "I gambled us into quite a bit of debt. Let's just say those replenished savings accounts are practically nonexistent. I realized what I did though. I knew how bad it was, how much I messed up. I wanted to fix this before you found out, Rachel, because I didn't want you to worry."

"Don't make it sound like you were doing me a favor by lying," she rolls her eyes.

"This is where Stephanie comes in. Steph and I were good friends in high school, and I thought she'd be able to help me out. I asked her for money, money that I would pay her back eventually. Just enough to keep us afloat for a while."

"I can't believe you went to Stephanie instead of me. We could've worked through this together."

"I should've gone to you, but I really was trying to protect you," he says, causing Rachel to just shake her head and roll her eyes. He shrugs his shoulders like he can't understand why she's so mad at him. "The thing is, Stephanie didn't want me to repay her the money. She was more than happy to give me what I needed and then some, but she wanted something in return. She asked me if I could get my hands on some pills for her, anything I could find around the hospital. I didn't want to do it, but I was desperate. I needed the money. And she was willing to repay me everything I lost over the course of a few months as long as I provided her with drugs and didn't ask questions."

Desperation is like a scuba diver who ran out of air under water. It's like running out of oxygen. You don't care about who you hurt or the rules you have to break, you just want to be able to breathe again. You'll fight for that air at all costs. But sometimes desperation makes you lose your mind, pushes you so far away from who you are. It makes you forget that all you have to do is stick your head above the water. All you have to do is break through the lies and the guilt and you'll be able to breathe.

"So let me get this straight," Rachel scowls at Sawyer. "You went behind my back and supplied Stephanie freaking Kester with pills in return for money?"

"That sounds about right," he nods his head. I feel like I'm watching a movie, like Sawyer and Rachel are actors on a screen and I'm just watching the scene unfold. "Rachel, you know how much I love you. I was trying to make it right."

"Oh save it!" she says. "Finish your story."

Sawyer seems almost amused with the attention this is bringing him. He stands there using his charming smile and calm and friendly demeanor to make his actions seem like they're not so bad. He takes another sip of his whiskey, swishing it around in his mouth, and then says, "She couldn't give me all the money at once for whatever reason, so we made a deal. Every Wednesday we would meet and exchange what we brought. It was pretty easy to get my hands on pills at the hospital."

"Why did she need the drugs?" I speak up.

He shakes his head, "I have no idea. Part of our deal was that I didn't ask her any questions."

"So you just blindly gave her highly addictive pills and didn't even worry about what she was doing with them?" Rachel asks. "You could've lost your job and your license to practice medicine and ended up in jail. Did you ever worry about what she was doing with the drugs you gave her?"

"Of course I worried about what she was doing with them. Every time I left one of our drop offs I had this sour feeling in my gut. At first I was just so thankful for the money, but as time went on I felt worse and worse. I couldn't sleep at night. I couldn't focus during any of my surgeries. I realized that I was gambling our entire future just to earn the money back. I told Stephanie that I wanted out, that I was done, that this was dangerous. She got angry. She told me if I pulled out she'd tell you. But I didn't care anymore. I was planning on telling you, just coming clean about everything. I knew she couldn't go to the police without implicating herself. Stephanie told me she'd kill me if I ever exposed her, but she was all talk most of the time so I didn't put too much weight on that. All of this happened and then two days later she ended up dead."

Rachel sits with her arms crossed and steam shooting out of her ears. She says, "I can't believe I'm married to a lying, gambling drug dealer." Sawyer better start packing his bags soon. I don't even want to think about the fight that's going to ensue after we leave. Sawyer's story explains a lot, but there's still one piece that doesn't add up.

"But if you didn't kill her, why do you have her cell phone?" I ask.

He sighs, "Stephanie was a ticking time bomb. Unpredictable and dangerous. She could be your closest ally, but she could explode on you at any second. She was so mad that I wasn't sure what she was going to do to bring me down. At the party on Friday I went to use Stephanie's bathroom and found her phone sitting on the sink. I grabbed it. I thought I could find a way to delete all of our messages and officially break ties with Stephanie. I slipped the phone into my pocket and then I got called in for an emergency surgery at work. I was at the hospital until eight a.m. Saturday morning."

"Why did you keep the phone?" Graeson asks.

"When I found out she was dead, I panicked. Do you know how guilty that would've made me look? I mean, you guys thought I killed her. I locked the phone in my desk and was going to get rid of it. I can show you the files on the surgery and can probably get my hands on the security camera footage if you still don't believe me."

"No, you don't have to show us any of that. I think you've got enough on your plate right now," I say shifting my eyes over to Rachel who looks like she's ready to beat the crap out of him.

"Now that you've questioned me, I have to ask you guys something," Sawyer tells us. "How did you get pictures of what was inside my locked desk drawer?"

"I'd rather not say," I respond. "Let's just say that paper clips work just as well as keys."

I thought he'd be angry, but Sawyer smiles and nods his head at me. "Impressive. Please don't go to the police," Sawyer begs. "I promise you, I had nothing to do with Stephanie's death. I just want a chance to make everything right for my family. I'm not a bad person."

I smile a little, "We won't go to the police. You should get a chance to make everything right."

I take the pile of pictures on the counter and rip them in half, which makes Sawyer's mouth turn up into a small smile. This time it isn't a charming or showboating smirk, it's a smile filled with genuine relief. I look over to Rachel as she twirls her auburn

312

hair around her fingers and stares at Sawyer with daggers shooting out of her eyes. Mascara gathers under her hazel eyes, showing the tears she's been fighting back. I think back to the day we broke into the Hastings' house and their back deck. I thought their life was so perfect. So simple. So easy. I thought they were living this beautiful love story. And maybe they still are. What's a good story without a few plot twists? I think they'll be okay. It might take some time and some tears, but I think they'll get there. I can't stop thinking about what Beckett said about second chances. He's right, you don't always get a second chance. But when you do, you better take it and run.

CHAPTER 16 - The Grey Area

I'm starting to realize that life isn't black and white. I'm starting to think that there's no such thing as good people and bad people. In the movies there's always the good guys and the bad guys, and there's always a clear line separating them. But in reality, there's no distinction. There's only people with flaws and issues and imperfections. Everyone has something, some sort of baggage, some sort of hardship, some sort of issue to work through. Most people I would define as bad are really just people who are struggling to cope with the hand they've been dealt. I used to see the world as black and white. I used to look at life like there was a clear right and wrong for every situation. I used to put people under the labels of either good or bad. But I'm starting to realize that there's this little thing called the grey area. The grey area is where black and white, right and wrong, good and bad blend. It's messy and blurry and uncomfortable, but that's where we live most of our lives. There's no definite answers in the grey area, which is why we don't like it all that much. When we think in terms of black and white, right and wrong, good and bad, there's clear boundary lines and definitions. But when you step into the grey area all hell breaks loose and there's so much uncertainty. When you learn to embrace the discomfort and the chaos, you finally start to grow and open your mind. Even though we cling to those simple outlines of black and white, right and wrong, good and bad, they're constraining. Those ideas make us prisoners in our own minds. But once you release yourself from those handcuffs, you see the world through a new set of eyes. Because life isn't about black and white, right and wrong, good and bad. It's about the grey area. And in the grey area, you'll finally see the world in color.

Stephanie's death has turned so many lives upside down and brought so many secrets to light. It feels like everyone here is hiding something and somehow it all leads back to her. It's as if Stephanie was the sun and everyone else just the stars and planets orbiting around her. So far everything we've uncovered leads back to her. In my head, there's this imaginary murder board with Stephanie's face in the middle and millions of threads of red string connecting back to her. There's so many people who had a reason to want her dead which makes me think back to what Graeson's mom said the night we found out Hannah died. She told us we were like foxes chasing our tails, that we were asking the wrong questions. We keep asking who would've wanted her dead. We keep searching for motives. We've found more motives than I can count, enough to fill a skyscraper. Maybe there was something to the drunken blur of words Evangeline Ambrose was spewing out of her mouth. Instead of looking for motives, maybe we should be looking into who had the opportunity and the means to kill Stephanie. Everyone had a reason, but who had the opportunity? Better yet, who was in the mindset to actually kill her? At least I feel like we're finally starting to make progress. I know from Detective Heights that Richard had a solid alibi, which counted him out from the start of the investigation. I've officially taken Beckett off my list because I just don't think that this grief stricken man is capable for a couple of reasons. Number one: he's not very clever or discreet. His affair with Stephanie was leaked so easily because of a stupid picture he took. I don't think he could commit the murder and then pin it all on his wife without slipping up. Number two: he seemed genuinely distraught when we talked to him. He loved Hannah. He's guilty of a plethora of things but I'm almost positive murder isn't one them. He's not a bad person, he just made some terrible mistakes. And then there's Sawyer. There's something bothering me about his confession. He seemed so smug and amused with the whole situation, like he didn't understand why his wife thought this was such a big deal. There was just something about his tone of voice and his mannerisms that made me feel like he was lying, or at least withholding some of the truth.

But right now, my mind is caught up on Forrest. For whatever reason, he's lying about his job. Alison also told us that Stephanie would give the bag of drugs she got from Sawyer to Forrest. But when we talked to Sawyer he had no idea what Stephanie did with the pills he gave her. Or at least that's what he told us. There's something very off about Forrest Shepard, something more than the mystery surrounding how he ended up with his drop dead gorgeous wife. Today the five of us are road tripping up to Paine's Creek to the lab Forrest claimed to own. We're hoping to find out more about him and how he fits into this whole puzzle. I told my mom we were heading up to Hazel's lake house for the day, and she seemed to buy it.

I see Shea's car pull up the driveway, and I make my way out the door with my little drawstring bag in tow to hold anything I might need for our day trip, including my phone, wallet, a sweatshirt, and pepper spray per my mother's request. I was given strict instructions to spray any stranger who came within three feet of me. As soon as I step outside I feel suffocated by the muggy late afternoon air. The sun seems to have disappeared, leaving the sky a hazy shade of grey. Despite Graeson's incessant pleading, we all decided that having Shea drive would be a much better idea if we wanted to make it to Paine's Creek alive.

Luke comes out behind me with his dark hair a ruffled mess on top of his head. He says, "Are you ready to go interrogate a couple of geeky scientists?"

I smile at him, "I've never been more excited."

We hop into the car, and I'm immediately grateful for the cool blast of the air conditioning. We pick up Hazel and then Graeson, who climbs into the car with one shoe on and the other in his hand and his t-shirt not completely on his body. He has a bad case of bedhead, and he still has that fresh out of bed look on his face even though it's almost three o'clock in the afternoon. The kid's a mess. A cute mess, but a mess nonetheless.

"Did you just roll out of bed?" Hazel laughs as he stumbles into the car.

"No I just rolled out of my afternoon nap," he smirks.

"You sleep more than anyone else I know," Shea shakes his head.

"What can I say? I need my beauty sleep to look like this," he replies arrogantly.

Once we're all settled, Shea starts driving down the street, his car rolling over the sleek, black pavement. I notice Cora Shepard strolling down the sidewalk with her daughters. She briefly glances over at us, her copper eyes so intense they seem to cut through the glass of the car window. There's something so odd about her. She's like an empty house with no lights on. Just skin and bone, broken furniture and decaying wood. No life. There's some sort of disconnect with the real world, a certain coldness in her eyes, in her face, in the way she carries herself. It's a certain mystery and coldness that I can't quite put my finger on, like a string of Christmas lights that won't light up. You can almost never figure out which light is the one causing the problem.

Cora looks away as quick as she can without waving, focusing her attention back on her daughters walking in front of her. She makes me feel unsettled, but I can't figure out why. I shrug the feeling off for now and turn my head away from the window and back to the road in front of us.

On the highway, miles of glossy black pavement stretch out in front of us, and leafy green trees line the sides of the road. Hazel and Luke are each listening to music on their headphones, and Graeson is fast asleep — as if he didn't get enough already — with his head slumped downwards. Every time we hit a bump his head flings back against the seat, but he still doesn't wake up. I steal a glance at Shea, his eyes glued on the road. There's something so adorable about him when he's focused. It makes me wonder what's going on in his head, if he thinks about the same things as I do.

I think for a moment and then say, "Shea, can I ask you something?"

He glances over at me, his blue eyes sparkling, and replies, "Of course."

"Are we . . . like . . . officially together?" I stutter.

He smiles as soon as I say the words, "I didn't want to push you, but I'd like to be . . . you know . . . official. But if you're not ready for that, I completely get it. We can be whatever you want us to be . . . I'm sorry, I'm rambling."

I laugh a little, "It's cute when you ramble like that. I'm ready. I want to be with you . . . officially."

He takes one hand off the steering wheel and places it on my knee. I take my hand and put it over his. It's so weird to think that a few weeks ago I was so sad and lonely and angry at the world. I never thought that I'd end up here with an improved relationship with all of my parents, a good group of friends, and a boyfriend who makes me feel like the luckiest girl alive. It's like I finally found my place in this world. It's right here, with Shea's hand in mine. This is where I belong.

✳✳✳✳✳

After about an hour and a half of driving, we reach the bioengineering lab in Paine's Creek. The lab is much bigger than I imagined it would be. I always pictured it to be this tiny little building, but instead, it's massive with large windows covering the exterior. The building has a modern look to it, which is surprising seeing that the rest of the town we drove through had a vintage and homey vibe. Hazel roughly wakes Graeson up by shaking him until he opens his eyes with a startle. All five of us get out of the car and stretch our legs, pausing for a few minutes in the large parking lot before we make our way into the building.

"What exactly are we going to ask the people here?" Graeson questions.

"We're going to ask if they know of Forrest Shepard and if he used to own this place. Hopefully, someone will know something about him," I respond. "We're kind of going on a whim, but it's better than nothing."

"We just have to remember to be calm and professional," Hazel says eyeing Graeson.

We begin to walk through the fairly empty parking lot, the air still unbearably humid and thick. I'm praying to God we can find out something about Forrest because we're running out of leads. We still haven't found much on Isla, but that's a different issue for a different day. We reach the front entrance and walk inside. Our footsteps echo off of the tile floor, and the air conditioning is turned up so high that goosebumps almost immediately pop up on my arms. The white tile floors and dull grey walls make me feel like I'm in a hospital. A few feet away, there's a front office where a middle aged woman with purple rimmed glasses waves at us cheerfully. Her strawberry blonde hair is tied up in a low ponytail, and her skin is dotted with freckles. The lady's name tag reads Laurie Piper, and a perky smile adorns her face.

"Well hello there!" she says enthusiastically. "What can I do for you?"

As we planned, Hazel steps up first to the lady, who is separated from us by a sheet of plexiglass, "Hi, how are you today?"

"Oh I'm great! No one ever asks me that, you are too sweet! How are you?"

"I'm good, but we need some help. My friends and I were wondering if we could talk to Mr. Wilkinson. We have a couple questions for him."

The lady thinks pensively for a moment, "Mr. Wilkinson is a very busy man. Do you have an appointment?"

Hazel shakes her head, "We don't have an appointment. I promise we won't take up much of his time. We just have a few questions. By the way, I really love those glasses. Purple must be your color."

The woman blushes and smiles, "Thank you so much, dear. You seem like a very nice group of kids, let me see what I can do for you."

"Thank you so much. We really appreciate it."

The woman disappears behind a doorway within the office while we wait around for an answer.

"Wow, Hazel," Graeson comments. "That was smooth. You buttered her up like she was a piece of toast."

Hazel laughs, "People will help you out if you're nice to them."

A few minutes later the lady comes back with a slight frown on her face. She says, "I'm really sorry, kids, Mr. Wilkinson is in a meeting right now. You can come back around six, and you'll have a better chance of getting his ear. Is there anything I can do for you in the meantime?"

"Actually," I step up closer to the glass. "You may be able to help us. Do you know anyone by the name of Forrest Shepard?"

"Hmm . . ." the lady thinks deeply, "The name does ring a bell, but I can't quite place it. Forrest Shepard. Hmm . . . I'm not sure that I know who that is."

I pull up his wife's Facebook page and find a picture of the two of them. I press the phone screen against the glass so she can see, hoping she'll recognize him. She scrunches up her face really hard, squinting her eyes to see the picture.

"I'm sorry, but I don't recognize him. The name sounds familiar, but I don't think I've seen him before. Can I ask why you want to know if I recognize this man?" she says.

"We think he used to work here," I reply, giving her the least amount of information possible. "We have a few questions about him and didn't know if anyone would be able to help us out."

"If you wait until 6:00 you may have a chance to talk to Mr. Wilkinson, but I can't guarantee anything. Unless, if you'd be willing to speak to one of our scientists instead, you may be able to get some answers quicker. Mr. Roland has been here since this laboratory was first established. If Forrest Shepard worked here at any point, Mr. Roland would know," she offers.

"That would be wonderful," Hazel responds. "You've been so helpful. Thank you so much."

Laurie Piper once again retreats behind the door and comes back a few moments later. When she returns, she says, "Mr. Roland would be more than happy to meet with you. Just wait here and he'll be over shortly."

It feels like we're finally getting somewhere. I'm not sure what Mr. Roland is going to be able to tell us, but hopefully it brings us closer to finding why Stephanie was giving him the drugs she got from Sawyer. I'm just happy Laurie Piper was so eager to help us out. She seems lonely, like someone who spends way too much time with her cats and is in serious need of some company.

A white haired man appears from another door down the hallway to our left a few minutes later. He wears a white lab coat with a button-up shirt underneath. He appears to be in his mid-sixties with large white eyebrows and saggy skin.

He walks over to us and shakes each one of our hands, "I'm Phil Roland. I understand you have a few questions for me."

"It's a pleasure to meet you. We only have a few questions. I promise we won't take up too much of your time," Hazel says, taking the lead once again. She's a very sweet and likeable person, and she seems to have a way with people.

"No worries," he smiles. "I was on my way out for the day, and I don't have too much going on. I'm happy to help you. Let's go into my office."

Phil Roland leads us down the hallway he appeared from. On our way to his office I notice multiple heavy wooden doors with names on plaques on the walls beside them. Once again, our footsteps echo off the tile floors. The atmosphere is so dreary I wonder how these people can possibly work here all day. When we reach his office, Phil unlocks the door and tells us to take a seat wherever we'd like. His office is underwhelming, neat and organized, not a piece of paper out of place. The room is filled with file cabinets with various labels, a small couch, a desk, and a few random folding chairs.

When we're all seated, Phil says, "What can I do for you kids?"

Something about him reminds me of my grandfather, or really just grandfathers in general. I reply, "We were wondering if you knew a man by the name Forrest Shepard? I can show you a picture of him if you'd like."

"Forrest Shepard," he says slowly. "I haven't heard that name in a long time."

"You know him?" I ask, hanging off the edge of my seat.

He nods his head slowly, like he's thinking really hard about how he wants to word what he says next. I show him the picture of my rat-like neighbor, and Phil heaves a great sigh.

"I remember Forrest Shepard. He used to own this place," his voice is steady paced and deep.

"Used to? What happened?" Shea asks.

"Before I tell you what happened I need to tell you kids that Forrest Shepard is not someone you want to get mixed up with. You seem like a great group of kids and I don't want to see you get in any trouble," Phil replies.

I feel my skin start to tingle and I get this strange sensation that there's something crawling up my back. There's this odd look in Phil's eyes that tells me that Forrest may be more dangerous than we thought.

Phil lowers his voice, like he's sharing a secret, "I'm not supposed to speak about this, so if anyone asks, you didn't find out from me." We all nod our heads anxiously, and Phil continues. "Forrest used to be a co-owner of this lab. He, along with another man, owned and ran the place. This was . . . let me think . . . about eight years ago when they established it. I will say, it was an excellently run program. Forrest was highly intelligent and very passionate about his work. We were becoming very successful in our field. However almost two years ago there was an issue, a *scandal* as they called it."

He pauses for a moment, and I feel like I'm reading a mystery novel, hanging on to every word that rolls off his tongue. He says the word scandal like it's a curse word, lowering his volume even more.

"Forrest's partner found out that he was selling drugs. He was running this drug ring where he used the lab as a distribution center. He would obtain pills from various suppliers, store them in parts of the lab, and eventually sell them for a profit," Phil tells us quietly. "He used the lab as a cover to carry out his operation."

Holy crap. I feel my heart drop into my stomach as shock begins to take over my body. Tiny, rodent-like Forrest was running an illegal drug ring through his lab. The thought bounces around in my brain, unable to sink in or be processed. Talk about a double life.

Phil continues his story, "When his partner found out about it, he was immediately removed from his position. His partner knew if he reported the incident to the board, their entire lab would be discredited and shut down. His hard work would have been destroyed. He made a deal with Forrest. If Forrest agreed to give up his half of the company and walk away silently, he wouldn't report him. Forrest agreed and left the laboratory. Luckily, it was taken care of before any of the employees or the public found out. The issue was swept under the rug, and no one heard from Forrest Shepard again."

I feel the wheels in my brain trying to fight against the shock and put the pieces of the puzzle together. My eyes stare intently at Phil, who seems internally distraught about the story. I feel like the dots are starting to connect. Stephanie took the drugs she got from Sawyer and gave them to Forrest. That means that Stephanie must've been one of Forrest's suppliers. But the timing doesn't exactly match up. This whole scandal took place approximately two years ago, and Stephanie had been giving drugs to Forrest up until shortly before she died.

"Do you know what Forrest does now?" Luke asks Phil, reading my mind.

Phil shakes his head, "I haven't the slightest clue. I hope he isn't continuing with his illegal activities, but I have no way of knowing." Phil seems so innocent, so genuine.

"Do you know anything else about Forrest? Anything at all?" Hazel questions.

"I've told you everything I know. You have to promise to keep this to yourselves. I only told you because I wanted to help you. No one's mentioned his name in a long, long time. Are you kids in some kind of trouble?"

"We're okay," Shea says. "Or at least we will be."

"May I ask what sent you searching for information about Forrest?" Phil asks.

"Something bad happened around where we live, and we think that Forrest may have had something to do with it," Shea answers as vaguely as possible.

"I'm just warning you kids, please don't get mixed up with Forrest Shepard. You seem like a nice group, and if you're in some kind of trouble you should go to your parents or the authorities. He's bad news," Phil warns.

"Thank you so much for your time. You've helped us probably more than you know. I promise, we're not involved with Forrest in any way. We'll steer clear of him. We really can't thank you enough, Mr. Roland," I say.

"It was my pleasure," he responds.

We say our goodbyes to Phil and thank him for all of his helpful information. On our way out the door, a thought pops into my head.

I stop and ask Phil, "You said they swept this all under the rug. How did you know about it?"

He half smiles, a reminiscent grin, "Because I, my dear, was Forrest Shepard's partner. We established the laboratory together. When everything went down, I realized I didn't want to spend the rest of my career managing a facility and dealing with problems like these. I just wanted to get back to my work, back to my love of science. I handed the company over to my nephew, Daniel Wilkinson. I don't know if I made the right choices, but I think it'll all work out in the end."

"So you were Forrest's partner?" I reiterate.

He nods his head and puts his finger to his lips, "Shh . . . it's our little secret."

*****

After our meeting with Phil, it was nearly 6:00 and no one was in the mood to cram into the car and drive another hour and a half home. We had so much to talk about, and the thought of the long drive was making everyone a bit annoyed. Hazel's family used to spend a few weekends each summer up here by the lake. They used to stay in this little bed and breakfast a few miles away from the lab. Hazel called and found out they had a couple of rooms available if we wanted to stay the night. We all decided that going out to dinner and driving home in the morning sounded like a much better plan for everyone's stomachs and brains to process all of the information we just learned. I called my mom and told her that we ended up deciding to stay overnight at Hazel's lake house. After about 20 minutes of convincing her we were perfectly safe on our own and eventually putting Luke on the phone to smooth everything over, she said it was fine.

The Free Hope B&B is a quaint and colonial style building made of bricks with a large front porch decorated with wooden rocking chairs, a chess board, strands of twinkle lights, and hanging pots overflowing with scarlet colored flowers. Creamy white, deep red, and pale pink roses fill large pots spread throughout the entire front porch. With our stomachs full after a very delicious dinner at one of the restaurants at the bustling and beautiful town center, we creaked open the red painted door and stepped inside the homey building.

The inside is even more charming than the outside, with dim lights and cozy tan walls. We walk down a short hallway, which leads to a small room. A silvery white haired woman sits at the front desk, reading a paperback book. A blueberry scented candle sits on the desk, along with a vase of pink peonies and a lamp with a cream colored shade. On the wall behind her are old mail slots they used back in the day for guests.

"Hello," she greets us warmly with a wide smile. "Welcome to the Free Hope B&B. It's wonderful to have you folks here! You, dear, look very familiar. Have you stayed here before?"

Hazel smiles back at her, "My family and I used to stay here when my brothers and I were little."

"Hmm . . ." the woman thinks. "Huntington, that was the last name I think. Your father was the football player and your mother was sweeter than a jar of honey. Wow, you've grown!"

"That's us," Hazel replies. "My friends and I were up shopping and walking around in town today and we just weren't ready to go home just yet."

"Well, I'm so happy you decided to stay with us again!"

The woman checks us in and hands us the keys to our rooms. She leads us up a pale grey carpeted staircase and down a hallway lined with black and white photographs set in distressed wood frames.

At the end of the hallway she says, "Here you are, room seven and room eight. Breakfast is served at nine every morning and there are fresh towels in the closets. Just give me a holler if you need anything else!"

"Actually," I speak up. "I have a question for you."

"I'm all ears," she smiles.

"Do you know anyone by the name Forrest Shepard?"

She thinks for a moment and then replies, "Actually, I do. He stays here from time to time. You don't forget a name like that one. It always made me think of the movie Forrest Gump."

"Has he stayed here recently?" I ask.

"Well you sure are an inquisitive little thing," she laughs. "Yes, he was here last week. He comes and goes periodically. He's always alone, which is a little disheartening. I don't think he's got a family to go home to."

We thank the kind woman and retreat into our rooms. Hazel and I go one way and the boys the other. The bedroom hits me with a wave of comfort and nostalgia, reminding me of my grandmother's house back in Portland. Three of the walls are painted a pale pink and the fourth accent wall is covered with pink swirl wallpaper. The beds are neatly made with red roses stitched onto the white comforter. A nightstand rests by each bed with a glass bottle of water and a small bowl of mints. It feels like a charming little bubble away from the harsh realities of the world, a refuge from the troubles right outside these four walls.

I change into the sweatshirt I brought with me and we head into the boys' room to talk more about Forrest. We sprawl out and put our minds to work.

"I can't believe he's been lying about his job for almost two years," Hazel says. "I wonder if Cora knows. He must still use the lab as a cover for his drug operation."

"I don't know, but there's something off about Cora too," I add. "This must mean that Stephanie was one of his suppliers. She wanted the drugs from Sawyer so she could give them to Forrest. But what do you think she got in return?"

"Money," Graeson replies. "Stephanie was greedy as hell. She loved her lavish lifestyle and would do anything for a little extra cash."

Shea says, "Why would she go to all that trouble for a little extra cash? She and Richard had more money than God. I feel like Stephanie would want more out their deal."

"You know what else doesn't make sense," I say. "The timing. Phil said this all happened almost two years ago, but we know Stephanie was giving Forrest drugs up until a few days before she died. It doesn't match up."

"Phil said that Forrest stopped selling drugs out of the lab but he never said that Forrest stopped selling them all together. I bet once he was fired he kept his drug trade running on his own. He had to make money somehow to afford his house and support his family. Drug dealing probably made him a ton of money," Luke theorizes.

"That must be why Stephanie was so mad at Sawyer," Hazel starts. "If Sawyer pulled out, her deal with Forrest would crumble."

"She was mixed up in so many awful things," Shea shakes his head. "It's weird to think about how much was going on that people couldn't see."

"Basically we need to figure out why Stephanie was involved with Forrest and what she got in return for supplying him. We also need to figure out what motive it gives him," I sum up our findings.

"I'm not sure of the exact motive, but this definitely adds to our case. Something went wrong with their deal, something that caused Forrest to pull the trigger on Stephanie," Luke replies.

"*If* it was him," Hazel says. "I still want to know more about Isla."

"I do too, but I'm exhausted," I say. "I think we all could use some sleep."

Hazel and I head back to our room, carefully tiptoeing across the hall so we don't wake any other guests up. Darkness pours through the windows of our room, which sends a strange and indescribable feeling through my body. I've never been a big fan of the dark. It makes me feel out of control, like there are shadows creeping and crawling around waiting to grab me when I least expect it. I close the curtains, trying to block out the eerie feeling the night sky gives me. I quickly climb into the bed and burrow myself under the comforter. Hazel switches off the lights and suddenly it feels like the darkness has infiltrated my little bubble. I close my eyes tight trying to drift off to sleep into a world a little different from the real one.

Suddenly, an image fills my head and I am hit with a strong sense of déjà vu. I squint my eyes shut even tighter, focusing in on the memory, which begins to play in my head like an old home movie.

Everything is black. Darkness swallows me up and surrounds me on all sides. I slowly open my eyes. I feel something cold on my back. What's going on? I'm laying down, the concrete

329

of the patio feels rough against my skin. Everything is spinning in slow circles. I look up. My heart stops. There's a pair of wide slate grey eyes staring back at me. Watching me. I feel my breathing pick up and I struggle to get air. The person, he's talking but I can't make out the words. Everything is blurry. I try to sit up, but a wave of dizziness crashes over me, and I lay back down. What is he saying? What does he want? "Are you hurt?" I hear him, his voice deep and robotic. "Are you hurt?" he repeats. I don't know. Everything feels numb and cold. Footsteps. I hear footsteps. Closer and closer. Quiet, secretive footsteps. Someone's here. Their presence makes me feel uncomfortable, like something's wrong. I feel a warm hand on my shoulder. My eyes are heavy. I fight to keep them open. There's a face, a different face. Everything is blurry. What's going on? The face inches closer. I feel their breath as they talk. My eyes can't fight anymore, and they shut tight. Everything is spinning. Everything is blurry. What's going on?

CHAPTER 17 - Ghost

They say once you know something you can't "unknow" it. That is unless you drank a whole lot of Tequila. Which in that case, you can "unknow" an entire night's worth of events, including the murder of one of your neighbors right in your own backyard.

The memory I recovered last night has me so deeply disturbed that I couldn't sleep at all. I keep feeling this odd chill in my core that causes me to shiver, the same one I felt from the concrete that night. I was lying outside, on the concrete in the dark, and someone was staring at me. But who? All I can remember are these unique, but familiar grey eyes. Whoever it was kept asking me if I was hurt, and I'm pretty sure the voice belonged to a man. And there was someone else. Someone else came over to me. I remember the feel of their hand on my arm, but I can't make out their face. I can't even distinguish if the person was a man or a woman. All I can remember is that someone was there. I can feel their presence, but I can't make out the face.

Grey eyes. That's all I can think about. Startling grey eyes. Concerned grey eyes. The early morning sun begins to peek through the curtains, signaling the start of a new day full of new problems. Hazel, an early riser herself, is flipping through her phone on the bed next to me while twirling her golden ringlets around her fingers.

"Hazel," I start, "Do you know anyone with grey eyes?"

"Huh? Grey eyes?" she answers, confused at my random question.

"Yeah, do you know anyone with grey eyes?"

"Let me think," she ponders. "I think Easton has grey eyes. That's the only person I can think of."

"Oh my God! That's it!" I practically yell. All at once, everything clicks into place. It was Easton standing over me, asking me if I was hurt. It all makes sense now. When we saw him the other day, he kept asking if I was hurt. I didn't think his words made any sense, but maybe he knew exactly what he was talking about. And if he's right about me being hurt, what else is he right about? He referred to a man with a gun and said that he hurt *them*. Maybe "them" was me and Stephanie. It's all starting to make sense. I walked outside because I heard a noise, and then I fainted or fell asleep either from the shock of seeing Stephanie's body or too much Tequila. For some reason Easton was outside when all this was going down. But who was the other person? Was it the killer?

I feel like I'm on the cusp of something, but it still seems so far out of reach. It's like climbing the monkey bars. Your fingers are close enough to reach out and touch the bar, but your grasp isn't strong enough so you slip and fall. If I could just recall who that person was. If I could just make out the face or the voice. Everything is becoming so much clearer, yet so much blurrier all at the same time. I have a strange feeling that that person who touched my arm had something to do with Stephanie's death. I'm almost there. Almost. I hate that damn word.

"What's the deal with grey eyes?" Hazel asks.

I quickly fill Hazel in on my frightening memory, and I watch her face turn a ghostly shade of white as I speak.

"That's terrifying. I don't like the sound of that at all," Hazel looks like she's just bitten into something disgusting.

"We have to talk to Easton again. We have to see what he knows. There's some truth to what he's saying, maybe not all of it but some of it."

"There's one problem. He and his mother just went away on vacation. They won't be back for a few days."

"Well, then we'll have to talk to him as soon as they get back. He was there that night, that's why he was asking if I was hurt."

"That just gave me the chills. Do you think Easton could've had something to do with the murder?" Hazel asks.

"No, I don't think so. He seemed so distraught and convinced that there was a man after him," I say.

"Does that mean we should rule Isla out?"

"No. His story was so all over the place that he may be mixing up the details, or he may be unsure about what he actually saw. I think Isla is still very much a suspect. We're so close, Hazel, I can feel it. We have to keep going."

"I'm on board, but I don't want to look into Forrest anymore. He gives me the creeps. Let's let the boys handle him and we'll take Isla."

"Agreed. On a much lighter note, you still haven't told me about your date with Luke," I smirk.

She blushes, "I haven't had a chance to talk to you without the boys around. And you haven't exactly told me that you and Shea are officially a couple."

My mouth drops open a little and my eyebrows raise, "How did you know about that?"

A wide grin spreads across her face, "My music wasn't turned up that loud in the car and let's face it, you're not that quiet."

I jokingly roll my eyes and toss the pillow from my bed at her and say, "I thought I was so quiet!"

"Think again," she smirks. "Do you want to go down and get some coffee? I'm in serious need of some caffeine."

"Definitely," I agree. "I don't think I slept at all last night."

The two of us make our way down to the common room of the B&B, passing through the hallway lined with black and white photographs and the grey carpeted stairwell. The smell of freshly brewed coffee, sizzling bacon, and maple syrup hits my nose and makes my mouth water. From the stairwell I have a clear view of the front door which creaks open sending a gush of cool, fresh air inside. A skinny, dark haired man walks in and when he turns his face in our direction, my mouth drops to the floor. I freeze instantly in my tracks, causing Hazel to smash right into me.

"Hazel," I whisper harshly and motion to the man with my head. "Look."

Hazel gasps loudly, causing the man to peer over at the staircase. I grab Hazel's hand and yank her to the ground, hoping the banister will conceal us. The two of us stay crouched down as we hear the man ring the check-in bell. He fidgets around, pacing back forth while he waits. Hazel and I are watching intently when, suddenly, I feel a tap on my shoulder. I jump so high I basically touch the ceiling and feel my heart rate skyrocket. I whip my head around and see Shea bending down, extremely confused by what's going on.

"Jesus! You almost gave me a heart attack!" I whisper intensely, my voice coming out more like a dull lion's roar than a whisper. "What are you doing?"

"Graeson's snoring, so it woke me up. What exactly are *you* doing?" he asks.

"Look over there," I motion at the familiar man with my head.

He goes to stand up but I grab his hand and jerk him downwards. He looks at me with slanted eyebrows and squinted eyes. I discreetly point at the man so Shea can see.

"Forrest?" he says quietly. Hazel and I nod our heads ferociously. "What is he doing here?"

I shrug my shoulders and continue to watch Forrest as he awkwardly paces and rubs his head with his hands. His chin is covered with a few days old stubble and from here his beady eyes look nervous and exhausted. The lady eventually comes and checks him in. He seems to be in a hurry, rushing to get to his room. They engage in brief small talk but I can't make out what they're saying. Forrest begins to walk away from the front desk and in the direction of the staircase. Oh no. I eye Hazel and Shea and begin to internally panic. There's no doubt that he'll recognize us. Oh no.

"Come on!" Hazel says as she quickly stands up and begins to speed walk up the stairs. We follow her lead, dashing up the stairs and down the hallway. Hazel ushers us into the room and slams the door shut behind us.

I heave in a major sigh of relief, "That was close."

"What's he doing here?" Shea asks.

"The lady who owns the place says he stays here from time to time," Hazel answers. "This is almost too good to be true. If we stick around for a bit, we may be able to figure out what he's doing up in Paine's Creek."

I hear footsteps outside our door and slowly crack the door open just enough to reveal a sliver of the hallway. I see Forrest anxiously creeping down the hallway until he stops at a door with the number 11 carved into the wood. He fumbles with the key, then shoves it into the hole. He slips inside, retreating into the secrets hidden between the walls of his room. He's hiding something. There has to be a reason he's still coming up here even though his job is gone. He's hiding something. He's hiding something big.

"Room 11," I whisper to Hazel and Shea.

I peek outside our room, then tiptoe down the hall in the direction of Forrest's room. Hazel creeps out after me, but Shea stays behind and gives us a look that screams "are you out of your mind?" Downstairs you can hear the clanging of pans and distant chattering of guests, but there's a strange silence that's settled over the upstairs portion of the B&B. My footsteps are muffled against the carpet and I lean my ear gently up against Forrest's door, feeling the smooth wood against my earlobe. Everything is quiet for a moment. But then I hear rustling, the sound of someone moving through the space and rifling through papers. I hear a muttering voice and press my ear harder against the door.

"Yes. I can meet this afternoon. I'll only be in town until early tomorrow morning . . . I'd be open to talking to him if he's interested. One of my suppliers just died, a tragic incident. Yes, yes. Business has to go on . . . two o'clock . . .yes. The protocol is the same as the last time we met. I understand. Two o'clock. Goodbye."

I'm trying to make sense of what he just said, that one of his suppliers just died. I'm willing to bet he's referring to Stephanie. This may confirm that Stephanie was partaking in Forrest's drug trade and that his illegal activities didn't stop when he was fired from his position at the lab. But I don't have time to think, because all of a sudden the door flings open leaving our cover completely blown. I guess we won't be joining the FBI anytime soon. His beady, electric green eyes bulge, his pupils darting around in their sockets. His nostrils flare and I feel my heart sink to the bottom of my stomach. My eyes are as wide as the moon. My mouth hangs open like the kid from Home Alone.

"Well this is awkward," I blurt out. There I go again, spewing unnecessary words out of my mouth to make awkward situations more uncomfortable than they already are.

Forrest narrows his eyes and lowers his chin to his chest, his evil look sending a wave of pure fear through my body. How do I keep getting myself into these situations?

"This is a private matter that does not concern you," he says robotically.

I keep my eyes glued to the floor, too scared to meet his terrifying glare. He clenches his hands into fists and it looks as if his entire body is shaking with rage.

"This is a private matter that does not concern you," he repeats even louder.

"We're sorry," Hazel's voice shakes. "We won't bother you again."

The three of us turn to walk away and escape this uncomfortable and possibly dangerous situation, but Forrest growls, "Stop."

I freeze instantly in my tracks when I hear the nasally, but intense rasp of his voice.

"Did you follow me up here? Who sent you?" he interrogates.

I want to answer but my mouth runs dry, and I feel like I'm choking on my own tongue. The look on his face is a mixture of panic and intense anger, which makes me unsure if he's going to kill us or if he's just as scared as we are. People always say that bears are more afraid of you than you are of them. I don't really believe that because the fact of the matter is that bears are massive and strong and could wipe you out with one swing of their paw. You see a bear and you run. You don't sit there thinking it's probably not going to come after you because it's possibly more scared of you. No. You run. So right now, I want to run. I want to run as far and as fast as I can.

"We didn't follow you," Shea answers. "We had no clue that you'd come up here. This whole thing is just a big coincidence. I swear. We're just as shocked to see you as you are to see us."

Forrest twitches and begins to tap his foot restlessly against the floor. He seems seconds away from losing control of himself, from falling off the edge of the cliff, the edge of sanity.

"We don't want any problems," Shea keeps talking, his voice calm and steady. "If you just let us go on our way, I promise we won't tell anyone we saw you up here. Let's just pretend this didn't happen."

Forrest's eyes seem to roll around to the back of his head while he thinks about Shea's offer. He releases his clenched fists and says with a shaky, but oddly monotone voice, "Fine, but if you ever speak of this encounter I'll . . . I'll . . . I'll make sure you regret it." He is breathing so heavy I can see his chest heaving in and out. And before we have the chance to run away, Forrest Shepard slams the door in our faces.

*****

Shea and I are hanging out at my house, enjoying the afternoon sun and each other's company. After our run in with Forrest, a little bit of relaxation is exactly what I need. I'm still reeling over the exchange with him. The strangest part was his mannerisms and the way he spoke, the words sounding so unnatural. The way he couldn't stop fidgeting and moving gave me a strange and anxious feeling. We're lucky that Shea was able to talk him down or else our cover would've been completely blown. But his threat. His threat is starting to make me think that Forrest Shepard is capable of far more than I ever imagined.

"Do you think Forrest killed her?" I ask Shea. You know, just casual conversation stuff.

"Possibly, he looks really guilty. But I don't know if I really trust Sawyer or Isla. We don't know much about her at all," he responds.

"She seems like a very private person. She doesn't have any social media. Luke can't find much on her. We have to find a way to catch her in the act of doing something she's not supposed to do. I don't know. I just feel like we're close." He smiles a little, so I say, "What?"

He shrugs, "You're cute when you're thinking really hard."

I giggle, feeling the butterflies in my stomach fluttering rapidly, "I really do feel like we're close to figuring this out."

"I know you do. I think we are too."

"I want to talk to Easton as soon as he gets back, see if we can pull any more information out of him."

"We should talk about something other than Stephanie's murder," he says jokingly.

"I'm sorry," I smile. "What would you like to talk about?"

"Hmm . . ." he smirks, "Who said anything about talking?"

"Wow, that was good," I laugh. "It sounds like something Graeson would say."

"I spend a lot of time around him."

We're going back and forth and I'm so close to standing up and kissing him right in my front yard, when I hear someone yelling Shea's name. Both of us turn to see where the noise is coming from, and I see Mr. Cavanaugh, the nice old man in the wheelchair I met at Stephanie's party, rolling down the street. Shea and I start walking down to see him.

"Hi Mr. Cavanaugh. How are you?" Shea greets the old man.

"I'm decent, how are you, young man? And who's this pretty lady?"

"I'm good, Mr. Cavanaugh. This is Izzie. I introduced you to her at Stephanie's party."

"Oh that's right," he says while he fidgets with his hat, but sounds unsure of himself. "I needed to tell you something, Shea."

"What's up?" Shea asks.

"I don't need you to come by tonight. My daughter's coming into town, and she's going to take me out to dinner," his voice is deep and steady.

Shea looks a little confused and says, "Alright. Are you sure?"

"I'm positive. You enjoy your time with your girl, you hear me?"

Shea nods and smiles at Mr. Cavanaugh, who switches his glance over to me. He studies my face for a moment, squinting through his large, square glasses, and then says, "Is he good to you?"

I smile, "He's great, the best I could ask for."

"Good, good," he mutters. "Who are you?"

I stutter for a moment, but then say, "I'm Izzie. I just moved here."

"Oh, I see. Great to meet you. I saw your dad at the hardware store last weekend. That nurse, the one I don't like, she took me to find some weed killer."

I can't tell if he's referring to my dad or Shea's dad, but either way, it doesn't make too much sense seeing that Shea's dad is dead and mine lives across the country in a rehab facility.

"My dad?" I ask.

Mr. Cavanaugh just smiles obliviously at me, his light brown eyes glowing, like he had no idea what I was talking about. "I better be on my way to the office. The boss will be mad if I'm late. It's always a pleasure, kids."

With that, Mr. Cavanaugh takes off in his wheelchair, rolling down the street until he reaches his house.

Before I can comment, Shea says, "He has dementia. Sometimes he says things that don't really make sense. He goes back to the past a lot or he gets confused. His daughter lives in California and hasn't come to see him in years, so she's probably not coming in for the night. And he doesn't work anymore."

"It was weird when he said that he saw one of our dads at the hardware store."

"A few weeks ago, he told me he saw my dad at the grocery store. It was after he died. That's probably what he was talking about again this time."

"It's sweet that you spend time with him," I say softly.

"It's no big deal. I'm just happy I can help him a little bit. He doesn't have much family around," he replies humbly.

The two of us start walking back up the driveway. I notice the way the sun hits Shea's hair, bringing out his blonde streaks and the way he's unsure of what to do with his long arms while he walks. We take our seats on the front porch again.

"Where were we?" I smile, remembering our conversation from before.

He turns to me and smiles, but something across the street catches my eye. I see Isla Grimaldi and her striking black hair walk out of her garage and into her car.

I turn to Shea with a mischievous sparkle in my eyes, "I have a wild idea."

"You do?" He looks at me unsure where my train of thought is headed.

"Let's follow Isla. We can trail her and see if we can figure anything out."

His face looks a little disappointed as he says sarcastically, "That sounds romantic."

"Come on! Please. She might lead us to some answers," I persuade while giving him the best puppy dog eyes I can muster.

"Okay, we'll go."

I dash into the house to grab my keys, and we quickly hop into my car. I force the keys into the ignition and jerk the car in to reverse, speeding down the driveway and on to the street. I follow her through the twists and turns of the Knox Hollow streets, trying to stay close enough to keep an eye on her car, but far enough away so she doesn't think we're following her.

After a while of driving, Isla pulls into the parking lot of a nail salon a few miles away from our street.

"We followed her to a nail salon," Shea says. "I don't want to ruin all the excitement, but there's nothing suspicious about a nail salon."

"Just wait," I reply. "This is just the beginning. She'll lead us somewhere worth our while."

Well . . . I may have been kind of far off with that statement. After the nail salon, we followed Isla to TJ Maxx, the local flower store, and then the package store where she purchased a bottle of white wine and a bottle of scotch. Exciting stuff. I'm so glad we were there to watch her run all her errands.

I look over to Shea with shame on my face due to overconfidence, "I think I may have been wrong with this one. We can just go home."

"We've followed her around for a few hours already. I'm not giving up now. Come on, let's go," he reassures me.

Isla begins to drive again, her car traveling down especially windy roads that I don't recognize. We come around a bend and take a sharp right as I start to feel a little sketched out by the unfamiliar landscape.

"Do you know where we are?" I ask Shea.

"I don't know where she's headed, but this is the way I go to get to the cemetery my dad's buried at," he answers.

I feel my face scrunch up in confusion. Why is Isla on her way to a cemetery? Sure enough, she pulls into Crownhill Cemetery, parks her car, and slowly emerges holding a bouquet of sunflowers. Huh? Sunflowers that's a strange choice. That was the same type of flower that Stephanie had in vases all around her house.

Even though Crownhill Cemetery is basking in the daylight there's still an eeriness to this place, which makes me wonder how strange it must be at night. I look out in the distance and all I see are miles and miles of smooth grey tombstones. It feels like there has to be millions of gravestones, millions of lives lost, millions of stories buried six feet underground. Everywhere I look, I only see death. Names carved into stone. Silent screams. I feel a chill run through my body. Some stones are crowded with various flowers, peonies and roses, lilacs and tulips. The worst part are the bare stones. The ones that aren't adorned with flowers or flags or teddy bears or wreaths. They're just empty. Who's thinking of those people? Who's keeping their memory alive?

Isla stands at her car, but does not move. She's frozen, like a dead body. Then she begins to walk. Slow and tiny steps, like she's trying to delay reaching her destination, like it's paining her to move. She reaches a grave only a few feet away from the car and carefully bends down. Gently, she rests the sunflowers against the stone. A breeze delicately swooshes through the graveyard, like a ghost dancing through the stones, ruffling the grass and Isla's sleek, black hair. Through the open car window I feel the slight wind against my face, the blowing air feeling like the cold, dead fingers of a ghost. Isla hangs her head so it's even with the top of the stone and brings her hands up to her face. I hear a noise. It's coming from her. She's crying. No. She's sobbing. Her sobs are quiet and high pitched, and it sounds like she's struggling to breathe. Her cries pierce the silence, like a hand making ripples in still water.

"I'm sorry," I hear her say in between sobs.

I lean my head closer to the window, straining to hear what she's saying.

"I'm sorry," she repeats. "I'm so sorry. I didn't want you to die. I didn't mean what I said. It was an empty threat. I'm so sorry. I didn't want you to die. When I sent those messages, I was just trying to save my relationship. I love Thomas. Our story wasn't conventional, but it was ours. But I never meant what I said. I feel like I wished this upon you. I'm so sorry. I want your forgiveness. I don't know if I'll ever find it, but I had to tell you. I'm sorry, Stephanie, I'm so sorry."

She chokes on the last few words, her quiet sobs becoming hysterical. I hear my own heart beating in my ears, echoing in my head. I glance over at Shea. His head is bent downwards, looking at his feet.

"I'm sorry," she sobs again.

A sharp pain hits the pit of my stomach. In that moment, I feel the hands of guilt drowning me in its rough ocean waves. She's seeking forgiveness, redemption, relief from the guilt she carries on her shoulders each day and night. I feel like I've intruded on her moment, on her privacy, that I had no right to follow her here.

I look back out to her, crouched down at the grave like she's praying. Her coal black hair blows in the wind and her tiny body is shaking with regret. Forgiveness. That's what she wants. Isn't that what we all want when we mess up? Forgiveness. Such a tricky thing. Forgiveness. I have no right being here, watching this, judging her. All she wants is forgiveness. But it's too late. Her time ran out. Forgiveness. Like a ticking clock. A second chance a minute too late.

C H A P T E R 18 - The Black Crow and the Silver Locket

I had a bad feeling about today. I don't know where it came from or why it was there, but I felt it. I felt it in the pit of my stomach, gnawing at my insides. I felt it in my chest when I tried to breathe. I felt it deep inside my bones when I first woke up in the morning. I had a bad feeling about today. It was random and strange. And when I looked outside my window a black crow flew across the grey sky, making an ear piercing sound. A bad omen and a bad feeling. But it probably meant nothing. Or maybe it meant everything. I don't know. It was just a feeling.

I'm sitting at the kitchen counter, eating breakfast with my mom and my sisters. Luke decided to sleep in today, and John has already started his job at the hospital. I try to eat some of my oatmeal, but something just doesn't feel right with my stomach. I don't feel nauseous or sick, just . . . I don't know . . . weird.

"What are your plans for today?" my mom asks as she sips her coffee.

"I'm not sure. I think Hazel and I might go out for coffee later," I reply.

"That sounds fun. I'm so happy you and Hazel are friends. I really like that girl. I think I'm going to take the girls over to the park by the elementary school today before it storms. I heard it's supposed to get pretty bad out later," she continues to talk about I'm not even sure what, but I don't hear any of it because I'm lost in my own thoughts. My head just feels empty, like I can't concentrate on anything, like I'm trapped in my own world.

"Are you alright, honey?" She eyes me concernedly.

"Huh? Oh yeah, no I'm fine. I zoned out for a minute. What did you say?"

"I just asked if you wanted a refill on your coffee," she smiles warmly.

I go to say yes, but then my phone buzzes. I pick it up, the bright screen hurting my eyes, and I see that I have a text from Alison Kester, which is strange for many reasons. Number one being that I never gave her my phone number and number two, I really can't stand her.

The message reads, *"Hi, it's Alison. I found something that might help you. Come over between two and five. It's important."*

After seeing Isla at Crownhill Cemetery, I've been a little reluctant to dive back into Stephanie's murder. But this text. This text is intriguing. Alison lives in the same house that Stephanie hid all of her secrets in. Now that I no longer think Isla is the murderer, I need something to prove that it was Forrest who committed the crime. It has to be him. I'm sure of it. He has a clear connection with Stephanie, and he seems insane enough to commit the crime. We still don't know why Stephanie was supplying him with Sawyer's pills, but maybe Alison can help. However, the thought of walking into the Kester house — aka Satan's den — alone is starting to freak me out.

"I'm all good on coffee. Thanks Mom. I'm going to clean my room. It's a mess," I say as I lunge upwards from the table and dash to my room, leaving my mom with a confused and concerned look on her face.

When I'm in the privacy of my bedroom, I call Hazel immediately.

"Hi, what's up?" I hear her voice on the other line.

"I just got the weirdest text from Alison. I don't even know how she got my number," I'm suddenly feeling more nervous than I originally thought I was.

"What did she want?" Hazel sounds surprised.

"She told me that she found something that could help us and to come over between two and five. How weird is that?"

"That's really strange, but she must *know* something. Alison's — how do I say this nicely — a little demon, but she's smart. She's sent us down the right path before. I would go."

I mull Hazel's words over in my head. I know she's right, but something about this whole situation is making me feel like I'm about to throw up my breakfast. Alison knows something, and she reached out to me. The last few times I met with Alison, I had to bribe her with cash to get her to talk. Now she's just offering up information for free. It must be urgent.

"Okay, I'm going to go, but if you don't hear from me by five, alert the cops. Tell them my body's at Stephanie's," I say.

"Stop it! You're not going to die. If you wait until later tonight I can go with you. My mom's making me babysit my brother all day, and he insisted that we go to Six Flags, but I'll be back around six. I hate that place."

"Thank you, but Alison said to come between two and five. I don't want to mess with her orders because knowing her she'll end up not telling me anything."

"Well best of luck my friend. If I don't hear from you by five I'll come looking for you myself. I may be exceptionally short, but I think I could take Alison if I had to," Hazel jokes.

I laugh at the image of tiny little Hazel kickboxing the devilish nine-year-old, "I appreciate it. And just for the record, you're not short, you're fun sized."

After a full day of procrastinating, I step out my front door and begin the trek to Alison's house around four o'clock. Doubt and anxiety swim in my stomach and the air feels heavy in my lungs. The sky is painted a gloomy shade of grey, like a sheet of freshly laid concrete. Off in the distance, a cluster of dark and ominous storms clouds are gathered, like a thick layer of fog. The weatherman said that these would be the worst storms Knox Hollow would see all summer. I walk over the Kester's front lawn, the grass itching my ankles. I start to feel water droplets trickling down onto my head, the rain bringing in unusually cold weather for this time of year. I hear birds crowing above me and I wonder if it's that same black crow I saw through my window this morning. Walking up to the Kester's front porch takes me right back to that Saturday night. The memories run in a loop around my head. My kiss with Shea. Graeson and his Tequila. The dead body.

I step up to the birch wood door and ring the bell. I hear the sound of it echoing inside the house as I look around at all the bushes in Stephanie's landscape. I can't shake the feeling that somebody is watching me, creeping around in the shadows.

I wait, but no one comes. I ring again, no answer. I watch the minutes go by on my phone, trying to be patient. Curiosity begins to take over, and I feel the strong urge to finish this business. I place my hand gently on the door handle and turn it ever so slightly. The handle slides downward easily, opening the door with a creak. I need to remember to remind Alison not to leave her door unlocked when she's home alone, especially not with a murderer running around and not when she's in the possession of massive amounts of cash.

I step inside the house and call out, "Alison!"

My voice echoes through the house, but Alison doesn't respond. I yell her name again and begin to walk down the hallway that leads to the kitchen. I notice their house is still a disaster, with dirty dishes thrown everywhere and piles of mail gathering on the counters.

"Alison! Are you here?" I call out again.

348

Silence. Complete and utter silence. I feel my heart beating through the cloth of my t-shirt. The logical part of me knows I shouldn't be here, but I want answers. No, I *need* answers. I make my way through the entire downstairs, but there's no sign of Alison or anyone else for that matter.

Upstairs. I haven't checked upstairs. The air conditioning is turned up so high that goosebumps reside on my arms and legs, and I start to shiver. The sound of my footsteps bounce off the walls and up to the foyer. All I can think about is the last time I was here when Shea and I were trapped in Stephanie's closet. I make my way up the stairs slowly, scared of what I'm going to find up there. I hear the faint sound of piano keys and then a massive boom of thunder that shakes the entire house. Rain pelts down from the sky, smacking the roof.

When I'm up the stairs, I begin to walk down the hallway in the direction of the sound of the piano melody. Thunder booms again, and then suddenly, the power flickers off, filling the house with shadows of grey and black. The darkness coats my eyes, making me feel like I'm wearing a blindfold.

"Are you freaking kidding me?!" I yell.

This is all I need right now. Not only am I trapped inside of the devil's house alone, there's no power. If only my mother could see me now, she'd be so proud of the decisions I'm making. It feels like the house is abandoned. Empty. Lifeless.

I hear the piano sound closer and closer, the melody eerie and haunting, reminding me of a jewelry box I used to have when I was little. I follow the noise until I reach a room with a white door. The sound is definitely coming from in there. I creak the door open and the noise immediately stops.

"Alison? Alison, is that you?" I say to the dark and silent room.

I watch a flash of lightning strike from the sky and I swear I see a shadow move through the room. Then, something touches me. Tiny, warm fingers. I scream as loud as I possibly can, a deafening cry that stems from my stomach.

"Relax, it's just me," I hear Alison's voice as she flicks on a battery powered lantern.

"Jesus Christ, Alison!" I yell.

"You're not supposed to say the Lord's name in vain," she retorts.

"And you're not supposed to blackmail people, but here we are! Why the hell would you scare me like that? I've been calling your name."

She sits at a bench in front of a grand piano. "I didn't hear you calling until you were already upstairs because I was playing my piano. And then the power went out, and I just couldn't resist the urge. I'm sorry. I didn't think I'd get you that good," she laughs, which makes me want to strangle her.

"You're a sick, twisted child. You know that?"

She shrugs, "I appreciate the compliment."

"Enough with the games," I start. "Why did you ask me to come over?"

"I'm getting to that," she says. "Follow me."

She takes the lantern and leads me down the long, dark hallway into Stephanie and Richard's room. Her mousy brown hair sways behind her as she walks. When we're inside their room, Alison leads me over to Stephanie's vanity, which is still perfectly intact.

"I was going through her jewelry today," Alison starts, her voice quiet but confident. "I saw this necklace I didn't recognize. I'd never seen her wear it before." She opens one of the small drawers with a crystal knob and pulls out a gorgeous silver necklace. Her tiny, skinny fingers delicately hold the necklace by the clasp so I can see. The shiny silver chain is strung through a beautiful heart shaped locket. Real diamond stones are carved into the smooth surface, causing the locket to sparkle in the darkness.

"What's so special about it?" I ask, unsure of what Alison's point is.

She turns to me, her hazel eyes illuminated by the glow of the lantern. Her eyes are wide and intense, almost fearful.

"If you open it, there's a date written inside. It was three years ago in August."

"I'm not following," I say to her.

"My parents got married a long time ago in June, so this locket isn't from my dad. I knew my mom was having some fun with Beckett, but I think that started pretty recently. I just thought it was strange. Someone gave this to her, and she never wore it. Doesn't that sound weird to you?"

"That's odd, but it doesn't prove anything," I reply. Something about this necklace is familiar, but makes me uncomfortable. I can't help but notice how well spoken and intelligent she is for only nine years old. I feel like I've seen this locket before, but I can't place where.

"I thought you'd say that," she says confidently. "So, I did some more digging. I found this locked box in her drawer, and I used a bobby pin to pop it open." She demonstrates, opening the red locked box. "The only thing in it was this letter." She takes out a piece of white lined paper and unfolds it. "You're going to want to read this."

I take the letter from her, careful not to bend or crease the paper. The letter reads as follows:

Dear Stephanie,

I miss you more and more with each passing day. Saying goodbye to you is the hardest thing I've ever had to do. All I can think about is our time together on the beach last weekend and how gorgeous you looked in that yellow dress. You know how much I love you in yellow. Like always, our time was too short, but I know we'll be together soon. I'm counting the days. But for now, this locket will remind you of me and that it won't be long until we see each other again. I love you with everything in me. Forever and always. Sending all of my love."

It ends there. No signature. No mention of who this mysterious love letter is from. For some odd reason, the handwriting is familiar, but I can't figure out why. It's like meeting a cousin you never knew you had or passing by an old friend you lost touch with in the hallway.

"Oh my God!" I gasp.

"Exactly," Alison says. "I don't think this is from Beckett. The handwriting is nice and why would Beckett talk about having to say goodbye to my mom if he lived down the street?"

"That's a really good point. I hate to say it Alison, but I'm impressed. You're really smart."

"Thank you," I'm surprised that she doesn't fire back a sarcastic comment.

"Why did you tell me this without making me pay you?" I ask her. Alison seems to shrink inside herself, and her fiery spark seems to have dulled. "You know, I won't tell anyone if you open up for a minute. It's okay to not keep a brave face every once in a while."

I notice a few tears well in her hazel eyes and start to stream down her tanned cheeks. Her voice is shaky, "If I'm being honest, I'm scared. I feel like there's someone watching me all the time. My dad's at work all day, and most of the time I'm all alone in this house. My mom is gone, Izzie. She was terrible and manipulative and mean, but she was my mom."

I feel my heart melting inside my body, and instinctively, I step closer to Alison and wrap my arms around her. At first, her body stiffens, but then she collapses into my arms. I feel her tiny body shaking, and I hug her tighter. She really is just a broken little girl, putting up a tough front because she has no one looking out for her. She's grown up thinking that she can't count on anyone, that she's all alone in this scary world.

She pulls away from me and wipes the tears falling from her eyes.

"You don't have to be scared, Alison. We're going to figure this out, I promise you. I'm sorry about your mom. It's okay to be sad. You're not alone. I know we haven't always gotten along, but I'm here for you. When you feel this way, if you want to talk, or if you just want someone to hang out with so you're not alone in this house, you can call me. You have my number now." She looks up at me and I wipe a tear away from her tanned cheek. "It's all going to be okay."

She takes a deep breath and smiles at me, which reminds me of a younger version of myself. She says to me, "If you tell anyone I cried, I'll hurt you." Even though she's already back to her sassy self, I can tell she's grateful for what I just said. How do I know this? Because I do the exact same thing to people who try to help me.

"Do you mind if I take this?" I ask Alison, referring to the letter and the silver locket.

"Go ahead," she answers. "I hope it helps."

"Can I ask you one more question before I go?" She nods her head so I continue talking. "Why is your sister so quiet?" I've been curious about Ella Kester since I met her the first time I kinda sorta broke into Stephanie's house. It was strange how quiet she was, it was as if the sound of her own voice frightened her.

"Oh, Ella? Believe it or not she used to be really outgoing and loud. She was a bit of a blabber mouth. There were a couple times where she almost told my dad about some secret my mom wanted us to keep. She got in a lot of trouble those few times. I'm not sure exactly what my mom punished her with, but she's never really been the same since. That's why she doesn't talk. She's scared to say the wrong thing."

353

That makes a lot of sense in a disturbing and sickening kind of way. These poor kids are growing up in such a toxic environment. I say goodbye to Alison and run back to my house with the locket and the note in tow, trying to shield myself from the pouring rain and booms of thunder.

A black crow sings out overhead. A bad omen and a bad feeling. My dad always told me to trust my instincts. I should've listened to him.

*****

I've been reading over the note for the past hour while watching the thunderstorm outside my window. Is it possible that Stephanie had another affair? Another life that no one knew about? There were so many sides to Stephanie, it was like she was ten different people all at once. It's bothering me that I can't figure out why this locket is so familiar. I feel like I've seen it before, but how could that be true? I called Hazel to fill her in, but she didn't answer. Luke's out running errands for my mom. I'd rather just tell him in person when he gets back. It'll be a lot easier to explain it all face-to-face than over the phone. Anyway, all five of us are meeting up tonight to discuss any new information, so I guess I'll just have to wait until then to share.

I comb back through the note, trying to pick out any details that might be useful. I notice that the letter is dated in the top right corner. July of last summer. There's no way this is from Beckett. The precise language and the talk about having to say goodbye would be so out of character for him. I hear the sound of the garage doors opening as John's pickup truck rolls up the driveway. Even though John and I have never been the best of friends, I'm thankful to have someone home with me while the power is out and the storm rages on.

"I'm home, Izzie," I hear him yell up the stairs.

354

"Okay!" I yell back, not in the mood to make conversation, but still happy that I'm no longer alone.

I feel like I'm overlooking something, like this note and this locket are more important than they seem. There's something right under my nose that I'm not seeing. I hear John walk up the stairs and into his bedroom, probably changing out of his preppy work clothes and into something more comfortable.

My phone starts ringing, and I see that it's Hazel finally calling me back.

"How was Alison's?" she asks eagerly.

"I think Alison's onto something. She found this love letter and silver locket in the back of Stephanie's drawer. She knows they're not from Richard, and we're pretty sure they're not from Beckett. It's hard to explain over the phone, but I'll tell you everything tonight," I lower my voice because I realize I'm talking extremely loud due to all of the adrenaline.

"Oh my God," she says. "I can't wait to hear. I'm about to get on the highway. I'll call you as soon as I'm home."

"Okay, bye. I'll see you soon."

I hang up the phone and see that I have a text from my mom, asking me if I can find some cake pan she needs for the dessert she's making tonight. Most of our baking stuff is still packed in boxes in the basement, meaning that I'm not only going to have to go down into the creepy basement while the power is off, but also search through an endless mound of boxes to find one silly little pan. I tell her I'll try to find it because I have nothing else to do and need something to keep me busy until I meet up with my friends later.

I walk down the stairs and find a flashlight in the kitchen. Slowly, I open the door to the basement, which is filled to the brim with thick, black darkness. I switch on the flashlight, which illuminates a narrow path in front of me. I don't know what it is about basements that I find so unsettling and creepy. I feel like most people, or at least most kids, have a weird, unexplained fear of their basement, especially when it's dark. In reality, it's just a room. But still, there's a strange and indescribable feeling in the pit of my stomach, and my heart is beating much faster than usual.

Ten. Ten stairs to take until I'm in the basement, submerged in darkness.

The hum of the furnace makes me feel like there's someone down here with me, concealed and tiptoeing around in the seclusion of the dim basement. I run my hand along the wall to orient myself, and my fingers brush against a cobweb. A chill surges up my spine. From here, everything looks like a shadow, a mysterious silhouette. Objects with no definition or shape. I take the last step down the stairs, careful not to trip.

Nine. Nine seconds tick by on the clock before I dive into the black hole that is our basement.

The letter and the silver locket. They must mean something. Stephanie was having an affair with someone else. Another mystery man. I walk through the unfinished side of the basement. The air feels damp and cold, and off in the distance, I can hear the roaring thunder and the pelting rain. It smells musty, like mothballs. With the flashlight illuminating my path, I inch my way to the back and to the area under the stairs where most of our unpacked boxes are. I crouch down, feeling the cold concrete against my knees and begin to rifle through our belongings.

Eight. Eight boxes stacked up under the stairs in front of me.

The black crow. The silver locket. I had a bad feeling about today. The thunder storm. The darkness. I feel it swallowing me up, its grimy fingers taking a firm hold on me. I go through a couple of the brown boxes with no sign of the cake pan. I push farther into the back, farther under the stairwell. I carefully open another box, and something catches my eye.

Seven. Seven thrums of my heartbeat.

In the back corner of the cardboard, there's a tiny black box. Gently, my fingers remove the top of the box. There's a letter, written in tiny, neat handwriting on white lined paper. A letter and a silver tie pin and an old plane ticket to California.

The tiepin and the ticket hold no meaning for me. My family's never been to California. I delicately open the letter, feeling the grainy paper in my fingers. I begin to read the letter.

My love,

Those few days on the beach were the best I've had in the longest time. I miss you so much it hurts to wake up in the morning. Every day I spend without you feels like a waste of time, a waste of life. You are my one true love, my soulmate. I love you more than all the stars in the night sky and all the gold this world has to offer. I can't wait until we're together again. I love you, J. The locket was the sweetest gift I have ever received. It reminds me of you even when you're so far away. With love, Stephanie.

I feel my insides constrict, and I feel like I'm choking on the heavy air. The blood in my veins runs bitterly cold, making it feel like there's a gush of wind dancing through the basement. My fingers are shaking furiously as I hold the white lined paper. J for John. John and Stephanie. I can't breathe. I can't breathe. I can't breathe.

Six. Six gulps for air.

The locket. My mom has the same locket. An anniversary gift from John. Suddenly, I can see it all so clear. The final missing puzzle piece. My mind goes back to that night. To lying on the cold concrete. To seeing Easton Black bent over me. To the person touching my arm. John. I can see it now. His cornflower blue eyes. His dirty blonde hair. Oh my God. Oh my God. It was him.

Five. Five booms of thunder shaking the house.

I feel frozen in time, like a paused TV screen. I can't move. I can't breathe. Then it hits me. I'm alone with John. My mom and my sisters are gone. Luke is gone. It's just me. And him. Oh God.

Four. Four footsteps on the floor above me.

This whole time I've been searching for the murderer, and he was living in my house. He was sitting across the dinner table. He was walking past me in the hallway. He was doing my laundry. He was sleeping in the room down the hall. I need to get out of here. Suddenly, my adrenaline kicks in, and I feel myself working in overdrive. I force the contents back into the black box and tuck it under my arm. I pull out my phone from my back pocket and dial Luke. I start sprinting as quietly as I can up the basement stairs.

Three. Three rings from the phone shrieking in my ears.

"Hey, Izzie, what's up?" I hear Luke's voice on the other line, which sends a wave of comfort throughout my body.

"Luke, I figured it out," I'm breathing so heavy it's hard to get the words out.

"Huh?" he sounds thoroughly confused. I dash through the kitchen and rifle through the drawers in search of my keys. I grab them and fumble with the door handle leading out to the garage. I feel like I'm being watched. Fear surges through my body. I'm trying to talk to Luke, but I can't even speak.

"Izzie, what's wrong?" he sounds worried. "Izzie, talk to me. What's going on?"

I dash out the door and walk through the garage, trying to make it out to my car in the driveway. The concrete feels cold and dusty on my feet, making me realize that I don't have shoes on. Screw it. I don't have time to go back for them. It is what it is at this point. I just need to get out of this house. I need to drive as far away as I possibly can.

Two. Two eyes watching me.

"It's John, Luke. He did it," I stutter, struggling to breathe and speak at the same time.

I'm halfway through the garage, when I hear the door creak open slightly. I can't see behind me, but I don't have to. I'm trying to run, but my body won't move. It's like my feet are cemented to the floor. I need to get out of here.

One. One murderer standing right behind me.

Suddenly, I am yanked back by my ponytail. I feel two massive hands ripping at my hair. My knees give out, and my feet can't hold their ground against John's sheer force. My body is dragged across the concrete while I thrash my legs around. I try to fight and break free of his grip, but I can't. The phone in my hand falls to the ground, shattering the glass, along with the black box, causing the contents to spill out. My head slams against the garage stairs. The room starts to spin, and I feel the metallic taste of blood in my mouth. A shooting pain fills my head until everything goes black.

Zero. I'm out of time.

CHAPTER 19 - For Love

"But surely for everything you love you have to pay some price" - *Agatha Christie*

My eyelids flutter open slowly, feeling heavy and sore, like there's tiny weights holding them down. Everything around me is pitch black. I feel like I'm awake, but all I can see is thick darkness smothering me. Where am I? I feel like I'm trapped inside a coffin underground like a dead body. I hear myself breathing shallowly, struggling to get air into my lungs. I feel cold metal against the back of my thighs and realize I'm sitting in a chair. I try to stand up, but feel something constricting my movement, something pressing against my stomach. My head is throbbing, a sharp pain shooting through my skull making me feel even more disoriented and dizzy. I try to move my hand up to the source of the pain. They won't budge. I feel the panic rapidly rising in my chest, and I begin to thrash around. There's something itchy and tight around both of my wrists, and my hands are tied behind my body. I kick my legs as hard as I can, but they're tied to the chair. I can't remember how I got here or what happened before, but I have this sinking feeling in my gut that it was something bad. I try to stretch my memory back. There was something about a letter and a thunderstorm. I must've hit my head at some point. Everything around me is moving, spinning in rapid circles like cars around a racetrack. This seems like a dream, some sort of horrifying nightmare.

Randomly flailing my limbs around doesn't seem to be helping my cause, so I do the only thing I can think of in the moment. I scream. I scream with everything I have in me, a desperate, horrified screech pouring out of my mouth. I howl until my throat burns and my voice goes hoarse. My screams turn into hysterical sobs. I feel my chest heaving up and down, and tears stream down my face. I'm trapped in the dark, tied to a chair with no idea where I am or what happened. I can't even wipe the falling tears from my eyes. There's no way out.

And then I hear footsteps. Slow, measured, calculated footsteps. Just like the ones I heard in Stephanie's house the day Shea and I were trapped in the closet. A beam of harsh light hits my face, stinging my eyes.

"Pipe down," I hear his familiar voice before I see his face, "The screaming is a bit much."

When my eyes grow accustomed to the bright flashlight, I focus in on the man in front of me. The cornflower blue eyes. The full head of dirty blonde hair. The reassuring smile. Everything about him is the same, but it feels so different now. The memories come crashing into me, like a head-on collision with a train. The locket. The letter. John.

When I see his face, I stop sobbing instantly and a fierce rage comes over me.

"Let me go!" I scream as I kick and thrash around in the chair. "Let me go! You killed her! You killed her! I trusted you!"

"Shh . . ." he puts his fingers to his mouth, his face illuminated by his flashlight.

I'm not sure why, but I lower my voice and try to take a deep breath in. "Did you kill her?" my voice is small and raspy.

"You're getting ahead of yourself, Izzie," he responds casually.

He seems emotionless, showing no signs of anger or fear or even amusement at the current situation. He's just his normal self, handling it like it's a typical everyday occurrence.

"Mom and Luke are both going to be home soon. They'll see what you're doing to me. And what you did to Stephanie!"

"I sent your mom on a couple more errands. She won't be back for a while. As for Luke, I texted him from your phone and told him that your call was just a misunderstanding and that everything was fine. He won't be rushing in to rescue you anytime soon," John says. He has the same steady and calming voice, but this time, there's an unsettling edge to it.

"So what's your plan? Hold me hostage down here and hope that my mom doesn't notice I'm missing when she gets back?" I yell.

"Sassy as always," he smirks.

"What did you do? Did you kill Stephanie? Did you kill Hannah?" I fire questions at him.

"What do you think happened?" he poses the question, which catches me off guard.

I think about it for a moment. What exactly do I think? Everything from the past few hours is still a little blurry. "You were having an affair with Stephanie. I saw the letters. You two were together while you were married to my mom. You killed her. I don't know why, but it was you. Wasn't it?"

"You're smarter than I gave you credit for," he replies. "If you just could learn to mind your own damn business, we wouldn't be in this situation. If you just left well enough alone Izzie, you wouldn't be living out the last few minutes of your life in this cold, dark basement."

My stomach clenches as the words pierce my ears, and I feel the lump in my throat grow so large it constricts my breathing. Every muscle in my body goes limp, and I feel like I'm about to vomit profusely. So this is his plan. To kill me. I'm going to die down here. I won't get a chance to say goodbye to anyone. To Luke, the person who's been there for me since day one. To Hazel, my best friend in the entire world. To Graeson, who always makes me laugh even though he's so stupid. To Shea, the first boy I think I may actually love. To my mom, who's loved me better than anyone else could. To my dad, my real dad, our relationship has come so far. To my sisters, they probably won't even remember me. This is where it ends for me. In this dark basement, tied to a chair. This is it.

Unless it's not. Luke knows me better than anyone. He'll know that something was weird about our phone call. If I can just keep John talking long enough, maybe Luke or my mom will come home. I take a big breath in, inhaling every bit of courage I can find. I just have to keep him talking. I feel my hands and legs violently shaking and take another deep breath. I can do this. I just need to keep myself together, retain as much composure as I can.

"So this is my fault?" I say sarcastically. "You murdered someone, but it's my fault. That makes perfect sense."

He laughs, "Always so sarcastic."

"You can't just tie me up down here and kill me. I want answers. If I'm going to die, I want to know the whole story," my voice is fragile, ready to break at any moment.

He doesn't say anything for a few minutes, a painful silence filling the space between us. He's mulling my words over in his head, deeply considering his options. Thunder booms off in the distance, the noise coinciding with the pouring rain. The storm is like its own little symphony — the rain, the thunder, the lightning — each their own instrument coming together to make one melody. John pulls up a folding chair a few feet away from me, sits down, and crosses his legs. He's cocky, proud of himself. I can sense it. This may work to my advantage. It had to be difficult keeping this entire scheme a secret. I bet he's itching to tell someone, to brag about his actions, about how brilliant he is for pulling the whole thing off.

"You want answers? Alright, I'll give them to you."

I release the breath I didn't even know I was holding, the smallest feeling of relief coming over me. I just have to keep him talking long enough for someone to come home.

"Stephanie and I met three years ago at a psychiatry conference. She was an adolescent psychologist who was interested in going back to school for a degree in psychiatry. She was captivating and beautiful and intelligent. I don't know what exactly it was about her, but she and I fell for each other fast," he speaks with a reminiscent tone in his voice. His eyes are glossed over, as if speaking about Stephanie is making him nostalgic, making him miss her. But he's the one who took her life away. He's the one who pointed a gun at her head. He's the one who ripped out the last chapters of their love story.

"What about my mom? And the girls? How could you do this to them? My mom loved you, she trusted you, she fought for you when I wouldn't give you a chance," I'm just trying to delay him, but I realize the tears streaming down from my face and the hurt in my voice is real.

"I loved your mom, Izzie," he replies nonchalantly. "I did. But then I met Stephanie and she stole my heart. Your mom is lovely, a beautiful human being. It wasn't anything she did, but I fell in love with Stephanie."

I feel a sharp ache in my heart for my mother. This was the man she loved. Her second chance after her first marriage fell apart despite everything she did to hold it together. All I can think about is how much this is going to kill her.

My face is pinched together in a hard, cold stare at John with daggers shooting out of my eyes. I can't even respond to what he just said. I can't find the words.

"Anyway, we spent a lot of time together at the conference, and when it was time to go home, we stayed in touch. I thought it was just going to be a one night thing. She lived in Massachusetts. We lived in Oregon. But we couldn't stop thinking about each other. We met up a few times, told our families different excuses for why we'd be out of town. That's why you found the love letter and the locket I bought for Stephanie. We quickly realized that this was more than we first thought, that we were meant to be."

He sounds like a sociopath, spewing all this "meant to be" crap out of his mouth. Life is not a soap opera. I don't care what his reasons are, he had no right to betray my mom.

"Can you just move on with your story? I don't want to hear about how you cheated on my mom." I know I'm supposed to be stalling him, but hearing this is physically painful.

"Someone's a little impatient. Stephanie and I decided to be together. For three years we met secretly and pursued our relationship. But the distance was tough. It was hard living a double life."

"Oh boo-hoo. Poor you, John," I mock him.

He shrugs me off, "We were going to leave our spouses and start a life together. And then your mom got pregnant with Olivia and ruined everything. I couldn't leave her just yet. We came up with an alternative plan. Stephanie said a house on her street was for sale, and she was able to pull some strings to get me the clinical psychiatrist job at the hospital. When I told your mom about the job offer she was more than excited to move. With all the problems with your dad, she was eager to get a fresh start."

He talks about Olivia like she was some sort of unwanted roadblock in his life, like she wasn't even a person to him. I used to be so jealous of Olivia and Madison, jealous that they had a stable home with two parents under the same roof. Those girls are going to have a tough time growing up.

"You used her. You used my mom to get closer to your girlfriend. You're sick."

"Stop with the drama, Izzie. You wanted answers and I'm giving them to you. So stop talking and listen for once in your life. We made the move to Massachusetts and everything was working out."

"Is that why Stephanie and Richard came over that first night?" I ask. "It wasn't them being neighborly. It was Stephanie coming to see you."

"Good catch," he smiles arrogantly. "That's right. Stephanie and I were happy to be closer. We were going to leave our spouses soon. This just bought us more time. It was a lot easier to be together secretly when we lived right next door. I loved her, Izzie. I loved her so much."

"But you killed her. She's dead, John. She's dead because of you," I say passionately.

Something in his calm and nostalgic demeanor changes. I can see it in his eyes. He suddenly becomes angry, vengeful even. He stands up from his chair with his fists clenched and an evil look in his eyes. He raises his voice, speaking intensely, "She's not dead because of me! Don't you see that!" His eyes appear to be bloodshot, and I don't think he's blinked once in the past few minutes. "I'm not the reason she's dead! She did this to herself!" He's screaming now, and he begins to rapidly pace the room, waving his hands in the air. I've never seen John like this. He's always so calm and collected. This is a whole new person. I feel my heart rate begin to accelerate as a cold sweat drips down my forehead.

"Then what happened?!" I yell to break him out of his hysteria. "If she's not dead because of you, then what the hell happened?"

He stops moving and looks over to me, the same rage bursting through his eyes even though his body has calmed. "We were at the party," his breathing is heavy as he talks, "And I saw her . . . kissing him. Behind her house, she was kissing him."

Beckett. John saw her kissing Beckett. Wow. They say it's always the boyfriend, which is why I pointed the finger at Beckett. But I pointed my finger at the wrong boyfriend.

"I saw her kissing him. Oh my God. I've never been more angry, more hurt in my entire life. I gave up everything for her! Everything!" he yells again.

"You were mad at her for doing the same thing that you're doing to my mom. Don't you realize that?"

He glares at me, "This was different! I walked away, but I was so angry I couldn't let go of it. I gave up everything to be with her! I moved across the country for that ungrateful bitch! And she betrayed me." He picks up the folding chair and hurls it across the basement. The chair smashes against the concrete floor with a clang and I feel my anxiety level skyrocketing. I severely underestimated John and what he was capable of.

"What happened next?" I ask, trying to bring him back.

"From inside our house, I saw her walking up to her house alone later that night. I slipped out while everyone was sleeping. Something came over me and I went after her. I needed to hear it from her. I needed to know what was going on. I told her what I saw and she tried to defend herself. Tried to tell me that it was just a one time thing, that she didn't mean it. I saw right through her lies. We fought in our backyard. She was crying, trying to make me pity her. She said he meant nothing to her, that it was me she loved. How dare she try to undermine me like that? How dare she make me look like a fool? I took the gun out of my back pocket . . . and I shot her. I shot her three times. I watched the life drain out of her eyes. If she wasn't going to be with me, she wasn't going to be with anyone."

I feel like someone's smacked me full force with a metal rod across my stomach. My lungs are refusing to breath, and everything in my head is spinning. Horrifying thoughts buzz around in my brain like a swarm of black crows. It's like our entire life with John has been one big act, one big performance. I never liked him. Since the first day he walked into our lives, I hated him. I always thought it was because he was replacing my dad, but maybe there was more to it. But this is the single biggest 'I told you so' I will never get to deliver to my mom.

I need him to keep this story going. I need to stretch it out as much as possible. I feel like he's fallen off the edge. Like he's lost control of himself. Like he could kill me at any moment.

"You shot her," I say with a hoarse voice. "You shot her three times. I don't remember everything from that night, but somehow I ended up outside on the concrete. Somehow there was a bloody shoe in my closet. And for some reason, I remember Easton Black being there. And what about Hannah? How was her DNA at the scene? What happened, John? What happened next?"

My questions seem to bring John back to a more sane state — if any of this can really count as sane. He takes another folding chair and sits down again. His voice becomes calmer as he says, "Slow your roll. One question at a time. I shot her in the backyard. On the patio. I knew I had to do something to cover it up. Beckett had gone into another neighbor's house, so I took it as a chance to place the evidence effectively. I snuck into his house, which was unlocked — I can't believe their stupidity. I realized I could place the blame on his wife so easily. She had a motive. She was at home sleeping alone. No one would be able to verify her alibi. I cracked open a safe in the back of their closet, wiped down the gun to clear my fingerprints and stuck it in the safe. I found one of Hannah's hairbrushes in their bathroom. I was able to sprinkle strands of her hair on the crime scene. It was the perfect set-up. The perfect crime!" His eyes seem to glow like those of a wild cat, filled with pride and admiration for his handy work.

I feel my heart sink into the bottom of my stomach as tears pour down my face. Hannah was painted as a murderer for a crime she didn't commit. John is the reason she's dead. The reason Beckett will have to carry around this earth shattering guilt for the rest of his life. The reason her kids won't ever see their mother again.

"How could you do that to Hannah? To an innocent person you hadn't even known? You're a monster! You're a sick, twisted monster!" I feel my emotions getting the best of me. I can tell I'm spiraling, the control I'd been fighting for slipping from my grip. I need to keep it together. I brace myself for John's reaction, waiting for him to stand up and flip out and kill me.

Surprisingly, he doesn't scream or throw anything. He just sits there with an amused look on his face. I hate him. I hate how he gets to sit here while Hannah is rotting in the ground.

"It's nothing personal, sweetheart. I did what I had to do. And if it came down to it, I would do it again," he says coldly.

In between tears, I ask, "What happened next?"

"I set up the scene perfectly. There was no way the blame wouldn't fall on Hannah. I was a genius. My quick thinking, my scheme, it was brilliant. When I came back with the hairbrush, I saw *you*. You were lying on the ground by Stephanie's body. I realized you were drunk out of your mind. I could smell it on your breath. You must've heard her scream and came down and passed out. I was planning on leaving you there. If they found you next to the dead body, it would help my case. Again honey, it's nothing personal."

I feel so many things right now that I can't comprehend. He was going to leave me out there. Let me take the fall for a crime I had nothing to do with. He's a disgusting excuse for a person. The memories of that night are starting to click into place, revealing a clearer picture of the puzzle I'm trying to put together. I heard a scream outside, so I opened the door. That's when I saw Stephanie's body. I must've passed out from shock. There was so much blood pooling underneath her head and her back. I'm not sure how I made it back up to my room, but now I know I didn't kill her. How could he do that to me? I know I never treated him nicely, but still, I don't think I deserved this. I so badly want to scream at him, to yell every nasty thing I can think of. But he's so

369

close to losing control again. I can't say anything to set him off because I'm not ready to die. I bite down on my tongue as hard as I can to stop the words from spewing out of my mouth. I taste blood on my tongue. I've never been good at filtering my thoughts, but I need to now more than ever.

He continues with his story, "Like I said, I sprinkled Hannah's hair throughout the crime scene and was going to walk away, but then Easton Black came around and ruined my plan. Seriously, I'm not sure who's supposed to be supervising him, but whoever it is is doing a terrible job. How was a mentally ill person able to escape their house in the middle of the night?" He talks about Easton's situation like he's above it all, like he's better than them. Get off your high freaking horse, John. Let's remember who the murderer in this town is.

"Easton came around to the back, so I snuck off behind the house. I wanted to watch, but I didn't want him to see me. I was hoping he would leave, but he didn't. He crouched down beside you and started asking if you were okay. The real problem started when you woke up. I had to step in and do something."

All this time Easton's been telling the truth. He knew exactly what he was talking about and no one believed him. The man with the gun. The man with the gun was John. Easton saw Stephanie's body with the pool of blood. He saw me unconscious on the concrete. He saw John with the gun. That's why he told me he didn't like my house the first time I saw him. That's why he incessantly asked if I was okay. He was scared, he was trying to protect me in his own odd way. No one believed him. No one listened to him. John was able to get away with it because of Easton's disability. The thought makes me sick to my stomach. I bite down even harder on my tongue, reminding myself to let him tell his story, to keep him from flying off the handle, to keep myself alive.

"I rushed over to you. I told Easton to go home. It took a while, but I was eventually able to get him to leave. I carried you up into your room and went to bed myself," he explains.

"What about the shoe? I found a bloody shoe in my closet. How did that get there?" I question.

"Oh, the shoe?" he chuckles maliciously. "I dipped your shoe in Stephanie's blood and stuck it in your closet. That way if the cops didn't think Hannah did it, the blame could be deflected to someone else. To *you*."

I start to sob hysterically, my chest rapidly heaving in and out. I thought I did something. I thought I murdered Stephanie. I was convinced I had done something terrible. How could he let me think that? He was so good at the mind games he played, skilled at manipulating people into trusting him, into doubting themselves. Our relationship had just turned a corner. I finally started to let him love me, to trust him, to accept him as part of our family. I thought I was guilty. I thought I did something awful.

"I thought I hurt her," I sob. "I thought I killed her. I couldn't remember anything from that night. You messed with my head. I thought I killed her." I choke on my own words as they spill out of my mouth.

He smiles like I'm one of his psychiatric patients, "I'm sorry you felt that way. I didn't mean to hurt you, but I had no other choice, Izzie. There was no other way."

"No, John! You had a choice! You had a freaking choice! You decided to cheat on my mom. You decided to murder Stephanie. You decided to pin it on Hannah. You decided to bring me into it. You had a choice," I yell. Okay, I need to reign it in. I've never been good with holding my emotions or my thoughts back. I need to get it together.

"How dare you talk about this like you know everything!" he roars.

He lunges upwards from his chair with such force the entire thing collapses to the ground with a bang. Suddenly, he pulls a gun out of his back pocket, the shiny metal illuminated by the flashlight. A petrifying fear fills my body as I try to swallow the lump in my throat. I don't have time to panic or freak out. I need to stay calm. I need more time.

He steps closer to me, holding the gun out in front of him. "Take it back, or I'll shoot you right now."

I breathe as deeply as I can and try to force the words out through the thick layer of fear inside me, "I'm sorry. I didn't mean that. I don't know what I'm talking about. You can't kill me yet. You didn't finish the story. I'm sorry. I shouldn't have said that."

Everything is silent for a moment. I clench my jaw and squeeze my eyes shut, bracing for the gunshot. Slowly, he lowers the gun.

"I'll finish telling you what happened, and then you're dead," he whispers.

He stands in front of me with his blue eyes penetrating through my soul and says, "My plan worked perfectly. I thought of everything. Your mom and I were questioned by the police just because it was our house. Oh . . . it was so easy to lie to them," he chuckles to himself. "They found nothing on me. No evidence. No motive. No conviction. Everything was fine. Hannah was arrested and awaiting trial. But then I caught wind of you and your friends' little detective scheme. I thought that you would all eventually lose interest. Hannah would be convicted and spend the next twenty or more years in jail. But I won't lie, I started to get worried. You were uncovering so many things about everyone. You started talking to Easton Black. You were getting too close for comfort."

"How did you know about what we were doing?" I ask.

He puts his hand to his chin like he's thinking hard, and then says, "I was always listening. Always watching. I would listen from behind the door when you and Luke were talking or when you had your friends over. You were smart, Izzie, but you weren't careful."

"So was it you that day in Stephanie's closet?"

He scrunches up his face, "How did you know I was in Stephanie's closet?"

"I was in there with Shea. Stephanie had said something to me about cameras, so we went to her house to look around. We hid in the closet while you searched it."

"Wow, that makes a lot of sense," he nods his head. "I found the burner phone in your room and was wondering how you got a hold of it. I knew she had a burner phone. I wanted to clear any messages to me that were still on it, but you got to it first. Lucky for me, Stephanie had already gotten rid of our messages and the phone only implicated some of our neighbors. When you left your phone in your room unattended, I saw the picture of Beckett and Stephanie. I leaked it to Facebook to further implicate Hannah." He's talking, but all I can focus on is the gun hanging at his side. One bullet. That's all it takes.

I'm just starting to realize how elaborate his whole scheme was. There were so many moving parts, so many little details.

"What about Hannah?" I say nervously, "Did you kill her too?"

"Right again, Isabelle!" He gloats. "I heard you and Luke talking about your little visit with Hannah. I heard you say that she knew something about the killer. I couldn't take the risk, so I went down to the jail and paid off some crooked guard to take her out for me. It's amazing the kind of scum you'll find in those places."

I look at him with a confused expression. The jail is filled with scum? How about him? He's dirtier than the gum that sticks to your shoe from a sketchy alleyway.

"We made it look like a suicide. Everything was tied up in a nice little bow. Hannah murdered Stephanie because of the affair, and then committed suicide in fear of retribution. It was perfect. I committed the perfect murder. I created the perfect crime," John says, glowing with pride.

It's taking everything in me not to break down. Stay calm. Breathe. Just breathe. I swallow hard and say, "What did Hannah know?"

John shrugs his shoulders, "I don't know. I had her killed before she sang."

I feel a sharp pain in the pit of my stomach. He's talking about Hannah as if she were nothing more than a pawn in his twisted game of chess.

"So was it you who chased us in the woods?" I question.

His face is smug as he says, "You were getting closer and I needed to take some precautions."

My mind instantly shifts back to Mr. Cavanaugh. Yesterday, he told Shea and me that he saw one of our dads at the store the past weekend. I thought he was referring to my dad in Oregon, and I also thought his dementia was just acting up. But he saw John. He saw John the weekend he was supposed to be away. The weekend he almost killed me. Almost. Maybe that word isn't so bad after all.

"So you sent Mom and the girls off to Boston and faked your mother's hip injury. You just stuck around town and tried to kill us in the woods."

"Stop being so dramatic, Izzie! I wasn't trying to kill you. I was only trying to scare you off. If you had just backed off then, if you had just let it go, Izzie, you wouldn't be in this place right now. You would be off living your life, hanging out with your friends. You got yourself into this damn mess!" he growls. "And now, now you're going to pay."

I need to stall him. I need to keep him talking. "Did you know all those secrets everyone was hiding? Did you know how Stephanie was involved in so many awful things?"

"Of course I knew! Stephanie told me everything. I knew all about Sawyer's gambling problem and how Stephanie agreed to help him in exchange for drugs. I knew all about Forrest's drug deal and how Stephanie supplied him in return for money. The woman would do anything for more money. She was greedy, never satisfied with what she had. She always wanted something more, something different, something better. She was always chasing after one thing or another. I knew all about Isla's inappropriate relationship with her college professor and how Stephanie threatened to go to the board and expose them. I know about how Isla threatened to kill her if she brought their relationship to light. The stupid little girl thought she could outsmart my beautiful Stephanie. I knew about Easton's mental illness and how I could use that to my advantage. I knew *everything*," he says.

This town is plagued with secrets . . . and he knows them all.

I can still see Stephanie craning her long neck down to whisper in my ear after a little too much wine. She told John everything. He knew the secrets that cluttered this street as well as she did. We went on this wild goose chase to dig into these people's lives when in reality, murder may have been the one thing they weren't guilty of. All of these people were red herrings. Like the smoke bombs magicians use to distract the audience from the actual trick.

"Stephanie told me all there was to know about these rich people and their dirty secrets. Everyone was hiding something. They were the perfect distractions when you and your friends decided to play detective. It sent you traveling down these crazy paths, searching for answers in a sea of questions."

"If you knew all of the awful things Stephanie was involved in, why did you stand by her?" I ask.

He steps closer to me, "Because I loved her. We loved each other. She was my soulmate." It seems like his eyes are tearing up, the blue pools above his nose appearing glossy and strained. I thought Luke would be here by now. I thought somebody would be here by now. I don't know how much longer I can hold him off. The rope around my arms burns my skin, and I'm becoming even more aware of the lethal weapon that John holds at his side.

He takes another step. He's so close I can feel his warm breath on my face, hear his heart beating, see the details on the gun's surface. This can't be it. This can't be the end. Slowly, he raises the gun, his grip so tight his knuckles are turning white. He takes the gun and presses it up against my forehead, the cold steel sending waves of fear through my entire body. I begin to hyperventilate, unable to get air into my lungs. This can't be it. This can't be the end. He slams the gun harder against my temple. I need to say something. I need to get his attention. My time is running out. I need something. Anything. Tick-tock.

"You killed her for love," I say quietly. "I read this quote once. It was by Agatha Christie. She said that you always have to pay a price for love. It's never easy or free. You have to give and take. You have to pay a price. You said you killed Stephanie because you loved her too much. You didn't want her to be happy with anyone else, but you were wrong about one thing. I'm not paying the price of your actions. You're going to pay the price for the rest of your life. You killed her. You have to live with that." I blabber on, talking about some philosophical shit that doesn't make sense. I'm just trying to buy myself some time.

"Shut your mouth!" he yells. "Don't you dare talk about Stephanie or me like you have a God damned clue about it!" He pushes the gun harder against my temple. The craziness, the rage, the fury, they're all back swimming around in his bloodshot eyes.

My heart is beating through my shirt, so fast I feel like I'm having a heart attack. This can't be it. This can't be the end. I haven't even lived yet. I haven't told anyone I loved them. I haven't seen the world outside of my town. I haven't gone off to college. I haven't found my passion. I haven't even figured out who I am yet. This can't be it. This can't be the end. There has to be more for me.

I begin to scream as loudly as I possibly can. A hopeless, horrifying, desperate scream. I'm just praying to God that someone can hear me, that someone can help me. It's all I have left. I'm not ready to die. Sweat trickles down my forehead as an ocean's worth of tears pour down my face. I scream and scream and scream and scream. I scream until my throat is burning and then some. I squeeze my eyes shut, trying to block out the horror surrounding me. Suddenly, John shoves a sticky piece of duct tape over my mouth, which muffles my cries. I feel like I'm drowning, trapped underwater with no way out. I try to scream, but nothing comes out. This is it. This is the end.

Out of nowhere, I hear an ear piercing bang and then a loud thud. I open my eyes and am utterly shocked by the sight. In front of me stands little Alison Kester with a shovel taller than her body in hand. Her mouth is hanging open, and I can hear her heavy breathing. John has collapsed on the floor in front of her, unconscious with blood covering the back of his head.

"Holy crap," she gasps.

Alison's eyes are filled with shock and terror as she rushes over to me. She rips the strip of duct tape off my mouth, which stings with a burning passion. I can't stop sobbing. I don't even have the words to say to Alison right now because my mind can't comprehend what's happening. Before I realize what's going on, Alison has untied me from the chair. I rub my burning wrists, and then my head, feeling a slimy liquid on my fingers. I'm bleeding. I stand up with my legs violently shaking and grab onto Alison.

"How did you — ?" I'm crying too much to finish my sentence.

"I had a bad feeling. I came over to see you and saw your phone and the box in the garage. Your spare key is under your welcome mat, which isn't very smart."

I cling onto Alison for dear life. I'm shaking so severely I can't even move.

"We need to get out of here, now," Alison urges. "I called 911. The cops should be on their way."

She guides me up the stairs and out of this house of horrors as the police come whizzing down the street. At the same time, I see Luke's car followed by my mom's. They pull into the driveway on two wheels, officers jumping out and running over to me. My mom springs out of the car, sprinting to me as fast as she can with sheer panic covering her face. I let go of Alison and collapse into her arms.

"It's John," I sob. "Mom —"

"Shh . . ." she says, "It's okay. It's okay, honey."

I hold onto her as tight as I possibly can, never wanting to let go of her. Luke comes running up behind her and starts talking to Alison, but I can't make out what they're saying. Everything around me is just a blur of colors and sounds and feelings, life moving too fast. I open my eyes for a moment and see Shea coming by. As soon as I see his face, I feel a sense of comfort.

"Shea!" I cry.

My mom releases me for a moment to talk to Luke and Alison to figure out what exactly is going on as I make my way over to him. He sees my distraught face and wraps me in his arms.

"It was my step-dad," I sob. "It was John." He lets go for a minute and looks at me with shock filling his eyes. "Please don't let go of me," I cry.

He hugs me, wrapping his arms around me as tight as he can, "I'm never letting go of you again."

CHAPTER 20 - See You Later

Three Weeks Later

I smooth out my jean skirt in the mirror and run my fingers through my hair a few more times. After everything I've been through this summer, the first day of school should be a breeze. But still, my hands feel clammy and the butterflies in my stomach are flapping around anxiously. I'm nervous for all the new people and the new environment, but I think I'm mostly scared because I feel like I already have a reputation going into the school year. I'm the girl whose sociopathic step-dad murdered two people. I'm the girl who was tied up in her basement with a gun held to her head. I'm the girl whose face and story filled the headlines of all the newspapers and was the lead story of the local nightly news. These kids I'm going to school with already know so much about me. It's strange, not exactly the clean slate I was hoping for. But who doesn't have a history? Who doesn't have a little bit of baggage? I wouldn't change anything that happened this summer — well except for maybe the part where I almost died, but that's beside the point. Everything I went through, brought me closer to who I am as a person. It led me to my best friends, to my boyfriend, to the real me.

I hear Olivia crying in her bedroom and walk down the hallway to get her. I quietly open her door and make my way over to her crib. Her tiny face is scrunched up with tears trickling down her cheeks.

I scoop her up in my arms and say, "Shh, it's okay. You're okay."

Three weeks ago, John was taken to jail where he will most likely spend the rest of his life rotting away in a cell. He's still awaiting his trial, but his chances of walking away free of charges are slim to none. The evidence piled against him combined with my testimony should be enough to put him away for life. But every time I look at Olivia and Madison I feel guilty. Three weeks ago, they lost their dad. Life for them is not going to be easy, especially in a town where there are enough rumors and gossip to fill all the oceans on Earth. They're going to need all the support they can get now that they don't have a father. I'm making it one of my top priorities to be there for them, to protect them from the harsh realities of this world. These girls are going to grow up to be strong. They're going to have to be.

I rock Olivia in my arms, swaying gently until she stops crying. I still can't believe how John talked about her like she was an unwanted roadblock in his way. Every time I look at her, I just see her innocent heart and her big blue eyes. I know I better get going if I don't want to be late. Shea is picking me up in twenty minutes and I haven't even made my way downstairs.

With Olivia in my arms, I start walking down the stairs. I stop suddenly at the last one, the sight at my kitchen counter taking me by surprise. My mom is standing at the granite counter with a cream colored mug of coffee in her hands. Across from her, my dad sits at one of the barstools smiling at something she just said and sipping on his own cup of coffee. My dad came in a few days ago after he heard about everything that happened. He's been helping my mom out, and the two of us have been able to spend a lot of time together. He's out of rehab and sober. I'm not used to seeing them in the same room together. It's weird, but a good weird. A very good weird.

"Good morning!" I hear my mom's cheery voice. "Senior year!"

I blush as she hands me a cup of coffee and bear hugs me so tight I feel like I'm going to pass out. After our hug, I transfer Olivia over to her. My mom's never faltered during any of this. She found out her husband — her second chance at love — was actually a psychotic killer, but she still shows up for us every day. I can't believe how incredibly strong she is. I used to think my mom and I were so different, and it's funny to think that a few weeks ago our relationship was so strained it was difficult to stay in the same room for too long. But here we are. All the fire we had to walk through, it got us here. To this place where she's my best friend, my role model, and my rock.

My dad steps up from his chair to hug me. He smiles, the familiar comforting grin I've been missing for so long. He says, "You look beautiful, kiddo. Ready for the first day?"

I smile as a strange sense of déjà vu comes over me. It takes me back to our small kitchen in Portland on my first day of Kindergarten. I remember my little pigtails and holding their hands as I walked into school for the first time. The memory was so far removed, but now it feels so close.

"I'm a little nervous, but I think I'll be okay," I answer.

"You're going to rock it," he smiles. "How's your ankle feeling?"

After everything with John happened, I had to go to the doctor because of the cut in my head. They just wanted to check everything out and make sure I had no other injuries. It turned out that my ankle was partly fractured from the incident in the woods. Apparently walking around on a sprained ankle for a few weeks is not a great decision. Well, now I have this gorgeous boot to accessorize my skirt.

"What time is Shea coming?" mom asks.

"He'll be here in a few minutes," I reply.

"Shea?" my dad raises an eyebrow.

My face turns crimson as I realize I haven't exactly told him about my boyfriend.

"Shea?" I say, "Oh, Shea. He's my . . . friend."

"Hmm," my dad eyes me suspiciously. "Just a friend, huh?"

"Oh, you're lying through your teeth," my mom jokes. "I would say Shea's a lot more than a friend. Just a friend who occasionally kisses you."

"Mom!" I jokingly roll my eyes at her and grab one of her homemade blueberry muffins on the counter to get some food in my stomach.

Luke comes walking down the stairs as I start to inhale my muffin. His mocha brown hair is styled neatly, and his bright emerald green eyes seem to jump out of his face. My mom rushes over to him to hug him and wish him a happy first day of school. He awkwardly half waves at my dad and says a quiet hello before he grabs his breakfast. At least Luke's acknowledging his presence. It's not perfect, but you've got to start somewhere. I know Luke will come around eventually, he just needs a little more time.

I hear a car pull up the driveway and then a knock on the door a few minutes later. Eagerly, I race to the door to greet Shea. He stands there with his caramel colored hair spiked up in front and his dimples hanging out on his cheeks. He holds a little bouquet of pale pink flowers and hands them to me with a sweet smile on his face.

"Just a little something," he says quietly.

"You're too good to be true, you know that?" I smile widely at him, and for a minute, I forget about my nerves.

I lead Shea inside where he greets my mom brightly, and I introduce him to my dad. His face is full of fear as he shakes my dad's hand and answers the questions he throws at him.

"How well do you do in school?" dad asks.

His eyes are wide as he responds, "Um . . . pretty good. Mostly A's."

"What are your career plans?" he fires another question.

"Not sure," he answers nervously.

"Alright, Tommy," my mom laughs. "Take it easy."

I say goodbye to my parents, hugging them both a little bit tighter than normal. Before I leave, I stop and say to my mom, "Are you going to be okay at home today?" It's the first time I've been without her since everything happened. I'm not sure if I'm asking more for me or for her though.

She places her hand lovingly on my shoulder, "I'm going to be okay, Izzie. We're all going to be okay."

Shea and I make our way out to his car, and he opens the door for me to get in. Luke walks out behind us on his way to pick up Hazel. The two of them are officially together thanks to my meddling.

"I'll see you there," Luke smiles. "Don't be nervous, Iz, you're going to be great."

I catch Alison out of the corner of my eye as we're about to get in the car. She's standing on the front porch in a light pink dress with her hair in two identical braids.

"I need a minute," I say to Shea.

I quickly walk from my driveway over to the Kester's front porch.

"Hi," she waves. "Aren't you going to be late?"

"Probably," I smile. "I just wanted to wish you a good first day of school before I left. And I wanted to thank you again. I wouldn't be here today without you."

A genuine smile comes across her face, "You were there for me when no one else was. I hate to say it, but I actually think I like you."

"I've got your back, kid," I laugh.

"Alright," she starts. "Enough with the sappy stuff. Go see your little boy toy before you're late on the first day. You're not really good at first impressions, so I would get going soon."

Typical Alison. Even though I've broken through to her, she never fails to throw in a dig or a sarcastic comment. I wave goodbye and head back over to Shea's car, nervous, but ready to get going.

Shea backs out of the driveway and down the street. I feel the sun glowing through the windows, daylight cutting through the glass. The air is warm, and I feel like I'm basking in streams of golden light.

We pull into Graeson's driveway, just as he's running out of the door with his backpack slung over one shoulder and his hair sticking out every which way on his head. At the beginning of the summer, Hazel told me that Graeson was one speeding ticket away from losing his license. Well, that third speeding ticket came around the other day, and now he can't drive anyone or himself for that matter for a while. So, lucky for Shea and I, he will be third wheeling in our relationship for quite some time.

He launches himself into the car, and says, "I can't believe they took my license away! I wasn't even going that fast."

I roll my eyes at him, "How many times do we have to tell you that a hundred miles an hour is over fifty miles over the speed limit."

"Oh please. I've never hit anyone, so what does it matter?"

"You almost killed me a few weeks ago," I laugh as he throws his hands up in the air. "Yeah, I haven't forgotten about that yet."

Hazel and Luke pull up beside us, both with bright smiles on their face. Hazel wears her signature cheetah print sunglasses and her golden curls are blowing around in the breeze.

"Are you excited!?" Hazel says to me. "We have the first two periods together!"

"I can't wait!" I reply with genuine excitement. "It's going to be our year, Hazel."

With that being said, both of our cars take off down the street and head toward our last first day of school. My head is full of wonderful possibilities for this new year and my heart is so full of gratitude and happiness because of all these people in my life. It's been a tough ride. But I like to think I've changed for the better because of it. I'm still a terrible person, but maybe a little less so than before.

I've never been particularly good at goodbyes. They're always sad and difficult and awkward. Saying goodbye is like leaving a piece of yourself behind. I guess I'm leaving a piece of myself here with you. But goodbye sounds too permanent. It sounds like the end of something you're not ready to leave. So instead of saying goodbye, I think I'll say see you later. For some reason, that feels different, a little bit better. Because this isn't the end of my story, this isn't goodbye. So I'll just go ahead and say it. See you later.